WEST ON GRAINGER

KC BURN

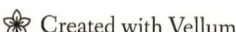 Created with Vellum

FOREWORD

So. Over the past few years, things have happened in the world. Difficult things. Bad things. But I write and read for escapism. And as such, the world of Sandy Bottom Bay has not experienced COVID, or hurricanes Ian and Nicole. This world may never experience those things, or they may be forthcoming in future books, but I do know I'm not at a place where I wanted to incorporate those things into this book. For the time being, assume Sandy Bottom Bay exists in a world that did not experience those particular events.

ACKNOWLEDGMENTS

This was a tricky book. Lots of people helped me get this one over the finish line, because there were times when I did not think it was ever going to happen.

Dolorianne, Dottie, Chudney, everyone in book club and in the CMC reading challenge group - thanks for being such great cheerleaders.

Jennifer W - thanks for helping me wrangle this sucker into shape.

Alex - love always, I wouldn't be where I am if not for you.

ONE

29 Days to Haunt Fest

"YOU HAVE ARRIVED AT YOUR DESTINATION."

Wendell Weston squinted at the GPS display, not sure if he should believe the smug, dulcet tone. The entrance of the bed and breakfast's parking lot was overgrown with foliage. For a brief moment, he imagined the vines and shrubbery coming to life, voracious, carnivorous, and seeking food. Then he shook himself. Lucinda would shit a brick and beat him with it if he sent her an idea for *Plants Attack!*

A niggle of fear slithered through his belly, leaving behind a sticky trail of unease. If this was the best his brain could come up with, his career might truly be over. Yoga and meditation weren't really his thing, but growing up in Los Angeles he could hardly avoid it. A few deep breaths and an attempt to clear his mind staved off the incipient anxiety, while he focused on guiding his car through the archway of green and pulled into a parking spot.

Wendell stepped out of the environmentally responsible car he'd rented, and stretched the muscles that had knotted tight across his shoulders. Fucking hell, but he'd thought traffic in LA was foul. To be sure, it was, but Floridian highway drivers were a nightmare of a whole different flavor. Completely unpredictable. They had to be either insane or lost. Or both.

The drive from Tampa International Airport to Sandy Bottom Bay had been far more harrowing than he'd expected, interspersed with long stretches where there weren't any other cars for miles. It hadn't helped that just about every vehicle he did see on the road was an SUV or pickup truck, which positively dwarfed his tiny, hybrid car.

Then again, any sort of scare on his first day in town boded well, even if he had yet to experience any supernatural activity.

He let out a rueful laugh. *Traffic Terror* wouldn't win any brownie points with Lucinda either. A yawn surprised him as he pulled his overnight bag out of the back seat. His suitcases in the trunk could wait until later. Tomorrow, even.

As much as he wanted to explore the town, he was exhausted. No way would he be receptive to inspiration while this tired. The last thing he needed right now was anything that made him doubt he still had a creative well to draw upon. Besides getting settled in, he also needed to figure out exactly what he was going to do over the next several weeks.

Before he continued on, he stood there and soaked in the atmosphere. Something about the increasingly sticky humidity, overblown greenery, and bright sunshine gave him a tiny sprig of hope. It was definitely different than home, for all that he wasn't much farther south. The differences were going to recharge him. Relax him. Refresh his creativity. As long as the people in town didn't take their reputation into the realm of the hokey rather than spooky, he had a chance.

The air was redolent with some tropical scent Wendell couldn't yet identify, but he inhaled deeply, adjusted the strap of his overnight bag on his shoulder, and pushed through the vine-choked archway to the front door.

Inside, Wendell's first impression was "Florida". He'd never been to Florida before, but between movies and television, the lobby looked about as expected. Theming was heavily nautical with a number of seashells, boats, and fish. The overall color scheme was white with accents of aquamarine and coral pink. Two white wicker chairs sat in the stark light streaming through a large window to the right of the door. The fabric cushions, once bright and cheery, had bleached over time in the harsh sunlight. Without a closer look, Wendell couldn't determine if the pattern involved fish or mermaids. Either way, it was delightful and charming.

Devoid of even a hint of terror.

He sighed. Disappointing. Especially as he'd read numerous accounts of spectral activity on the premises.

Inside, the scent was no longer herbaceous but salty and almost musty, like stormy weather on the ocean. Which made sense. Despite the heat, the atmosphere was heavy with moisture and the Gulf of Mexico lurked a couple of minutes' walk from where he stood. The bed and breakfast, named the Orange Lady Inn, looked like it had been here for a hundred years, although given the extremes of wind, water, sun, and heat, any structures undoubtedly aged quickly.

In short, the Orange Lady looked like any accommodation found up and down the Florida coast. Not at all what he'd expected from the second most haunted town in Florida. He hoped that they'd named the B&B for a local ghost story, but it might have been nothing more than a reference to the interior color scheme or the vast orange groves he'd driven past on the way from the airport.

He couldn't lose hope yet. The town did, apparently, dive whole-heartedly into the paranormal waters, from the write-ups he'd read. Inspiration may yet be found. Even if it wasn't, there were worse places to spend his desperately needed break. Sabbatical? Working vacation?

Wendell strode over to the tiny desk. The peg board behind the desk boasted large keys with clear resin fobs encasing real sand dollars. Old-fashioned, campy, and surprisingly reminiscent of the hotel desk in one of his earlier features, *Dead Eye Dance*, except that had been set in 1920's Hollywood. Granted, the scene in the hotel had been memorable, despite having only minutes of screen time. Didn't mean he wouldn't be accused of being derivative of his own damned work, if he could scrape together a decent script set in a haunted, tropical-themed resort in present day. Which would rely entirely on this town kickstarting his elusive creativity.

Plants attacking, traffic jams, or recycling old material. Wendell closed his eyes and stifled a groan. If those were his only options, he was going to have turn this sabbatical into early retirement. He could afford to retire if he wanted, but he was only thirty-fucking-two. What would he do with the rest of his life?

His pulse kicked up, and Wendell took a deep breath. He needed to not be so hard on himself. This was his first day in Florida. Miracles were not required, he had three months to relax and let his creative juices replenish. The first step for recovery was getting settled and—showering, possibly napping. His eyes were gritty from fatigue, and thinking wasn't on the agenda for today.

He stood alone in the lobby. There was an old-fashioned desk bell that looked every bit as old as the building itself and he stared at it for a moment.

Living his whole life in Los Angeles, he was used to being invisible. After all, he didn't look like typical leading man material, and for most of the glitterati, that was enough for their gaze to drift over him as though he were a set piece instead of a person. Mostly that suited his personality and often gave him a front row seat to a lot of drama, as he was considered an inconsequential observer.

When he had to draw attention to himself, like ringing a loud brass bell in the middle of an empty room? That was far more discomfiting.

But standing here all day was stupid.

Wendell reached out and hit the bell, cringing. Announcing his presence was required, but he did not love how imperious it seemed.

A few moments turned into a few minutes, and Wendell stared at the bell. Should he ring again? Would that create a worse impression than simply waiting until someone, eventually, appeared?

Gritting his teeth, he rang the bell again.

An older woman with a wide smile and grey hair piled haphazardly on the top of her head pushed open the door behind the counter.

"Well, hello there. I'm sorry for the wait. How can I help you?"

"Morning. I'm Wendell Weston. I think you were expecting me?"

"Oh, honey. Is it Friday already?"

Wendell nodded. "Are you Sandra Chavez?"

"Yes, I am. And I can't tell you how happy I am to see you." In contradiction to her words, her smile fell away, and her shoulders drooped. And Wendell saw, clear as day, the stress she'd been hiding with her cheery facade. Shadows beneath her eyes, a sallow tinge to her complexion, and deep grooves that had once been laugh lines.

Exactly what he'd expect if he believed someone was enduring a haunting they couldn't ignore, but in this case, there was a more prosaic explanation.

"Can you show me to my room? Then we can get started." His nap could wait. Sandra and the Orange Lady needed his help, and the sooner he proved himself, the sooner she could whisk her husband away.

"Yes, of course. Follow me."

Sandra led him through a long room with lots of windows and more wicker chairs with fat, fluffy cushions and tiny side tables, all set up in the sunshine. The room was narrow, and it appeared to be a former wraparound porch. They went through a doorway into a dark hall, and passed another hall leading to a couple of other doors and a staircase. Sandra ignored them in favor of continuing straight, out through a door that led them back outside.

They emerged onto a covered walkway, bordered by almost intrusive foliage. A few steps further and the foliage broke on the right to reveal a sunny patio with umbrellas that resembled grass hut thatching. The wall at the back of the building was covered in bamboo, except for a small opening to order a cocktail or perhaps a sandwich.

The opening was shuttered and the patio empty, and there wasn't a menu to be seen. It wasn't at all clear what sort of service could be expected but Wendell had plenty of time figure that out.

His guide showed no signs of slowing down and he followed her down the path, which strangely reminded him of some sort of Hawaiian wilderness. For now, he resolutely didn't think of bugs or gators or other various critters that might be sheltered by the greenery, but the little shudder in his gut held promise. Nothing he could build an entire script around, but definitely potential for some foreboding atmosphere. He hoped. Because with the bright sun almost directly overhead, it wasn't easy to imagine horrors in what was shaping up to be a quaint little seaside resort.

They broke through a stand of palm trees and Wendell realized they were on slightly elevated ground. From here, stairs led down to another path, and he could see the beach and the ocean. They were so close, much closer than he'd realized. The concrete path petered out shortly after the stairs ended, becoming a hard-packed... sand surface? If it weren't a golden, sandy color, Wendell would call it a dirt path. But when they crunched down on it, it was obvious the "dirt" was composed of seashells mixed with the sand.

To his left, a path led to a building that looked like it was off limits to guests, due to the way bushes practically hid it. To the right, the path continued to a string of beachside cottages with privacy fencing extending about ten feet or so from the back of the cottages, separating the cottages and their patios from each other but not closing off access to the beach.

Sandra stopped at the spot where the path diverged, and pointed at the small building to the left.

"That's our place. Well, normally. I think I mentioned when we spoke that my husband and I had to move into one of the accessible rooms on the first floor, at least temporarily."

"Yes, you did."

He did have mixed feelings about capitalizing on Sandra's, and her husband Bill's, misfortunes. But Wendell was getting desperate. He hadn't been able to write in months. It was like his entire creative essence had been drained, but if he didn't get something written soon, he'd lose the momentum he and his siblings had been building.

They were well on their way to creating a paranormal empire that may well rival Blumhouse's success, but if he couldn't get another script written, they'd have to start shopping for outside offerings, and Wendell didn't want that. Nor did his sister, Lucinda. They'd have to do it at some point, but preferably not yet.

Lucinda had ordered him to take some time off, which was unlike his ambitious, cutthroat sister. Wendell wasn't nearly as much of a workaholic, but neither could he imagine going somewhere and doing nothing. He'd spend all his time getting depressed about his lack of ideas.

Getting out of LA was a smart move. If nothing else, a change of scenery, a change of pace, would do him good. While he'd been considering options, he'd seen a repeat of the *Phantoms* episode that featured Sandy Bottom Bay, and had a gut feeling that visiting over the town's Haunt Fest he'd find something to write about. Ideally, the haunted bed and breakfast itself. He did like the idea of mashing together the idyllic vacation nature of a beach with a haunting. Better than any plan he'd come up with since his muse went on strike.

The fates had smiled on him, because when he'd called to book a room, there had been a cancellation that allowed him to book for a full three months, with the exception of the first weekend of Haunt Fest. Fortunately, he'd also been able to book a room at the nearby, but much less infamous, hotel for that weekend so he wouldn't have to sleep in his rental car those few days.

When he'd proposed the idea that he also work as an unpaid intern at the B&B in order to do some in-depth research, as well as give him something to do besides brood about his uncooperative muse, Sandra had been lukewarm. Until he explained he did have relevant experience.

He hadn't worked in the hospitality industry in years but during college, he'd worked at a boutique hotel his parents had owned as part of their extensive property portfolio. He'd been fully trained and more than competent. It had been a great way for him to earn some money while in school—his parents had not handed him or his siblings everything they asked for. And after he graduated, it had also provided a schedule flexible enough to get their fledgling movie studio up and running.

That previous experience had been enough for Sandra. Especially given her current predicament. Her husband, Bill, had recently had a triple bypass, and he wasn't recovering as quickly as he should. His cardiologist had ordered a complete break from stress. Due to the expected rush during their busiest season, Sandra had hired a temporary manager, but additional backup, one who paid for room and board, wasn't something she could pass up.

Besides, not much had changed in the hospitality industry since he'd last worked a concierge desk. Whatever time he needed to invest in dusting off his slightly outdated knowledge would be worth it to get backstage access, so to speak, to a location that appeared to have a legitimate ghostly presence.

His only concern was that he hadn't seen a computer during those few brief moments at the lobby's check-in desk. He saw the appeal of going old school, but he didn't relish the idea of doing everything by hand or via phone.

"As you can see, this path leads to the beach. There's a mudroom by the patio door for people to de-sand before entering the main house." She gave a weary chuckle. "But it doesn't help much. There's always sand everywhere. All the time."

Sand. Everywhere. Wendell filed that little tidbit away. *The Mummy* had done a good job of making sand creepy and foreboding —no reason he couldn't also. But he laughed politely anyway.

"And I presume those are the cottages?"

"Yes. I've set you up in the first one."

Wendell blinked. "Oh. Thank you, but doesn't that make it inconvenient to assist guests? What if they need something overnight? For that matter, how could you possibly hear the counter bell from way back here?"

There was no reason to assume guests would have middle of the night requests, but he'd worked enough overnight shifts to know that one could never count on a quiet night. He'd also known, based on his previous discussions with Sandra, that he'd be sharing overnight coverage with the new temporary manager.

Hearing that bell in the main building would be a challenge on its own. Utterly impossible to hear from an exterior building.

Sandra grinned, the first genuine smile he'd seen on her. She pulled out her smartphone and waggled it. "There's a motion sensor at the front desk. I get a notice on my phone when it goes off."

"Wow. That is very clever." Wendell grinned back at her. Security equipment had come a long way in recent years. With next to no effort and little expenditure, there could be fully functional cameras all over the property.

"Thank you. My son set it up for us." Her smile faltered a bit. "He's the one we're going to go stay with while Bill recuperates."

He didn't have a suitable response to that, so Wendell simply nodded.

"Kelpie's Roost is the first cottage, and is yours for the duration." Sandra started walking again, and Wendell followed her. At the door —painted a cheery sky blue with a navy trim—Sandra pulled a large ring of keys from her waist and unlocked the door, gesturing for him to proceed her.

Wendell strode in. This was full-on nautical theme with anchors and ropes and navy blue accents. Pirate's Roost would have been more expected and cliched. Kelpie was a better choice by far. Sounded innocuous but kelpie meant water demon. Had them leaning right into the paranormal without sounding scary for those only interested in a lark or a regular beach vacation. Good thing Wendell wasn't superstitious.

After dropping his overnight bag off in his cottage, Sandra separated a carabiner on her key ring, and handed him a ring of keys identical to the one left in her hand. "Here. This will get you in pretty much everywhere on the property."

"Everywhere?"

"Yes. Including our cottage, but as that is where Jackson will be staying, please don't use it except in case of emergency."

Wendell nodded. That went without saying, as far as he was concerned. But he was glad Sandra had reminded him the temporary manager's name was Jackson.

"That's a lot of keys." Even though it had been years ago that he'd worked in a hotel, anywhere that didn't open with a swipe of a passcard used a single master key. No one carried around a different key for every guest room. Super old-fashioned, to be sure.

Sandra shrugged. "Probably we should update the locks and all, but our customers like the classic feel of a key with a fob."

"Oh, of course." Wendell's mind was already whirling. Surely there was a way to embed sensors into a key that only looked old-fashioned but still acted more like a modern security system rather than a lock that could get picked by some rando with a paperclip or hairpin. Had story potential but a bit terrifying for real life.

But he was only here for the short term. Any suggestions for improvements would be overstepping in the extreme. And if anyone understood the value of atmosphere, it was him.

"At the moment, the other three cottages farther down the beach are occupied through the weekend. Bill and I are in the Friar's Lantern room on the first floor of the main building. The other accessible room on the first floor is unoccupied, as are the four rooms on the second floor. Daisy's up there now. She's our full-time housekeeper, and she does most of the cleaning, but we also have a part timer who helps her out when things get busy. We have a few other people who are in and out to help, and there will also be additional backup Jackson can call in if needed. This is the calm before the storm. There's always a lull in occupancy prior to Haunt Fest."

"Okay, sure." Wendell sucked in a breath, marveling at how a different ocean carried its own scent and character. And despite the common sight of palm trees, this didn't seem anything like home. Hopefully, he hadn't made a big mistake signing up for this. Jackson would be here and in charge, but this was someone's livelihood he was potentially fucking with.

Sandra laughed. "Oh, honey. You looked like you saw a ghost. Don't worry. You and Jackson will be fine. I've got a binder of information at the desk, that should cover off everything, including contact information for employees and backup. It's not just you and him against the tide."

Wendell took a deep breath and sighed. "Are we expecting any new guests this weekend?"

"Not until Sunday afternoon. And it's only one room at that. All the other guests will be clearing out early in the week, then you'll have a bit of break until the following weekend. You've got a chance to get your feet under you."

Not much of a chance, though. Haunt Fest would be here really damned fast. Sandra and Bill were planning to depart as soon as they could after Jackson arrived. Now that Wendell was here, the task he'd taken on for himself was more than a little daunting. He'd wanted to be kept busy enough that he didn't dwell on his lack of creative progress, but now he was afraid he was going to be overwhelmed, even with Jackson bearing the brunt of the work.

"It'll be fine, honey. By the time Haunt Fest comes around, you'll be an old hand. No one needs to be on the desk all the time. Mostly, you can just lock the front door and put up a sign with the main phone number. You can forward it to your cell or Jackson's—whoever is on duty."

Sandra led him back up the path toward the main building, talking all the way. It was almost like she'd been afraid to scare him off, but once his bag was in the cottage, the dam broke.

"All the outdoor maintenance has been arranged for. They'll keep the lawn mowed, the vegetation tamed, and the place sprayed for bugs."

"Bugs?" An involuntary shiver danced up his spine.

"Just life in the tropics. Don't panic the first time you see a palmetto bug."

Wendell grimaced. "I'll try not to." Maybe there was more inspiration here than he'd realized.

After his second movie, *The Missing Sarcophagus*, which featured so, so, many flesh-eating dermestid beetles, Wendell had developed a definite aversion to bugs. The research had been… intense.

He plucked at his t-shirt, already damp from the heat and humidity. The moisture in the air wasn't the only difference to home. Instead of a steady background hum of traffic, he could hear the surf. Having been born and raised in LA, he'd never lived right on the water. And although Hollywood could be incestuous and insular, it wasn't the same as a living in a small town. He was looking forward to the change. Maybe he'd feel differently come December, but so far, this seemed a small sacrifice.

"Laundry is taken care of by a service, but there are a couple of coin washers in the mud room for guests who need them and a couple of industrial machines in the storage area behind the kitchen for emergencies or for your personal use."

By this time, they'd reached the back door. Sandra opened it and a whoosh of cool air wafted over him. He hadn't realized how hot he'd gotten and the drop in temperature was incredibly welcome.

Wendell glanced into the mud room as they passed, but Sandra didn't slow down until they'd reached the lobby. She held up a key and unlocked the office behind the desk.

Not a window to be found, and looked exactly as one would expect.

Sandra tapped a plain green binder on the desk. "Everything you need is in here. I've created a profile for you in the computer system.

The login information and how to set up the motion sensor alarm on your phone. But if you don't mind, I have to run some errands while Bill is still asleep."

Wendell squinted at his new boss. She looked almost like a whole different woman from the one he met just twenty minutes ago. One who couldn't get out of here fast enough. "Are... is everything okay?"

Sandra smiled, wide and happy, right up to her eyes, like a modern, well-tanned Mrs. Claus in a mint green pant suit. "Wendell, honey, just talking about handing this over has been such a relief. Once Jackson gets here, I'm going to believe this is really happening."

Then, like a curtain falling, her smile dropped and her eyes filled up with tears. She sniffed, and grabbed a tissue to dab at her cheeks. "I'm so, so sorry. But the last six weeks have been hard, and I've been worried the whole time. I've been stressed about Bill, and Bill has been so stressed about being laid up and not able to help me... he just hasn't been getting better. I've been..." She hiccupped. "I've been afraid this place was going to kill him."

Wendell reached out and squeezed her hands. "It's okay. Whatever comes up, we can handle it. You can take Bill away and relax. I promise."

Hopefully Jackson wasn't going to be an asshole, but Wendell navigated the treacherous waters of movie star wannabes on the daily. He ought to be able to get along with one man for a few months.

"Thank you. Thank you."

"Anything else I need to know before you leave?"

"I shouldn't be too long, but breakfast has already been served. During the week it's continental breakfast, catered by Mysteriously Good Confections—they've already been and gone. They also bring in afternoon tea every day. On the weekend, we have a cook come in to prepare a full breakfast for the guests."

"Oh, that makes it easier."

Sandra shrugged. "There was a time when I made breakfast every day myself, but I just can't anymore. And having breakfast and tea catered only made sense." She fluttered her hands around. "Please, just, wander around and get to know the place. I should be back by lunchtime, then you can explore the town a bit."

"Go. I'll be fine." Probably. He managed to bite back a question about Jackson's arrival time. He was a grown man with all the knowledge of the world at his fingertips, in the form of a phone with an unlimited data plan. He would be fine until Jackson showed up.

Just in case, though, the first thing he should look up in the employee binder was the Wi-Fi password.

TWO

29 Days to Haunt Fest

"MORNING, KYLE."

Kyle Grainger looked up and waved. "Morning, Mrs. Williams."

He loved starting his day walking down Main Street, even when he ran into teachers who'd known him as a small boy, like Mrs. Williams, his first grade teacher. One day, he might even feel mature enough to call her Miriam, but today was not that day.

Sandy Bottom Bay was such a quintessential small Florida town, overlaid with the kitsch of the paranormal. Considering its claim to fame as the second most haunted town in Florida, everyone was quite friendly.

The thing he couldn't quite wrap his mind around today was that his best friend, Drew, was married and had flown out last night for a three week honeymoon in Paris.

Paris.

Kyle wasn't teeth-gnashingly jealous. Not even a tiny bit.

Okay. Maybe a minuscule bit.

A week ago, he'd been caught up in the frenzy of preparations leading up to Drew's wedding. Without his best friend in town, and nothing to occupy his time other than his normal work, Kyle was... empty? Bored? No, he hadn't didn't really have time to be bored, and in a few short weeks, Sandy Bottom Bay would be heading into their peak tourist season. Kyle wouldn't have time to breathe, much less worry about this feeling of discontent curdling his mood.

Normally the town had two peak seasons, in the spring and fall. Spring saw an influx of college students, as did most of the state, giving the town a welcome economic boost.

The fall season started with Haunt Fest in first week of October, and the town was overrun pretty much from Haunt Fest through Day of the Dead in November, filled with the most rabid of the paranomalists and those looking for an unusual vacation experience. Given the crowds they'd already seen so far, everyone was anticipating a much busier Haunt Fest this year, too.

Paranormal aficionados visited all year around, keeping the town busy. The winter saw a number of snowbirds who didn't give a fuck about hauntings. The past year had been different. After the episode of *Phantoms* featuring Sandy Bottom Bay had aired, nearly six months after filming, business had picked up and even off-peak times saw more tourists than ever before.

Fall peak season also meant Kyle would be guiding more haunted walks than he did during any other season and he wasn't going to be able to relax much. Drew, aka Malachi the Mystic, owned a psychic tarot reading business, supplemented by selling herbs, candles, incense, and the like.

While Drew was on his honeymoon, Kyle was minding the store. The brick and mortar store. He was already in charge of Drew's online business, which had supplied them both with a much-needed steady source of income. For the first time in a long time, he and Drew had been able to unpinch a few pennies. They hadn't been forced to buy fucking ramen or peanut butter just to survive.

Not that Kyle did tarot readings. Hell no. Cold reading took way more patience than Kyle had, and besides, since Drew started to show evidence of true second sight after a head injury two years ago, Kyle had even less interest in trying to give anyone a reading that made sense. But selling the bits and bobs that went along with all the mystical hocus-pocus was something Kyle could do. A week or three behind the counter wouldn't hurt, and might give him a few ideas to update the web store.

Keeping busy had the advantage of keeping him from getting envious—much—about Drew's happy love life. After Haunt Fest last year, Drew and his big strong cop had driven up the coast to see the fall colors—Drew had never been on vacation, nor had he ever been out of state—and to celebrate their one-year anniversary. When they'd returned from that trip engaged and planning a wedding, Kyle had been thrilled. Mostly thrilled. Almost entirely thrilled.

Jealousy occasionally wormed its slimy, green tentacles into his heart, but only because Kyle wanted a man who loved him as much as Cliff loved Drew. His best friend deserved nothing less, and ugly emotions withered and disappeared in the face of Drew's delighted happiness.

The wedding had been beautiful, and a goodly chunk of towns-people had participated in the festivities. They'd had a few days to breathe and recover, then late last night, Cliff had whisked Drew off to the airport. Watching Drew's business for him while he was away was a no-brainer.

And if Kyle felt a little adrift, that was normal. Not only was there a gap in his life where Drew had always resided, but he also wanted his own boyfriend. But the last thing he wanted was for Drew to witness his increasing dissatisfaction with his so-called love life and feel guilty for being happy. Drew deserved the best, and he'd fought through a really shitty childhood to get it.

Kyle's life hadn't been a bed of roses, but neither had it been a bed of nails. He just hoped love would come his way. Or even a little fling. There hadn't been time in months to socialize, but maybe after

Haunt Fest he could find someone. A winter vacation fling? Surely that wasn't too much to ask for.

Kyle snorted. He didn't like his chances of that happening. Most of the people who vacationed in the winter were snow birds, and not to be ageist, but he wasn't interested in any dudes who already had grandkids.

With a sigh, Kyle plucked Drew's keyring out of his pocket and turned up the path to Malachi's. Drew's grandmother had left him the tarot business, along with the property. At one point it had been a tiny house fronting on Main Street, but it had long since been split into an actual store front with the original living room and dining room converted to a waiting room/sales floor and a private reading room. Drew and Cliff lived in the back half of the building, with a new addition to give them an office/guest room and a proper living room.

A bright pink piece of paper on the front door caught Kyle's eye, and he squinted. Surely that couldn't be....

A few swift strides put him within reading distance.

Kyle ripped the paper down and crumpled it in his fist.

Fucking Eddie Price.

Drew hadn't been gone one damned day and already Eddie was trying to divert Drew's business. Again. Not that there was a huge amount of overlap between those people wanting a medium and those wanting their cards read, but Eddie did his damnedest anyway. When Drew had been recovering from his concussion two years ago Eddie had tried the same garbage, but he'd swiftly been put in his place by Drew's brother, as well as Cliff, and Cliff's mother, Helen Somerset, Sandy Bottom Bay's unofficial matriarch. Since then, he'd shifted his feud, such as it was, to Kyle.

At least Eddie's feud with Kyle didn't impact anyone's livelihood. Kyle didn't care about Eddie not talking to him, or glaring at him or whatever. Three or so years ago, Kyle and Eddie, who was bisexual, had spent a week boinking like bunnies but there hadn't been any real emotional connection. And while Kyle didn't have anything against decent, no-strings sex, he wanted the strings, and the sex hadn't been anything special.

Didn't help that most of the young single women in town had been pissed off at him for taking Eddie out of circulation, however temporarily. Competition for dates and boyfriends was practically a blood sport in this tiny town.

Kyle strode down the street as quickly as his bum knee would let him, turned the corner to circle the village green, walked another three blocks, then stormed up the path.

After stumbling slightly on the steps, he took a moment to steady himself, and took another fortifying glance at the aggravating, irritating, presumptuous-as-fuck message on the flyer in his hand. After half a mile in the Florida heat, even this early in the day, he felt more wilted than wrathful. Although he still had a vicious little thrill that Eddie's location wasn't nearly as prime as Drew's. Not as much tourist foot traffic here by the bank and the medical offices as there was on Main Street.

He flung the front door of Eddie's Ghost Whispers open and blew inside. Fortunately, Eddie was right there. It would have been a lot harder to hold on to the full head of steam if he'd had to wait.

"What the fuck is the meaning of this, Eddie?"

Kyle ripped the notice to shreds and tossed it in the air in a dramatic flourish, letting it flutter to his feet in a cloud of large pink confetti.

Eddie blinked his long, Bambi-like lashes at him and attempted an innocent look. "You've made a mess, Kyle. What's the meaning of *that?*"

Kyle gritted his teeth. "Haven't we warned you about the signs? Cliff won't be happy to hear about this. Nor will the twins."

Ha. Like Kyle would seek out Drew's twin brothers to tell them about this. He was still mad at them. But this feud, perpetuated almost entirely on Eddie's side, was ridiculously childish and undermined both Eddie's and Drew's credibility. It had tapered off almost as soon as Cliff moved in with Drew, but apparently Eddie was taking advantage of Drew's much-deserved honeymoon and the corresponding absence of Drew's big scary cop, Cliff Garcia. Even more ridiculous that Drew—and sometimes Kyle—at nine years Eddie's junior, was the more reasonable party.

Eddie gave him another attempt at an innocent look and an unconcerned shrug. "Just trying to make sure Drew's customers are happy. After all, he's not here. And neither is Cliff."

Anger boiled up in Kyle and he gritted his teeth. It would serve Eddie right if he did march right over to Rob and Wyatt's place. Not that he ever would. But it made a nice dream. Both of Drew's brothers were redneck assholes, but they were also sexy as hell and super protective of both him and Drew. Also, super straight. Sexually, anyway. Their morals were about as straight as rotini. There was a good reason the extended Drummond family were likened to rats and had very little respect from the townspeople. Drew and his late grandmother were the sole exception to the brush that tarred the whole family, although lately the twins had been trying to up their game and become more respectable.

But running to Rob and Wyatt might result in a brawl, and oily Eddie would probably squeak out of jail time. Drew's brothers might not be so lucky, and Kyle would rather bust his other knee than make Drew cut short his honeymoon to come bail out his brothers.

"Cliff isn't the only cop I can call about harassment."

Eddie shrugged again and pointedly turned his attention to the tablet in his hands, typing out something. "I'm just trying to do a nice thing for a friend."

Oh sure. Just like Kyle was currently starring in a Broadway musical.

"Right. Because the needs of others are just so damned important to you." Kyle glared, only slightly mollified by Eddie's reddened cheeks.

The door opened behind him, preventing Kyle from rehashing that useless argument. Kyle had his suspicions about why Eddie had bothered to seduce him in the first place, but things had gone from bitter to downright sour since Drew had gotten engaged.

"If you'll excuse me, Kyle. I actually have a customer that needs attention." Eddie set the tablet on the counter and turned his back on Kyle to fawn greasily over the newcomer, who clearly sensed she'd walked in on something.

Eddie's words were reasonable, but the tone implied Kyle was a waste of time and couldn't possibly have to worry about paying customers.

Kyle curled his lip up in a sneer, noticing Eddie had left his tablet unlocked. Kyle's next self-appointed task was to get Drew to upgrade from computer and paper calendar to a tablet that would both schedule appointments and process payments. So damned annoying that Eddie already had made that transition. A quick glance over his shoulder confirmed Eddie was still pointedly ignoring him. Kyle leaned over the counter, tapped quickly on the tablet, then picked up one of Eddie's business cards as plausible cover. He'd throw it out later or stuff it in a voodoo doll or something.

"Thanks for the business card, Eddie." Kyle swanned out, putting a little extra swish in his hips. He'd much rather wait around to see Eddie's face when he tried to compose an invoice or schedule a new appointment and realized his tablet's default had been changed from English to Japanese, but Kyle really couldn't neglect Drew's business to indulge in this stupid, useless feud. Unless Eddie didn't back off, like a reasonable, adult, human being. Then he was fully prepared to bring the big guns—whatever those might be. Lube in his hand sanitizer? Hidden speakers in the ceiling with a porn soundtrack? A pair of lacy underwear on the pathway? He'd come up with something.

A new spring in his step, Kyle strode down the street like he owned it. If only. Until recently, he'd been working four part-time jobs, but he'd been able to shed the least rewarding—both mentally and financially—once Drew's online business had picked up. He had flexible hours as Drew's eCommerce manager, and had been able to move into a better apartment a couple of months ago.

Ditching the cheerleading choreography at the high school had been the best thing he'd ever done. He'd hated it, and the cheerleaders didn't respect him at all.

But he hadn't been able give up all the part time jobs. His other two jobs were labors of love, and for the most part, kept him too busy to bemoan the utter wasteland of his love life. He hadn't had a boyfriend since he'd left college. The busy tourist seasons were enough to bring in a stray hookup here and there, but even that could be a challenge because he was often too busy and too tired to put in the effort required to pick someone up.

Back at Drew's, he unlocked the front door and flipped on the lights. After locating the sign that explained the storefront was open but no readings were available, he popped it in the door then sat behind the counter and fired up the computer. Orders needed to be fulfilled and inventory needed to be replaced.

After a few minutes, Kyle huffed out a sigh and wandered to the front window. A fairly steady trickle of foot traffic passed by, heading for the beach. If he craned his neck and popped up on his toes, almost en pointe, he could see the ocean from here.

Should he go to the beach this afternoon? More fun to go with someone, but it was still a workday for most of his other friends. Even if Drew hadn't been gallivanting off on his honeymoon, Kyle would have been hard pressed to convince him to play hooky.

With the sun shining so brightly, he didn't expect many takers for smudging sticks or incense. Despite preparing for the uptick in tourists over the next couple of weeks, Drew had explicitly said Kyle didn't have to sit around keeping the front shop open the whole time.

Sadly, Kyle didn't have anything else to do. At least he had some bookings for his ghost walk that evening. He'd be too busy to dwell on the fact he had nothing to do on a Friday night besides work.

He tweaked a display of meditation candles then pulled out his phone. No messages, no texts, and he didn't have the mental energy to open up any of the dating and/or hookup apps he had. While he appreciated the sight of a well-formed dick, and appreciated a man who could verbalize what he wanted, Kyle was over the whole "wanna fuck?" plus dick pic that seemed to be the sum total of app users' communication skills.

He was old-fashioned. Or perhaps jaded, but he craved a tiny bit of conversation. Even a minimalistic "Hi" before launching into a request for sexual preferences and positions would be nice. There just weren't enough single, decent, non-weird gay men who lived locally. He loved Sandy Bottom Bay and its quirky claim to fame, he loved the close-knit nature of the community, and he even mostly loved the influx of tourists, but sometimes it was hard to believe he was going to be stuck here for the rest of his life. Mouldering into the woodwork, leaning into eccentricities, contributing to the general Floridian weirdness.

He leaned over and rubbed his knee, which had been aching all morning. Not a storm coming in this time; he'd only slept on it funny. His righteous march over to Eddie's had not been wise, with respect to his bum knee.

Dancing was supposed to have been his way out. Dancing was going to take him places. And then it had all gone so horribly wrong. The only thing that made sense was coming back home. Without dancing, he wasn't motivated to move away, or find another career aside from the one he was currently carving out for himself. Not a calling or a passion like dancing had been, but respectable.

Now that he was no longer holding body and soul together with dental floss and ramen, where an unexpected twenty dollar expense might mean the difference between eating regularly and not, he wanted someone to share his life with. Drew might be his best friend, but he had Cliff now. Kyle would always be the third wheel. And that was no longer enough. He'd always had a competitive streak and coming in second didn't cut it.

Unfortunately, wishing for a man to appear didn't make it so.

A small, bright blue car crawled past the window.

"Who the hell is that?" Kyle didn't love his new habit of talking to himself but there wasn't anyone around to hear him, so it didn't matter.

Hardly anyone in town owned such a small car, and definitely not in that color. It could be a tourist who'd lost their way, but there wasn't any beach parking here on Main Street, and the signage for that was pretty damn clear at the roundabout by the village green.

Kyle pressed himself closer to the window, and saw the hybrid turn into the overgrown parking lot at the bed and breakfast.

Mystery solved. And kind of a letdown. A new guest at the Orange Lady Inn wasn't newsworthy.

Another vehicle stopped in front of Malachi's, a large brown truck blocking his view. The UPS delivery was probably going to be the most exciting part of his day. Kyle stared at the inventory for a few minutes before he pulled out his phone. Maybe read a quick chapter or two of his book before he dove into work.

THREE

29 Days to Haunt Fest

AS SOON AS Sandra returned from her errands, Wendell picked up a map of Sandy Bottom Bay from the display of pamphlets in the lobby and headed straight for the food trucks. He'd spent more time than he should have back in LA seeking out food trucks, but he just loved the idea and the food was usually so good.

The trucks were slightly off the beaten path, which made sense since they didn't exactly fit the whole spook-a-rific reputation of the town, but they were still within walking distance of just about every item of interest highlighted on his map. Wise, as far as Wendell was concerned.

He had his choice of three today, and he stood on the sidewalk, considering. Fish and chips, burgers, or burritos. The selection was a little slim but they all sounded good.

An angry grumble not unlike a nether demon on the prowl came from the vicinity of his belly. A quick glance around assured him that no one was close enough to hear the yawning emptiness in his gut.

He should have eaten on the plane but airplane breakfasts were the worst, and by the time he'd picked up his luggage, he'd just wanted to get on the road.

Burritos. Definitely burritos. They had to be the most filling. Wendell ordered, a line starting to form behind him composed of both beach-attired tourists and fully dressed business people. He'd gotten here just in time.

"Are you here every day?" Wendell handed over a twenty to a guy about his age while another, older man started putting his burrito together. While he could probably eat burritos every day, it might be nice if there was a little variety. He wasn't entirely sure how he felt about packing in with the tourists at the Specter Smorgasbord, and while Sandra had given him run of the kitchen, he wasn't much of a cook.

"Nah. We rotate out with a few other trucks, but I'm usually here Thursdays and Fridays."

"Good to know."

"You new in town?"

Wendell lifted a shoulder. "Yes, as of today actually. I'm here for a few months."

The dude raised a brow. "Oh yeah? Well, I hope to see you back here again." And he handed Weston a bottle of water and a foil wrapped brick of a burrito.

"Uh. Thanks. Have a good one."

"If you don't have anywhere to be, head up to the clock tower. There's a garden there with benches and some shade." The young guy winked at him then moved on to the next customer.

Wendell stepped out of the way and looked around. A garden bench in the shade definitely held more appeal than the few picnic benches on asphalt that had been set up to accommodate the food trucks' customers. He'd walked right past the garden but he'd been so focused on getting food he hadn't noticed any benches.

A few minutes later, Wendell had claimed a prime bench under a fat-trunked tree with crazy overhanging branches. He thought it might be an oak tree but it definitely wasn't something he'd seen in LA. The bench faced the traffic circle that surrounded the village green, where a clock tower featured prominently.

Wendell leaned back against the bench for a moment, just taking it all in. It was fucking hot, and the humidity would really take some getting used to. He plucked at his short-sleeved shirt. So glad he hadn't opted for a long-sleeved one. With all the moisture in the air, being in the shade didn't make it that much cooler. Shade was a far more effective cooling device in the desert.

He drained half his water, then picked up his burrito.

"Jeez. I could eat for a week with this thing." But he was going to eat it all right now, as long as it was decent. If weight was any indication, it was going to be an excellent burrito.

He unwrapped it and took a bite. "Oh my god." He didn't even care if anyone heard him moaning over his burrito because it was like manna from the heavens. Next time he'd ask for extra hot sauce, but otherwise it might have been the best burrito he'd put in his mouth and that was saying something.

Perusing the map while he ate, he made some mental notes about what he wanted to check out first. Not today, of course. He had one more stop after this, but he didn't want to spend all afternoon exploring, no matter that Sandra had said he should.

So far, nothing he'd seen gave out any creepy vibes. Palm trees and sunshine had a way of mitigating anything scary. It was a minor miracle that he'd managed to write as many scripts as he had, because Southern California had a similar problem. He sighed and focused on his lunch. No need to overthink himself into a corner.

After a leisurely lunch, Wendell stood and threw his garbage in a nearby trash bin. If he'd sat there any longer, the heavy but delicious burrito and the muggy early afternoon heat would have lulled him to sleep, right there on the park bench. He had a lot to do today, but an early night was definitely on the agenda.

By the time he walked the few blocks to Mysteriously Good Confections, he was more awake and substantially sweatier. As soon as he opened the door, chilly air hit him in the face and the scent of sugary treats slapped him all the way awake. He could *live* here, just for the smell alone.

Although it was almost one, the bakery still had a number of patrons lunching around tiny tea tables. Wendell had only come in intending to introduce himself to the manager since getting to know the caterers for the inn only seemed wise. And the bakery's name had also intrigued him. Despite his good intentions and the mammoth burrito, no way he'd be able to leave here empty-handed.

He approached the counter, but not near enough that anyone would assume he was ready to order. The selection of savory items had been well picked over by now, but he was pleasantly surprised to see quiches, Cornish pasties, and empanadas, alongside tasty-looking sandwiches. He'd remember that for the future. But it was the sweets that had his attention now. Most of the cakes, cookies, and cupcakes had ghosts or tombstones or the like adorning their glossy frosting. Halloween-like, and probably available all year round. But even the ones that weren't haunt-themed were frosted in glorious shades of purple, blue, teal, red, and pink. Even the shelves of bread looked enticing.

The only thing to do was to get in line and order quick, otherwise he'd buy one of everything, and that was the last thing he needed on top of his lunch.

Within moments, he was at the cash register.

"Can I get a few things to go?"

The grizzled older man behind the counter smiled pleasantly. "Of course. What would you like?"

The ghost gingerbreads and tombstone sugar cookies were tempting, but for today...

"I'll have two cupcakes, please."

"Which flavors?"

Now the pressure was on, and he perused the case like his life depended on his choice.

"I think I'll take a Kraken." Mostly because of the swirled shades of blue frosting. "And a Vampire Kiss." Which looked like a chocolate cupcake with chocolate frosting decorated with a set of molded white chocolate fangs, but he loved a good chocolate cupcake and the name intrigued him.

So far, the bakery appeared to be the best source of inspiration in Sandy Bottom Bay.

"Very good choices." The man's gaze dropped to Wendell's pale peach shirt. "But be careful. The cupcakes can be a little messy."

"Thanks, I'll keep that in mind." Could they possibly be messier than his lunch? Doubtful, and he'd managed to keep that from dribbling down his shirt.

As soon as he paid, Wendell glanced around. Only two people in line behind him. Good. "Would Lisa Watson be here by any chance? I'd like to speak with her."

That got him a narrow-eyed look. "She's here, but she might be in the middle of something. If you want to take a seat, let me finish up with the line and I'll go see."

"Thank you, I'd appreciate that." He'd been hoping to get back to the inn within an hour and if he didn't have to wait too long, he'd be back in just over that.

"Did you want a cup of coffee while you wait?"

"Actually, yes, that would be great."

Mr. Grizzled turned to a coffee station that looked like it came from an old-school diner—no fancy lattes or cappuccinos here. He poured coffee into a plain white ceramic mug and handed it to Wendell.

"I'll bring your pastries over to your table. Did you want to eat any of them with your coffee?"

"No, thank you. I'm saving them for later."

He took the mug to the coffee fixings bar and doctored it to his liking before sitting at a recently vacated table. Then he took a sip and almost moaned. Definitely something to be said for a good cup of coffee, and this qualified as great. If the pastries were as good as the coffee, it was a no-brainer that Sandra had asked them to cater for the inn. But he wasn't about to do any taste testing at the moment, partly because he was too full and partly because he didn't want to have his mouth full when Lisa showed up.

After Mr. Grizzled served the two remaining customers, he brought over a glossy black paper bag with the Mysteriously Good logo embossed on the side in silver foil. Eye-catching for sure, especially in a beachside town.

"Thank you." Wendell peeked inside. A bright teal bakery box sat inside, with a black sticker on the top, also with the logo. Elegant, understated, and yet thoroughly striking. He definitely admired the marketing. A discreet sniff inside the bag had his mouth watering, but he was definitely going to save these. For a couple of hours at least.

A few sips later, a woman approached his table. Her hair was scraped back in a bun and she wore an apron streaked with color like a Pollock painting.

"Hi. I'm Lisa Watson. Tony said you wanted to speak with me?"

That'd teach him to assume. Because this woman was nothing like he expected as the owner of clearly successful bakery. He'd been vaguely expecting an older woman, grandmotherly. In fact, he'd swear Lisa was a few years younger than him.

"Hello. Would you care to sit for a few minutes?"

There was some indecision in her expression, but there was also ample evidence of fatigue. With a quick glance at Tony, she shrugged and sat.

"How can I help you?"

"My name is Wendell Weston. I'm going to be helping out at the Orange Lady while Sandra and Bill are away. And since your excellent bakery is catering, I thought it would only be polite to pop in and introduce myself."

"Nice to meet you, Wendell Weston." Lisa extended her hand and Wendell shook it. "I look forward to working together."

"As do I." Wendell flashed her a grin.

Working together might be an exaggeration, especially as he wasn't sure how much or how little Jackson would want him to do, but making friends with a baker like Lisa Watson was no hardship at all.

"I also wanted the chance to check out what sort of treats a place called Mysteriously Good had on offer."

Lisa smiled at him. "You could have taste-tested after tea time this afternoon. Sandra doesn't mind the staff having the leftovers."

Wendell's grin stretched wider. "Maybe I didn't want to wait that long."

That coaxed a little laugh out of Lisa.

"I hope you enjoy. Have you met the temporary manager yet? I know Sandra is planning to head out as soon as she can. Not a lot of time to acclimate yourself. I'd be terrified to be left in charge with only a few hours training, and that's not even counting the ghosts in this town."

"True, I am little terrified." Although he didn't actually believe in the supernatural, he wouldn't really mind a spectral encounter, or even a reasonable facsimile. Anything to jumpstart his muse. As long as he didn't seriously fuck up anything at the inn while he did it. "I assume Jackson will be okay with it all, but he hasn't arrived yet."

Lisa thrust her chin in the direction of Wendell's bakery box. "Those for you?"

Wendell's cheeks heated. "I have a bit of a sweet tooth."

"Then you're my kind of person."

Wendell laughed, then drained the last of his coffee. "I'd better get going. I don't want Sandra to have to worry about packing and covering the desk."

"You and Jackson will have help around town if you need it. We all want to Sandra and Bill to be okay. Don't worry, everything will work out fine."

"Thank you." Wendell stood and shook Lisa's hand again before grabbing his bakery bag.

Weirdly, Lisa had known who he was, but hadn't said anything about his research. Normally, when he did research like this, people asked a lot of questions, but Lisa didn't ask one. Had Sandra not mentioned it? She did have a lot on her mind, and Wendell's research was likely a distant second to his value as an additional unpaid employee.

Or maybe a lot of people came to Sandy Bottom Bay for research. Enough that it qualified as ho-hum.

He opened the door and stepped back out into the saline-scented heat and sighed. At least the inn had excellent air conditioning, but if he sweated any more today, he'd have to change his shirt.

"Excuse me."

Wendell focused on the guy who'd spoken. Suddenly, the day got a lot warmer, and he plucked at the neckline of his shirt.

An adorable man with wild blond waves smiled up at him, making him feel every bit as hulking and ungraceful as did most of the wannabe actors in LA. But this time it was also compounded by a solid thump of desire, right in his gut. Was it the hair that wasn't perfectly coifed? Or the sparse sprinkle of freckles across a pert nose? Or maybe it was simply the snug yoga pants that revealed strong, muscular legs.

The man's smile got wider. "Hi. I kinda need to get in there."

"Oh, right." Heat crept up Wendell's neck and he stepped out of the doorway. "Uh, sorry about that."

"No worries."

Wendell twisted to watch the guy's retreating form, but the shapeless T-shirt hung too low to get a good glimpse of what was undoubtedly a spectacular butt.

He sighed. While he hadn't exactly signed up for months of celibacy, neither was he ready to drop trou for a midday hookup on his first day. Assuming the hot blond was into guys and also into him. He'd been born and raised in a town filled with movie actors and models—he was definitely no stranger to rejection and that guy was easily as good-looking as any of the actors he'd come across. Out of his league, for sure, but certainly nice to look at.

A tiny glimmer of an idea flickered in his mind. The first real hint of inspiration he'd found in Sandy Bottom Bay.

Then he shook himself. Staring after some guy like a lovesick puppy wasn't going to make a good impression on anyone.

He tugged on his neckline again, and headed back to the inn. He'd already been gone longer than he'd intended.

Somehow, Kyle managed to keep on walking to the bakery counter. The very attractive guy he'd passed on the way in had flustered him. Enough that he hadn't even added an extra butt wiggle because O-M-G he was wearing yoga pants and a t-shirt that could double as a yurt.

Probably a good thing, though. The last thing he needed was another meaningless fling with some guy on vacation who was going back home to a boyfriend, husband, wife, or even the closet. Not that he usually had time to fuck around with tourists anyway. Because the more tourists that were around to catch his eye—and this one was definitely eye-catching—the busier he was.

Besides, seeing his best friend fall in love and get married had stoked the embers of hope inside his chest. Not that there were many husbandly—or even boyfriendly—prospects in Sandy Bottom Bay, but that didn't change his heart's desire any.

Instead of sighing or moping, Kyle plastered a smile on his face as the door closed behind him with a tinkle of bells. "Hey, Tony. Hey, Lisa. Don't see you on this side of the counter too often these days."

Tony nodded and continued wiping down the counter but Lisa smiled back and came over to hug him.

"Looks like you've got an admirer," Lisa whispered in his ear.

Kyle turned his head in time to see the attractive guy avert his eyes and rub the back of his neck. Even at this distance he could see a sudden flare of red in the guy's skin, but that could just as easily be a reaction to the sun and heat as embarrassment. Gave him a little flutter in his belly all the same.

"Another tourist." He quashed that flutter with disdain as he extricated himself from Lisa's hug.

"Not exactly."

"What do you mean?"

"He's helping out at the inn. Not the temporary manager, but... backup?"

Kyle put a hand on his belly, hoping to calm the sudden, aggressive resurgence of butterflies.

"You mean, he's going to be here for a while?"

"Three months, I believe. And I think he likes you."

Kyle shrugged and waved off Lisa's words. Plenty of time to assess that, if the guy was going to be around for the next few months.

"How did you even manage to find that out so fast?"

Lisa waggled her eyebrows. "I am just that good."

"Uh-huh. You're going to get a reputation for being psychic."

"In this town? I don't think so. Drew has that job all locked up. But if you think gossip doesn't flow through here faster than I go through sugar, you're being willfully obtuse."

Gossip. That made sense. It travelled faster than wildfire. Kyle tamped down a little spurt of irritation. Although he'd hated choreographing cheerleading routines and had been more than grateful to ditch that particular job once he no longer needed it to make ends meet, he did miss the unending font of gossip. When he wasn't actively coaching the cheerleaders, it was like he'd been rendered invisible. But he'd overheard a crazy amount of confidential information as a result of teenagers talking in front him, utterly heedless of his presence.

"You're like the queen bee in her hive, and all the little worker bees bring you tidbits of information."

"You better believe it, buster." Lisa laughed. "You in for lunch? I've got goat cheese and sun-dried tomato quiche today."

Kyle groaned. "I was only going to have a ham sandwich." Half of one, more like. No cheese, no mayo. With his bum knee and lack of intense dance rehearsals, he worried about putting on weight. It had been a lot easier to not indulge when he'd been flat broke.

"You sure?"

"Fine. Quiche it is." He'd known he was going to cave the

moment he decided to come to the bakery for lunch. Honestly, he'd wanted a little comfort food and Lisa made the best quiches.

Kyle slid into a chair near the window and pulled out his phone. Drew had texted him a picture of the Eiffel tower. Lucky bastard.

He pulled up one of his time-wasting games and played a few levels before Tony came over and placed a plate with warmed up quiche on it, along with a fork.

"Oh, thanks, Tony." He'd sort of hoped Lisa had been going to sit with him while he ate, but she was busier than ever these days. After the fire that destroyed a good portion of the bakery, the previous owner decided to sell up. Lisa and her husband Mateo bought it, and she'd gone from assistant manager and part-time baker to owner and full-time baker. It was great to see the place thriving under Lisa's stewardship.

Nevertheless, Kyle felt a little sorry for himself.

No more than ten minutes later, the quiche was nothing more than a few crumbs, and he should really be getting back to his work. Not that anything was all that pressing, but he didn't exactly have anything else to do.

First things first. He checked the confirmations in his email. Seven people signed up for the tour. A dozen cookies should do. If he didn't have any late sign-ups, he could give out doubles to most of the people. Or just hang on to them until tomorrow's tour. Save him a trip back to the bakery.

At the counter, he picked out a dozen individually wrapped sugar cookies decorated with various haunt-themed images, and Tony put them in a black bag with a handful of teal business cards.

Kyle got a discount, and a number of his tour clients hit the bakery at least once during their stay in Sandy Bottom Bay.

He managed to walk the few blocks back to Drew's storefront before he realized something rather important. Important enough to send a wave of goosebumps up his spine. He craned his neck to get a glimpse of the inn down the street but the box hedges and slight curve of the road blocked most of the view of the first floor from here.

Tonight, he'd be meeting his ghost walk group in the same place as always, the front porch of the Orange Lady Inn. It was his customary starting point, and Sandra was always happy to have the group as she frequently got new business from Kyle's tours. Although there wasn't normally anyone covering the desk at that time of night, Sandra often came out to introduce herself to the tour group.

But tonight, would Sandra show up? Would it be the temporary manager? Or would he see the other guy? The guy who had so flustered Kyle that he'd fucking forgotten to ask Lisa what his name was.

Then again, if the guy was as attractive as he'd seemed at first glance, Kyle wouldn't be able to get a word out anyway. For someone who was far more likely to forge ahead in life than hang back, he was awkward and uncool in the presence of guys he was attracted to. Not that he never got laid, but every crush he'd ever had in life turned him into a voiceless, too-smiley weirdo.

At least the events of two years ago had cured his very X-rated crush on Drew's older twin brothers. Not only were they straight, but their carelessness had almost gotten Drew killed. He appreciated their protectiveness over the years, but he no longer became completely mute in their presence. Better for everyone involved, really. But this felt very much like the stirrings of a new crush and that... Would. Not. Do.

A long, low growl of thunder made him lift his eyes to the horizon out over the ocean. Somehow, he'd missed the darkening of the sky, lost in his thoughts, on the walk back from the bakery. Angry clouds piled up over the lighthouse in the distance, heading southeast, as in directly for Sandy Bottom Bay. Looked a little more intense than their normal, daily summer deluge.

Like it was only waiting for Kyle to notice, his knee twinged and he glared at the offending joint. Being a human weather vane at the grand old age of twenty-four had not been a life goal.

A fresh breeze brought a hint of cool moisture to ruffle his hair, and he scrambled up the path to Drew's storefront. Getting caught out in the rain was definitely not on his list. He managed to unlock the door and get it shut behind him before the air turned gray with sheets of water.

Kyle took in a deep breath, and lit a couple of calming lavender-scented candles to chase away the gloom rather than turning on any more lights. He grabbed a bottle of water and settled in the chair behind the counter, soothed by the drumbeat of rain on the roof, a roof that wasn't going to leak after Drew's he-man of a boyfriend—er, husband—had re-shingled it.

Better to get the rain over with now, because if there was anything both he and his knee hated, it was having to conduct a ghost walk in the pouring rain.

One of the candles he'd lit flared up, then sputtered out.

Odd. Kyle squinted at it before getting up to relight it. The flame took as expected. He held up a hand, testing for a draft, but there wasn't any movement of air. Imperfection in the wick maybe. He'd keep an eye on the reviews for the candles, see if he had to source another supplier.

While in front of the window, he glanced in the direction of the inn.

Wonder if the new guy likes thunderstorms?

FOUR

29 Days to Haunt Fest

SINCE JACKSON WAS NOW NOT EXPECTED until sometime the next morning, Wendell took the employee information binder back to his cottage. He could review Sandra's notes, unpack, and maybe make a grocery list.

The sunlight faded and disappeared as he walked along the beach path, as dark, angry clouds pushed in over the ocean.

Fascinated, he wandered through his outdoor sitting area and over the sand to stand closer to the water, clutching the binder to his chest. The water that had, just a few hours ago, looked so blue and inviting with flirtatious little waves, now looked like the realm of a vengeful sea god, gray and stern with roiling white caps. Icy bright lightning flickered in the clouds, and a damp, misty wind tossed his hair about with utter disregard for his styling products.

Thunder boomed, making him jump. He did not want to get drenched, so he strode back to his cottage. From the look of the clouds, the storm was going to be quite major. How had he missed a warning? He'd been listening to a local radio station on the drive from the airport, and neither Sandra nor Lisa had mentioned anything.

Was this a hurricane? He knew what he was supposed to do in the event of an earthquake or a wildfire, but he failed to research—stupidly—what to do to prepare for a hurricane. He shut the door firmly behind him, tossed the binder on the coffee table and slumped down on the sofa, pulling up his weather app on his phone.

All it told him was that heavy rain was expected.

Another bolt of thunder rattled the glass of his sliding doors, and he realized how dark it had gotten inside, despite the relatively early hour.

In desperation, he turned on the television and quickly found the weather channel. They also claimed only heavy rain was on the way, not a hurricane. Wendell tried to relax back into the sofa. Before long, he heard a pattering sound.

Rain. Just rain. He could handle that. He got up to turn on a couple of lights when the sound changed to something akin to running water in a bathtub. He turned toward the sliding glass doors. The water pouring from the sky was like nothing he'd ever seen before. Gushing, splashing, heavy enough to obscure the view of his patio furniture, and forget seeing the beach.

This is what he imagined a blizzard would be like if he were up north, and he was sincerely grateful he was not currently trying to drive through this mess. Or even walk in it.

A rivulet of water streamed along his patio stones, heading for the lower ground of the beach.

So much water had fallen from the sky there was already mini damned rivers forming around his shelter. What madness was this?

As he watched the world drown, the meteorologists on the television spoke of the rain passing. Sure enough, about twenty minutes later, the sky outside began to lighten, and the shapes of the patio furniture came into sharper focus.

Wendell took a deep breath and began to investigate his current lodgings. He wasn't about to head out to the grocery store in the middle of the deluge, but he could prepare a list of what he'd need.

The cottage contained one small bedroom, but the majority of the space had been given over to an open concept catch-all room that was living room, dining room, and kitchenette. It would be a lovely place to write.

He wandered over to the kitchenette. No oven, but the double hot plate, microwave, and tiny gas barbecue on the patio should take care of any of his cooking needs. He opened the few tiny cupboards and found dishes, spices, and a couple of pots, but no teapot or kettle. His grandmother would keel over dead if he told her he'd ever heated up tea water in the microwave, but then she already thought he was crazy for using teabags instead of loose tea anyway. But teabags were easily portable, and the microwave was convenient.

He pulled out his phone and started a grocery list in his notes app. First things on the list were teabags and an electric kettle. He also added a few staples. He wasn't the world's best cook, but he didn't want to have to eat takeout or at restaurants three meals a day. He might be doing fine financially but that would be a lot of money out and a lot of extra calories in over the next few months. Not acceptable.

With a glance out at the steadily decreasing rain, he added umbrella and raincoat to his list, as well as a couple of frozen dinners. Something he could toss into the microwave for a few minutes was about all the effort he wanted to make for dinner tonight, especially since he wanted nothing more than to have a nap.

Once he'd finished his list, he noticed everything had brightened up. Outside, aside from an extremely wet ground, there was no sign of the storm. The sky was blue and the sun was bright and hot enough, he sort of expected to see everything start to steam.

Wendell shook his head. How often did it rain like that here? Guess he'd find out. Although he didn't write it down, he tried to make a mental note to find out what he should do in the event of a hurricane. Probably they were unlikely to have one here, but he did know this was the middle of hurricane season.

He rubbed at his belly. Yeah, that storm had made him just a bit nervous. He'd never thought much about the terror of too much water, but water in large amounts was very powerful. He'd have to remember that.

The real question now was had the storm moved on enough for him to risk trying to drive. He stepped out onto his patio. Half of the patio was covered, and half wasn't. The furniture had all been pushed out to the uncovered part, probably from a previous guest wanting to soak up the sun. Wendell would have to move it all back under the covered area because he sure as hell wasn't going to sit out in the Florida sun, nor did he want to have to worry about getting his pants wet when he sat down.

Problem for another day. He moved out onto the uncovered part of the patio and looked up to the sky. The storm had truly passed, like it had never been there at all.

He went back inside, grabbed his car keys, and headed back along the beach path to the inn's parking lot.

Later that evening, after a spectacular shower with incredible water pressure, Wendell dried himself off and glanced at the time. Around forty-five minutes until sunset. As much as he'd like to just faceplant on his bed, he wasn't keen on the idea of waking up before four in the morning after having a solid eight hours of sleep. Better to push himself to stay awake a little longer. And that meant a cup of tea, a cupcake, and watching the sunset over the water from his private patio.

This was exactly the sort of relaxation he needed to recharge. An immersion in a life far from his own was either going to reinvigorate his creative muscles or was going to precede a different career path. The next few months were going to be his watershed moment, but tonight he was going to enjoy nature as Florida served it up.

He pulled on a pair of baggy cargo shorts and a t-shirt. No point in underwear when he was just going to strip down again when he hit the sack. Wendell ran his fingers through his damp hair and left the bedroom. Normally he'd do a little more to style it, but he was planning to shower in the morning too, and there wasn't anyone to impress between now and when he was going to sleep.

He stood at the sliding glass doors and stared beyond the patio at the small patch of ground sparsely covered in the wide-bladed grass that did not at all look inviting to walk on bare-foot—even if he hadn't been warned about fire ants.

Wendell shuddered. Fire ants. Sounded horrifying, and they'd probably end up having a starring role in a future movie, but he didn't want to tangle with them. Everyone joked about the wildlife in Australia trying to kill people, but Florida had some scary stuff too.

But he could wear his flip-flops, and he had a straight shot down to the beach, so he might go for an early morning swim when he got up. He'd heard the water was warmer here, and he was looking forward to finding out for himself. For all that he'd lived in the Los Angeles area his whole life, he'd never lived anywhere this close to the water. And it was pretty fucking cool.

He wandered over to the kitchenette and started up the kettle for his tea, playing a game on his phone until the water boiled.

Once he had his tea steeping, he turned to the fridge to grab his bakery box. Kraken or Vampire Kiss? Whichever one he didn't eat would end up as breakfast.

Shit. He'd left the box in the staff's mini-fridge in the office. He hadn't even needed to heat up his frozen meal, because he'd simply grazed at the leftovers from the cookies and tea sandwiches that the bakery had catered and set up in the sun room. Between his exhaustion and the giant burrito, he'd had plenty to fill him up, but he'd been looking forward to his cupcakes all afternoon.

Another quick glance at the microwave clock convinced him he had enough time to go grab his baked goods and return before sunset. He slipped on his battered canvas flip-flops, snagged the employee binder to return it to the office, and headed for the inn's main building.

Minutes later, he'd popped into the office and grabbed his bakery box and cradled it close to his chest. He couldn't wait.

A flicker of movement outside caught his eye and he moved closer to the front window. Four people, likely parents and two teen children sat in the rocking chairs on the front porch area, the teens engrossed in their phones.

They didn't have luggage, and Sandra had confirmed that there weren't any new check-ins expected today. They looked harmless enough, but he didn't feel quite right abandoning the front desk with people lurking outside. The door was locked, and if they wanted in, all they needed to do was follow the instructions on the sign, but nevertheless, he went back behind the check-in desk and sat down.

When a trio of mid-twenties girls showed up moments later and also sat down, but not in a manner that suggested they knew the family of four, Wendell was glad he did. If there was anything funny going on, better he know about it now. None of them looked like they were looking for drugs or ready to vandalize the inn, but he would die of shame if anything bad happened on his first day.

Too bad he hadn't brought his tea with him. But he was going to eat a cupcake while he observed. If anything suspicious occurred, he'd be ready to call the cops.

Kraken first or second? First, definitely. Chocolate on chocolate he knew and loved. But Kraken flavor was an unknown entity. The bright teal frosting edged in blue was still alluring, even in the low, after-hours light at the front desk. He peeled back the paper and took a big bite. Lemony fresh flavor burst over his tongue, tempered with a hint of something herbal. Basil maybe? He moaned. It was fucking delicious. He wanted to savor it, but it was so good. Another bite in he discovered a delightful pocket of blackberry compote.

Perhaps he'd binged too many episodes of the *Great British Baking Show* while trying to come up with a new script. Because those words shouldn't easily come to his mind—he was not a baker, and despite the cravings those bakers induced, he'd not had any inclination to try his hand at baking. Besides, anything his amateurish ass could come up with wouldn't be near as good as Lisa Watson's cupcakes.

What an excellent town he'd managed to find.

He retreated back into the office to grab a bottle of water and some napkins to wipe off stray streaks of frosting from his lips and fingers. As much as he wanted to dive right into his second cupcake, he really did want to wait until he had a cup of tea. He settled himself back behind the desk and closed up the bakery box before shifting his gaze back to the group on the porch.

An eighth person had showed up, and Wendell nearly gasped aloud. It was that sexy blond man who he'd spoken to briefly in the doorway to Mysteriously Good Confections. At least, Wendell was almost certain it was the same man. This version was snappily dressed in a white pirate shirt, snug black pants, and black boots. His wild blond hair had been fiercely tamed into finger waves evocative of screen idols from the early days of Hollywood. But the detail that brought it all together into a composed goth-slash-steampunk style was the thick black eyeliner and the hint of artificial pink shine on full lips.

He was fucking glorious, although Wendell wanted to muss up that precise hairstyle, wanted to see what that eyeliner would look like when the guy woke up after a night in someone's—Wendell's—bed. Wondered if the lipgloss had any flavor.

Wendell stood up and moved closer to the window to get a better look. The guy was so far out of his league, and while he hoped he was gay, he didn't know for sure, or if he was out.

The guy opened a battered leather messenger bag—which did nothing to detract from his ensemble—and handed small bottles of water and cellophane bags out to each person in the group. The bags seemed too large for drugs, but it was about time Wendell confirmed everything was on the up and up.

He unlocked the door and opened it, leaning halfway out the door.

"Hey there." Everyone looked at him, the steampunk cutie wide-eyed and stunned, the rest with mostly bored expressions. Wendell didn't know exactly what to say. If the guy was dealing drugs it would be a shattering disappointment, and also might not necessarily be wise to just come out and ask. Colossally stupid might be a better description. Probably he should have located the light above the door and turned it on too.

The blond blinked a couple of times, then shook himself before turning back to the group. "I'll be back in a minute, and we'll get started."

He strode toward Wendell like he owned the place, and Wendell gaze followed the V of the shirt's neckline to the bright, oversized silver-toned belt buckle. There was nothing stopping him from letting his gaze dip a little southward, and he swallowed past a suddenly dry mouth.

Wendell had no idea what to do until the guy waved a hand at him, ushering him back inside. Without a better plan, he obeyed. Stupid, if this guy had bad intentions, but Wendell couldn't believe he wouldn't be able to sense it. Couldn't believe he'd be so fucking attracted to the guy if he was up to no good. Bad boys had never been Wendell's thing. No denying that this guy was his *thing*, however far out of his league. He was, however, regretting his decision to go commando. Because his dick was taking a serious interest, and he didn't need that humiliation.

The door shut behind them both, and they stared at each other in silence for several moments.

Whatever the hell was going on here, Wendell wasn't sure he wanted to break the spell.

"Kraken or Mermaid?"

Wendell frowned. "What?"

The blond leaned toward him and aimed a finger at his mouth as though he was going to touch Wendell's lips. His dick fully woke up at that, not nearly as confused as Wendell himself was.

"The blue. Lisa's Kraken and Mermaid cupcakes are the worst offenders for staining."

A wave of heat swept up Wendell's neck and into his cheeks, but he laughed weakly. "It didn't even occur to me that the frosting would stain." But his reference to Lisa indicated he was likely local rather than a tourist.

"Like a blue freeze pop," the other guy chuckled and wrinkled his nose, which made Wendell laugh for real.

"Or I've been chowing down on Smurfs."

The blond snort-laughed, and covered his mouth with his hands.

"Actually, it was a Kraken," Wendell said in between chuckles. When they'd both calmed down, Wendell spoke again. "Look, I don't mean to be a buzzkill or anything, but is Sandra okay with you hanging out around here?" If he had to, he'd call her and find out, but he was reluctant to disturb her and Bill unnecessarily.

"Oh, yes of course. This is the first stop."

Just like the first question the guy asked him, Wendell was super confused. "The first stop for what?"

For a split second, the guy looked nervous. But he rallied quickly.

"The ghost walk?"

"Are you asking me?" Otherwise, why make it sound like a question.

The man in front of him closed his wide anime eyes for a second and took a couple of shallow breaths.

FIVE

29 Days to Haunt Fest

THIS WASN'T HAPPENING. The new guy Sandra had hired had such a laid-back, calming aura. Maybe it was the hipster bear vibe? Whatever it was, Kyle wanted to kiss him, climb him like a tree, and snuggle with him in equal measure—with a few other sex-type activities thrown in the mix.

Already he'd sounded like an idiot. Pointing out the blue coloring on his lips was bad enough but snorting? He was such a fucking dork around guys he liked. At least this time he hadn't been struck mute, but speech was *not* working to his advantage. Did he ask the man out for dinner? Compliment him? Introduce himself? Nope. Just spewed the ridiculous after the inane.

But he needed to not be his normal, tongue-tied self. Because the last thing Kyle needed was to tangle with the Orange Lady's... assistant manager? Interim assistant manager? He needed more information.

Ugh. Not the time to get side-tracked. He had this ghost walk down to a fucking science and he didn't want to throw off his game dealing with a botched professional relationship.

He tried to center himself, and took a few breaths—probably closer to hyperventilating than meditating—before he opened his eyes.

"Hi, I'm Kyle Grainger." He held out his hand, letting out a tiny huff of relief when it was taken.

"Wendell Weston. Nice to meet you."

"You too." Kyle smiled up into bourbon brown eyes. Wendell's blue-stained lips made him less intimidating, but no less attractive.

"Uh. So…" Wendell glanced at their hands, which were still clasped. Kyle laughed nervously and let Wendell's hand go.

"Right, sorry."

Blue Kraken frosting wasn't enough to *completely* cure Kyle's dorky awkwardness. Better luck next time.

"No worries. You run a ghost tour?"

"Yes. Sandra keeps flyers here for me." Kyle pointed to the small stand of attraction advertising near the registration desk. "Sandy Bottom Bay's Official Ghost Walk. It's sponsored by the chamber of commerce. You should come along some time. I'll give you a freebie."

Although he might just choke and die if Wendell actually showed up to listen to him. He'd definitely need some advance warning about that, otherwise it'd take a miracle for him to be able to speak coherently.

"A freebie? You don't have to do that."

No, he didn't, but he did want to make nice with this man, only partially for professional reasons.

"It only makes sense that you know what I do, since we'll be meeting on the front porch of the inn anywhere from one to six evenings a week, and at peak season, often more than once a night."

Wendell's eyebrows raised. "That often? Wow."

Kyle shrugged. "It's a popular tour."

Not that he'd seen one single, solitary ghost in the hundreds of tours he'd conducted.

"Is it spooky?"

Kyle laughed. "Well, it's a ghost tour. It's supposed to be a spooky. But I've been doing it long enough that I can alter the creep-factor depending on the audience."

"Yeah, I'd like to take you up on that."

Movement outside the window caught his attention. The group was getting restless. As much as Kyle wanted to stay and take advantage of his no-doubt temporary ability to speak to an attractive man, he had a job to do.

He grabbed a flyer off the rack, strode to the front desk and snatched up a pen. After he scribbled his cell number on it, he thrust it at Wendell.

"The info's all on the website. Text my cell and let me know what day you'd like to go. Don't sign up through the site, though, because you'd have to pay and the refund process is a bitch."

Wendell smiled at him. "Okay, thanks. Kyle."

Kyle bit his lip then slipped out the door.

"Everyone ready to get started?"

All of his charges nodded, and he stepped back from the porch, gesturing for them to follow him so they could better see all of the inn.

"The Orange Lady Inn was built on the foundation of an older house, built by a wealthy family invested in the development of this region. After an arranged marriage, Katherine Mercer spent many a lonely night here, waiting for her husband to return. Some say he ran away. Others say he was killed in a skirmish with Native Americans. Then there's a third faction that believes she herself did away with her husband and he's buried somewhere on the property. They also believe that her grieving widow act was designed to divert suspicion."

"So, he just disappeared one day? With no record of his death or anything?" One of the teens asked, with a tiny frown.

Kyle nodded. "Yes, record keeping was a lot more challenging back then. If he was ambushed while travelling and no one survived, how would anyone know where or how he died? And likewise, if he returned home late one night, with none of the other townspeople seeing him—and they were spread out enough back then it was surely possible—she could have killed him and hidden all traces of his return before dawn. There were no forensics, no cadaver dogs, nothing." Not like in his murder shows—his new binge-able favorites.

"What do you think happened? And why is it called the Orange Lady if her name was Mercer? Don't they usually call these types of spirits white ladies?"

Kyle smiled at the other teen who'd spoken. Clearly a budding paranormalist who'd dragged her friends along with her.

"Sure. But they're usually called white ladies because when they're seen they're dressed in white. Or appear as whitish smoke. Katherine Mercer also wears white when she's seen, but she would often wander the nearby orange grove, crying, so she became the Orange Lady instead."

"Probably she buried the body in orange grove." The elder son of the family group spoke, a hint of contempt in his words, but he definitely wanted to make a good impression on at least one of the girls.

Kyle didn't mind a bit of discussion about theories, but he still had a schedule to keep.

"It's possible that guilt is what keeps her spirit roaming, but I believe she's searching for a husband who never returned and that grief is why she's not at peace. But there are those who claim she walks the halls of the upper floor of this inn at midnight, usually appearing to couples who are in need of help. Other times, people have gotten a whiff of orange, like the scent of an orange grove, there and then gone again."

Scent would be the easiest way to fake a haunting, but Sandra had never, to Kyle's knowledge, ever perpetrated any sort of hoax at the inn. He couldn't say with any certainty about previous owners of the inn, which had passed through several hands over the decades prior to Sandra and Bill buying it.

"Have you ever seen her?" This time it was the third girl. He did so like to have an engaged group.

"Ah, well, I have never stayed overnight at the inn, and the upper floors can only be accessed by staff or guests."

Lies. Well, not exactly, but he was skirting the truth pretty hard. He'd done some temp work at the inn on occasion, and had twice stayed late enough to try and see the Orange Lady, but never saw a slip of smoke, never mind a whole ghost. And the only time he'd smelled oranges had been when Sandra or the cook had offered him juice.

But he believed one day he'd see a ghost, and he definitely didn't want to ruin anyone else's experience with his inability to see those of the otherworld.

"Let's move on. Lots to see tonight."

The front door of the inn clicked shut, and Kyle smiled to himself. He was ninety percent sure he'd be hearing from Wendell. He led his charges down the path and gestured for them to proceed through the boxwood hedge ahead of him.

He tried to get one last glimpse of Wendell through the window, but it looked like he'd already gone. A wisp of movement caught his eye, drawing his gaze to the darkened windows of one of the guest rooms on the second floor. No white dress or ethereal hair was visible through the glass.

Nothing there. Nothing at all, unless one of the inn's guests was lurking about in the dark. Unlikely. Must have been nothing more than a passing palmetto bug, and Kyle had just managed to freak himself out. Kyle shivered and rubbed at goosebumps that had sprung up on his arms for no apparent reason.

As soon as Kyle shepherded his group down the path toward the sidewalk, Wendell moved quickly. He shut and locked the door, grabbed his bakery box, and sped back to his cottage.

It had gotten dark while he'd listened to Kyle's introductory spiel about the reputed ghost at the inn, and Wendell couldn't stop thinking about it.

He wasn't quite ready to get out his laptop to start writing, but he'd book a ghost tour of his own soon. No way to know yet if the story was enough to jumpstart his creativity, but Kyle had enthralled him with just a few sentences.

It didn't hurt that Kyle was gorgeous, sexy, nice, and seemed to have a sense of humor. But it wasn't just Wendell's libido he'd tied up in knots. Kyle had a gift. The group listening to him had been every bit as spellbound, and Wendell had no doubt he made excellent tips whenever he led a ghost tour. If there was anything in this world Wendell could appreciate, it was the talents of another storyteller.

The only thing that had broken Wendell's trance had been getting caught listening to Kyle's tour from the cracked open door. And frankly, he'd already had more embarrassment than he was comfortable with, after Kyle had identified his cupcake snack from no more than the stain on his lips.

Wendell put the kettle on for a fresh mug of tea. Sure, he could have popped his now-cold tea into the microwave, but he'd sooner microwave the water to begin with than warm up some too-strong tea. Yuck.

While the water heated, he slipped into the bathroom and stared at the mirror.

"Oh my god. That is some fucking blue." He really did look like he'd been snacking on Smurfs. A wave of heat swept into his cheeks. Kyle had been amused, and not in a mean way, but Wendell was going to need a few days to live this down before he signed up for a ghost tour. And he'd definitely take more care with future cupcakes flavors. Fear of a little food coloring wasn't going to keep him away from Mysteriously Good, that was for damn sure.

After he'd set his tea to steep, he entered Kyle into his contacts on his phone, making sure to include the cell number, then carefully tucked the card into his laptop bag for safekeeping.

Despite having missed sunset, Wendell decided to take his tea outside. He lit the citronella candle in a stand near the edge of the concrete patio tiles and sat.

The rhythmic crash of waves on sand was a significant improve- ment over the white noise app he'd used on occasion to help him sleep. Assuming he could hear this from his bed, he was going to sleep better than he had in a long time.

Between the lulling rhythm of the ocean and his red-eye flight, he was just about ready to call it a night.

He walked toward the water with his mug and stared out at the ocean, starkly lit under a bright, almost-full moon. Beautiful but with a lonely, and perhaps menacing aspect that wasn't apparent during the day. With the sun shining, and the water in cheery hues of blue and green, it wasn't as easy to recall how dangerous the ocean could be.

No, still not ready to write, but the promise was there, buried deep under the dead leaves and soil of mounting pressure, expectations, and crushing writers block.

Wendell gazed up along the coast toward the lighthouse. Whether it was also supposed to be haunted or not, whether it was functional or not, he couldn't wait to check it out. Lighthouses had great atmosphere.

Also on his list was an overnight stay in the main building of the inn, to see if he could encounter the eponymous Orange Lady, aka Katherine Mercer. He strongly suspected the original owners of the inn had made the whole thing up to get their share of the economic pie. According to his brief internet research, Sandy Bottom Bay had been investing in paranormal tourism since the late sixties, but no sense in ignoring a potential story idea so close to his temporary home.

Not that he was a professional skeptic or debunker. He'd not had a single paranormal encounter in his life, and yet, he'd found inspiration for creating supernatural horror tales in any number of places. The Orange Lady Inn at midnight was as good as any other option.

When his eyes got too heavy, Wendell extinguished the candle and went inside. Even though the waves were muffled, they were audible enough to lull him to sleep in minutes.

SIX

28 Days to Haunt Fest

THE NEXT MORNING, Wendell's alarm startled him awake and he sprang out of bed. He resolutely did not calculate how much earlier it was back home, because that way lay madness and jet lag. Jumping right into the current time zone was the only way to deal with it. Regardless, he'd be grabbing a cup of coffee or two to fire up his day. Tea wasn't going to cut it.

He quickly showered and dressed, then remembered his cupcake in the fridge.

Cake of any sort was the best breakfast ever, and he'd woken in plenty of time to eat before starting work. Sandra had already told him he could help himself to any of the catered breakfast items as long as the guests had first choice, but he didn't know how long he'd have to wait for it to feel appropriate to pick over the offerings. Definitely not while Sandra was still around to oversee things. He was doing himself a favor by eating the cupcake now, really.

He pulled the bakery box out of the fridge and opened the lid.

The aroma of rich, pure chocolate hadn't lessened one bit overnight. In the bright light of the morning, he couldn't see any mouth-staining coloring, just luscious chocolate. He popped the white chocolate fangs in his mouth and savored them. Then he took a big bite of the cupcake.

And discovered an entirely unexpected pocket of filling that spilled down his chin and dripped onto his fresh, white, golf shirt. Lurid red jam, raspberry according to the burst of taste on his tongue, splotched his shirt, every bit as bright as blood.

Blood. Wendell laughed as best he could around the delicious confection in his mouth. Of course a cupcake called Vampire Kiss would be filled with crimson jam. Only made it tastier, and he didn't regret for one second the need to change his shirt and do a serious rewash of his hands.

It merely confirmed that the next time he ate something from Lisa's bakery he was going to have to be careful, and have plenty of napkins on hand.

Safer, too, if he avoided eating any cupcakes in front of Kyle. Not until he got to know the man a little better, at least. No sense in making a total fool of himself yet again.

As soon as he'd fully savored the joy that was a vampire-themed cupcake, he washed his hands, changed his shirt, and eradicated any evidence from his lips and chin.

He made it up to the main building with ten minutes to spare.

Wendell observed Sandra during the Saturday breakfast service, helping where he could. He was painfully aware that Sandra planned to depart later this afternoon, and he'd have much rather known that Jackson was here to observe as well, rather than relying on the binder and Wendell's memory. There was still Daisy, and the cook, and any other seasonal employees, but the whole idea unnerved him more than he'd expected. Tomorrow morning, it would be him and Jackson, on their own, and he still had no idea what Jackson was like or if they'd get along.

Shortly after ten, when just one table lingered over coffee and fruit, his and Sandra's phones pinged with a notification of someone at the front desk. Wendell smiled at the proof that the system was in good working order, and he followed Sandra to the lobby.

Standing there, looking just a trifle lost, was an attractive older man, maybe mid-forties. He had a few threads of silver in his dark hair, and although he looked solid and lean, he also had an air about him. Delicate, like he needed a good night's sleep, or a hug, if he didn't seem so brittle. Or maybe it was pain Wendell sensed.

"Jackson. You made it," Sandra exclaimed. "I hope the traffic wasn't terrible." She folded him in a hug, disregarding or not realizing how tense Jackson was.

Jackson smiled wanly and hugged her back, but didn't lose that aura of brokenness.

"It's good to see you again."

Wendell let out a tiny breath as his shoulders relaxed. Jackson wasn't a newbie. That made him feel ever so much better, because he definitely didn't want the inn to be an even greater source of stress for Sandra and Bill.

"Jackson Este, this is Wendell Weston. He'll be staying at Kelpie's Roost for the next three months, and will be helping you out."

Jackson reached out a hand. "Nice to meet you. I look forward to getting to know you."

Wendell shook Jackson's hand. "Thanks, me too."

"Wendell, honey, would you mind overseeing the end of breakfast while I get Jackson up to speed? I'm hoping to get a few hours of driving in while it's still light."

"Of course. And if you need any help getting things in the car, just let me know." He smiled at Jackson, and returned to the dining room.

Jackson seemed nice enough, but hoped the oddness he'd sensed wouldn't have any unpleasant repercussions over the next few months.

Once the dining room had been returned to rights, ready for breakfast on Sunday, Wendell went back to the lobby, and found

Jackson listening raptly as Sandra spoke, the employee binder clutched tightly to his chest.

They both turned to him, and Sandra heaved out a sigh.

"Just about ready to get on the road. Can you both help me with a few last minute things?"

Jackson disappeared into the office, and returned without the binder, locking the door behind him.

In less than an hour, Sandra and Bill were driving off, leaving him and Jackson staring at each other.

Jackson cleared his throat. "I admit, Sandra hasn't told me much about you. Can I 'buy' you a cup of coffee and we figure out how we're going to go forward from here? I really don't want to let Sandra and Bill down. I've known them both for a long time."

"I don't want to let them down either. Coffee would be great."

Wendell followed Jackson into the now deserted and spotless dining room. There was a little coffee station along the wall that guests could access most of the day, if they didn't want to make coffee in their room or make the short trip to Mysteriously Good. Jackson quickly put together a couple of mugs and turned to Wendell with a questioning expression, which he correctly interpreted.

"Two sugars, please."

Jackson doctored his own brew then sat across from Wendell.

"So, Sandra says you've got some past experience in a boutique hotel, and that you're working for room and board?" Jackson took a careful sip of his coffee. "Don't get me wrong, I'm going to need your help, but it doesn't quite feel right that you're not getting paid for anything, at least in this situation where we're going to be under the gun in just a few weeks."

Wendell blinked at him. Sandra really hadn't told anyone about his research. He hadn't asked her to keep it quiet—screenwriters never garnered the interest and adoration that actors and directors did—so he hadn't been worried about fans or paparazzi. She had either taken it upon herself to keep quiet, or there must truly be so many people who come through this town claiming research with nothing that ever came of it, that she hadn't bothered telling anyone about him.

Or she just could have simply been stressed enough that she wasn't paying attention to much besides her concern for her husband.

"That's not quite the situation. I'm paying for my room, full price, like any other guest. I'm a writer, doing research. Since I had the hospitality experience, I offered it up to Sandra in exchange for letting me have full run of the inn. Turned out, I was sort of in the right place at the right time, because not only was a cottage free for the stay I proposed, she had just arranged for you to come and take over, but was concerned about you being on your own."

Jackson sucked in a breath, almost like he'd been slapped, and blinked furiously.

Wendell took a few sips of coffee, worried that Jackson was going to be a dick and refuse to work with him.

"Oh. That's... would I have read anything you've written?"

Wendell laughed. "Unlikely, but perhaps you've seen *Shadow Stalker*?" It had been his most recent release.

"*Shadow Stalker*? Uh, no, but I did see a trailer for it. These days, I pretty much confine myself to comedies and action movies. But you wrote that?"

"I did."

"That's amazing. And you're going to do a movie about the inn?"

Wendell shook his head. "Not directly. I have some ideas I need to flesh out." As in, get some—any—ideas more concrete than 'haunted tropical resort', but he wasn't about to admit that to just anyone.

Better to get the focus off him and his issues, though.

"So, what's your story?"

Jackson stared down at his cup and his fingers twitched like he wanted to peel a label off something.

"My husband and I came here regularly, and even had an idea that we might want to open our own B&B after he retired. We worked it out with Sandra and Bill, and would take over for them occasionally to give us practice to make sure it was something we wanted to do. It also allowed them to take vacations without having to close down. When Sandra was in need, she called me first thing."

Wendell was as curious about everything as any writer, but the white strip of skin where a wedding ring would normally sit told part of the story. And it was clear Jackson didn't want to discuss why his husband wasn't with him. Wendell came from a town where no one gave a fuck about privacy, especially when related to the movie industry, and he kind of hated that. So, he wasn't about to pry and invade someone else's privacy if he could avoid it. But he would happily listen if Jackson ever wanted to talk.

"Do you live far away?"

Jackson bit his lip and looked up. "Upstate New York."

"And you *drove* here?" Wendell was aware people did that, but he would have gone completely nuts all by himself in a car like that.

"It's not that bad, really. And I'd rather have my own car with me instead of a rental."

Jackson glanced away and fiddled with the handle of his coffee mug.

"Anyway, this is maybe a horrible thing to ask, but I was hoping you could be on call tonight. I've got to run some errands before I settle in, and I've got a friend who wants to meet up for dinner, to welcome me back to the area."

"Sure, not a problem." *Probably* not a problem. He hoped.

Jackson finished off his coffee. "I'm going to check in with Daisy and make sure everything's ready for tomorrow, so it really should be nothing more than responding to any guest issues."

And with that, the guy was gone, taking his mug into the kitchen.

At least he didn't seem like a dick. Time would tell if they'd become anything like friends. Knowing he was gay or bi was a comfort because that meant Wendell wouldn't have to worry about whether or not to hide anything from him.

Later that evening, Wendell sat in the chair behind the check-in desk and shuffled a small stack of handwritten notes. The front door was locked, as they weren't expecting any more registered guests tonight. Of course, he was still on call if the guests needed anything, but with less than half of the rooms currently occupied, he didn't think there would be any requests.

He was itching to write but there still weren't any good ideas kicking around in his brainpan. With a sigh, he unlocked the inn's computer, intending to review the system a little more. Maybe it was stupid to be here, pretending to work when he could barely sit still.

Someone knocked at the front door, interrupting his downward thought spiral, and he sprang out of the chair to answer the door.

"Thank you, I'm starving." He took the pizza box from the delivery kid's hands. The box was hotter than the muggy air outside, and that was saying something.

"Enjoy!" The delivery person turned and bounced away with far more energy than Wendell would expect from anyone not dressed in a bathing suit on the beach in this heat. Back home, as evening drew in, the temperature would definitely be getting cooler, but not here.

He took his pizza back to the check-in desk and munched distractedly while he sorted the notes that needed to be entered into the system.

Lisa had sent a box of cupcakes just for him along with the afternoon tea delivery, as well as something separate for Jackson.

Wendell had already texted her to thank her for thinking of him, but he was saving them for later—once he was back in his cottage and had easy access to a bib, facecloth, and a toothbrush. According to the enclosed note, she'd sent him a Mermaid and a Fire Demon—he couldn't wait to find out what flavors they were—but he wasn't about to risk another shirt to her frosting-festooned alchemy.

By rights, he could have retired back to Kelpie's Roost, for the night and have his pizza on the deck while watching the ocean. The vista was beautiful, and somehow different than watching the ocean up by Malibu.

But he had his sights set on a different visual tonight. Maybe. Even better, he didn't have to admit or explain *anything* to Jackson.

He'd never actually confirmed if Kyle was hosting a ghost tour tonight, although weekends were more popular days to book on. Or so he inferred based on some light research on his phone during the few moments he'd had to take a short break.

Not stalker-y at all. Just... interested. For all Wendell knew, Kyle might not be the only ghost walk guide Sandy Bottom Bay had, and someone completely different could appear on the inn's front porch.

Or maybe there wouldn't be a tour at all.

Nevertheless, he'd chosen eat at the desk instead of in his cottage for the chance to see Kyle again.

Stupid, really, since he didn't have a good reason to interrupt Kyle's tour again.

He'd managed to eat one slice of pizza, that unfortunately didn't hold a candle to yesterday's burrito, before his phone rang.

Lucinda.

He stabbed the speaker icon.

"Hey, sis. How's it going?"

"Hey sis?! Is that all I get? I guess you landed okay. Yesterday. And you weren't kidnapped or eaten by crocodiles."

"Alligators."

"What?"

Wendell sighed and shook his head. He'd texted his parents that he'd arrived okay, and assumed they'd pass on the message to his siblings. Although, they were prepping for a month-long South Asian cruise, and might have been too busy. Hell, for all he knew, they *had* passed on the message, but Lucinda never let facts get in the way of her overblown dramatics.

"Never mind. I'm fine. What's up?"

"Got any writing done? Fresh ideas? I can't believe you're going to be in Florida of all places for the next three months. If you manage to get a decent script together soon, surely you can cut your exile short."

Wendell drew in a deep breath, even as his neck and shoulders tightened right up.

"Luce, this isn't helping any. I just got here, I'm spending the next few months doing a job."

"You have a job already. And if the creative well had dried up, so what? There's still plenty of other work you can do with the company. I don't see why you have to do this."

Wendell shoved the pizza away from him as his stomach soured. He knew damn well his sister didn't understand, but she was the arm of Lucky Weston Studios that focused on budgets, casting, and marketing. But mostly budgets. His brother, Byron, directed the majority of their movies, and their eldest sister, Felicity, wasn't usually an active part of the business, but she had invested when they were just starting up.

Of all of them, Lucinda was the most analytical and practical. But creativity couldn't be boiled down to spreadsheets and balances. For someone who had such a keen eye for what plots or casting would result in good press or big box office sales, she didn't comprehend that the thought of no longer being able to write was simply... devastating for him to contemplate.

He badly needed to restock his mental pond with fat, juicy idea koi. He rolled his eyes. And if that ill-conceived metaphor didn't illustrate how bad the writer's block was, he didn't know what would.

He needed a break, and the pressure cooker of expectation in Tinseltown only made things harder. Especially with the added bonus of Lucinda's nagging and Byron's silent, worried glances.

"We talked about this." Many times, but reminding her of that would only make them both cranky. "I needed a change of environment."

"But running a motel?"

"Managing a bed and breakfast. And only assisting, really."

"Whatever. How could that possibly help?"

One, he wouldn't have her dropping by his workspace every other day, demanding to know his progress. Two, he wasn't qualified to do anything else. Hell, he was barely qualified for this. Of course, he could afford to rent a house somewhere and just stare at a blank computer screen all day for the next few months, but that wasn't going to convince the words to come.

Whether this temporary relocation would coax words out of his brain remained to be seen, but he was convinced he needed a drastic change to jumpstart his mental engine. If nothing else, working at the inn would keep him busy enough to avoid wallowing in melancholy. The memory of negative emotions provided depth and nuance to writing, but it was really fucking hard being creative whilst in the grips of them.

"Luce, seriously, you can't keep asking me when I'm going to have something." Because he might never write another script, and confronting that thought was more painful than anything he'd ever done. "Can you do that? Can you wait until I'm ready to talk about it?"

There was silence while she contemplated his request. Then she heaved out a sigh.

"I suppose so."

"Thank you." Wendell was going to avoid the next few calls from her, though, just in case.

They chatted for a few more minutes before Wendell ended the call and did some deep breathing to release some of the tension Lucinda had brought back. Then he went back to his pizza.

He'd had one more slice before another knock came at the front door. He patted himself down for crumbs and wiped his mouth. Perhaps a walk-in guest? He'd posted the sign with the inn's phone number on the door—anytime the door was locked, guests could reach him via that number. Maybe he was still somehow visible to someone standing outside? He'd never thought to check sight lines.

Whoever it was, he wanted to get rid of them quick so he could settle back and be done eating before Kyle—hopefully—arrived for a ghost tour.

He flipped the lock and opened the door without paying attention to whomever was on the other side. Big mistake.

"Oh. Uh. Hi, Kyle." Please, *please* say he wasn't stained or wearing any food this time. At least he hadn't gotten into the cupcakes yet.

Kyle glanced up at him then directed his gaze back down at his feet, almost bashfully. Kyle wore a pair of artfully distressed skinny jeans, a snug white t-shirt, and a stellar pair of purple Converse All Stars. And he looked every bit as delectable as he had in his pirate getup.

"Hey. Um. I thought you could use this." Kyle thrust a fistful of papers at him.

Wendell didn't care what was on those papers, but he would definitely find a use for them, and took them without inspecting them.

"Why don't you come in? You could share my pizza if you haven't had dinner yet."

Wendell bit back a groan. How dare his tongue just spit out an invitation like that, without any input from his sense of self preservation? Guys like Kyle probably had a shitload of options for dinner, better-looking and buffer than Wendell, on a Saturday night, since it looked like he wasn't hosting a tour tonight.

"Oh. Well, I have a salad waiting for me across the road at Drew's place, and all my stuff for tonight's ghost walk."

Stomach crashing into his feet, Wendell dredged up a smile. Was Drew Kyle's boyfriend? A truly disappointing turn of events, but since Wendell's dating life was always disappointing, he shouldn't be surprised.

"Drew's place?"

"Yup. He owns the psychic tarot place. Malachi the Mystic. If you stretch, you can probably see it from the front window.

He wasn't in a hurry to do that. But he wasn't about to let his disappointment get in the way of making a new friend, because he could definitely use more of those. Especially so far from home.

"Doesn't make sense for us to eat alone, across the road from each other, does it? Bring your stuff over here. You can change in the office or the staff bathroom for your tour, and you can tell me about what I've got here."

Wendell waved the pamphlets in his hand. But seriously, how desperate did he sound? Begging for Kyle to spend time with him.

Kyle's swept his gaze up, peering at him through thick black eyelashes and Wendell's heart fluttered like it never had for any big screen ingenue.

"That sounds good."

Wendell cleared his suddenly dry throat. "Yes. Good."

Kyle stood there for several moments, looking at him, and Wendell's neck got hot. Was he supposed to say or do something else?

Then Kyle shook himself, and he gave Wendell a half-grin. "I'll be back in a few."

Wendell allowed himself a few seconds to admire Kyle's pert ass as he strutted away, then the reality hit. He was going to have dinner —however simple—with an attractive man. Not a date, obviously, because Kyle had a boyfriend or harem or something, and there was no way Wendell could compete. But that didn't mean he didn't want to make a good impression. And that meant at least another paper plate for Kyle's pizza.

And, of course, double checking that he wasn't currently wearing any of his previous slices.

SEVEN

28 Days to Haunt Fest

KYLE MANAGED to saunter nonchalantly until he'd passed through to the sidewalk, then leaned heavily against the low stone wall that contained the boxwoods.

"Oh my god. I can't believe I did that."

A family of four, sunburned and sandy, passed him as they returned from the beach, the mom looking puzzled. He gave them a lazy salute and smiled ruefully, because there was no way to pretend he was on a call via Bluetooth headset. He'd been talking to himself out loud and got heard. Embarrassing, as the heat in his cheeks attested, but not nearly as traumatic as what he'd just done with Wendell.

The family continued on, and Kyle took in a couple of deep breaths.

Making the first move was not in his comfort zone, no matter how much he liked being the center of attention. And for anyone else, handing someone flyers wasn't even a big deal. For him, though, it had taken several minutes pacing over this same strip of sidewalk to gather the courage to walk up and knock.

He hadn't even considered that Wendell might not have been at the front desk, and he should have. He'd spent his fair share of time working for Sandra over the years and the amount of time anyone spent at the desk, especially at this time of the evening, was minimal.

Then again, maybe the part of him that was so scared of rejection had sort of hoped Wendell wasn't around, so Kyle wouldn't have to go through with his admittedly weak plan. But he hadn't been able to come up with any other ideas, aside from either hoping he ran into Wendell accidentally in town, or striding into the Orange Lady and asking him out.

However, his plan can't have been as pathetic as he'd initially believed, as it garnered him a dinner invitation—of sorts. He couldn't even call it a date, because he wasn't sure how Wendell viewed it. Wendell could be married, have a significant other, or just be in the market for a friend.

There had been a moment last night, a terrifying, exciting, breathless moment when Kyle had been sure Wendell was going to kiss him, but the moment had popped like a soap bubble, leaving Kyle second-guessing if he'd seen true attraction or the simple politeness of a man in the service industry trying to avoid making waves.

Stop freaking out. If he wanted a semi-relaxed dinner with Wendell, he needed to get his butt over to Drew's to grab his stuff. Not haunt the sidewalk and stew.

Across the road, he rolled his eyes and snatched Eddie's stupid flyer off the glass pane on the door. Asshole. But also, not the response he'd been expecting after he'd changed the language on Eddie's tablet to Japanese.

Hopefully this meant Eddie was getting bored with their skirmishes, or was attempting to de-escalate, but Kyle didn't think Eddie had that much self-preservation. At some point, if Drew's new husband, Cliff, didn't step in officially as a member of the police force, one of Drew's idiotic brothers were going to, and no one was going to be happy then.

And Kyle wasn't about to stand down. Not until Eddie stopped trying to sabotage Drew's business, however ineffectually.

He ripped the flyer into shreds and dumped it in the trash. He definitely didn't want to waste any more time fuming about Eddie Price.

But neither did he want to keep Wendell waiting.

To center himself, and to purge Eddie's possible retaliation from his mind, for at least the next few hours, Kyle dropped down into cross-legged position and closed his eyes, focusing on breathing. If he'd been wearing yoga pants, he'd have done a few asanas, but he'd found out the hard way that balls plus tight jeans plus yoga equaled eyewatering, soul searing agony.

Kyle let his mini-meditation and Drew's new and effective air conditioner cool him down before he gathered up all his stuff and went back across the road. Last thing he wanted to do was show up sweaty and flushed. That particular look should be reserved for after a really good dance number, or a really good workout, sexual or otherwise.

Living in south Florida made that a difficult rule to follow, but he still wanted to make a good impression.

On the inn's front porch, he raised his hand to knock, but Wendell was there, opening the door, before he had a chance to connect knuckles to glass.

"Hi." Wendell smiled.

"Hi." Kyle smiled back.

Silence hung in the humid air for a few moments, until Kyle realized he was staring like an idiot and shifted his gaze away from Wendell's face.

Wendell shook himself, and moved back out of the doorway.

"Please come in."

Kyle stepped in, and Wendell locked the door behind him.

"C'mon. You can leave your bags in the office. The door is right here."

Wendell led him to the Staff Only door that Kyle was well familiar with and led him inside. Nothing much had changed.

"I should probably tell you that I've filled in on the desk before," Kyle said as he set down his messenger bag, bulging with his change of clothes, and the reusable grocery sack that held the cookies from the bakery.

Wendell blinked owlishly at him, and for a second, Kyle expected to see glasses on the bridge of his nose. "Oh. So, uh, I don't think I saw your name in the list of people to call in case we need extra help."

Kyle smiled. "Yeah, I wasn't a regular or anything. I did some shifts in high school before I went away to college, then one here or there after I came back. But Sandra took my name out of the book once Drew hired me on full time. Kind of like, I don't know, a milestone."

"You said Drew was a tarot reader?" Wendell's question was tentative but Kyle wasn't sure why. Probably Wendell was another skeptic. Or religious. But what if he thought Drew and Kyle were involved?

"Yup. He's my best friend. He's really good at the readings. When he gets back from his honeymoon, you should have him do the cards for you."

Kyle held his breath for a brief second, hoping to see... something in Wendell's face now that Kyle had laid it right out there that he and Drew weren't lovers or something.

Unfortunately, Wendell did not immediately prostrate himself and declare his undying love, so Kyle let out the air in his lungs. Friends were never a bad thing, right?

"Anyway, you have my number. You can call me if you have questions or anything about how the inn works. And I don't mind pitching in to help out, if I don't have any other obligations."

"Thank you, Kyle. I really appreciate that. C'mon, I set up another chair behind the desk."

Kyle grabbed his kale salad and water bottle and followed Wendell.

Once they'd both sat down, Kyle had to smile. Wendell had set up a couple of plates, cutlery, and napkins out on the desk beside the pizza box.

More conscientious than Kyle's last so-called date, but was this standard Wendell, or Wendell trying to make a good impression on a man he was interested in?

Wendell frowned a little. "Is this okay? Maybe we could go sit in the library? Or the sun room?"

"This is fine. Everything is all set up here." He wasn't about to tell Wendell that he'd never really loved the library. Sandra had put a lot of effort into some sort of period decor that was supposed to evoke the spirit of Hemingway. Not that Hemingway had ever darkened the door of the Orange Lady.

The guests loved it but it felt utterly oppressive to Kyle. And the sun room probably got a lot more traffic from guests than where they were right now, even this late in the day. Privacy was definitely on Kyle's mind. Hopefully Wendell was on the same wavelength.

Wendell flipped up the lid of the pizza box. "Please, help yourself."

Kyle sucked in the scent of melty cheese and tomato sauce, although it was clearly starting to cool down.

"Thank you, but I'll stick with my salad." He shook the container to redistribute the low fat, low calorie dressing, then popped off the top and grabbed a fork.

Wendell snorted. "Kale salad? I feel like I'm back in Los Angeles."

Kyle shrugged. "I know. People think of Florida and assume we're eating fried seafood platters and key lime pie every day. Don't get me wrong, I love me some fried clams, but I like kale, too, and it's better for me." And less likely to pack on the pounds.

"So, no pizza at all? I can cut a slice in half. Or do you not like pizza?" Wendell blinked at him, as though the very idea was alien.

So sweet of him. But still no indication if his motivation was attraction or just that he was too damned nice. Kyle would rather bite of his tongue and eat it with his kale, rather than ask outright.

"I like pizza just fine, but most pizza around here isn't worth the calories." He'd been dancing so long, he really didn't eat pizza very often, and if he wanted to treat himself, there were other things he preferred.

Wendell wrinkled his nose. "Yeah. I mean, there are some gourmet and artisan pizza places in LA that are okay, and I've had a few decent vegan pizzas, too, but they're nothing like a good New York style pizza. I gotta say, they're all better than this."

"Vegan pizza? Not a thing in Sandy Bottom Bay, although there are more vegetarian and vegan options than there were a few years ago."

"Vegan stuff isn't so bad, although I don't eat that way all the time." Wendell tilted his head at his pizza. "So, if you don't eat pizza, I guess you don't have any recommendations for a better one?"

"When I went away to college I developed a fondness for the deep-dish pizza. There's a place not far from here called Giordano's that does them, and when I choose to indulge, that's where I go." Not that he'd ever travelled far enough to try Chicago style pizza in Chicago, but one day he would.

"Well. Maybe when you next indulge, we could go together."

Wendell busied himself with pulling a slice of pizza out of the box and fussing with it on his plate, not looking at Kyle at all. Random conversation, or was Wendell actually asking him out? If he only had the guts to actually ask outright. Being attracted to a guy trapped Kyle in a quagmire of indecision, unless the other guy was willing to lay his cards on the table. Hookups weren't the same. When there was potential—or hope—for more, that's when Kyle lost what little mojo he had.

"Sure. Sounds good." Kyle did his best to sound *all bros together* just in case. Then he stuffed another forkful of kale into his mouth, to give it something to do besides saying something stupid.

"But you know, this isn't truly bad pizza. I mean, pizza's kinda like sex," Wendell said, then coughed and turned red.

Kyle's heart rate sped up, afraid Wendell was choking. He braced himself to leap up, when it became clear Wendell had only been embarrassed.

By the mere mention of sex? Kyle didn't usually see this sort of squeamishness, except in a few straight guys when they mentioned sex around him. Like Drew's brothers, assuming that just mentioning the word would get Kyle all inappropriately hot and bothered.

To be fair, he had been crushing on them for the longest time—so, so many taboo fantasies over the years—but in reality? No. He wasn't about to become a sex-crazed maniac over the drop of a single word. Straight guys were so weird.

Kyle sighed. Just his luck. A cute, sweet, bearish man dropped in his lap—figuratively speaking, sadly—and he was straight and repressed. Probably just wanted a buddy. At least he wasn't homophobic, because Kyle was pretty sure he hadn't been mistaken for straight since he'd hit puberty.

But Kyle could use a new friend to occupy his time anyway. Even after Drew came back from his honeymoon, he'd be spending the majority of time with his new husband, and Lisa's hours at the bakery did not mesh with Kyle's free time at all.

"So. You were saying about bad pizza?"

Wendell cleared his throat. "Uh, yes. I mean, uh, sex can be great obviously, but rarely bad. Just like pizza."

Kyle rolled his eyes. "Oh, trust me. Sex can be pretty damn bad."

Wendell froze, pizza slice halfway to his mouth.

"I meant, uh, *consensual* sex. Of course."

"I know you did." Kyle patted Wendell's knee. Nevertheless, he definitely didn't want Wendell associating bad sex, or even worse, assault, with Kyle. *Alert! Alert!* They needed to divert from this topic immediately, if not sooner.

Wendell took a bite then set his pizza down on the plate. "It does taste better hot." He cleared his throat again. "And it's not as bad as the worst pizza I ever had."

"Once, my roommate in college ordered pizza and they sent him one that had anchovies on it." Kyle shuddered. Looked like cat whiskers and smelled like rancid cat food. They'd been commiserating about his roommate Alex's sudden and unexpected breakup. The foul pizza had at least put a smile on his friend's face.

"Yikes. Anchovies suck, I agree. One time I was in Germany working, and I'd ordered room service. I guess I never realized uncooked pizza dough had a specific scent, but I could actually smell that the dough underneath was completely raw. And yet, the cheese was melted and the basil burned, so I'm not sure how they managed it."

Kyle held in a sigh. Germany. He'd love to travel someday. Tallahassee was the furthest he'd ever been from Sandy Bottom Bay. Not even outside of Florida. So pathetic.

"If I ever went to Germany, I'd probably order... well, not pizza."

Wendell laughed. "Fair. I should have known better. Room service food is a crap shoot at best, but this particular hotel was very utilitarian and their menu limited, and I really didn't have the time to go out anywhere."

They continued chatting idly while they ate, and Kyle finished his salad right around the time half of Wendell's pizza was gone, and he closed the lid.

"So, tell me about these." Wendell picked up the papers Kyle had brought over as an ice breaker, which was the only excuse Kyle was willing to admit to.

"I don't know how much time you'll have on your hands while you're here, but I thought you might like some info on things the locals do."

Kyle spread out the papers, separating the pamphlet from the flyer. "Sandra has the display with all the nearby touristy things, if you want those, but this here is from the community center. It lists all the classes, meetings, and other gatherings that happen there, and nothing is that expensive."

Expense was a relative term, of course, but as broke as Kyle had been most of his life he still considered the fees to be quite reasonable.

"Anything in particular you like? I mean, I'm pretty sure the mom-and-tot movie matinee isn't exactly up my alley."

Kyle laughed. "No, I don't suppose so, unless you've got a baby stashed around here somewhere."

Wendell let out a laugh, gratifying Kyle.

"I usually go to the fitness classes, especially yoga."

Wendell wrinkled his nose and smoothed a hand over his shirt. "I know I should be more active, and eat less pizza, of course."

"I wasn't suggesting... anything..." Shit. "I'm sorry. I feel like I'm giving you a healthy lifestyle lecture tonight, and that's really not my intention." Stupid subconscious letting his own hang-ups ruin this beta test of a date. His cheeks heated like he'd just finished an hour-long hot yoga session. Wendell might not be totally buff, but he looked both sexy and comfortable at the same time, and Kyle wanted that more and more with every minute.

Wendell winked, and Kyle let out a breath, unaware he'd been holding it, waiting for Wendell's reaction.

"No worries." Wendell flipped to the section on dance classes. "Hey. This is you."

Kyle rubbed his hands together. "Yes, yes, it is. I, uh, teach beginners ballet." He swallowed heavily as his salad shifted. Most of the time, people were cool with it, but not everyone. Sometimes telling a new person he was a dancer was almost as scary as the few times he'd actually had to *tell* someone he was gay.

"Ballet? For real? Those dancers are fucking hardcore."

Kyle blinked. Then blinked again. "Not too many people seem to realize that."

Wendell's ears reddened a bit. "My brother dated a ballerina for a short time. But her career took her out of LA too often and they weren't in a place to make a long distance relationship work. But it gave me some real insight into the dedication, strength, and pain threshold they have. So, you dance ballet professionally?"

The stab of pain wasn't quite as sharp as it usually was when he considered his failed dancing career. And it was a bit joyful to discuss it with someone who didn't sneer at him.

"No, ballet wasn't my specialty. I went to school for dance and I mostly focused on musical theater. But I have a grounding in a large breadth of styles. Definitely enough to teach the basics to kids who've never done it before."

He smiled.

"What's that smile for?" Wendell asked.

Kyle's cheeks heated. "I only teach a couple of classes a week, but my favorite class was this morning. It's the four and five year olds. They're so fucking cute."

Wendell laughed good-naturedly. "Oh, that is awesome. My oldest sister has two kids, six and eight, and they love dancing. I'd love to see you teach someday."

The heat in Kyle's cheeks intensified. Most times guys wanted to pretend he didn't dance at all, never mind having anything to do with a bunch of tiny kids.

"Are there any playhouses around here that put on musicals? There must be, right, if that's what your degree is in."

Wendell flipped through the flyers Kyle had brought, pausing on the playhouse one. Right now, they were advertising A Streetcar Named Desire. So boring. The playhouse had never put on anything that had required his skills. Even if they did, it wouldn't matter. Debra Pearson, the theater director, would rather lop off her right hand than have Kyle in one of her productions, never mind choosing a musical that Kyle would shine in.

Kyle grimaced. He didn't enjoy discussing his failures.

"I damaged my knee during a college performance of *Chicago*. I had to switch majors to business for my final year."

Wendell sucked in a breath. "Oh, I'm so sorry."

For a change, the sentiment seemed heartfelt, rather than a standard platitude.

"Thanks. It was, well, it still is hard to deal with. I love dancing, and musical theater is a lot of fun."

"And you didn't decide to go into acting, instead? Even if the playhouse doesn't do musicals, I would think a lot of the skills would be transferrable. Business seems like the polar opposite, and I heard the introduction to your ghost tour. I bet you'd be a great actor."

Kyle snorted. "Maybe yes, maybe no. The theater director here does not like me at all. So, there's that. And when I hurt my knee, I also got dumped. I needed a big change—distance from performing, distance from my ex, and hopefully landing a career that had a shot at paying the bills."

Instead of answering, Wendell blinked at him. Kyle could have kicked himself. That was a lot of information to pile on someone he'd effectively just met. What was wrong with him? At the moment, he'd give anything to return to his awkward inability to speak around a man he was crushing on.

"Um. Sorry."

Wendell's eyes widened. "What for? None of that sounds like your fault. I applaud you for holding it together and making reasonable decisions faced with such a big change in your life."

Holding it together? Reasonable? Kyle wasn't sure that those described him, but as more time passed, he was better able to accept things without becoming a raging, strident, ball of emotion.

"Thank you." Things weren't all bad. He had a good full-time job, got to hang out with his best friend, and also got to indulge in fun activities that also paid him. He occasionally missed being in the limelight, but disappointment was a part of life.

However, he appreciated Wendell's support, more than he could say. It fostered a sense of closeness, and Kyle hoped it was the beginning of something good, whether it be friendship or something more.

In the confines behind the check-in desk, it seemed like they were all alone. Wendell leaned forward slowly, like he was either preparing to share a secret or land a kiss. At this point, Kyle still had no idea which was more likely. Perhaps he could put his newfound speaking ability to use and actually ask.

Maybe later.

Kyle leaned in, too, hoping things were heading toward a kiss.

A crash broke the silence, shattering the sense that they were alone in the world together.

EIGHT

28 Days to Haunt Fest

IN UNISON, they both stood up, Wendell's heart pounding as he strained to listen.

"Did someone fall? Should I call the police or an ambulance?" He couldn't hear any cries of pain or pleas for help.

Kyle darted his gaze around. "It sounded more like some*thing* fell? Not heavy enough for a person, I don't think."

True. And maybe not thump-y enough to be a body hitting the ground. But better safe than sorry.

"I need to check this out. If it's something critical, we may need to call... someone." The police? Sandra? Interrupt Jackson's dinner plans? He didn't want to do any of those things.

"I'll come with you."

Wendell smiled gratefully at Kyle. He'd much rather not be alone if there was an emergency. He snatched up his phone and keyring, then led Kyle into the lobby.

"Where do you think it came from? Upstairs?"

Kyle shrugged. "Maybe. But it sounded closer than that. I think."

"There shouldn't be anyone in the kitchen at this time of day." A few steps, and Wendell was able to see the whole of the sunroom, and nothing looked out of place. "Let's check out the other rooms down here."

He hoped he wouldn't have to start knocking on doors. Like Kyle said, it didn't sound loud enough to be a human body, but if someone was hurt in their suite, well, he had a responsibility for that, didn't he? Or did he? It wasn't something that ever came up when he'd worked in his family's boutique hotel.

Oh, sure, people fell and even died. He'd facilitated his fair share of health checks, and not all of them ended happily. But he'd never had to go *searching* for such a thing. The rooms were sound-proofed enough that he never heard any guest activities while at the front desk. Unlike the Orange Lady, which was an older building with suites directly overhead.

They peeked into the tea room and the main dining room, both of which were dim and obviously empty. Wendell flicked on lights but that only confirmed that the rooms were empty and undisturbed, ready to serve guests tomorrow first thing.

"Library's next." Then the game room. Then opening unoccupied rooms. Not long before he'd have to figure out if he had to start knocking on doors. Pretty much the last thing he wanted to do.

Kyle nodded, and gestured for Wendell to proceed. Thankfully he'd spent some time prowling around the building and knew where everything was already. It wasn't the most efficiently laid out building, but repurposing a Victorian homestead into a bed and breakfast can't have been simple, and it was clear the work had been done long before they had to consider things like accessibility, network cabling, and air conditioning. The subsequent adjustments for which had been a little slapdash, in Wendell's opinion. But the place was charming enough, and if it were up to Wendell, he wouldn't bother spending money on aesthetics until something needed to be repaired or replaced, and then improve on things at the same time.

"There really ought to be an entrance to the library from the main hall." The door to the library was quite a way down a side hall that led to a secondary staircase to the guest rooms above.

"My understanding is that Sandra and Bill had to put a fair amount of money into sprucing the place up when they bought it, and didn't want to mess with the built-in bookcases. The library apparently just needed some paint and accessories, not the expense of a new door. I guess it also maybe makes it quieter?"

There was an odd note in Kyle's voice. An edge that Wendell couldn't interpret, but there wasn't time to figure out what was wrong. He needed to know now if that sound they'd heard had heralded an emergency.

Wendell flicked a switch by the door and various tabletop lamps flickered to life, filling the room with a serene yellow glow. This particular room had no windows—the one existing window had been blocked up at some point to accommodate the later addition of a fireplace—and as such, always required lighting.

Unfortunately, given the maze of additional bookcases and high, wing-backed chairs, the sight lines weren't anywhere near as clear as they were in the previous rooms. Wendell strode into the room, almost at the far wall, when he spotted it.

"This must be it." He turned back to Kyle, who hovered in the doorway. "Is something wrong?"

An indecipherable expression crossed Kyle's face, before he sucked in a breath and walked into the room.

"Nothing's wrong."

"Uh. Okay." Something definitely was, but Wendell wasn't about to poke his new friend about something sensitive. "Anyone else here?" Wendell called out.

"Don't say that," Kyle said from just inside the doorway.

"Why not?"

Kyle rolled his eyes. "This town is full of ghosts. You don't want to accidentally invite one in."

Wendell's eyes widened. "For real?"

"Eh. I don't know. I've never seen a ghost, but Eddie—he's a medium—and he says stuff like that all the time." Kyle got a look on his face that Wendell would never tell him made him look constipated. But it was fairly obvious Kyle didn't have a lot of patience for this Eddie character.

Nevertheless, Wendell made a mental note to seek him out at some point during his stay. Interviewing a 'real' medium would be excellent research.

Then Kyle approached close enough to see what Wendell had found. "What the hell happened here?"

It looked like someone had swept an arm across an entire shelf of books, sweeping them to the floor, along with some sort of ceramic sculpture, which lay in shards on the floor amongst the haphazard pile of hardcover books. This had to be the source of the crashing sound they'd heard.

Wendell frowned. "If we were back home, I'd assume we'd had an earthquake, and these books hadn't been shelved securely or something. But you don't get quakes out here, do you?"

Kyle shrugged. "Not that I've ever heard of. I guess there's a first time for everything, but wouldn't we have felt an earthquake strong enough to dump books off their shelves? I've never been in an earthquake."

"Yeah, we definitely would have noticed that."

"Kids, then? A stupid prank?"

Wendell chewed at his bottom lip. "We don't have any kids in residence at the moment. Not even college kids. Think there's any way outsiders, like kids from the town, could easily get in here and do this? Although I have no idea why they would."

It could have been an adult having a bad day, but even if they'd run upstairs in order to avoid getting caught, surely he and Kyle would have heard that.

"The Lady isn't exactly Fort Knox, but I also don't see any reason why anyone, kids or not, would sneak in here to do this. And it's not like there aren't any security measures. People need to feel safe, you know?"

"Yeah, I know. So weird." Wendell had just reviewed the binder with a tab carefully labeled Security. But it wasn't a prison, it wasn't a palace, and any number of employees, past and present, could have either gotten around the current security, or let slip to someone else how to do it. Maybe it had been a localized weather phenomenon? He'd much rather think that, than someone was mean-spirited enough to harass Sandra with everything else she had going on.

And just like that, Wendell could believe it was a freak weather thing as a gust of chilly air swept across his neck. Must be an air conditioning vent nearby.

Kyle also rubbed his arms. "It's cold in here."

Wendell wasn't so sure he'd go so far as to call it cold. Finally comfortable, maybe. But Kyle did not look too happy.

One of the table lamps nearby flickered, then the bulb blew with a sharp pop.

Kyle yelled, and clutched at his chest. Wendell flinched, then curled a lip at the shards of lightbulb glass that had been added to the mess on the floor.

"Can you grab me a broom or something to clean this up? I'll start putting the books back."

A quick nod, and Kyle turned on his heel and dashed out of the room. Wendell couldn't help himself but admire Kyle's rear view. It was pretty fucking spectacular. He sighed. He was shitty at reading guys' signals. There were times he thought Kyle was interested. There had been that one shining moment when he'd thought they might kiss. But the moment had literally been shattered, and he didn't have the guts to just ask Kyle... anything.

As soon as he finished returning the books to their shelf, Kyle returned with a dustpan and broom. Within minutes, the mess had been cleared up but the vibe between him and Kyle was still weird.

"You sure you're okay?" Wendell asked as they returned to the lobby.

The question got him a big sigh. "It's stupid but I've never liked that room. I don't know why."

"Haunted? The Orange Lady?" Wendell could not be that lucky. But Kyle snorted and rolled his eyes.

"Not hardly. I don't think there have ever been any sightings of her in the library. Besides, I'm sure I'm not sensitive to ghosts, or I would have seen one at least once during the many, many ghost tours I've done. But I've never seen any."

Wendell could one hundred percent agree with the disappointment in Kyle's tone. A real ghost would jumpstart his creative juices like nothing else. And it would be really fucking cool to encounter a ghost, however much he didn't, deep down, think they existed.

"And you don't think hating a room for no good reason might be a haunting?"

Kyle smirked, and Wendell smiled back, relieved to see Kyle's good mood returning.

"Nope. It's probably something wonky in the proportion of the rooms and it's messing with my equilibrium or something. Maybe asbestos."

"Asbestos?" That was the sort of horror story Wendell was not interested in living. Not a tiny bit. "Wouldn't there have been inspections or something to correct that?"

"I'm just kidding. I know Sandra's passed all the building inspections. But I wasn't kidding when I said that room hadn't been changed since the house was built. Aside from blocking the window to put in the fireplace, and the decor, I'm pretty certain it's original."

"Original? That's pretty cool, actually. What about the rest of the place?"

"The guest rooms upstairs are mostly original too, but between modern safety codes and plumbing requirements, they've had more work done than the library. Of course, the rest of the ground floor has had substantial upgrades to accommodate paying guests, rather than one wealthy family."

"I suppose so." Nevertheless, the mental gears that Wendell had feared were rusted over for good had, well, they hadn't started moving. Nothing as solid as a faint idea. But this simple discussion tweaked something in his mind. Like it was lubing his gears, or scrubbing away the rust. Preparing for work. Too soon for hope yet, but if he relaxed and let it happen, he might be able to coax his muse back.

"What about the cottages?"

"Built in the fifties, I believe."

"And I guess you haven't seen the Orange Lady, have you?"

"Nope. But I haven't been here overnight, either. She doesn't show herself during the day, or so I'm told."

Wendell opened his mouth to invite Kyle to ghost watch with him some night, but something stopped him. Mostly the fear of looking dorky. Also, it really would need to be at a time when ghost watching wouldn't disturb any of the paying guests, and Wendell didn't recall when the upstairs was scheduled to empty out. Another thing to run past Jackson.

It was a question he could keep in his back pocket to ask Kyle at a later time, if it seemed appropriate.

Kyle's phone buzzed and he pulled it out of a tight pocket.

"Shit. I have to get ready or I'm going to be late for my tour. Did you want to join tonight?"

"Raincheck. I'm still getting my feet wet here, and I think I'd be more comfortable going some night when there are fewer guests and Jackson was on the premises."

"Okay. Just let me know." Kyle grabbed his bag and swanned into the employee bathroom.

While he changed, Wendell tidied up the mess they'd made from dinner, and shortly after he'd finished, Kyle emerged wearing the same pirate-esque outfit he'd worn the previous night, except this time his eyeliner was thicker and more dramatic.

Butterflies swooped and soared in his belly. Kyle was just so beautiful. Too beautiful for a writer nerd like him.

That didn't stop those damned butterflies.

As much as Kyle had been enjoying Wendell's company, he also couldn't wait to get out into the humid heat of the evening. He'd gotten very cold in the library, cold enough to raise goosebumps. He wasn't sure if it was a malfunction of the air conditioner, or if it was simply the willies knowing someone had been in the library moments before they got there, and had been angry enough to create such damage.

All of his registered attendees were present on the porch, waiting patiently. Kyle smiled at them, and began his spiel, but was very thankful that he could do his tour in his sleep because he couldn't focus one bit.

Tourists were a funny bunch. Often times, things they would never do at home they felt more than free to do while on vacation. Like vacation had no consequences or something. Cliff and Scott, the members of the police force that Kyle now socialized with, of all bizarre things, would be the first to tell anyone that consequences existed, and those consequences kept them on their toes, especially during the fall and spring.

Nevertheless, there was something malicious about the havoc that had been created that bothered Kyle. A maliciousness that didn't feel like a tourist with imagined free rein. He'd been at odds with Eddie for such a long time, but they'd never done actual damage to either's place of business. Not even anything as inconsequential as breaking a dollar store vase. And Kyle had a feeling the broken sculpture in the library cost rather more than a dollar.

He wasn't about to forgive Eddie for the things he'd done. Not yet. But he suddenly understood that their so-called feud had a much different feel to it. Mostly harmless.

If he and Wendell hadn't been close by, would the unknown intruder have done more damage? Could Wendell have woken up to a completely trashed library, or had that shelf been a one-off expression of frustration and rage?

Kyle shivered again.

"Did you see the ghost?"

The unexpected question from one of the younger members of the tour pulled him out of his thoughts.

"No, I didn't. But I did feel a chill, which as you know is definitely the sign of a haunting." He smirked and lunged forward. "What was that?"

He was well rewarded with many shrieks, including a few from the guys, followed by a round of nervous laughter.

Kyle smiled gently at his charges. "Oh, my mistake. I guess it was nothing."

Just like that, he was back to normal. He didn't know why the library spooked him so much, but there was really nothing to worry about.

Later that night, Kyle settled into bed, hair still damp from his shower. His knee ached just a touch from all the walking on two back-to-back tours, which thankfully only occasionally happened during the offseason. The first couple of years, he'd had to wear a brace on his knee in order to do that amount of walking, and sometimes still did during Haunt Fest. His knee had improved, but it was never going to be fully normal again. As much as he enjoyed the tours, he didn't think he'd have the ability to continue doing them at this pace. Especially as the tourism rate picked up.

But that was a problem for another time. He picked up his phone and texted Wendell. It might be too soon to text after a date, but since no one had explicitly called the evening a date—even assuming Wendell was into him—it might be okay to open lines of electronic communication.

Kyle: *Everything okay after I left?*

He rolled his eyes. Like he had some magic forcefield that had protected Wendell while they were together.

If only he'd thought of a cool opening salvo before firing off that limp fizzle of a text.

He threw his phone down the bed beside him. He could be such a loser.

After he turned off the light, he laid back with a huff and crossed his arms, staring at nothing, wondering if he'd be able to fall asleep. As cars drove past his apartment building, streaks of light and shadows of palm fronds chased each other across the ceiling.

The vibration of an incoming text made him smile, although he cautioned himself against getting his hopes up. It might just be another picture from Drew of the Eiffel Tower or the Louvre or something. A dick pic from one of his dating apps. Or worse, a spam notification.

He forced himself to move slowly, and not snatch at his phone like a hungry, hungry hippo.

Wendell: *All good. No one has owned up to it, but I guess that's no surprise.*

Kyle flopped back on the bed, smiling at his phone's display. He was such a dork. Wendell's reply had been utterly neutral, but Kyle couldn't stop grinning. Friend or fling, he was going to see where this went. Even if it meant more time in the Lady's creepy library.

NINE

23 Days to Haunt Fest

THURSDAY MORNING, almost a week since he'd arrived in Sandy Bottom Bay, Wendell emerged from his cottage into the bright sunshine. Although still well before noon, the humidity made it almost hard to breathe. On Sunday, his jet lag had caught up with him. He'd dragged his sorry carcass around the inn, helping Jackson out, but he'd been about as witty and charismatic as a zombie. Aside from a few texts, he hadn't done anything to further his connection with Kyle because he wanted to present his best self, and the past few days had not seen him at his best.

But this morning, he'd awoken refreshed. Energetic. Ready to explore, research, and perhaps book a ghost tour. Or even just invite Kyle to lunch. Or dinner. Definitely he needed to see Kyle in person.

He made his way to the main building of the inn, and wended his way toward the front desk. Considering the noisy chatter from that direction, it wasn't hard to figure out where Jackson was. He popped into the dining room to snag a croissant and a cup of tea, then gave

Patricia a little wave as he left. Patricia had checked in on Monday, also a writer and also doing research, but for a romance novel. She was as yet unpublished. Wendell had admitted to also being a writer, but he generally didn't admit much else to strangers because then he'd be bombarded by people wanting to "collaborate" on screenplays, or hoping to get introduced to someone who could get them a juicy acting role.

Perhaps not such a concern out here in Florida, but as a writer, he was also happy to let others talk about themselves. He'd learned so much about human nature over the years.

In the sunroom Mr. and Mrs. Lee sat sipping coffee, presumably waiting for their two teenagers to emerge from the depths of sleep. The Lees had arrived Sunday, well after the incident in the library, otherwise Wendell would have considered their children as possible perpetrators. He nodded to them and to Chester Peterson, who'd checked in yesterday. Chester was the first of the guests scheduled to be at the inn through Haunt Fest, and had booked Greenbriar Lodge, the cottage next to Wendell's.

Although they looked nothing alike, something about Chester reminded him of Jackson, and vice versa. Very weird, but with Chester here for a month, he'd have plenty of time to figure it out.

As he got closer to the front desk, the din got louder, and when he stepped into the lobby, Jackson turned to him with a relieved sigh.

"I was just about to text you. Can you help take bags upstairs? Some of the weekend's wedding party has arrived."

Wendell smiled at the chattering group of women. "Of course." He looked back at Jackson. "Pixie Light and Will 'o' Wisp rooms?"

Jackson nodded. "Yes. They're going to head over to the venue now. You can just put all the luggage into Pixie Light, and they'll sort it out when they decide who is sleeping where."

Wendell got started. They had a full house this weekend between the wedding party, the bride's parents, and the groom's parents. Wendell wondered if the wedding was going to be paranormal-themed, or if they'd just wanted a tropical destination wedding that didn't require travel out of the country. The ceremony and reception were slated to be held at the founder's residence, which was reputed to be haunted, but it was also the best venue for a wedding in the area.

Ten minutes later, Wendell had all the luggage stowed upstairs. When he returned to the lobby, Jackson was alone at the desk.

"Going to keep us hopping this weekend," Wendell commented.

"For sure. They seem nice enough so far. But I haven't seen enough of the bride yet to be sure. Her attitude usually sets the tone, I find."

Wendell frowned slightly. "How do you know that? Been to a lot of weddings?"

Jackson laughed, the first genuinely happy expression Wendell had seen from him since he'd arrived.

"You could say that. I spent many years as an event planner and I've overseen dozens of weddings."

"Ah, well, of course you'd be an expert then."

Jackson shrugged sheepishly. "About as expert as it gets, I bet." Then he cleared his throat. "Had time to do any research?"

Wendell had been going to ask more questions about Jackson's life and how he could just pick up and babysit a bed and breakfast in another state, but the change of subject was a clear indicator Jackson was done sharing anything personal for the moment. Which Wendell was happy to respect.

"Some. But I think there's a lot more exploring I need to do." The lighthouse, the clock tower, and the old cemetery were tops on his list, based on the perusal of the tourists maps the inn had in the lobby. He'd also gone through the pamphlets Kyle had brought him but wasn't sure which of those activities would be appropriate. Or which would be more likely to let him spend more time with Kyle. There were plenty of fabric arts options but he wasn't ready to dive into those.

"You ever seen the ghost here?" Wendell asked.

Jackson winked. "I haven't made the lady's acquaintance yet, no."

"But you think this place is haunted?"

"I'm willing to keep an open mind."

Wendell held back a frown. Jackson's non-committal answer would have made Sandra proud, as one of her main rules was never shut the door on a guest's beliefs. But Wendell wasn't a guest. Not exactly.

"Sure, sure. Once this wedding party is gone, there's a couple of days with almost no bookings. Would you be okay if I stayed overnight in the inn itself? I'd like to try to see the Orange Lady with my own eyes."

Because seeing a ghost? That would be incredible. Not probable, because Wendell didn't truly believe in ghosts, but it would make damn fine story fodder if it were true.

Jackson shrugged.

"I don't have a problem with it, as long as there's no disruption for the guests that will still be here."

"I can't see any reason why there would be." Wendell bit his lip. "What about if I asked a friend to join me? Help keep me awake and all that." Because *that* was the only reason he wanted to invite Kyle.

"A friend?"

"Yeah. Um, Kyle Grainger? Do you know him?" In a surprise move, Wendell's cheeks heated. Living in Hollywood, he thought he'd long since lost the capacity for blushing, but something about Kyle brought it back.

Jackson grinned at him. "Kyle's a good kid. But no shenanigans."

Unexpectedly, Wendell's blush got worse. Shenanigans? So, so many possible definitions of that.

Jackson calling Kyle a kid made Wendell feel a bit like he was also a kid asking someone to prom. Then again, Kyle was a few years younger than Wendell, and while he didn't know Jackson's age, there could easily be twenty years between them. Kyle probably was young in Jackson's eyes. But that didn't change the fact that Kyle was all man and Wendell was a hundred percent down for any and all shenanigans.

Perhaps not in the public areas of the inn, however.

Wendell glanced down at his phone, then through the front window. He couldn't see Drew's storefront from where he stood, but he was tossed up between going over there and talking to Kyle in person, or texting him.

They'd been texting off and on over the past couple of days, but maybe if he could see Kyle's face when he asked, he'd have a better idea where he stood.

He glanced at Jackson. "You okay if I take off for a bit?"

"Go. I'll text you if something comes up, but until the rest of the wedding party arrives, it should be pretty slow around here."

Wendell made a mental note to be back well before the rest of today's guests were scheduled to arrive.

He took a quick check to make sure he wasn't too rumpled or covered in crumbs, and headed out the front door.

It wasn't totally clear if Malachi's was even open. Kyle had told him he was trying to keep the storefront open as much as he could but that the hours had been irregular while Drew was away.

Nerves rattled his belly. Should he hope Kyle was there? Or hope he wasn't?

Sucking in a deep breath, he strolled as casually as he could across the road. There was a bright pink piece of paper on the window, but from the street, Wendell couldn't see what it said.

He approached the door slowly, and stalling for time, he leaned over to read the pink notice thoroughly before peeking through the window to see if Kyle was there.

Disappointment made his shoulders droop. The store did not look open, and he didn't see Kyle inside.

Then a little flicker had him trying the door, and it opened immediately, accompanied by the tinkle of a bell.

The nerves swooped as Kyle turned to him, but when the generic smile on Kyle's face immediately morphed into a wider and warmer one, Wendell couldn't help but smile back.

"Hey there. Jackson finally letting you out, is he?"

Wendell chuckled. "You know it isn't like that."

"No, I know. But you're free now. What are you up to?" Kyle set his clipboard down on the desk. "Did you want some tea or something? Drew usually has instant coffee available for clients when he's here, but I could easily boil some water for you."

"I'm fine. I got my fill during the breakfast service today."

"That's good."

An awkward silence filled the space between them, and Wendell cleared his throat.

"I don't want to interrupt you while you're busy." Shit, why couldn't he just spit out the question?

Kyle smiled shyly. "I'm not really that busy. I've actually got everything for the store ready for when Drew gets back and Haunt Fest gets into full swing. Mostly I'm just killing time."

Wendell couldn't ask for a better opening than that. "Um, then maybe I will have some tea, please?"

Because he could barely swallow around the dryness in his throat. Which was stupid. He'd been rejected before, plenty of times. It wouldn't be the end of the world. Hell, he wasn't even sure Kyle was into guys. Mostly sure, but not completely. But for some reason this felt more important than just a hookup. More significant than ships passing in the night.

Kyle nodded and disappeared around a corner. Rustling and clinking sounds assured Wendell that he hadn't gone far, and Wendell took this time to take a few deep breaths. He also wandered around the tiny storefront, inspecting the products for sale. They appeared to be decent quality, and while a number of the scents were unfamiliar, they were quite pleasant.

Soon, Kyle returned with a steaming cup of tea. Wendell took it from him and fiddled with the teabag string.

"What are you up to today?" Kyle asked.

Okay, this was an even better opening.

"I was going to explore some of the sights. Did you want to come with me?"

Wendell couldn't breathe while he waited.

"I'd love to. I just need a few minutes to finish up what I was doing and we can head out."

"Good. Great." Wendell took a big gulp of tea to keep himself from saying any more synonyms for 'good' but had forgotten the water had just finished boiling. He spit the tea back into the cup and moaned.

"Did you burn yourself? I'm so sorry." Kyle grabbed the tea and disappeared while Wendell tried to suppress the tears of pain.

It was official. Wendell had zero game. If he was movie star hot, that might not matter, but he wasn't. He was going to be alone forever with his permanently singed mouth.

Kyle burst out through a curtain covered in mystical symbols, carrying another cup. "Here's some ice. Pop one in your mouth."

Wendell did as instructed, the relief immediate. He tried to thank Kyle, who shook his head and rested his hands on his waist.

"Nope. Not a word," Kyle scolded. "You sit down and finish the ice while I finish up here."

Wendell blinked and noticed the chair next to the counter. Although part of him wanted to run back to the inn and never let Kyle see his extremely uncool self again, he was a little intimidated by Kyle's take charge attitude, and a lot intrigued. But he didn't want to make Kyle angry, and he suspected if he didn't sit and eat ice, he might see Kyle in a temper.

Kyle mumbled a little to himself as he worked, shaking his head. Wendell just watched patiently as the pain in his mouth receded.

Once the ice was gone, Wendell found the courage to speak.

"Eddie Price is the town medium?" Kyle had briefly mentioned a medium a few days ago, but Wendell hadn't recalled the name at all, not until he'd seen the flyer.

Kyle whirled, eyes narrowed. "Where did you hear that name?"

"It was on the flyer on the door."

Kyle's nostrils flared and he stomped to the door, wrenched it open with a cacophony of bells and ripped the pink paper from the door.

"I swear, that man is the worst." The tirade continued while Kyle shredded the paper into pieces and jammed them into a wastebasket behind the desk.

He had never understood the concept of people looking attractive while angry, but Kyle managed it. He was incandescent and Wendell was glad he wasn't the subject of Kyle's ire.

Kyle turned on him. "What? Is he like your best friend or something?"

Too stunned to do anything other than respond truthfully, Wendell spoke. "You're beautiful."

Which made Kyle freeze. Great. All he'd wanted to do was invite Kyle to show him around town. Maybe ask him to ghost watch with him some night soon. Instead, he burned his tongue, spat tea back into his cup, stepped into some ongoing feud with Kyle and this Eddie person, and then just blurted out that he found Kyle attractive. If there was a tiger pit in front of him, he'd probably jump right in.

But then, Kyle's cheeks reddened and the ire in his eyes softened to something like wonder.

"I am?"

Wendell jumped into the pit with both feet because why the hell not.

"You must know you are. You're stunning, and what I really would like is to date you. Get to know you better."

Kyle rubbed at his cheeks, eyes shining. "Just that?" His voice had a little purr to it, one that heated Wendell's cheeks too.

"Not just that, no. But I understand if you're not interested. I'm... friends is good, too."

Kyle stepped closer. Close enough Wendell could smell his citrusy soap.

"I'm interested. Of course, I am. Friends would be good, but maybe we can be more."

"Maybe we can." Was this really happening? Wendell could

hardly believe it. Now, as long as Kyle didn't pull out a script for him to review or ask if he knew any casting directors, then maybe he could start believing it.

Kyle licked his lips, huffed in a short breath, then shook himself. "I, uh, I need to close up, and then we can get going."

Yeah, making out in a friend's shop maybe wasn't the best place to have their first kiss. Wendell was hoping for something super romantic. Maybe with proximity to privacy also. Wendell licked his own lips and grimaced slightly. Maybe wait until his mouth wasn't burned to a cinder also.

It didn't take long for Kyle to finish up, and he led Wendell out of the store.

"I'm sorry for losing my shit back there." Kyle turned right at Main Street, and Wendell followed. At this point, he didn't much care where they went—there would be plenty of time to hit his mini bucket list for Sandy Bottom Bay.

"You don't have to apologize. But I will admit to insatiable curiosity. What was so bad about that flyer?"

Kyle rolled his eyes. "Eddie and Drew have this weird rivalry, or more like, Eddie keeps trying to foster one. I don't really know why, or what his end game is, but Drew's new husband is a cop and Drew's older brothers are brawlers who hit first and ask questions later. I'm not sure why Eddie is courting either a harassment charge or a broken nose."

Wendell's mind immediately compiled reasons for Eddie to act that way, which grew increasingly improbable, as they didn't live in a world where the paranormal happened, but it didn't stop him from smiling. Been a while since his mind churned in that particular manner, a manner he associated with the creative process.

"And I guess you've tried asking him?"

Kyle stopped so suddenly in the middle of the sidewalk that Wendell took a few steps before he realized he was walking alone, and turned back to face him. Kyle appeared absolutely stunned.

"You know, I haven't. And I don't think Drew has either. I've been too caught up in the outrage of it all, and Drew hates conflict."

"Maybe you should give it a try. You might be surprised. And I can't imagine a feud is good for business." If Wendell knew anything at all, it was that people could do things for the strangest reasons.

Kyle stood completely still, expression thoughtful. "That's a good idea. When Drew gets back, we'll do it. I know he wasn't that upset when we stopped messing around."

Then he blinked at Wendell, and flushed a dark pink. "I mean, we were never a thing. And it was over a long time ago."

Hey, good one, Wendell. Suggest your new crush patch things up with his old boyfriend. Forget having zero game, your game is somehow in the negatives.

"I don't... I don't want to step on any toes."

Kyle's eyes narrowed. "You wouldn't be. And also, even if you were, step away. Eddie's made today a bit of a disaster. I don't really want to think about him anymore. And I have no interest in that direction. If you were wondering."

"Okay by me." He hadn't loved hearing that Kyle had messed around with this Eddie character, but it wasn't like he had any right or logical reason to be jealous of things that happened before he showed up. Hell, it wasn't even like Kyle was his boyfriend. But Wendell would be just as happy to forget about Eddie Price, and he was a bit sorry he'd brought him up in the first place.

"Where did you want to go first?"

"The old cemetery, maybe?" Cemeteries were always ripe for inspiration, and he hoped this one would be no different.

Kyle nodded and they continued down Main Street.

Kyle stood under the shade of an old oak tree and watched Wendell peer at the engravings on various gravestones. One of his teachers had brought his class on a field trip here to do rubbings of gravestones and something else historical related, but he didn't recall anything of significance, historical or otherwise, in the gravestones they looked at. But he'd rather hang out in this cemetery than the library at the Lady. Perhaps he was just allergic to books that weren't on his Kindle.

Wendell would occasionally pause and take a picture of various stones, rub away some of the moss, or pull back creeping ivy.

He could hardly believe Wendell had blurted out that he wanted to start dating. Amazed and thrilled, but so surprised. Sure, Wendell was only in town for a short amount of time, but that could be a good thing. A test run. Or, if things went well... no, he wasn't going to leap ahead like he often did. He was going to be chill. Take things as they came. Be a normal person. The complete opposite of what he'd been when Wendell had asked about Eddie. Damn Eddie and his flyer fusillade.

A breeze from the ocean ruffled Wendell's hair and he brushed it out of his face in a distracted manner. Definitely more intense than the average tourist, but maybe not as intense as some of the hardcore paranormalists?

"What made you come to Sandy Bottom Bay?" Kyle wandered over to the tombstone Wendell was crouched over. He wasn't going to stay out in the sun long. It might be edging into autumn but the sun was still strong and Kyle had not applied his heavy-duty sunscreen this morning, since he'd anticipated hanging out in Drew's store most of the day.

"Oh, well, I saw an episode of this show, *Phantoms?*"

Kyle's earlier anger came boiling back. "Oh really?"

Wendell rocked back on his heels and stared up at Kyle, who had been unable to hide his ire about the host and the damage that man had nearly done to people he cared about.

"You don't like *Phantoms?*"

"The host is a total dick and I refuse to even speak his name."

"Agreed, he's a total dick. Did you meet him when he was filming here?"

"Yes, and I hope to never repeat the experience. He needs to drop off the face of the earth."

Wendell laughed. "I could get behind that."

"How do you know he's an asshole? I mean, he seems so charming on the show. It was a real disappointment to find out how self-centered he is in person."

Wendell stared at him for a moment before standing. "We're going to try dating, right? We agreed to that? I mean, I'm only here for a few months, but I don't really like casual, and I'd like to see how it goes."

"Yes..." Although Kyle had no idea how those two ideas were connected. "I'm interested in that too. If it's a vacation fling, that's fine. If it gets more serious than that, we can talk long distance stuff later."

Wendell nodded and blew out a breath. "And no one told you what I'm doing here?"

"You're helping out at the inn. That's all I've heard." And somehow, it had never come up in their recent text conversations.

This time, Wendell's laugh was rueful. "I honestly thought the small town gossip network functioned better than this."

"Well, I heard that you were coming long before you got here." Kyle frowned. "But it sounds like you've... got a secret?"

"It's not really a secret. But I guess it could change things. I probably should have told you earlier."

Oh great. Just what he needed. "Let me guess. You're married?" Kyle wasn't going down that road again. No way, no how.

Wendell's eyes widened. "Oh, no. It's nothing like that."

"It's getting hot out here. Let's go by the Dairy Devil, and find a quiet place to talk."

"Dairy Devil?"

"Yup. Soft serve ice cream. It gets mobbed in the summer, but it shouldn't be too busy right now."

"Maybe some lunch afterward?" Wendell was hopeful.

"Yeah, maybe." Although it would depend entirely on what this 'secret' was. Because if it was Wendell was married or had an open marriage or whatever crap guys tried to pull when they wanted their cake and to eat it too, Kyle wasn't going to stick around for a meal.

Ice cream was more carbs than he needed, but he had a bad feeling he was going to need the ice cream therapy after this discussion.

"Lead the way."

They left the cemetery, and Kyle only hoped this fledgling relationship wasn't as dead as the cholera victims whose graves they walked over on the way out.

TEN

23 Days to Haunt Fest

KYLE LED them to a park bench behind the Dairy Devil. He and Drew had eaten many an ice cream on this bench when they were kids. And a few after they grew up, too.

Wendell had gotten a strawberry chocolate twist, but Kyle had gone for the classic chocolate. Drew would say plain vanilla was the true classic but he was wrong.

"What's the big secret?"

"I mean, I never really meant for it to be a secret, actually. I told Sandra everything, and didn't ask her to keep it confidential. I mean, almost no one ever does anyway."

"How bad is it?"

Kyle stuck a spoonful of ice cream in his mouth—no cones for him, too many wasted carbs—to prevent himself from asking any more stupid questions. He suspected there would be plenty of opportunity for stupid questions.

"It really isn't bad," Wendell replied. "At least I don't think so, and I hope you don't either. I'm here to do research. I'm a writer, but I've lost my mojo, and when I saw the episode of *Phantoms*, I hoped coming here would spark some fresh ideas."

"You're right. That doesn't sound bad. What sort of writing do you do?"

Wendell's face and neck went a blotchy red that Kyle found utterly charming. As long as Wendell wasn't a dirtbag, anyway.

"Um. So. Have you ever seen *Dead Eye Dance*? Or *Shadow Stalker*? The *Missing Sarcophagus*?"

What the hell? Kyle set his cardboard cup of ice cream down on the bench beside him, and turned more fully to face Wendell. "You're not... are you the scriptwriter for Lucky Weston Films?"

"Um, yes."

"You're Wendell *Weston*. Like, for real?" Kyle waved his hands around like he often did when he got agitated or excited. He'd nearly punched several noses over the years and had lost a number of drinks, too.

"Um, yes?"

"I love those movies. All of them." Because there were definitely more than the three Wendell had listed. "They're go-to movies for scaring the crap out of ourselves on Halloween. Drew is gonna shit a brick."

"Really?"

"Yes! Seriously, that's one of the reasons why I was thrilled when I found out *Phantoms* was going to film here. Ghost hunting shows are almost as much fun as horror movies." Kyle squinted. "You're not an asshole, right? Because for real, dude who shall not be named was a giant jerk."

"Believe me, I know. We'd considered him for a leading role in one of our movies, and fine, he's allowed to turn us down, but he was a complete ass about it, and strung us along while he did so."

"Then he got that other stupid movie. It just burns my ass that acting like an entitled jerk can still get beneficial results," Kyle replied.

"But despite it all, it was his *Phantoms* episode that brought me here."

"You're writing about Sandy Bottom Bay? That's cool. And I can't believe no one knows!" Kyle fanned himself. This was so exciting. Okay, maybe it was him, not Drew, who was going to shit a brick. Although Drew did prefer Lucky Weston movies to *Phantoms*.

Wendell sighed. "I didn't ask Sandra to keep things quiet, nor Jackson, but I'd rather not advertise. I don't have any definite plans for a script."

Melancholy surrounded Wendell, smoky and sad. Kyle did not want him to feel like this.

"I'm sorry. I mean, I won't talk about it." Although he wasn't sure why Wendell had suddenly seemed to... deflate.

"It's just that, well, I haven't been able to write. For a long time. And I'm worried I won't ever write anything else. I'm hoping being here will fix that."

Kyle reached over, grabbed Wendell's hand, and gave it a quick squeeze. Wendell's sorrow was so familiar, it was like a knife to his gut.

"I can't tell you it's going to work out the way you hope. Because I know better than most that sometimes your life changes in unexpected ways."

"Change is scary. But however scary, it doesn't make for a good horror film."

The comment surprised a rueful laugh out of Kyle. "True. Might make for a good film in a different genre. But seriously, whatever happens, you're going to be okay. You have to believe that. You've got friends and family and that's not going to change, even if your profession does."

Wendell squeezed Kyle's fingers, and they just sat there for a few moments, breathing. Then Wendell started and let go of his hand.

"Shit." He slurped at his cone. "This is going to melt away if I don't get to it."

Kyle paused, as frozen as their ice cream had been a few minutes ago. Wendell was licking his own hand, cleaning up the drips, then continuing to lick right up to the peak of the soft serve. He... wow... he wanted. Blood flowed south, but Kyle couldn't do anything but stare, ever so jealous of an ice cream cone and Wendell's hand. If they were to kiss right now, Wendell would taste of strawberries and chocolate.

He had to stop thinking about it. Had to stop staring. But he couldn't.

Never had he found Dairy Devil products to be arousing, and he wasn't entirely thrilled to discover that fact today.

"Hey, Kyle."

Kyle yelped and pulled his knees up to his chest. "Scott. What the fuck?"

Scott Hunter stood before them, in full deputy uniform.

"Hello, Kyle, nice to see you, too." Scott's acerbic tone was at odds with smirk. Kyle rolled his eyes.

"Hello, Scott."

Scott shook his head, and directed his attention to Wendell. "Hi. I'm Scott Hunter with the Sandy Bottom Bay Police Department."

"Oh. Um, Wendell Weston. I'm helping out at the Orange Lady Inn for a couple of months." He glanced ruefully at his hands and the cone that was almost completely gone, eaten or melted, Kyle wasn't entirely sure which. "I'd shake your hand but I'm a little sticky right now."

What Kyle wouldn't do to make this man a little sticky, too. Maybe a lot sticky. And slick. Naked, also.

Fuck. He tucked his knees even closer to his chest, attempting to strangle his errant erection with his tight jeans.

Scott darted a sly glance at him, and for a split second, Kyle was afraid he'd said that aloud. But apparently his face was an open book, because it was clear Scott knew he was all the way into Wendell.

Hopefully Scott hadn't seen any physical evidence of Kyle's attraction before he scared the life out of him, because Kyle definitely didn't need any arrests for random erections in public parks. Getting on the sexual offenders list was *not* a life goal.

"Good to meet you, Wendell. We're glad Sandra and Bill could get you and Jackson to help out." An odd expression crossed Scott's face. "How is Jackson holding up?"

Wendell crinkled his nose. "Seems fine. Definitely knows the ropes. Is there something I should be worried about?"

Scott slipped into what Kyle thought of as his "cop" face. Impassive, emotionless, implacable. Cliff had one, too, but Kyle usually only saw it on either of them when they were actually working, and usually with difficult people or situations.

"Nope, nothing. Just a big responsibility, is all. I was going to stop by the inn to check on him, but I came across you first."

This time it was Kyle staring at Scott. Normally Scott reminded him of a big golden retriever puppy, not this stiff man of the law he was currently portraying. Weird.

"I'm sure Jackson will be touched by your concern." Wendell's voice lifted slightly on the last word, making his statement more into a question. Wendell didn't even know Scott and he was able to tell that Scott was being weird.

Scott cleared his throat. "Uh, well, see you around. Nice to meet you, Wendell."

Then he was gone before either of them could respond. Clearly Scott was aware he was acting weird and didn't want Kyle to call him on it. Like that was going to stop him. Next time he saw Scott—well, in civvies, because Kyle had some sense of what was appropriate—he was going to grill that man.

Wendell got up and rinsed his hands off in a nearby water fountain, drying them on his pants before returning to sit on the bench. Kyle spared a glance for the unappetizing dairy soup in the cup beside him. He'd sadly only had a few bites, but then again, he didn't need a whole cup of ice cream anyway.

"Was that strange?" Wendell asked. "Does he know something

about Jackson? Surely Sandra wouldn't have hired a murderer, right?"

Kyle chuckled. "Yes, Scott was being weird but I don't think it's because Jackson is a murderer. I don't really know Jackson at all, but he seemed perfectly normal when he'd been here before. Scott is a bit of a dork, though, so maybe that's all it is."

"Ah. You're friends with Scott?"

"Sort of. It's new. He's a friend of Drew's husband, who is also a cop, and I've gotten to know him through Cliff. Scott and Cliff were seniors in high school when the two of us were freshmen."

"Speaking of the inn, did you want to stay over sometime next week?" Wendell asked.

Kyle blinked at him. Did not sound like an invite to sexy times. "Um."

Wendell blushed. "I mean, to try and get a glimpse of the Orange Lady. Over night."

Nothing to think about there, even if sexy times weren't on the menu. "Of course. If I saw her, I could kick some serious ass on my ghost walks."

"I bet. I assume seeing a real live ghost might stir up the creative juices, too."

A chill crept down Kyle's spine. "We won't have to stay in the library, will we?"

"Seriously, why don't you like the library?"

"Honestly, I don't know." Kyle grimaced. "Feng shui? An architectural oddity? Regardless, I'd much rather sit in the sunroom or the dining room. Besides, the Orange Lady is only supposed to haunt the upper floors."

Wendell gave him a gentle smile. "I think it's kinda funny that you've got an aversion to the library, but are okay with the idea of seeing a ghost."

Kyle shrugged. "I know, it's weird."

"I thought we'd stay upstairs anyway. Unless we have to follow her into the library, that is."

Goosebumps sprang up all along Kyle's spine. That was a scenario that didn't bear thinking of. But then again, he did want to see a ghost. It wasn't fair that Drew got all the paranormal fun.

"Deal. Where did you want to go to now?"

Wendell glanced up at the sky, which had started to darken and cloud over. "Lunch? Inside somewhere?"

"Sounds good. How about the Angry Parakeet?"

Wendell stared at him for a minute. "Sounds better than the Specter Smorgasbord."

"Yup. It is."

Wendell stood and held out his hand. Kyle took it with a little flutter in his heart.

"Lead the way," Wendell said, and didn't let go.

Kyle could get used to this.

Wendell couldn't remember the last time he'd had such a good connection with a man, especially one he wanted in all ways. Kyle was definitely special.

They'd made it to the Angry Parakeet just before the rain hit, and the sound of the downpour thumping on the roof was almost soothing. He'd not really expected so much additional sensory input from Florida, but he knew he'd make the most of it going forward in his creative endeavors.

Lunch had been spent mostly chatting about movie making. Kyle had asked a lot of questions, but questions that had nothing to do with trying to break into the business or how he could sell the script he'd kept in a lockbox under his bed. Wendell loved what he did for a living, and it was exhilarating to share some of that knowledge with someone he was certain wouldn't turn around and exploit it, either directly or via the tabloids.

In return, Kyle told him all about growing up in Sandy Bottom Bay, and the things he and Drew had gotten up to as kids. Mostly it was avoiding trouble caused by Drew's older twin brothers, who Wendell needed to meet, if only for the character ideas.

They made plans to visit some of the other places on Wendell's list the following week, after the wedding party was gone, including an overnight visit to catch a glimpse of the Orange Lady. If they didn't do it next week, it would be well after Haunt Fest before the inn would be similarly empty—Sandra had definitely been right about a significant lull just before the festival.

If they weren't too busy, Wendell also had a couple of date nights in mind. During the week, of course, because Kyle's weekend nights were full of ghost tours.

After lunch, they walked leisurely through the center of town, and headed down Main Street toward the beach.

All too soon, though, they stood in front of Drew's place, which fortunately had no signs courtesy of Eddie Price, because Wendell definitely didn't want to ruin the lovely day they'd had. Although Kyle in a tizzy with his arms waving around, ranting, had been quite the sight.

"Text me later if you want." Wendell tried not to grimace. That was a stupid thing to say, wasn't it?

Kyle simply smiled. "Can't wait to see you again." Then he blushed. "Sorry, that was too much, wasn't it?"

Wendell laughed softly. "Maybe we both just need to say what we mean. You're not going to scare me off, if that's what you think."

"Really? Because a lot of guys get hives if I want to hang out with them for two days in a row."

"Nope. No hives on this guy." Wendell smiled, then lifted his hand to Kyle's cheek, sliding it around to cup the back of Kyle's neck.

Kyle sighed, and leaned toward Wendell, who bent his head. Their lips met, gently, chastely, for all of one second. Then Kyle breathed out, lips parting, and Wendell dove in. The kiss turned frantic, hungry, and their mouths clashed, eager to lick and nip and taste.

Kyle pressed himself to Wendell's chest, and Wendell slid a hand down to cup Kyle's perfect, pert ass, pressing them closer, nestling their erections together.

A wolf whistle from down the street shattered the fog of desire and they split apart. Wendell was pleased to see Kyle was breathing every bit as heavily as he was, although he was less pleased that Kyle was no longer in his arms. Wendell had never had a kiss so explosive, and if it wasn't for the awareness of their surroundings rushing back in like a slap across the face, Wendell might have tried coaxing Kyle to the ground.

Then Wendell remembered that this was Florida. Where they had fire ants. There would be no naked outdoor dalliances for them.

A charming slash of pink had colored Kyle's cheekbones, and he stared at Wendell's lips, eyes dark and sultry.

"I'll see you later," Wendell said, less tentatively this time.

Kyle snorted. "Yes, you definitely will. Now go before I have to explain to Drew that we did unmentionable things in his psychic reading room."

Wendell laughed, although it was going to be a while before he fully calmed down. He'd known from that very first day that Kyle was something special. He brushed a quick kiss over Kyle's lips, backing away before Kyle's magnetic pull sucked him back in.

Suck. Nope, he wasn't going to think about that *at all.*

Wendell discreetly adjusted himself, hoping that his burgeoning hard-on wasn't too obvious in his sturdy jeans.

He nodded at Kyle, then spun on his heel and headed to the inn.

Outside the inn's front door, Wendell ran his fingers through his hair and sucked in a deep breath. The short walk from Drew's place had mostly taken care of his hard-on, but he didn't want it to be obvious he'd been kissing... his boyfriend? Too soon for that sort of label, and yet, the term felt right. His creative juices might not be getting the workout he wanted, but meeting Kyle had been a welcome surprise. A stupendous, mind-blowing surprise, and no matter how early it was, Wendell didn't see ever wanting it to end.

He opened the door, a smile on his face.

Jackson looked up from the desk. "Hey. Have a good time?"

"Yes, I did, thanks." Neither of them commented on Wendell's suddenly warm cheeks, thankfully. Maybe blushing was a Florida thing. Nah. Definitely a Kyle thing.

"Lisa's setting up the tea things. Go on in and have some, I got word that the rest of the wedding party was delayed and won't be here until after dinner. There's going to be lots of food, and then some."

Wendell had eaten plenty at the Angry Parakeet, but he wouldn't say no to some of Lisa's cookies.

"Sure, thanks, I'll do that."

"How's Kyle?" Jackson asked, with the barest hint of a wink.

Completely without his permission, Wendell's cheeks heated even more. "Fine."

"Just *fine*? Odd."

Wendell spluttered out an embarrassed laugh. "Stop it."

"Go on. Relax a bit. We'll be busy enough once the bride and bridesmaids get back from the wedding venue." Jackson shooed him away, and Wendell obeyed.

He'd like to get in some quiet time, because it turned out a bunch of women in a bridal party could be very loud.

"Hey Lisa," Wendell said as he entered the tea room.

"Hey Wendell. Nice to see you. Come get some cookies and scones." Lisa arranged the displayed baked goods with practiced ease.

"Scones! Honestly, though, I just ate lunch. Scones are maybe too much."

"So, no sandwiches either? If you don't have dinner plans, you might have enough leftovers to feed yourself and Jackson."

"Not a bad idea." Especially if they were going to be dealing with an influx of new guests. Leftover tea sandwiches might be the perfect thing to eat tonight. "For now, though, I'm going to grab some cookies."

Wendell put a couple of tombstone sugar cookies and a ginger-bread ghost on a small plate before preparing a mug of tea.

Lisa was just about to take her leave, and Wendell knew she'd be too busy to sit and chat with him. He also didn't totally love the ambiance of the tea room. Slightly too frilly and fussy for his tastes. But neither did he want to go back to his cottage—he'd rather be close by so he could easily jump in and help Jackson when the bridal party returned.

"See you later, Lisa. Thanks for the cookies."

She saluted him and sailed out of the room. He'd actually been surprised to see her in person. Usually she sent Tony. Wendell took his goodies and headed for the sun room.

"Hello, Chester. Mind if I sit with you?"

Chester was their other long-term guest, an elderly man who'd arrived shortly after Wendell and took up occupancy in Greenbriar Lodge, one of the cottages further down the beach.

"Of course not. Please, sit down."

Wendell wasn't the most extroverted person in the world. A lot of writers weren't. But he had found that casual conversation could sometimes lead to a lot of story ideas. And he was much better one-on-one than he was in group situations anyway.

He set down his plunder from the tea room, then noticed Chester didn't have anything. Although the man was mobile enough to walk to and from his cottage, he did at times seem frail and washed out, more so than he'd expect from a healthy man in his seventies.

"The tea service has been laid out, can I get you anything? Aside from scones and cookies, there are number of delicious-looking sandwiches."

Chester smiled at him, serene, like a male version of the *Mona Lisa.* He was no doubt been a heartbreaker in his youth. He was still great-looking for an older guy.

"Thank you, that's sweet, but I haven't got much of an appetite at the moment."

"What about tea or coffee? There are some herbal teas there as well, if caffeine isn't your thing."

Chester's grin widened, going from serene to almost wicked. "I appreciate your wording. Most people would just ask if I can't have caffeine because I'm too old."

Wendell shrugged. "Well, I am a writer. Words are my thing." Even if he seemed to forget how to use them around Kyle sometimes.

"Are you, now? Fascinating. As for the tea question, if there's some peppermint tea, I would be happy to have some of that."

"I'll be back in a second."

A few minutes later, Wendell settled back into his chair, a cup of fragrant peppermint tea on the table. Chester wrapped his hands around the cup as though seeking the warmth, which boggled Wendell's mind. It was air conditioned inside but the sunroom was still the warmest spot in the inn, and if it weren't for Wendell's tea addiction—especially when eating pastries—he'd want something cold to drink.

But then, his grandmother was just the same, in the desert heat of LA. She said it helped her joints, although Wendell suspected she was older than Chester.

Wendell took a bite of his gingerbread ghost and barely held in a moan. If there was magic in this town, it was all in Lisa's bakery.

They sat in silence for a few minutes, then Wendell took a careful sip of tea.

"What brings you to Sandy Bottom Bay, Chester?" Already Wendell knew there could be a million reasons why a person might show up to this particular Floridian town, but he really wanted to know if Chester was a secret ghost hunter. Or tarot enthusiast.

"Going to put it in your book?"

"I write screenplays, not books."

Chester nodded. "Well, then probably not, because my story isn't that interesting."

"I don't believe that."

"My life hasn't been all explosions and intrigue, which is what the kids watch these days, isn't it?"

Wendell shrugged. "I could probably write a dissertation on different genre types and how they relate to societal issues." Mostly because his sister made a point of imparting that information to him ad nauseum because of how it all related to marketing. "I'm frankly just curious. I don't need explosions."

Although maybe an explosion might be an interesting departure from his normal gore and psychological horror.

"You know Haunt Fest has been going on for a long time, don't you?"

Digging through his memories, Wendell pulled up a stat from his admittedly limited research before booking his stay with Sandra. He really had been escaping LA more than he'd been actively trying to find an inspirational venue.

"It started in the early seventies, I think."

"It did. I wasn't here for the first one, but one of the earliest. I'd turned thirty, and a few of us decided to road trip down from Iowa as a lark. It was expected upon my return that I would propose to my girlfriend. So, it wasn't exactly a birthday party or a stag party, but it did feel a bit like my last hurrah before settling down."

Wendell grinned. That sounded like something he'd have done, too. Not getting engaged to a girl, but going someplace off the beaten path like Sandy Bottom Bay, as opposed to Las Vegas or Atlantic City.

"It was so fantastic. I mean, it wasn't all free love or anything, but there was a freedom of expression, a mix of people, the likes I'd never seen before. Being gay back then was no picnic, and I was completely in the closet."

Chester paused to blow on his tea, and take a few prolonged sips.

Unexpected. Wendell leaned forward, waiting anxiously for Chester to continue. What did Chester's sexuality have to do with the festival?

Was it a man? Maybe he was crushing on one of his friends? At this rate, Wendell was going to have to start writing romances.

"Although completely in the closet, it was easy to tell there was a small group of, well, I guess they'd be called LGBTQ folks these days? Anyway, I don't think they knew each other before, but they'd sort of gravitated to each other. Not obvious, exactly, unless you knew what you were looking for. I think it was because the whole ghost thing was so... unusual. The addition of gay men and women... not that much more unusual. And I think the fact that it was still men and women in the group, well, things got overlooked by people who maybe wouldn't have overlooked them in other situations."

"I guess I can see that." Wendell's coming out had been relatively painless, but there were still times where he had moments of nervousness about revealing his sexual orientation, and he couldn't imagine how terrifying it would be to have to be on guard all the time.

"I met a man. He was incredibly cute. Younger than me. Carefree. His name was Sam Kerwin. And he changed my life."

Oh, Wendell was definitely going to have to seriously consider writing romances. This was awesome. For all that his professional life was gore and blood and violence, in his personal life he was a bit of a marshmallow. And right now, he was feeling very sweet and gooey inside.

"Tell me more," Wendell demanded, taking a bite of the sugar cookie and waiting impatiently.

Chester smiled his Mona Lisa smile. "Sam was twenty-two, I was thirty. And we spent that weekend finding every dark corner we could. Not to get too graphic, but we spent so much time rubbing up against each other, there was chafing. We probably took a lot of chances that neither of us would have dared if we had been in either of our respective homes. Broke a few laws, too."

Still adorable, even if it wouldn't be a storyline suitable for all viewers.

"That weekend changed something for me. It made me... realize truly who I was and how little I wanted the joyless half-life I'd been preparing myself for. When I returned to Iowa, I made preparations. Instead of staying at my very religious father's company and becoming the successor he expected, I hightailed it out to San Francisco. Burst out of the closet. Met the love of my life. Lived life to the fullest. Traveled, made lifelong friends."

"Wait." This was totally not how Wendell had expected the story to go. "Sam wasn't the love of your life?"

Chester laughed. "No. I never saw Sam again after that weekend.

But I am incredibly grateful I met him. I have so many good memories of that Haunt Fest weekend, and the life that came out of it."

Wendell sat back his chair, a tiny bit disappointed, but also so happy for Chester. It can't have been as easy to do as he made it sound. But the next free moment he had, he'd jot down some notes about this, because he wanted to be able to reference it all later. He nibbled on more cookie and sipped at his tea.

"And you came back just to relive that weekend?" There was definitely something missing in Chester's recitation. Wendell was a storyteller by trade. He knew better.

"Not exactly." Chester glanced down at the plain gold band on his left hand. "My husband, the one I would never have met if it wasn't for Sam Kerwin and Sandy Bottom Bay, passed a year ago. It's been hard. Very hard. But this place was magical for me back in the seventies, and I just wanted to, I don't know, pay my respects. Maybe see if there's still a little magic here for me."

Wendell blinked furiously, as his eyes suddenly burned.

"I'm so sorry."

Chester smiled, and now Wendell could see the sorrow he was hiding.

"Not to worry."

"I hope you find your magic."

"I hope you find yours. But I think I'll head back to my cottage. I could use a nap."

Wendell watched Chester shuffle away, and a gust of cold air swept across his neck. It wasn't the first time there had been a weird cold patch. Maybe he'd have Jackson call someone to check the air conditioner. Be nice if it was a ghost, but surely there would be something more significant to the chill. How would anyone even determine what was A/C and what was ghostly in origin? Maybe in the days before modern indoor climate control such things were more noticeable. Or less explainable.

Still, he finished his tea and cookies in silence, wishing Kyle was here beside him so he could hold his hand. Or kiss him. Things

Chester probably hadn't dared do openly, even while here on vacation.

Considering how hot and uncomfortable he'd been since he arrived in Florida, this temporary cold breeze was not as comfortable as he'd have expected, and as soon as he finished his snack, he cleared it away and went to hang out with Jackson to wait for their slew of guests from the wedding party to arrive.

ELEVEN

19 Days to Haunt Fest

KYLE PACED ALONG MAIN STREET, peering into the inn's parking lot every time he passed it. When the hell was that wedding party going to leave? Although the weekend had been busy for both him and Wendell, they'd texted fairly often and he knew the bride and groom had left yesterday evening for their honeymoon in Europe.

He and Wendell had speculated on whether they were going to spend their honeymoon like any other newly married people, or if they were going to chase ghosts through whatever medieval castles they came across. Jackson was the one who'd interacted with the bride and groom, though, and he refused to ask them that very pertinent question. Party pooper.

Sunday evening was a respectable time to check out, and in spite of insatiable curiosity about what the honeymooners were going to do —outside of the bedroom—he couldn't be mad at them. The wedding party that stayed on another night to today and dawdled as they packed up their cars? Yeah, they were starting to annoy him. And the parents of the bride, and the groom's two brothers, who were all staying on yet another night, and not leaving until Tuesday morning? They were responsible for an extra dose of annoyance.

Still, as soon as the lion's share of the bridal party left, Kyle wouldn't feel like he was imposing on anyone by casually wandering into the inn. Texting wasn't enough. He wanted to see Wendell. Hang out with him. Maybe get in some more kissing. It already felt like an eon or twelve since they'd locked lips on Thursday, and he hadn't been able to stop thinking about it. He was almost a hundred percent certain Wendell felt the same, but he hadn't overtly said so, and it was making Kyle nervous.

He could understand Wendell might not want to be too obvious. But surely, they had both experienced the "I've said three words to you in text, so here's a close up of my erect cock" phenomenon on the dating apps. Wendell had a long way to go before reaching that level of forwardness, and for a change, Kyle might have liked a dick pic to keep him company until he got to meet the real thing.

No, scratch that. He'd rather meet the dick live and in person before getting any sort of commemorative photo shoot on his phone. Porn was one thing. Porn was a *good* thing. It was the sheer presumption of random guys that irked him on the dating apps. Fortunately, Wendell was the farthest from irksome that Kyle had come across in... maybe ever.

He peeked through the box hedges for a fifth time and groaned. What the fuck did they bring with them to Florida? He was half-tempted to offer his services, just to get them on the damned road. They were also far more interested in yapping than packing. Which he'd done after Drew and Cliff's wedding so he couldn't be too mad about it, but the wait was making him nervous.

This relationship was still so new. And shiny. And he was terrified of fucking it all up.

Huffing, he spun on his heel and headed back toward the village green. At this rate he was going wear a rut in the sidewalk.

Halfway to the green, a now-familiar blue minivan drove past him.

Was that the one?

Kyle forced himself to continue on to the village green before turning around and walking—sedately—back to the inn. Because bursting in the front door mere seconds after the wedding party finally drove off was just going to make him look desperate and stalker-y. He and Wendell might have passed a milestone, but that didn't mean he didn't want to keep making a good impression on the man.

The sixth time was the charm. This time, when he looked through the hedges, the parking lot was as empty as it was going to get today. With a little extra spring in his step, Kyle practically bounced up to the front door and flung it open.

He smiled at Jackson and Wendell who were both behind the front desk.

Jackson just winked at him and disappeared into the office. Wendell smiled back, and he came out into the lobby.

"Want to do something tonight?" Kyle nearly clapped a hand over his mouth. He hadn't meant to blurt it out like that.

"Yeah, I would. No ghost walks tonight?"

Whew. He liked that Wendell didn't need him to play games or play a role just to spend time together.

"No walks tonight." And he was unlikely to have any until the weekend.

"What did you want to do? I'd like to grab a shower, but then I'll be ready."

Kyle adored the fact that Wendell had so little artifice. It made him a lot more confident and less wary. "I was thinking mini golf, dinner, then stream a movie either here or at my place?"

No, he wasn't expecting to them to have sex tonight. But he had an idea, and he hoped Wendell wouldn't assume "stream a movie" meant "Netflix and chill".

"Ooh. Mini golf. I haven't done that in forever. What's the theme?"

"Pirates!" Mostly because it had been built before that asshole William Morales had been mayor, back when the chamber of commerce thought catering to the town's pirate origins would serve the tourists better rather than doubling and tripling down on the paranormal. If William Morales had had his way, they'd have been knocking golf balls through gaping skeletons and around fake tombstones. Kyle didn't have a problem with the paranormal kitsch of his hometown, but he personally liked a little variety too.

"Sounds awesome. Did you want to come back to the cottage while I shower and get ready?"

"No, I'll come back in half an hour or so. I have to close up Drew's first."

"It's a plan." Wendell leaned over and gave him a quick kiss. It was over so fast, it shouldn't have been enough to make him weak in the knees, but it did.

"Okay then. I'll see you soon." Kyle wasn't quite able to hide his sudden breathlessness, and it must have communicated itself to Wendell, because his pupils flared and he cleared his throat.

"I'll, uh, just get going."

But they stood there, staring at each other.

"Go shower already!" Jackson stuck his head out of the office, breaking the trance and making Wendell's cheeks redden, fast and furious.

"I'm going, I'm going."

Jackson covered a smirk with his hand and ducked back into the office.

"I guess I'm going too," Kyle said. His own cheeks weren't entirely unaffected, but he didn't think he'd blushed quite as strongly. Not this time, at least.

A few hours later, they pushed through the door of Wendell's cottage, takeout bags in hand, flushed and sweaty.

"That was so much fun." Wendell set the bags on the counter and started rummaging for plates.

"It was. I haven't been there in a couple of years." Mostly because there were a lot of stairs, far more than one might expect of a mini golf course, and he wasn't sure if his bum knee would hold up. But it had been years since his injury and he figured Wendell would enjoy it. He hadn't been wrong.

"However," Wendell turned to him and smirked. "I still think you cheated on the seventeenth hole."

Kyle put on his most innocent face. "Hey. Don't hate the player, hate the game!"

Wendell laughed. "Yeah, not buying the big eyes this time, Bambi."

"Sure, sure. But just remember who won." It wasn't his fault if Wendell got so distracted when Kyle bent over that his ball had sailed right over the hole, over the barrier, and into the chest of pirate "gold" on hole five, which due to the serpentine nature of the course was right alongside where they were on hole seventeen.

"Yes, you won. And you get to pick the movie." But Wendell was still smiling, and Kyle was secure that Wendell hadn't minded losing one bit.

He was even more convinced when Wendell took a few steps closer and kissed him.

Light, sweet, with the promise of more.

But then Wendell's stomach growled, making Kyle laugh. The man was definitely ruled by mealtimes.

They broke apart and Kyle got out drinks.

Wendell checked his phone. "Hey. Want to watch the sunset while we eat? This is really good timing."

A little flutter came to life in Kyle's belly. There hadn't been any big, sweeping romantic gestures—that wasn't Wendell's comfort zone, being the center of attention—but there had been a lot of small ones. Like this suggestion. And Kyle was a fucking fan.

"Sure. I'd love to."

They carried their food and drinks outside to Wendell's small patio table. Wendell arranged the chairs so they'd both be looking out over the water. The sun loomed large and red over the horizon, ready to put on a spectacular show.

Right as they finished eating, the sun gave its final curtain call, the ocean waves crashing on shore and reflecting streaks of orange and yellow and red. Wendell reached out to take Kyle's hand.

He had never seen a more beautiful sunset.

But then, he'd never held hands with a wonderful man while watching one before.

They sat in the growing dark, fingers entwined, for a few minutes longer.

"Movie?" Wendell asked, softly, like he hadn't wanted to shatter their bubble of solitude.

"Movie," Kyle confirmed.

Fifteen minutes later, Kyle stared in bemusement at Wendell's lightly snoring form. Kyle had been scrolling through the options on the streaming service when he'd heard the first snuffly breath. When he turned to look, he heard the next, deeper breath. Noisier. No doubt Wendell was sleeping, rather than dozing. Apparently, the exertion of mini golf on top of a rather demanding wedding party had exhausted Wendell.

This wasn't exactly how he envisioned the night ending. But he couldn't be mad about it. He liked that Wendell felt comfortable enough to fall asleep, and the evening had been a lot of fun, with Wendell behaving like a dream date. Falling for this man was going to be the easiest thing he'd ever done. Now he just had to hope Wendell wasn't going to eviscerate him when he left town.

Kyle stared at the movie he'd been about to ask Wendell if he wanted to watch.

Screw it.

He covered Wendell with the knitted blanket that lay over the back of the couch, and snuggled in. If Wendell woke up during or after the movie, they could figure out something else to do. Otherwise, Kyle would head home after the movie was over. He wasn't about to crash here without an invite.

Tuesday morning, Wendell stood beside Jackson as they watched the final members of the wedding party depart. Over the past three days, they'd trickled away, along with the Lee family, which left a few days free before the inn filled up again for the weekend.

"They kept us busy," Jackson said with very little inflection in his tone. Wendell snorted in response.

"Understatement." Jackson had borne the brunt of it, as he was the official interim manager, but since Wendell wasn't a dick, he'd pitched in as often as possible, and they'd both still been run off their feet.

In the sudden and welcome silence, Wendell's stomach let out a loud growl.

Jackson snickered. "Go get some food. There should be more than enough to fill you up."

"Can I bring you anything?" Wendell liked hearing Jackson laugh. He got the feeling it wasn't something the man did very often these days, and after almost two weeks of being comrades in arms, he found he liked the guy.

"No, I'm good for now. I'll grab something a bit later."

Wendell nodded and headed back to the dining room. The departing guests had barely touched the offered breakfast, and with only two guests remaining, Wendell and Jackson could probably get by on leftovers for the next few days. Anything they didn't think they'd eat or need for guests, Wendell would drop off at the homeless shelter.

He dashed into the dining room and set about making tea and a makeshift breakfast sandwich with a croissant, cheese, and sliced ham.

No one else was in the room, so he sat a table and ate his breakfast. Pulling out his phone, he scrolled through his texts with Kyle. In the midst of some genuine conversation, there had been definite flirting. He didn't know how he'd gotten so lucky to have Kyle's attention, but he was going to enjoy every moment.

He wanted to plan their next date, because their date last night had ended in such an embarrassing way. How could he have fallen asleep in the presence of the most attractive man he'd ever spent time with? Way to show the guy how much he meant. Tonight, he wanted to set up an overnight for them to do some ghost hunting in the inn. He started to type, then frowned. He could just go across the road, see if Kyle was in Drew's shop. Ask him in person. After all, there wasn't much Wendell needed to do today, with most of the guest rooms currently empty.

Slipping his phone back in his pocket, he smiled then scarfed down the rest of his breakfast, along with a blueberry muffin for good luck.

On his way back to the front door, he passed through the sun room and saw Chester.

"Morning, Chester."

Chester had a cup of coffee and a crossword puzzle book open on the small table in front of him. He looked up and smiled at Wendell.

"Morning, Wendell. What are you up to today?"

"Gonna see if I can get myself a date." Wendell tried to control the flush that heated his cheeks, but to no avail. It was stupid to be embarrassed to talk about Kyle, especially since the whole inn, and as a result, probably the whole town, knew Wendell was sniffing around the man.

"Good for you. Make use of that Sandy Bottom Bay magic." Chester grinned.

"What about you?"

Chester shrugged. "Finish my crossword, take a walk on the beach. Catch up on some reading, maybe."

Wendell wondered if community activities would be available to someone like Chester. It might be better for him to do something a little more active, because the man before him did not seem like a man on vacation. Not that Wendell was entirely certain what

Chester had hoped to get out of his pilgrimage, but he didn't seem to be enjoying himself. As a dedicated loner, he could recognize the signs of someone enjoying his own company, and Chester didn't seem like he was.

Then again, the man was also still grieving and Wendell could understand the desire to do that in solitude, even if he wasn't sure it was the healthiest option.

"Listen, if you'd like company... we could always play a game sometime." The game room had a few games that were decent, although if he had to play Monopoly, he might lose his shit. Just like he hated storylines that were too predictable, the winner of Monopoly was obvious early on, with no plot twists to make the inevitable interesting. A long, slow, slog to the end.

Chester smiled wanly. "Thank you, Wendell. I might just take you up on that. But I think you had a date to acquire?"

Wendell jolted. *Kyle.*

"You're right, I better get going."

Chester's expression lightened. "Maybe brush the crumbs off your shirt first."

Wendell glanced down and rolled his eyes. Honestly, he had no game whatsoever, despite watching actors ply their trade for so many years. He hadn't picked up one scrap of cool.

"Thanks, Chester, I owe you one."

He brushed himself off and continued on his way.

"Hey, I'm just going to head over to Malachi's, see if Kyle is there. Everything good here?" Wendell asked Jackson when he got to the front desk.

"All good. I'm going to give Daisy a hand getting the laundry downstairs, but today and tomorrow should be quiet."

"I was thinking I might do some ghost hunting tonight. See if the Orange Lady wants to make an appearance."

"It's a good night to do that, with no guests in the upstairs rooms. Let me know for sure, so I won't worry if I see lights or anything."

"Will do."

Wendell braced himself for the humidity onslaught, and walked out the door. It wasn't quite as oppressive as a sauna outside, but it wasn't great.

He did like the scent of the sea on the air, and the sense that he was not in the same old rut as when he was at home. He was enjoying himself, and more than once he'd had a little spark of life in his muse. Nothing concrete, nothing that he could hang a whole script on, but enough to hope that... well, hope that there was still hope for him yet.

He didn't want to acknowledge how much he had riding on his attempt to see the inn's infamous ghost.

At this point, he was more invested in spending time with Kyle. Who was more fascinating than any scary story Wendell had ever come across.

He walked up to the door and opened it, the bell announcing his presence.

"Hello, how can I help you?" Kyle was staring intently at something on the computer, and hadn't looked up. Wendell was almost positive it wasn't porn.

Wendell grinned. "Wanna have a slumber party tonight?"

Kyle lifted his head and grinned as he rounded the counter.

"Hey there. I wasn't expecting to see you."

"Wedding party left. It's going to be pretty dead over there." Wendell waggled his eyebrows at the incredibly obvious pun.

Kyle rolled his eyes. "I see. Have a seat. I have a couple of orders I have to finish off, but we can head out to the lighthouse today, if you want. Or the founder's residence, since you didn't get a chance to see that during the wedding."

"I'd love that."

"Oh, wait, you mentioned a slumber party?"

Wendell tried not to grimace. Why had he used the word slumber in his invite? He wanted to forget falling asleep last night.

"Yeah. I'm going to check out the upper floors of the inn tonight, see if I can find the Orange Lady. Did you still want to, uh, do that with me?" Wendell groaned inwardly. Seriously, he was the worst at asking guys for dates, even ones who clearly indicated that they were interested. And he was damned lucky Kyle still seemed interested, even after Wendell's poor showing last night.

"I would."

Wendell checked the time on his phone. "We could check out the lighthouse, grab some lunch and hang out at my cottage. Have a nap."

Heat climbed up his cheeks. Did he seriously just offer to nap with a man who filled his dreams with a number of X-rated fantasies? Kyle was going to think he had narcolepsy.

"That sounds great." Kyle smiled at him. "There's nothing better than an afternoon nap by the ocean."

Kyle was just too kind. And out of his fucking league by a mile.

"Maybe I could also, uh, take you out for dinner? There should be plenty of time before ghost hunting."

"As long as we can also stop at my place so I can pick up some things, like a change of clothes, I'm in."

A flutter of nerves tickled Wendell's stomach. Spending time with Kyle was becoming his new favorite activity.

"Maybe grab some swim trunks? I haven't had much time to get in the ocean and the weather looks great."

"Swim trunks? I can probably do that, although it'll depend on when the rain comes this afternoon."

Wendell opened his mouth to ask "what rain?" but stopped himself. Yes, the sky was as blue as could be, with just a few cheery white fluffy clouds to break up the monotony, and no hint of a storm on the horizon. But even after just a few days in Sandy Bottom Bay, he quickly learned that this was rainy season in Florida, and almost every day saw afternoon rain, whether it was a full-on thunderstorm or not. He'd never seen so much water fall from the sky in all his life.

"You're okay if I wait here?"

"Yup. It'll be like ten minutes or so."

Wendell sat down and scrolled through his social media while he waited, but he had a hard time sitting still.

Today was going to be so much fun.

TWELVE

18 Days to Haunt Fest

"IS THIS OKAY HERE?" Kyle made another minor adjustment to the digital camera Wendell had brought with him.

Wendell peered at something on his laptop.

"Yep, that's perfect."

Kyle didn't know anyone these days who still used a camera that wasn't a part of their phone, not even Drew who until a year ago barely had a pot to piss in. Wendell had brought a camera with him, which he said he used to take pictures of settings that inspired him in his writing.

Again, not entirely sure why a camera phone wouldn't do the same, but who was Kyle to say. One of the many things they'd managed to cram into their day had been a trip to a big box store to get... some piece of equipment that would allow Wendell to take pictures remotely as well as to trigger photos from a motion sensor. Or maybe it was something to do with time lapse? Kyle wasn't sure.

He'd seen equipment like this on *Phantoms*, but hadn't paid it much attention.

It was sort of refreshing to note that Wendell hadn't arrived in Sandy Bottom Bay with all that equipment. He obviously hadn't planned to do any serious ghost hunting. He wasn't like the host of *Phantoms*. Not that Kyle wanted to be suspicious, but he had been duped by a man who'd been married. Also, they'd recently had a murderer in their midst who'd fooled the whole town. Kyle wasn't exactly ready to take people at their word.

And he'd never tell that the moment he'd gotten home after Wendell had told him what he did for a living, Kyle googled the shit out of that to confirm his Wendell and Lucky Weston's Wendell were one and the same. Because that was the sort of thing assholes said to get in your pants, but Wendell hadn't been lying.

In this case, though, Kyle hoped Wendell wanted in his pants. He'd wanted to test the waters this afternoon, but between lunch, the lighthouse, having to drive to Hell's half acre—or at least, almost all the way to Tampa—to find an electronics store, there hadn't been a lot of spare time.

They'd ended up napping through the afternoon rain, because apparently Wendell had been serious about that, but Kyle loved curling up with a strong, warm man who wasn't only interested in one thing.

Still, Kyle was hoping they'd get to that one thing soon. Or his hand might just chafe. He and his spank bank had been getting quite a workout since Wendell rolled into town.

But Wendell had been serious about getting to know each other. Kyle truly appreciated that, because Wendell had made him feel more special during their low-key activities than any man he'd ever dated before.

To top it all off, Wendell had treated him to a late dinner, exactly as promised, without any expectations or quid pro quo.

That wasn't the only reason dinner had been more romantic than just about any date he'd been on. They'd talked about so many things.

Real things, not fake "trying to impress you" things. Which, ironically, impressed the crap out of Kyle. Wendell had been genuinely interested in Kyle's thoughts and experiences, every bit as interested as Kyle had been about Wendell's life.

And if Kyle hadn't eaten so much, he'd have suggested a moonlight swim before ghost hunting. Instead, he was doing his best imitation of a well-stuffed turkey after leaving the Angry Parakeet, and he wasn't at his seductive best.

"Think we're ready?" Kyle fluttered about the cameras, wanting everything to be perfect.

"I think so. We just have to sit back and wait."

"How long do you think we should wait?" Kyle checked his phone. It was just after eleven.

Wendell shrugged. "Of the stories online that mentioned a time, all agreed that events happened between midnight and one, but traditionally the witching hour is supposed to be between three and four. So, I think we wait until one, and see how we feel. If we're tired, we leave the cameras to cover us the rest of the night."

"Sounds like a plan." At the moment, Kyle thought he could probably stay awake all night talking to Wendell. Or sexing him up. But as someone who relied on their body to be in top shape, he'd long ago realized the value of getting a good night's sleep on a regular basis and hadn't pulled an all-nighter since his first year of college.

Kyle took another glance at their set up. Not bad for a couple of amateurs. They both might have professional interest in the outcome of this little ghost hunt, but neither of them were ghost hunters by trade.

They'd set up the equipment, not nearly the amount a real ghost hunter would have, in the small sitting area at the top of the stairs. Kyle had never been sure why there had been a sitting area here, when anyone upstairs had a room they could go into, but it certainly came in handy now.

Also, none of the rooms on this floor were occupied right now, so if they wanted, they could go in and check out the situation. Both

Marsh Mist and Pixie Light had a few Yelp reviews Kyle had read that mentioned cold spots and the sound of weeping, so the rooms were other possible avenues of exploration.

Drew was going to be so fucking jealous when he found out what Kyle was doing tonight. Neither of them had ever had this kind of opportunity, and he likely never would have if it hadn't been for Wendell's unusual and fortuitous situation.

He sat next to Wendell on the sofa, and barely suppressed a nervous giggle when Wendell interlaced their fingers. Including Wendell, Kyle could count on his nose the number of guys he'd dated who'd been interested in holding hands.

How had he met what was shaping up to be the perfect man? There had to be a shoe waiting to drop. Possibly an entire shoe store poised to rain down like an avalanche.

"Did I ever thank you for this?" Kyle asked.

"Thank me? I should be thanking you. As much as I'd love to see a ghost, it'd be pretty lonely doing this by myself."

Kyle stroked his thumb against Wendell's hand. "Are you kidding? An overnight in the Lady if you're not staying in one of these rooms? Just doesn't happen. Although I could probably afford to stay here sometime, now that Drew's store has been doing so well. There was a time when I never thought I'd have that sort of disposable income, so a chance to see the Orange Lady was nothing but a dream."

"Oh. Well, I'm glad I could be of service." Wendell gave a sly little twist to his words that gave Kyle hope that they weren't going to be exploring this relationship platonically for much longer.

Kyle grinned, but bit back a salacious response. "If we see a ghost, my tour attendees are gonna be so damned jealous."

"So, you never see ghosts when you guide those groups around town?"

Kyle shrugged. "It gets pretty spooky near the end of the tour, and I've had people swear up and down that they've seen a smoky wisp or felt a cold spot or the brush of an insubstantial being. I play along, but I've never seen diddly-squat."

Wendell snorted out a laugh. "Diddly squat? Not sure the last time I've heard someone say that."

Oh Kyle. So suave. "Drew's grandma, the one who bequeathed him Malachi's, used to say it all the time. Not sure why it popped out now."

Kyle wasn't averse to swearing, but most of his paying jobs required him to rigidly police his language and apparently it was becoming second nature.

He mock-glared at Wendell. "Anyway, it would be a real coup to see a ghost for real."

"I agree." Wendell's sincerity was obvious, but equally apparent was his skepticism. Kyle had thought the existence of ghosts was a plausible possibility even before Drew developed his psychic mojo. Afterward? He was more convinced than ever that ghosts were out there somewhere, he just had to find them.

And thinking of Drew...

"I can't wait for you to meet Drew." Especially if Drew pulled out some his freaky woo-woo shit. Wendell would get a real kick out of that. Maybe he'd even write a character based on Drew. That would be a lot more satisfying than seeing asshole-who-shall-not-be-named in that ridiculous action movie.

He glanced at Wendell who had a weird look on his face and extremely flushed cheeks.

"What's wrong?"

Wendell cleared his throat. "None of my boyfriends cared if I met their friends before. I mean, not that I was a secret or anything, but it happened organically, not as a result of any active desire."

Now it was Kyle flushing. "I... I..."

"Oh, no, I wasn't insinuating anything bad about anything. I just meant, it means a lot to me that you want me to meet Drew."

Kyle swallowed heavily. He'd mentioned his previous relationship briefly but it had thrown him for a loop. Being kept a secret, and finding out his boyfriend had been in another relationship, the one he'd shown to the world, had really done a number on his self-confidence. He'd clawed his way back to mostly his old self, but for a moment, he'd thought Wendell was making a dig, and the pain had been sharp and deep.

Wendell squeezed him tight, and lifted their hands so he could brush a kiss across the back of Kyle's hand. The whisper of sensation sent blood thrumming south, and he shifted in his seat.

"If it makes you feel any better, I wouldn't keep you a secret. I'd be happy to introduce you to my family."

"I can't believe I met you." Kyle was still in awe.

The blush in Wendell's cheeks intensified, and Kyle couldn't help himself. He pulled his hand free just long enough to cup Wendell's stubbled cheeks and brought their lips together.

The kiss remained sweet for no more than a second or two before becoming as carnal and molten as any kiss Kyle had ever experienced.

Within seconds, he was so fucking turned on he straddled Wendell's lap as they devoured each other's mouths. Wendell gripped his ass tight and Kyle bucked his erection against an answering hardness.

A loud thunk, like a thick hardcover book falling from a shelf, startled Kyle out of the kiss.

"Did you hear that?" Kyle wasn't sure why he whispered, because they were supposed to be alone.

"I did," Wendell whispered back. "Did something fall?"

"Jackson is for sure back at his place, right?"

"Yes, I'm almost sure," Wendell replied. Then he said, a little louder, "Jackson? Is that you?"

They both listened intently, but the air around them was still as... well... still as the grave. Kyle shivered and slowly climbed off Wendell. Standing up, they both scanned the sitting area.

Nothing appeared out of place, and even if someone had lifted one of the armchairs and dropped it, it likely wouldn't have made a sound like that.

"Do you think it was Katherine, the Orange Lady?" Kyle asked.

Wendell shrugged. "I'm sure there's a logical explanation. Maybe she doesn't like seeing men kiss."

Kyle scoffed. "Yeah, right. Or maybe she was cheering us on."

Wendell let out a breathy little laugh, and the tension eased off.

So far, no concrete evidence of ghosts, although they'd managed to scare themselves. Or at least, Kyle had managed to scare himself. He wasn't sure if Wendell had been affected or not.

"Maybe we should check the rooms. Make sure there aren't any open windows or anything," Wendell suggested.

"Sure. Or prowlers." Kyle shivered again. Why had he brought up that possibility? It might be intruders in truth, and Kyle wasn't prepared for a confrontation with criminals.

Wendell shook his head. "Really? Why would anyone break into the second floor of a currently unoccupied inn?"

Kyle shrugged. "I don't know. But maybe a burglar wouldn't know there wasn't anyone here?"

"Please. They'd be more likely to strike during the day anyway. After all, it'd be much easier to rob the place when they didn't have to worry about waking up people who were sleeping in a strange bed and catching them in the act."

"That makes sense." Kyle took a couple of slow breaths, and his heart rate started to slow.

"It's probably a draft. Let's check the guest rooms, make sure nothing is broken. If one of the wedding party left a window open, there could be a wet mess to clean up after the rain this afternoon."

Wendell unlocked a room, opened the door, then offered his master key to Kyle.

"We'll split the rooms. Sooner we check the rooms, sooner we can get back to waiting for the Orange Lady."

Kyle grimaced. "You write horror movies for a living. And you're suggesting we split up? For real?"

Wendell laughed. "It does make for great story tension. But seriously, we're not lost in the woods or in a sketchy part of town. We're going to be mere feet from each other. It's not really splitting up. Besides, that trope works best when there's a basement. Florida buildings don't have basements, do they?"

"Not usually," Kyle muttered. He took the key from Wendell. "See you on the other side."

He was probably overreacting. Maybe that was something humans did in the middle of the night. The dark outside made them hypervigilant or whatever. Evolution at its best.

Kyle eased the door open to Marsh Mist and tried not to think about the fact that if evolution had favored hypervigilance at night, there might be a good reason for that.

Ambient light from the moon bleached out the decor, and the shadows stretched in a way that, well, looked normal. He flicked the light switch by the door.

The sitting area of the suite, done in shades of green, appeared as pristine as Daisy had undoubtedly left it.

"Hello?" His voice wasn't anywhere near his usually sonorous greetings.

There was no response, not even a flutter of mint curtains. After glancing around the room, he couldn't spot anything out of place. In deference to Wendell's theory, he walked over to the window. The window was closed and locked. No wayward draft from there.

"Hello?" Kyle called again as he moved toward the bedroom. "Anyone here?"

He flicked on the light. A cheery warm glow lit the room from the two bedside lamps. He smiled, imagining a romantic weekend with Wendell, curled up on the spacious king sized bed.

But just beyond the bed, something caught his eye.

He held his breath as he crept further into the room. Then let out a relieved sigh. A book lay on the floor, open.

Exactly what it had sounded like. A book just fell on the floor.

He bent over to pick it up, and noticed it was open to *Macbeth*.

Against the undivulged pretense I fight.

Huh. Hopefully that line wasn't an omen. He flipped to the

flyleaf. Shakespeare. *Major Plays and the Sonnets*. And it had still sounded like a brick. The complete works might have gone right through the floor.

He flipped through the pages, grinning a bit at the nostalgia. There had been a lot of suckage in high school around reading these damned plays for English, but it had been a whole different experience when he'd done it with the drama club.

Not *Macbeth*, mind. He'd spent enough time in theater circles to have absorbed a healthy superstition about saying the play's name aloud in a theater, and had never been involved in a production of it. And given his career-ending injury, *Chicago* was also verboten for him.

A cold hand on the back of his neck startled him.

"Jeez, Wendell, your hands are freezing. We need to do something about that."

"What was that?"

Kyle froze. Wendell had sounded... very far away. He turned slowly, his nape still clammy. He was utterly alone in the room. Just him and the book of Shakespeare.

Which couldn't have fallen from any surface in the room and landed where he'd found it.

"Who is in here?" Kyle could hear the panicky tremor in his voice, but there was absolutely no way he could control it. Even if someone was in the bathroom, he would have heard them run in there, right?

Or under the bed?

Kyle gripped the book tightly, brandishing it like a weapon and slid his foot under the bed. It quickly encountered a barrier.

Not too surprising. He remembered when Sandra had replaced all the beds with ones that were standard hotel style so guests wouldn't leave things behind under the bed. And also, it made it easier to clean.

Okay. No one was under the bed. He flung open the wardrobe door.

Empty aside from a few wooden hangers and some spare pillows.

He forced himself to step toward the bathroom. It took only a second to confirm Kyle was alone. The shower curtain had been pulled to the side, allowing him to see into the tub without any barrier.

An odd scent hit his nose, like the time the plumber had showed up to his old apartment to fix a leak. Musty and damp, overlaid with the old-penny scent of copper piping.

"What the hell is going on?" Kyle whispered. "Is there a leak in here?"

Then, he blinked, and suddenly the white tile of the small bathroom was streaked in blood. It pooled dark and crimson under the sink, flowing along the grout to the toilet.

Kyle's heart rate shot up and he had a hard time catching his breath.

And he needed his breath. Needed it to scream.

The blood began to flow toward him, and he couldn't move. It was going to touch him. Get on his shoes. He gripped the book against his chest as tight as he could, like it could somehow protect him. But how could anything protect him from this?

Kyle...

His heart pounded like a frightened rabbit trying to escape from his chest. Was that whisper by his ear? Or in his mind? He didn't know that voice.

"Kyle, did you find anything?"

Wendell's strong voice, closer this time, shook him out of his paralysis and he sucked in a breath to call out when the tang of oranges filled his nose, a welcome antidote to what he believed to be the odor of death.

He staggered back against the bathroom wall, rattling the tiny shelf that held toiletries. He glanced at it and reached out a hand to steady himself, and when he turned back to the blood streaked scene, there was no blood at all.

The bathroom was as pristine as Daisy had left it.

What in the ever-loving fuck had happened?

"Hey, what's up?" Wendell appeared in the doorway, and Kyle jumped.

"Sorry, I didn't mean to startle you. I checked the other three rooms, and didn't find anything. Doesn't look like there's anything here either."

Kyle rubbed the back of his neck with one hand, trying to get it back to his normal skin temperature. The weird smells had dissipated, leaving behind a faint whiff of bleach. He brandished the book at Wendell.

"I found this. On the floor by the bed, but I don't know where it came from."

He sure as shit wasn't going to mention the bathroom of blood. Because he was definitely chalking that up to a momentary mind glitch. Like going into a room and forgetting what you were there to get. Except this one had clearly been brought on by ghost hunting at midnight, and perhaps flavored by a faint memory of Lady Macbeth and her "out, damned spot".

The last thing he was going to do was let the very sexy horror writer know he'd managed to freak himself out, in a way he'd not once done on the hundreds of ghost tours he'd hosted.

Wendell took the book from him and inspected it while Kyle got the hell out of that bathroom. The bedroom was far less disturbing. Hoping to suppress the jitters, he discreetly hugged himself.

"Shakespeare? And you think we heard it fall on the floor?"

Thankfully, Wendell followed him out into the bedroom.

"I think so? I didn't see anything else out of place." Mentioning it was open to the Scottish play would ascribe more meaning to it than it really had. Wouldn't it? And none of the scents had lingered long enough for Wendell to smell, which meant they may have been a figment of his imagination.

The last thing he needed was Wendell thinking he was lying about a ghostly encounter to impress him. That's something Eddie would do. Kyle had more self respect. Besides, he had no proof and he wasn't sure he wanted to believe anything had happened anyway.

"Maybe it accidentally got left on the bed and fell off?" Kyle didn't believe that, but it was the most rational explanation.

"Wouldn't Daisy have returned it to the library?" Wendell asked.

"I suppose. But no one's perfect. Maybe she forgot it after she'd cleaned the rest of the room."

While Kyle sounded reasonable, the shivers were out of his control. Wendell frowned at him.

"Are you cold? The temp is a bit lower in here than I'd expect, but maybe that's a requirement for guests."

"Yeah, I'm a bit cold." He wasn't sure he'd be warm again, especially the clammy patch on his nape. Maybe that was how the zombie infection started.

He let out a burst of nervous laughter because that was too ridiculous, even for him. Wendell squinted at him.

"Nothing. Just imagining the cold signaled my impending transformation into a zombie."

Wendell paused for a moment, looking thoughtful, but then shook his head.

"Nope, I can't use that for inspiration. Lucinda is convinced zombies have been done to death, er, so to speak."

That surprised a real laugh out of Kyle and Wendell smiled before wrapping him in his arms. So warm and safe.

"Besides," Wendell spoke into Kyle's hair. "While I love zombie movies, I've never been too inspired to write them, not even a few years ago when Lucinda hounded me to get on the zombie train."

"Okay, well, but has there *been* a zombies-on-a-train movie?"

Wendell's chuckle rumbled through his torso.

"Honestly, there probably has. There have been so many zombie movies over the years. Zombies, in my opinion, aren't very versatile as a creative medium, so we still haven't solved my writers block."

Kyle took a deep breath and pulled himself out of Wendell's embrace. "Then I guess we ought to try and see a ghost, right?"

They settled back on the loveseat, book on the end table. Wendell wrapped an arm around Kyle's shoulders and he snuggled into the warmth. Kissing could wait until they were done up here. He glanced balefully at the giant book of Shakespeare. He wasn't about to get interrupted again by some moldering old book.

THIRTEEN

18 Days to Haunt Fest

THEY SPENT the next hour talking about everything and nothing, until Wendell caught Kyle yawning and looked at the time. He had to concede that it was well past any previous anecdotal sightings of the Orange Lady, and he was tired too.

The only real disappointment had been the kiss. And only because it hadn't been longer or been more than one. Otherwise it had been an awesome fucking kiss.

"C'mon, let's call it a night. I think if the Orange Lady was going to show herself to us, she'd have done it already."

"Are you sure?" Kyle asked, the last word muffled by another yawn and Wendell chuckled.

"Yes, I'm sure."

"Are you disappointed?"

Wendell shrugged. "Of course, I am, but considering I don't actually believe in ghosts, I'm not exactly surprised."

Kyle pressed his lips together and nodded. He'd been a little tense the whole time they'd been up here, and if it hadn't been for him cuddling up against Wendell on the love seat, he'd have assumed Kyle had lost interest.

He might just be tired. For sensible adults on the East Coast with day jobs, it was late.

"We can try again sometime. Maybe after Haunt Fest." Kyle frowned. "No, I bet it would have to be after Halloween. I'm pretty sure the inn is fully booked up, or close to it, for all of October."

Wendell stood and held out a hand to help Kyle up. He pulled a bit too hard and Kyle stumbled into him. He had no choice but to wrap his arms around Kyle to steady him.

Kyle smiled up at him. "Oh, I see why you're throwing in the towel so early."

It wasn't what Kyle thought. At least, not entirely.

"Any objections?"

Kyle's arms tightened around his waist. "Not a one."

Wendell bent his head to kiss Kyle, but it threatened to go nuclear within a few moments, and he pulled back.

"Better not start that just yet."

Kyle smiled impishly but stepped out of Wendell's embrace, and Wendell missed him immediately.

They packed up Wendell's equipment and at the last minute, Wendell noticed the book of Shakespeare. He picked it up and tucked it under his arm.

Downstairs, Kyle walked past the library.

"Hold up, I want to put this away."

Kyle halted, and stood still for a moment before he turned around.

"Now? Can't you do that later? Like tomorrow?"

Some of Kyle's odd tension had returned, and it wasn't eagerness to get in Wendell's bed.

He didn't think he'd disturb anyone by rummaging around in the library, and he didn't think there was any shelf organization he needed to worry about, but neither did he want to make Kyle wait around while he made that determination.

The books in the library were available for guests to borrow, and there was no reason Wendell couldn't borrow this one for the night. Like anyone would notice.

"You're right. Let's go."

Just like that, Kyle relaxed.

Outside, Wendell shifted his equipment and the book so he could take Kyle's hand in his.

The air was redolent with salt and vegetation, warm and sultry. For the first time since he'd arrived, Wendell could understand the appeal of the Floridian climate. There was something about it, walking toward the beach, pinpricks of starlight overhead and the rhythmic pounding of waves as a backdrop. Romantic. Sensual. Lush.

In other words, nothing that would help him professionally, but with Kyle by his side, he was far more concerned with his libido than his muse. Which he could not ever confess to Lucinda. Byron would understand, but Lucinda had her eyes firmly on the business.

Kyle's thumb stroked over his knuckles, driving away any stray thoughts of family and sending a spark right to his heart. And other places, but it was the heart that was going to cause him the most problems. Problems he couldn't bring himself to worry about right now.

They walked up to door of the cottage, and Wendell had to let go of Kyle's hand in order to get the key out.

Once inside, he set everything down, stared at Kyle, then started to sweat, just a bit. He really wasn't in Kyle's league, and he didn't want to disappoint. He wasn't an athlete, he was a writer. One who didn't go to the gym nearly as often as he should. One who had a sweet tooth. He sucked in his belly, then let it out again. Unsustainable.

"Oh fuck." Wendell bit his lip before anything else could slip out.

"What?" Kyle asked.

"I don't have... anything. I mean... I wasn't exactly expecting this." Hoping, yes, but that hope hadn't been strong enough, despite their developing friendship, to go to a pharmacy and pick up condoms. Lube, he had, as he'd expected to spend his sabbatical engaging in some self-love. But having sex with another person, he hadn't really planned for. Stupidly hadn't planned for.

Kyle smiled. "Plenty we can do without that, you know."

Wendell smiled back, unable to help himself. Kyle just made him so damned happy.

"Did you want to shower, or something?"

"I wouldn't mind freshening up a bit."

"Oh, yeah, me too." Wendell had rather less flop sweat than if he'd only just met Kyle, but he wanted their first encounter to be as perfect as possible.

"You go first." Kyle gave him a gentle shove.

"Are you sure?"

"I am. I'll just get comfortable in your bedroom, if that's okay."

"Oh, yes. More than okay." Wendell blushed a little at how eager he sounded, but Kyle just gave him a quick kiss and they parted at their respective doors.

Wendell stared at himself in the mirror over the sink. Wipe down or quick shower? He'd already had a shower today. But he really, really wanted to make a good impression. So, shower it was.

After less than ten minutes to shower, wash, and dry off, he realized as he stood naked in the steamy room that he hadn't brought any other clothes with him.

Despite their intention to share a couple of orgasms together, walking naked into the bedroom seemed a trifle presumptuous. Not to mention, his body wasn't nearly as sleek as Kyle's. Hands down, Kyle would win any competitions between them. Flaunting his less than stellar form maybe wasn't in his best interest. Neither did he want to put on his still slightly sweat-dampened clothes.

Towel around the waist was going to have to do, despite it not hiding his burgeoning erection with any success.

He grabbed his clothes, made sure his towel was secure, and headed into the bedroom, lit only by the dim bedside lamp.

"Bathroom's all yours," he said as he dumped his clothes on top of the dresser.

When he got no response, he screwed up enough nerve to look at the bed.

Kyle was curled up under the covers, fast asleep. Wendell smiled. Even though there was no sex on the table tonight, having Kyle in his bed was not a disappointment. And suddenly he realized why Kyle hadn't been angry about Monday night.

As quietly as he could, Wendell rooted around for a pair of sleep shorts and pulled them on before sliding into bed beside Kyle. He took a minute to just stare at the man who was quickly becoming the one guy he wanted to spend all his time with.

Although sorely tempted to brush a finger over the light dusting of freckles on Kyle's nose, he refrained. Ten years ago, he hadn't cared about sleep, but that attitude had quickly changed, and he suspected Kyle, as athletic as he was, likely believed in the benefits of getting good sleep on the regular.

Wendell wasn't about to disturb him in order for them to get their rocks off. Not for their first time, especially.

He clicked off the light and settled in, not sure how much contact Kyle would be comfortable with. Wendell liked a good cuddle, but his previous boyfriends hadn't cared to snuggle in bed once the orgasms were done.

Red flags right there, showing that none of them had been destined to be truly long-term.

But dredging up memories of men long gone wasn't going to help him sleep. Instead, he closed his eyes and ruminated on what he and Kyle might do the next day. There was still a day or two before the inn would be too busy for Wendell to spend a lot of time in Kyle's company.

Just as he was drifting off to sleep, Kyle rolled over and tucked himself against Wendell, one hand resting on his belly.

With a little smile, Wendell wrapped an arm around Kyle and slid the rest of the way into slumber.

Wendell blinked awake, buoyant mood instantly deflated by a distinct lack of Kyle in the bed next to him.

He hadn't exactly shown Kyle the best time. Again. His choice of date activities was at best, weird. At least Kyle hadn't laughed directly in his face. But Wendell had had such a good time. He always did with Kyle. He couldn't deny the overwhelming disappointment that Kyle had snuck out of the cottage while Wendell was asleep. Again.

This was going to be a long, long sabbatical if he had to avoid awkward encounters with Kyle for the next several weeks. And without any real jumpstart to his muse, he was already avoiding awkward encounters with his dusty laptop.

Moving with the speed and enthusiasm of a depressed sloth, Wendell brushed his teeth and pulled on a pair of swim trunks. Maybe an ocean dip would get him out of his funk. He picked up his phone and flicked through his notifications.

Nothing from Kyle. Not like the little goodnight text he'd sent Monday night before returning to his apartment.

He huffed out a breath. His gaze caught on the book of Shakespeare, weirdly sitting open to *Macbeth*. Seemed an odd choice of early morning reading material for Kyle. Perhaps it had fallen open when he'd dropped it on the dresser last night.

Against the undivulged pretense I fight.

Wendell didn't recall that line from the play, but he certainly didn't have any of the plays memorized.

After his swim he'd walk the book back to the library. See if Jackson had any errands that would keep him busy.

With a half-assed plan in place, he slathered himself with sunscreen and grabbed one of the complimentary beach towels provided with the cottage. He couldn't be bothered with his contacts —he had no one to impress—so he grabbed his glasses out of the bedside table.

He trudged out the sliding doors, past the small patio set, and onto the sand, which was not too hot this early in the morning.

A sand-covered swath of colored cloth sat on the beach not too far away. He'd grab it after his swim and throw it out at the cottage.

He fussed with his towel, placing his flip-flops in such a way that he hoped would keep it flat until he got out of the water. He flung his glasses down on a corner and headed to the surf.

As he got closer, a shape appeared on the water. A coconut? He squinted.

Then it rose. And resolved into the sleek shape of Kyle wearing the most indecent pair of blue briefs he'd ever seen. And he'd seen a lot of indecencies on LA's beaches over the years.

Frozen in the sand, Wendell could do nothing but sweep his gaze over Kyle's wet form, blond hair darkened to gold.

"Hey. I thought you were going to sleep longer. Otherwise, I would have waited for you."

The words broke the spell Wendell had been under, and he sucked in a breath as relief and lust swept through him like an inferno.

"Come on in, the water's great."

Wendell nodded, and hurried to the water, splashing in like an ungainly otter in order to hide just how happy he was to see Kyle.

"Hi," Kyle said as he waded closer.

"Hi." Wendell's response was breathless.

Kyle pulled him into deeper water, the gentle waves breaking over his shoulders then moving on to slap at Wendell's sternum.

"I'm sorry I fell asleep last night."

Wendell reached out and placed his hands on Kyle's waist.

"I'm not mad. I'm glad you stayed."

Kyle quirked his lips. "Me too. But I had plans for last night."

"Plans?" Wendell's swim trunks were getting tighter by the second, based on the look in Kyle's eyes.

"Plans," Kyle confirmed, and hooked a finger in Wendell's waistband, pulling him closer.

Wendell half floated, half walked into Kyle's orbit, his lips inexorably finding Kyle's. The sea water still clinging to them gave them a briny flavor that Wendell wanted to devour forever.

Kyle's fingers delved down, pressing his palm against Wendell's growing erection. He gasped and pulled out of the kiss, taking a look around, but there was no one to see them. The waves were active enough that even if someone were to glance out of a window, there wouldn't be anything to see.

Without any hesitation, he dove back into the kiss.

Even though Wendell had known a number of extroverted exhibitionists who thought nothing of getting a blow job in the alley behind a club or a hand job in a car, Wendell's sexual exploits had all taken place behind doors and walls. The most daring he'd gotten were a few escapades in a club bathroom.

This was reckless and freeing at the same time. Exciting because it was Kyle, and thrilling because it was also taboo as shit.

Kyle's nimble fingers loosened the ties at Wendell's waist and plunged his hands into Wendell's trunks, stroking fast and hard.

Wendell gasped as those skillful fingers worked. He kissed Kyle's lips, already salty from the sea. He dragged his mouth along Kyle's jaw and was rewarded with Kyle's hips bucking against his side. He latched on to Kyle's neck, also delightfully salty, and licked. But he couldn't keep his hands away from Kyle's sleek form. Especially since Kyle had already brought him to the brink of orgasm, with just a few strokes, virtually out in the open.

Kyle's briefs were tight, but Wendell was determined, and he slid them down Kyle's thighs. His cock was warm and heavy in Wendell's hand, and as much as Wendell wanted to see everything. Taste everything. Touch Kyle from head to toe. There was an urgency, to get done before anyone came along and saw them.

With the urgency transformed into mad desperation, Wendell took Kyle's lips again, and moaned out his delight as he crested a wave bigger than the ones slapping against their skin. Kyle bucked against him again, and pulsed in his hand. Wendell slumped, thankful they weren't out so far that his post-orgasm legs would cause them to drown.

Fast, dirty, and sweet at the same time. It had never been better.

KYLE LAUGHED a little as Wendell chased after his swim trunks, trying to grab them before they were swept onto shore. Somehow, the little devil had managed to keep his tiny scrap of briefs close at hand and strode out of the surf like a sea god. Wendell scrambled into his trunks and pulled them on just before the lowering sea level put him at risk of indecent exposure.

Wendell's arrival on dry land was far less graceful than Kyle's, but Kyle's smile was nothing but good-natured, and engaging enough that Wendell smiled helplessly back.

Then he bent over and picked up his glasses. Mostly because he didn't want to accidentally sit on them.

"I didn't know you wore glasses."

"Ugh. Yeah. I prefer my contacts, but I was feeling a bit lazy today." And he hadn't thought Kyle would be around to see him at his geekiest. Not yet, at least.

"I think they're adorable."

Adorable. Not Sexiest Man of the Year, but he'd take it. Especially since Kyle's smile still appeared genuine.

Wendell sat on his towel while Kyle shook sand out of his own before placing it next to Wendell's and taking a seat. He should have seen earlier that the cloth on the beach was a towel. Leaping to the conclusion that Kyle would treat him like a one-night stand did a disservice to them both. Wendell really needed to place more faith in the man he'd gotten to know over the past couple of weeks.

Because there wasn't a hint in Kyle's demeanor that indicated he was tired of Wendell or that he wanted to move on. And Wendell was getting to be an expert on that particular piece of body language.

Fuck it. If this sabbatical broke his heart, it wouldn't be because he didn't give it his all.

"Did you want to get breakfast somewhere? Then maybe do something today? If you can take the time off work, that is."

Kyle winked. "Didn't we just do *something*? I mean, I need a little rest time in between, but definitely interested."

Wendell's cheeks heated up from more than just the increasingly hot Florida sun.

"Uh, yeah, I would totally be into that. But I did mean sightseeing, or maybe something at the community center. Anything really."

Which maybe sounded really pathetic, but the previous week they'd stopped at a grocery store for Kyle to grab a few things, and the simple domesticity of it still made Wendell all warm and squishy inside. It was far too soon to be pretending to play house with Kyle, but he'd suppressed the desire for a partner for so long. This path they were on just felt so right.

"Anything?" Kyle wiggled his eyebrows. "Just kidding. Maybe we can go to the bakery for breakfast. I have to pick up some cookies for tonight's ghost tour. But if we do that, I have to hit the gym today as well as get a few things done at Drew's. But we could head over to the lighthouse afterward. Maybe the pumpkin patch."

"Sounds good."

Despite wanting to spend the day with Kyle, Wendell resisted suggesting going to the gym with him. First, he wasn't as fanatical as Kyle was regarding working out. Obviously. A daily swim in the ocean was plenty for him. And secondly, he ought to check in with Jackson. Maybe do a little daylight reconnaissance of the upstairs area. There had been a moment last night when he'd thought he'd smelled oranges, but it had been so fleeting and possibly more wishful thinking than fact, he hadn't wanted to mention it to Kyle.

"Did you maybe want to tag along on tonight's tour?"

"How many people?" Wendell had wanted to take up Kyle on his offer before, but he'd been wary. Now that they'd gotten to know each other better, he was anxious to check out the ghost tour, see Kyle in action.

"Just four tonight, unless someone signs up last minute."

Wendell bit his lip. "I'd rather wait until there were more people, if you don't mind. I'd like to be able to not only fade into the background, but also have a bigger group to observe."

Kyle leaned over and gave him a quick kiss. "You're welcome to join whenever you want, even if it's more than once. I don't mind."

What he really needed to do was sit his ass down and do some brainstorming. Without getting distracted by the activities in this town, or its very distracting ghost tour director.

As they lay there in drowsy silence, Wendell stretched out a hand, and Kyle tangled their fingers together, sending a curl of pleasure through him.

After baking for several minutes, Wendell realized he needed to get up and get moving or he was going to fall asleep. He'd fallen asleep on the beach once before and that was a sunburn he was in no hurry to revisit. Sure, he'd put sunscreen on before his swim, but he hadn't brought it down to the beach with him, and he wasn't ready to put full trust in the "waterproof" claims on the bottle. Especially since he'd started to sweat again under the sun.

"I think I have to head back in," Wendell said regretfully as he sat up.

"Can I borrow your shower?" Kyle asked.

"Of course." Part of him wanted to suggest sharing the shower, but like many things shown in the movies, shower sex was more dangerous and a hell of a lot harder to accomplish in real life. Even basic blowjobs were fucking hard on the knees in the shower. And they'd have to be contortionists anyway to fit both of them in the cramped shower stall.

Although it might be nice to attempt sex in the shower when he didn't have to feel guilty about wasting water in the middle of a drought. Was Florida ever not wet?

"Then let's get going."

Kyle stood and Wendell had to tear his gaze away from those tiny blue trunks. Because if he didn't, he would definitely suggest spending the rest of the day in his bed.

They grabbed their towels and walked hand in hand back to the cottage.

After getting showered and dressed, interspersed with not a few kisses and gropes, Wendell grabbed the book of Shakespeare and they walked back on the path to the inn.

Again, hand in hand, which pleased Wendell all out of proportion.

If only his professional life would go as smoothly as his romantic life appeared to be going.

When they got to the door to the library, Kyle hesitated again.

He didn't know exactly why Kyle didn't like the library. Maybe there was something skewed in the architecture. Wonky architectural lines had been theorized by some to be the source of unconfirmed paranormal activity. Wendell had never experienced anything himself, but he had a friend back home who'd done her undergrad schooling at the University of Toronto, and got woozy every time she had to go into Robarts Library, the main library on campus.

They'd also speculated on issues of air quality, but considering she'd never had problems in any of the other campus buildings, or any allergies, Wendell thought it could just as easily be a sensitivity to an architectural anomaly. Because why not? And Robarts Library, built to resemble a peacock, was undoubtedly filled with architectural anomalies.

Kyle was definitely too smart to be spooked by books.

"You can wait out here, if you want."

FOURTEEN

17 Days to Haunt Fest

KYLE BIT HIS LIP. He dreaded going into the library even more than before. In the comfort of Wendell's cottage and under the bright heat of the sun, he'd been able to forget the scare of the previous night. Amazingly, he'd even slept as solidly as he'd ever done, although that could just as easily be attributed to the solid warmth of Wendell's body curled around his.

But it was fucking stupid to be afraid of a library. He wasn't in a rush to head back up into Marsh Mist, but the library had never done anything to offend him. He liked books. He liked reading.

He also liked that Wendell was offering him an out, without any judgement in his voice or scorn in his expression.

He just plain liked Wendell.

"No, it's fine. It's just a library. It's just a book."

"And no harm ever came from reading a book," Wendell intoned with a waggle of his eyebrows.

It took a moment for Kyle to figure out he was paraphrasing from *The Mummy*. The one with Brendan Fraser. He rolled his eyes.

"You do remember what happened in that movie, right?"

Wendell nodded a gleam in his eyes.

"It's your favorite movie, isn't it?" Kyle should have known. For a man whose life work was writing horror movies, *The Mummy*, despite its comic and romantic elements, had to be a benchmark of sorts. Perhaps even an aspiration.

"It's not my favorite, exactly, but I do love it. It is definitely one of my early inspirations, that's for sure. Both professionally, and um, personally."

"Yeah, I can see that." A fun movie, filled with horror elements and beautiful people. What more could a gay boy with aspirations to screenwriting ask for? Kyle would have been happy to discuss the movie for hours with Wendell, except he was well aware that would simply be stalling.

Then Wendell's stomach growled, loudly, and he blushed. Kyle laughed.

"And we're burning daylight here. Let's get that book put back and get some breakfast."

If they got to the bakery early enough, there would be some baked egg white bites left, otherwise he'd have to consume even more carbs.

Wendell smiled and went into the library. Kyle sucked in a breath, pulled up his big boy pants, and followed.

There was a slight chill in the air, but Kyle could blame that on the inn's overactive air conditioner. Or his own trepidation. It didn't have to be a harbinger of ghosts.

Wendell flicked on a light and spun slowly near the wingback chairs.

"Do you know where the Shakespeare section would be?"

Kyle snorted. "It's not a library with a Dewey decimal system. It's basically a glorified book storage room."

"Yeah, but there's probably some sort of organization, right? Otherwise how would anyone find anything?"

"Well, I'd assume that anyone relying on the library offerings of a haunted bed and breakfast for their reading material wouldn't be too particular. Unless it's actual ghost stories they want, or histories of Sandy Bottom Bay, which Sandra keeps over there."

Kyle pointed to a low-slung double-sided bookshelf that partially divided the fireplace seating area from the rest of the room.

"I don't suppose Sandra has a lot of time to spend reshelving books anyway," Wendell commented.

Kyle nodded. "I know she putters in here during the slow season sometimes, but it really isn't critical that we put the book back exactly where it came from."

His objections had nothing to do with wanting to get out of here as soon as possible. Not at all.

He glanced at the tall bookcase that extended to the ceiling behind one of the wingback chairs.

"What about right there? There's a gap on the top shelf."

Wendell twisted around to follow the direction Kyle pointed toward.

"Good eye." Wendell slotted the book in between two other weathered hardcover books. "It fits perfectly. And these other books are also books of plays. This might be where the book came from in the first place."

Kyle didn't want to think about how perfectly the book fit in the gap. He didn't want to think about how neatly the other books sat on the shelf, no disturbance. Or the fact that Wendell had had to stretch a bit to get the book back in place, and at that height, it would have been very difficult to read the faded title on the spine of the Shakespeare book.

It was *just* a book. And the weird vision he'd had last night had been something he'd done to himself by being too suggestible. Everything was normal.

Wendell brushed his hands against his jeans. "Breakfast?"

"Breakfast," Kyle confirmed.

The moment they left the library, Kyle breathed a bit easier, and his shoulders unclenched.

As they passed by the dining room, Wendell detoured.

"Good morning, Chester," he greeted the only occupant.

"Morning, Wendell." The old man glanced at Kyle.

"Chester, this is Kyle. Kyle, this is Chester. He's staying in the cottage next door."

"Nice to meet you." The tips of his ears got hot. Had Chester seen them in the water this morning? He'd sort of forgotten there were any guests at the inn right now.

"Nice to meet you, too, Kyle." Chester looked back at Wendell. "This your young man?"

Wendell's face went red and coughed.

Kyle recognized that twinkle in Chester's eyes, though. A kindred spirit. He threaded his arm through Wendell's.

"I am indeed his young man."

Chester merely smiled.

Wendell's embarrassment abated quickly, and he smiled down at Kyle. They exchanged a few more pleasantries before continuing to the lobby.

Jackson greeted them both when he looked up from the computer. He also had a knowing look in his eyes.

"Did you have any luck last night?" Jackson asked.

Wendell again lit up like Rudolph's red nose and Kyle laughed and shared a glance with Jackson. If Wendell had hoped to keep anything under wraps, he was going to have to stop broadcasting his feelings.

Then again, Kyle much preferred being able to interpret Wendell's expressions over his earlier confusion about whether Wendell was attracted to him or even gay or bi.

Kyle slid an arm around Wendell's waist and hugged him.

"He means did we see a ghost last night. Not if you got your rocks off." Kyle sniggered again. Somehow Wendell's face managed to get even redder. Probably because they had just gotten their rocks off less than an hour ago, practically in public.

Wendell laughed nervously. "I knew that."

Kyle and Jackson exchanged another glance. They weren't exactly friends—Jackson and his husband hadn't covered for Sandra all that many times in the past few years—but their encounters had been friendly. And he sensed that maybe he could be friends with the older, somewhat reticent man, who had a deep well of loneliness that he tried to keep hidden.

"Well? Did you see the Orange Lady?"

Wendell scowled. "No. The most excitement we had was a book falling to the floor and startling us."

"A book?" Jackson asked.

"Yeah. I guess it got left in Marsh Mist and fell on the floor. A collection of Shakespeare's major plays. Real old version, from the forties. I suppose if it had been the complete works, it would have felt like an earthquake."

Jackson smirked. "Seems a weird thing for anyone to read on vacation. Especially the wedding party that just left, but I guess you can't judge a bridezilla by her dress."

That startled a little laugh out of Kyle. He hadn't realized Jackson had a little snark in him, and he liked that spark of humor. Boded well for Jackson getting past whatever he'd run down here to escape. Because no one left their job and their life on short notice to man the desk at a bed and breakfast during what was shaping up to be one of the busiest Haunt Fests the town had ever seen. Not unless one were related or indebted to the owners.

But maybe Jackson was. Not related, but had somehow become indebted to Sandra and Bill.

After all, Kyle no longer had his finger on the pulse of all the gossip in Sandy Bottom Bay. He got a lot of it, but ditching his job as high school cheerleading choreographer had cut off a vital source of gossip. He was going to have to take up knitting or something at the community center to replace that pipeline.

"Anyway," Wendell continued. "A falling book wasn't enough to convince me we had a supernatural visitor, although I haven't reviewed the footage from my camera yet."

Kyle shivered and rubbed the back of his neck as he remembered the clammy chill. There was no way his little episode had been supernatural. Absolutely no way.

"Did you want us to pick you up anything from the bakery?" Kyle definitely wanted to change the subject.

"Oh, I don't think so. There are plenty of leftovers from breakfast and yesterday's tea."

Wendell smiled ruefully at Kyle. "But have you ever eaten a Kraken?"

Kyle let out a soft chuckle as a confused frown crossed Jackson's face. Then he realized something.

"You haven't been here since Lisa took over the bakery, have you?"

Jackson shook his head.

"Really?" Wendell glanced between him and Jackson. "She has a gift for cupcakes. Seriously, the Kraken cupcake was one of the best things I've ever eaten. The Vampire Kiss was equally good."

"He's not lying." Cupcakes weren't Kyle's kryptonite, but he enjoyed having a taste now and then. Especially Lisa's. "They're all themed after mythological creatures or horror movie monsters."

"And I guess if cupcakes are a premium item for her, I assume they never show up in the catering. Okay, you've talked me into it. Pick out something delicious for me."

"You got it. Any allergies or dislikes?"

"No allergies, and when it comes to baked goods, I like just about anything."

"Got it." Wendell opened his mouth to speak again, but his stomach chose that moment to growl again, and they all laughed.

"Go on and get some breakfast." Jackson shooed them out of the lobby and they burst out into glaring sunshine. The temperature wasn't as bad as it had been, though, simmering down from a full boil as autumn slowly encroached.

If Kyle had been alone, he would have been practically pirouetting up the path to Mysteriously Good's door. Then again, the reason he wanted to dance unabashedly was because he wasn't actually alone. As it was, Kyle was doing his best to tone down his elation to the occasional squirm.

He was Wendell's "young man," at least for now. Wendell didn't have a problem holding his hand in public, didn't object to announcing they were together.

This was everything he'd ever wanted, and he was trying very hard not to acknowledge the fast approaching sell-by date on their relationship. In the surf this morning before Wendell had showed up, he'd caught himself trying to figure out how many days were left before Wendell's scheduled departure date. But it had been too damn depressing and he'd firmly put it out of his mind.

Drew was not going to be super thrilled about picking up the pieces of him after Wendell left, but he'd have no choice. Married or not, Drew was still contractually obliged by the best friend pact.

Kyle gave himself a little shake. No depressing thoughts while out with a man who... Well, no, he couldn't finish that thought either. Because it would be the epitome of stupid to fall for someone on what was basically an extended vacation.

Wendell glanced down at him and gave his hand a little squeeze. Kyle smiled back. He was going to enjoy the fuck out of the next few months. He could worry about his broken heart after Wendell left.

"I am starving." Wendell opened the door for Kyle. "And this place always smells so good."

"I'm hungry, too." He glanced at the cupcake display case. Which was stuffed to the gills with colorful swirls of icing. They must have just filled up with the day's selections. "And it looks like we're going to have a hard time deciding on a cupcake for Jackson."

In a few minutes, they'd ordered breakfast—a fat slice of quiche, a gingerbread zombie cookie, and a caramel latte for Wendell, two red pepper and mushroom egg white bites and a skinny decaf latte for him. Tony was going to bring everything over when the drinks were made and breakfast items heated up.

"Maybe we wait until after we eat to get cupcakes," Wendell suggested.

"Sure."

"There's an open table." Wendell pointed to a two-seater table in the corner, and started walking toward it.

Kyle, unfortunately, hadn't paid attention to the neighboring patrons, because as soon as he pulled out the chair, a familiar voice spoke.

"Good morning, Kyle. What are you doing here? I thought you didn't eat carbs. Ever." Eddie's sneering tone made Kyle's jaw clench.

"Eddie. My food choices are none of your business." Then Kyle clamped his jaw shut and plopped down into the chair. They'd been enjoying a temporary truce, or so Kyle supposed, as he hadn't seen any recent attempts to boost Eddie's business at Drew's expense.

He wasn't interested in renewing hostilities, but neither was he interested in listening to Eddie snipe at him.

"And who are you?" Eddie's voice now dripped in saccharine sweetness as he addressed Wendell.

Kyle didn't buy for one second that Eddie didn't know Wendell was helping out at the Lady. The only thing Kyle knew for sure was that Eddie didn't know Wendell was involved in Hollywood. Otherwise he'd have been stalking Wendell at the inn a hot second after he'd found out.

More than likely he was trying to charm Wendell simply because he'd seen them walk into the bakery holding hands. He'd never seen Eddie actively try to break up a relationship, but if Eddie was going to start, it would be with Kyle.

"Er, hello. I'm Wendell. I'm staying at the Orange Lady for a bit, helping out."

Kyle refrained from rolling his eyes. Eddie for damn sure knew that.

"I'm Eddie Price. And if you ever get bored with Kyle, here, please give me a call. I'd be happy to show you around town. Also, I'm a gifted medium. If there's anyone from beyond that you'd like to contact, I'd be happy to give you my friends and family discount."

Eddie fluttered eyelashes, that yes, were long as Bambi's, and had perhaps been the primary reason Kyle had caved that first time and slept with Eddie, but offering a discount with such heavy-handed flirting had been a new low.

"He's not interested in your lame flirting or your theatrical charlatanry. So, knock it off, Eddie."

Eddie's face flushed purple and he pushed back his chair hard enough that it rocked as he stood.

"Why you little—"

"Is there a problem here?" Scott Hunter stood tall and broad behind Eddie, all official sounding, despite his current lack of deputy's uniform.

Eddie's mouth opened and closed like a stunned goldfish for a second or two before he found his voice again.

"No problem here. I was just leaving." Eddie spun on his heel and practically sprinted for the exit. If it wasn't for the pneumatic hinge on the door, that door would have slammed and the glass shattered. Dick.

Scott grabbed a nearby chair, flipped it around and sat on it backward like a total bro.

"Thanks, Scott. Please, join us." Kyle had a bit of bite in his tone, however unfair that was. He wanted to have his breakfast with Wendell uninterrupted by exes or cops.

Scott sighed and gave him a disappointed look.

Kyle frowned at Scott. "I'm not in the wrong here."

"No, you weren't. Exactly. But you do press his buttons, and that's not going to smooth this over."

"Smooth it over?" Kyle waved his hands about, nearly knocking Scott's coffee out of his hand. "Er. Sorry." Like *Kyle* was the only one pressing buttons.

Scott carefully placed his coffee out of Kyle's reach.

"I know this falls on deaf ears for both you and Cliff, but I think if you ignore Eddie's pranks, he'll get bored of all this and it can finally be filed as past business."

Kyle gritted his teeth. Because there may be some truth to it all. He had sort of flung himself into the feud between Drew and Eddie, like it was a well-loved hobby.

"Fine. I'll do my best to turn the other cheek."

"That's all I ask." Scott took a sip of his coffee and showed zero intent to get the fuck up and leave. Wendell had been watching their exchange in silence, and Kyle had no idea what he was thinking.

"Did you just come over here to scold me?"

Scott lifted an eyebrow then casually took another sip.

For a guy who could imitate an over-enthusiastic puppy with the best of them, he'd certainly learned a few techniques over the years that must have perps falling all over themselves to confess.

"Fine. Sorry. That was uncalled for." Scott had surprisingly become a good friend once Drew and Cliff had gotten together.

Scott smiled and ruffled his hair like Kyle was a younger brother and Kyle mock-glared at him.

"It's all good. But seriously, I think you should sit down and talk with Eddie. You and Drew, both, maybe."

"If I promise to discuss it with Drew when he gets back, can we drop the subject for now?" Because Kyle could tell he was going to have to have a rather awkward conversation with Wendell as soon as Scott left. Even Wendell had suggested that he just talk to Eddie, but as soon as Kyle had heard Eddie's snide remark, he just hadn't been able to help himself.

Scott huffed. "I'll take what I can get, but it'd be good if you could get this shit cleared up before Haunt Fest. This year is going to be crazy enough."

Kyle wasn't entirely sure if Scott's objections were coming as a cop who was worried things were going to escalate into felonies, or as a friend who was tired of listening to him bitch about Eddie Price.

He grimaced. Yeah, he needed to let this go. He was acting, well, *they* were acting like children, but Kyle could prove he was the bigger man—and better.

Scott and Wendell exchanged a few pleasantries, and after Scott drained the last of his coffee, he tilted his head at Wendell and winked at Kyle before he stood up.

Kyle rolled his eyes. It didn't take a super cop to figure out his relationship with Wendell had changed, since they'd arrived hand in hand.

Scott laughed and clapped Kyle on the back with just a bit too much strength, like the big ox he appeared to be, and left with a cheery wave.

Almost immediately, Tony arrived with their breakfast and set it on their table.

"Thanks, Tony," Wendell said, and got a tip of the head in return.

Kyle stared at his breakfast, irritation wiping out his appetite.

"So," Wendell began.

Gathering his courage, Kyle looked up. Only to find Wendell's lips quirked up.

"Charlatanry?" Wendell's grin widened and Kyle sputtered out a laugh.

"I had to look it up, but it really does push his buttons, hard. Which maybe means I need to retire it."

"It could be defensiveness talking. Maybe he is a fraud."

Kyle shrugged. "Maybe. But I'm probably not as skeptical as most people about the existence of the paranormal." He wasn't about to go into Drew's new psychic abilities. No point in trying to convince Wendell, who appeared to be a true skeptic, without Drew around to demonstrate his abilities.

And he'd rather enjoy his time with Wendell and not have to worry about Wendell thinking him deluded.

"What was that dig about carbs?"

Shit. Kyle's ears heated. He'd completed forgotten Eddie's comment about his eating habits.

He huffed out a sigh. Not that long ago, he wouldn't have been able to talk about this at all.

"Dancing is hard. Harder than people realize. And it's very competitive. When I was in college, I developed an eating disorder. The physiotherapist that treated my knee discovered it and made sure I got help for that as well. I still have a... fear... of gaining weight, and as a result tend to avoid certain foods. Especially carbs. But I'm much better now, and I focus on eating healthy foods."

Wendell scowled. "That's a shitty thing for him to say. I don't blame you at all for trying to push his buttons. I might have slugged him, if I were you."

Kyle sighed again. "In all fairness, he didn't know. I'm not sure anyone here knows. They all know I'm careful about what I eat, but I never told anyone in town about it, except for my doctor. And, well, now you."

Wendell blinked and gently took Kyle's hand in his.

"Thank you for sharing that with me. What about Drew, though? Or your family?"

Wow. So much baggage getting laid on this tiny bistro table today. It'd be a miracle if it didn't collapse.

"Drew grew up dirt poor. If you stick around a while, you might hear a lot of not nice things about the Drummonds. Drew, once his grandmother took over his upbringing, isn't included in that. And his older brothers are slowly digging themselves out of the Drummond abyss, but the extended family are all petty criminals, with the majority of them either in jail or on parole or probation. Or in juvie."

Wendell frowned in confusion. "Okay. That sucks for him, but I don't quite understand."

"They were so poor, they ate whatever. I personally know that Drew has existed on nothing but peanut butter and stale bread for weeks at a time, because that was all he could afford. He wouldn't recognize an eating disorder if it kicked him in the balls, because he's never had the opportunity to eat properly. So, it was actually easy to keep it from him.

"As for my family, well, I was a late in life baby for parents who were well entrenched in their childless existence. They didn't quite know what to do with me, a bit distant even before they realized I was gay. They sort of washed their hands of me once I reached eighteen, and then retired to Arizona."

Wendell blinked at him. "Your parents lived in Florida and moved somewhere else to retire? Isn't this state chock full of retirees?"

Kyle shrugged. "What can I say? Anyway, I get cards and the occasional phone call, but it's basically been Drew and me against the world for quite some time. There's been no one else to tell."

His relationship in college didn't count, that was for sure. Not only did Kyle think his eating was under control at the time, his ex wouldn't have wanted to deal with such heavy emotional shit anyway.

"I'm truly sorry. But I'm glad you had Drew at least. And even if you didn't have an eating disorder, it was still shitty of Eddie to denigrate your choices. You're an athlete. Of course, you're going to be more careful about what you put in your body than schlubs like me."

This time, Kyle squeezed Wendell's hand. "You know that my choices aren't a judgment of yours, right? I can't tell you how much I wish I could enjoy my food the way you do."

"I would normally make a joke here about me and my food choices, but that feels super not respectful. Because I'm aware I could eat better than I do, but expedience and a pretty insistent sweet tooth win out over my better intentions most of the time."

"If you ever want to start eating healthier, I can help. I've done a lot of reading on the subject in the past few years—it's helped me a lot, actually. But I'm a hundred percent never going to judge you for what you eat."

"And I won't either."

Kyle smiled at him, and then Wendell's stomach growled again, making them both laugh.

Maybe sharing wasn't such a bad thing, because Kyle's appetite had magically returned. They ate in near silence, and Kyle even took a bite of the gingerbread zombie when Wendell offered it.

The rest of the day passed by in a blur of domesticity. They took a couple of cupcakes back to the inn for Jackson—Fire Demon and Hydra. Wendell grabbed a change of clothes suitable for the gym and accompanied Kyle there. They went to the grocery store and Kyle replenished the staples in his pantry. Kyle prepped one of his favorite lunches, with zucchini 'zoodles' standing in for pasta, super thankful that he wasn't still living in the shitty studio he'd been renting last year at this time.

Then they wandered around the old graveyard again before heading back to Drew's store so Kyle could get some work done.

Wendell sat in a client chair and tapped out notes on his phone. Kyle was pretty sure his writing mojo was gearing up. He'd seen a lot of thoughtful expressions on his face while they'd been walking around the graves.

Like he could sense where Kyle's thoughts and gaze were, Wendell looked up.

"I had a great time today."

"Me too." They smiled at each other, and as much as Kyle wanted to kiss him, he knew damn well if he started kissing Wendell now, he wasn't going to stop until they were naked.

Drew would not appreciate hearing about an erotic tableau enacted in his front window.

"Maybe, uh, after your ghost walk we could spend the night at my place?" Wendell asked.

"We are definitely on the same page." Kyle wanted to taste Wendell all over. Take the time to enjoy each other.

Kyle couldn't remember the last time he'd been this happy.

Then the sirens started.

FIFTEEN

17 Days to Haunt Fest

"THOSE SIRENS SOUND CLOSE." Wendell got up to look out the window, only to see flashing lights heading down the street. Pedestrians had stopped to look, and a couple of business owners on the street, many of whom Wendell now knew by name, came out on the sidewalk.

"Car accident?" Kyle moved closer to Wendell's side.

"I don't think so. I don't know where—" Wendell broke off when a fire truck screamed into the Orange Lady's parking lot. Closely followed by an ambulance, siren wailing.

"Fuck." It had been a long time since Wendell had felt this sort of gut wrenching fear. Fire or injury, there wasn't anyone at the inn who hadn't wormed their way into Wendell's heart, even after this short time.

"Go. Find out what's going on. I'll lock up here and be over in a few minutes."

Wendell gave Kyle a quick kiss, then sprinted out of Drew's store and across the street.

He burst into the inn, following the emergency services personnel, and trailed them to the library.

At the door of the library, a firefighter blocked his way.

"Please let them do their job."

"What job?" Wendell asked. "What happened? Who needs help?"

"Please just stay back, sir." The fireman was implacable.

"Excuse me," a voice came from behind him.

Wendell whirled around to find two women wheeling in a gurney of sorts. Not a full sized one like he'd seen in hospitals, but a more compact version that was presumably more portable.

He stepped out of the way to let them in, but the mass of bodies in the room obscured whomever they were working on.

"Wendell!"

He spun around to find Daisy wringing her hands.

"Daisy. Shit, do you know what happened?"

"No. I was in the laundry room checking supplies with my earbuds in. I freaked out when I came out into the hallway to find it, well, full." She waved a hand at the people milling about, which had added a couple of police officers.

"Where's Jackson?" Wendell asked. If it wasn't some random person who'd broken into the inn's library, there were only three people who could have had a medical emergency, and Jackson was one of them.

"I don't know. I haven't seen him in hours."

At that moment, Jackson pushed through the throng of people, face pale and tear streaked. He saw Wendell and headed straight for him, flinging himself at Wendell in such a way that all he could do was wrap his arms around Jackson and let him sob.

Daisy looked as horrified as Wendell felt. Intense relief that Jackson was okay warred with growing dread as the possible victims narrowed down.

Eventually Jackson's tears slowed to a trickle and he pulled back. He hiccupped and wiped at his face. Daisy raced away and swiftly returned with a box of tissues that Jackson grabbed and made quick use of to blow his nose.

"What happened?" Wendell made sure to keep his voice low and gentle.

"I don't know. I don't even usually go into the library. I had just finished checking Patricia out. I remember thinking it was going to be odd just having one guest at the inn after she left. Then I heard a weird sound. And... and..." Jackson sniffled and wiped at his eyes with a tissue. "Chester was dead."

The words were like a fist to the stomach. Wendell had really liked the old guy. Tears burned his eyes, but Jackson's reaction seemed excessive. Unless he'd maybe never seen a dead person before. Most people had by Jackson's age, but that didn't make it true for everyone.

"Oh no," Daisy sniffled, and took a tissue for herself. "He was so lovely."

"He was a good guy, that's for sure." Wendell's voice wobbled only a little as he spoke.

He kept his arm around Jackson, who seemed to be in no hurry to leave.

"Are you okay?"

"I don't know," Jackson mumbled into his shoulder.

"How much longer do you think they'll be?" Daisy asked.

Wendell wasn't sure. He'd never attended a death in person and while he'd done a lot of research into death for his writing, how long things took had never been a pertinent detail.

"I don't know. I can hold the fort down if you need to get going." He didn't imagine an old guy dying of natural causes would require much of an investigation.

"I was just wondering about tidying up in there," Daisy waved toward the library door.

Oh, right. That was a topic that he had come across in his research, and odds were good that they'd need more intensive cleaning than simple tidying up.

He waited for a moment, because technically Jackson was in charge.

When it appeared Jackson wasn't going to say a thing right now, Wendell spoke up.

"Don't worry about cleaning. We might have to call in a service, actually, depending on exactly what's going on in there. Maybe you could make sure there's coffee available in the dining room? Then I think you could just go home."

Daisy nodded distractedly and wandered back toward the dining area.

It wasn't far off her normal time to knock off for the day anyway. Hell, they could all use some time off to deal with the shock.

Unfortunately, with a few new guests expected in the next couple of days, they wouldn't have the luxury of a long break.

If there was a protocol in the employee handbook for this situation, he hadn't seen it yet. If the Orange Lady, with its reputed haunting, hadn't yet seen the death of a guest within its walls, it was a very lucky establishment.

The hotel he'd worked at while in college had seen a couple of deaths and everything had been so discreet none of the other guests had ever realized. Between the small town and the screaming sirens, news of Chester's passing was probably already widely known.

"Hey Jackson," Wendell said softly. "Can I take you back to your place? Or maybe there's someone we could call for you?"

He didn't hold out much hope. Even if there was anyone to call, they were probably all back in New York and couldn't be here to comfort Jackson anytime soon.

"No, no. I need to be here." Jackson's words cracked and he sucked in a deep breath. "This is my responsibility and I need to be around in case anyone has any questions."

Jackson pulled back, face reddened and blotchy. On most people, that type of crying made people look like shit, but Jackson somehow managed to look younger, vulnerable, and still stupidly good-looking.

"Sorry, Wendell. I'm better now. It was just a shock."

"I have no doubt." Wendell did, however, doubt that Jackson was better.

After blowing his nose again, Jackson pocketed the tissues, and began rubbing his hands together like his fingers were cold.

Jackson was quite slim, and it was possible he was truly cold, but more likely he was still reacting to the shock. He was pointedly not looking in the library, not that there was anything to see yet, with everyone milling around.

He wasn't about to insist Jackson leave, because truth was, this was his responsibility. And if Jackson didn't want to call Sandra and put this back on her, Wendell wasn't about to either. He also wasn't about to force another hug on Jackson, but he did wish there was something he could do.

Probably he should have just sent Daisy home and gone to make the coffee himself.

As he watched, it looked like they were getting ready to transport the body.

"What the hell happened?" Kyle skidded to a halt just short of knocking into Jackson. "There's a deputy at the front door. I had to call Scott so I could even get inside."

Kyle glanced into the library just as they lifted the black body bag onto the gurney. He gasped and the color left his cheeks.

Wendell didn't have time to explain. "Can you do me a favor and take Jackson to the office? I can't remember when the next guests are due to check in, but we should probably block any new reservations until then."

Kyle swallowed heavily but nodded and gently took Jackson's arm.

Wendell moved into the cross hall to watch their progress. As soon as the office door closed behind the pair, he let out a breath, and moved back to the library door.

But the truth was, he didn't think he could bear to watch them take Chester out of the building. He'd only chatted with the old guy a few times, but he was going to miss him.

He snagged the attention of the nearest officer.

"Yes, sir?" She wasn't Scott, that's about all Wendell knew.

"I'll be in the dining room at the back of the building if anyone needs anything. There's also fresh coffee ready there. You're all welcome to it, if you want."

"Thank you, sir."

The gurney trundled closer, and Wendell wasn't too proud to admit he pretty much ran away.

In the dining room, he contemplated the coffee for a few minutes, despite it not being his preference, but sleeping tonight was going to be a challenge, without a doubt. No point adding all that extra caffeine.

Daisy was already gone, hopefully safely. He probably should have ordered her an Uber or something to make sure she got home okay.

He set a reminder on his phone for thirty minutes to check in on her, then he prepped a cup of tea and sat down at a different table than the one Chester usually sat at.

Hands wrapped around the warm mug, he stared into the amber depths, trying to figure out what to do next. It didn't take a genius to realize he'd also had a shock, too, despite having encountered death before. But there was no other explanation for his fractured, wayward thoughts and inability to corral them.

He pulled out his phone again, opened the notes app and stared blankly at the blank screen. There might be a joke in that, or maybe even a comic relief scene for a movie, but at the moment, nothing was funny.

After he managed to jot down a couple of items that would have to be taken care of, three of the emergency services personnel trooped into the dining room, including the officer he'd most recently spoken to.

Wendell stood up. "There's coffee over there. Please help yourselves."

The other two, both firefighters, headed straight for the sideboard, and began prepping coffees, presumably for the rest of the crew, based on the number of to-go cups.

The officer, on the other hand, walked over to Wendell.

"Please sit down."

Wendell sat, and the officer also took a seat across the table.

It wasn't a full-on interrogation, but the officer—Sanchez, Wendell thought she'd said—was definitely intent on making sure she had copious notes about the "incident" as she'd called it.

Wendell provided whatever information he could, but he couldn't access any of Chester's personal information on his phone. He'd need to get into the office and pull it from the computer there.

Once the interview was over, Officer Sanchez made herself a coffee to go as well, and asked Wendell to lead her to the office.

Kyle was still inside with Jackson, who looked a little worse for wear.

"Everything blocked out?" Wendell asked.

Jackson nodded, and Wendell squeezed his shoulder. Then he turned to Sanchez. "Do you need to talk to him, too? Because this has been real hard on him."

Sanchez took a long look at Jackson's tear-ravaged face and blank expression.

"Not today. Not as long as you can get me the contact information for the deceased."

All three of them flinched at the officer's reference to Chester as the deceased.

"Kyle, can you take Jackson to his place, please?"

"Of course."

Wendell squatted down so he could look directly into Jackson's eyes.

"Go on and have an early night. I'll take care of things here. And if you need me for anything, even if it's just to talk, call me. Okay?"

Jackson nodded absently, but did reach out and pat his arm. That didn't mean Wendell wasn't going to worry about him all damn night.

Once Kyle had escorted Jackson out of the office, the room seemed far less claustrophobic. It had not been designed to hold four adults at the same time.

Wendell quickly printed out the information from Chester's file, grateful that Officer Sanchez was going to inform the family.

But there was the number one item on his list still to address.

"Uh, Officer, does Sandy Bottom Bay have any sort of biohazard cleaning service?"

Sanchez's eyes widened briefly. "No. You'd have to bring someone in from Tampa. I'll text you a number when I'm back in the office. I know it's not a pleasant thing, but I think if you assess the situation, you may find it won't require that level of expertise."

Oh. That was... promising? Wendell didn't know what to say in response to that, though, so he merely nodded. Then he led Sanchez out the front door and made sure everything was locked up tight, with a sign in the window informing people that the inn was closed for the next couple of days.

He definitely wasn't ready to "assess the situation" in the library. And the coffee clean up could wait until morning.

What seemed like hours later, but in reality had been almost no time at all, Wendell stood under the shower in his cottage, not washing, not thinking, just standing there, still stunned.

When the water began to run cold, he stumbled out. He dried off, wandered into the bedroom, and dressed in sweats on autopilot.

"Hey there." Kyle popped his head into the bedroom, making Wendell jump and let out a rather embarrassing squeak.

"Oh, hey, didn't mean to startle you."

"I thought you'd left."

Kyle wrinkled his nose. "I absolutely would not leave you here like this. I went out to grab a couple of pizzas. Not that either of you are interested in eating, but I did leave one with Jackson before I brought the other one here."

Weird. For the first time in a long time, Wendell wasn't interested in eating.

"Come on."

"I..." Wendell wanted to say he was just going to go to bed, but surely this incident shouldn't be affecting him this badly. And it wasn't even eight yet. If he went to sleep this early, he'd likely wake up in the dead of night.

Sometimes, he did his best work in the wee hours, but at the moment he could barely string together a sentence to fall out of his mouth. He certainly didn't trust he'd be able to write anything coherent, now or in the middle of the night.

"Just a few bites. Please," Kyle cajoled.

Wendell nodded and followed Kyle out of the bedroom.

After he settled into the couch, a fuzzy blanket wrapped around his shoulders—a blanket he'd wondered when anyone would use—Kyle brought the pizza box and some water over to the coffee table. He flicked on the television and found a rerun marathon of *The Big Bang Theory*.

Wendell wasn't able to focus well enough to follow along, but he appreciated the mindlessness of it all.

"I'm not very good company tonight. You can go home if you want to. Or, wait, don't you have to host a ghost walk tonight?"

Kyle snorted. "Obviously, I cancelled the tour. And I don't need you to entertain me. Just eat, okay?"

Wendell obeyed, although he could have been eating cardboard for all that the flavor registered.

At some point, they'd eaten most of the pizza, drank all the water, and Kyle tugged him toward the bedroom.

Since he was more than ready for this day to be over, Wendell slid under the covers without an argument. Somewhat surprisingly, Kyle grabbed a pair of his workout shorts from the dresser and disappeared into the bathroom for a few minutes.

When he returned, he was wearing Wendell's shorts and nothing else. He flicked the light off and slipped into bed beside Wendell.

His bafflement disappeared when Kyle wrapped arms around him, in a move that was clearly designed to comfort rather than seduce.

"I'm sorry. This isn't how I wanted this evening to go," Wendell whispered as his eyes burned, thankful for the dark.

Kyle kissed his temple. "Don't apologize. This isn't your fault. I'm just glad I could be here for you."

"Thank you." Wendell settled into Kyle's arms and closed his eyes.

The waves crashed against the shore, almost in time with his breathing.

Tomorrow had to be a better day.

Then he slept.

SIXTEEN

16 Days to Haunt Fest

THE BUZZING of his phone woke Kyle. He rubbed at his eyes, and found Wendell still sleeping peacefully beside him. As quickly as he could, he slithered out of bed, grabbed his phone, and dashed to the living room. The last thing he wanted was Wendell to wake up before he had to.

By the time he got out there, his phone had stopped ringing, but he'd missed a couple of calls and several texts. He wasn't about to answer nosy questions from anyone. Partly because he didn't know much, but mostly because he was sure neither Jackson nor Wendell wanted any kind of spotlight on what had happened. Sandra wouldn't be pleased when she found out, either. Kyle wasn't about to take on the job of informing her, because he, like most everyone in town, didn't want to add to her stress levels.

He couldn't think of any good reason anyone had to reach him urgently.

Then his phone started ringing again.

Lisa.

He sighed. One of his best friends. He couldn't shut her out. But like normal people, she usually texted. Calls weren't common when they weren't related to her business.

"Hey Lisa," he answered.

"Finally," she huffed out.

Kyle rolled his eyes, thankful she couldn't see him.

"What's up?"

"I can't get a hold of either Jackson or Wendell. Do you know where they are?"

"What's wrong?"

"Nothing. But I've got breakfast and lunch here, and no one is opening the door."

"You're at the inn? Right now? You don't usually do the deliveries." And he was pretty sure Jackson had cancelled the breakfast delivery yesterday when he was blocking out the room reservation system.

"Of course, I do deliveries, for special situations. And this qualifies. I can't stay gone long, but I wanted to make sure they were okay. If you don't know anything, I'm going to call the police. Because, well, they both had a terrible shock and they might not be okay. You know?"

Kyle smiled. Lisa was good people.

"Hold on, I'll be there in a minute to let you in."

He disconnected the call quickly, before she could ask any impertinent questions. Not that she wouldn't ask them to his face, but at least he'd have a few minutes grace to prepare.

After a quick bathroom visit, he scrawled a note for Wendell in case he woke up, then Kyle left the cottage and headed for the lobby.

Lisa stood on the other side of the glass door, a mound of bags on the ground at her feet.

Kyle unlocked the door and grabbed a few bags. Lisa scooped up the others and led him toward the kitchen. Kyle had never actually been in the inn's kitchen. The few times he'd assisted on the desk, there had been no reason for him to go in there, but Lisa knew exactly where she was going. Probably because she'd done deliveries on a regular basis, back before she'd owned the bakery.

She unpacked and sorted everything with ruthless efficiency. Then she typed something on her phone before she dragged him into the dining room. It was filled with shadows and not exactly welcoming until Kyle flicked on the lights. She flopped into one of the chairs and gestured for him to sit with her.

"I thought you were worried about Jackson and Wendell."

"Oh, I was. Until I realized you were here." Her face went through a complicated contortion. Kyle knew her well enough to realize she wanted to tease him about staying overnight, but under the circumstances it was hard to feel good about teasing anyone.

"Still," she continued, "I would have been happier if either of them had answered their phones."

"Wendell was still asleep when I answered the phone. I haven't checked on Jackson yet, but I know he took a sleeping pill last night, so I'm guessing he's also still out."

Lisa nodded. "Sleep will do them good. I brought enough sandwiches and muffins and things that they should be set for the next couple of days if they don't want to forage for meals. But I guess maybe you could do that for them." She let a tiny smirk cross her lips.

He smiled back at her. "I'll look after them. Don't worry."

"Good, good. So tell me, what the fuck happened? There are so many stories swirling through the bakery I've barely got a lick of work done."

"Honestly, I barely know. Wendell and I were spending the day together. I had a few things to do at Drew's and he was keeping me company."

Lisa nodded and gestured for him to continue.

"Anyway, we heard the sirens and realized they were turning into the inn. Wendell ran over there first while I closed up and by the time I got across the road, Peter was standing in front of the door and wouldn't let me in because I was a *bystander*."

"He can be such an officious ass. But I suppose he was also just doing his job."

"Doesn't mean I'm not pissed. Maybe I can convince Drew to give him a scary prediction next time he comes around with some bogus complaint from Eddie."

Although it *had* been a while since Eddie had tried to involve the police in his feud with Drew. Right around the time Drew got involved with Cliff.

"So then what?"

"No one would tell me anything, especially not Peter. I texted Scott, and he came right over, got me past Peter. Then I figured out one of the guests had died in the library. I'd just met him this morning, but I know Wendell chatted with him a number of times, and well, Jackson must have known him even better because he was a fucking wreck."

Kyle thought for a moment, then continued. "Or maybe that was just because he'd found Chester. I mean, even Wyatt, who pretends he doesn't have any feelings, got messed up by finding a dead body."

"Bound to be a shock, for sure. And you can't predict how someone will react to an event like that. Hell, I have no idea how I'd react. I'm just glad you're here for them, and that they have the luxury of shutting down for today. Imagine if this had happened during Haunt Fest? With the place full of people?"

"That would be awful." Kyle shuddered. "I just hope this doesn't bring Sandra and Bill back. This is the last thing Bill needs."

"Tell me about it." Lisa tilted her head, staring at Kyle. He waited, because it was obvious she had something else to say.

"And it definitely wasn't murder, right?"

"Murder?" Kyle gasped. "What are you talking about?"

Lisa shrugged and tugged on her ponytail. "Well, I said there was a lot of swirl. Murder was suggested by more than one person."

"I swear, this town needs more things to occupy its time. Of course it wasn't murder. I've watched enough shows and listened to plenty of podcasts. There's no way they'd have been in and out so quickly if it was murder. There's no crime scene, and aside from asking a few questions about Chester's profile in the hotel registry, no one was interrogated. It was all very sad and shocking, but the guy was getting up there in age. He probably just had a heart attack or something."

Lisa let out a tiny sigh, like she been at least a little bit afraid someone had gotten murdered at the inn. There were bound to be other people who'd be disappointed by that. With Sandy Bottom Bay's reputation, there had to be a few residents hoping for a fresh influx of ghosts.

"That's a relief. Well, if you've got this in hand, I'll get going."

"Thanks, Lisa. I really appreciate it, and I know the guys will as well."

She gave him a hug and took off at her normal brisk pace. The sound of her footfalls receded, leaving him in the almost unnatural silence of the inn.

He'd never been entirely alone in this place, and it was unnerving as hell.

Although he wanted nothing more than to head back—run, run—to Wendell's cottage, he decided to start a pot of coffee first. If Wendell had slept this long without benefit of pharmaceutical assistance, he wasn't going to worry about Jackson just yet.

While he waited for the coffee to brew, he checked his messages to make sure there wasn't anything critical he needed to respond to. And there wasn't. He shoved his phone back in his pocket.

The rich scent of coffee filled the air, making it seem like he wasn't quite so alone anymore. He poured himself a small cup—he didn't often drink caffeine, but his sleep hadn't been as restful as he could have wished—and poured the rest into a large insulated urn. Wendell preferred tea to coffee, but one of the many things he'd already learned was that when Wendell was sleep deprived, he reached for the coffee, with lots of sugar.

He suspected, despite how long Wendell had been asleep, that he'd need the coffee today. And Jackson drank the stuff like it was more necessary than air.

Did he wake Wendell? He didn't know if there were things Wendell needed to take care of today. But he was inclined to let Wendell sleep as long as he needed. The next guest was expected to arrive tomorrow evening. There was plenty of time—he hoped—to let Wendell and Jackson recover.

Almost without thought, his feet led him to the library, and he stood by the door. Just the thought of going inside raised goosebumps on his arms. Even if he turned on the lights, he wouldn't be able to see from here what sort of mess had been created.

The previous day, he'd done his best to avoid looking at what was going on, but he'd seen enough to know the EMTs had been working by the fireplace, the view of which was blocked by a chest-high bookcase.

However much he wanted to help Wendell, and Jackson, out, there was an absolute zero chance he was setting foot in the library while he was alone in the building.

A gust of chilly air swept out of the library and curled around his ankles. Which was his engraved invitation to go the fuck somewhere else.

He briefly considered the sunroom, but really didn't want to stick around inside. Instead, he made up another cup of coffee, the way Wendell liked it, and trekked back to the cottage.

A couple of hours later, Kyle found himself standing outside the library again, waiting for Wendell.

When he'd got back to the cottage, Wendell had still been asleep. Kyle had picked up an old thriller from a shelf by the television and had gotten caught up in a rather improbable action story from the nineties.

By the time Wendell had woken, his coffee had been ice cold. But Kyle had been glad to see Wendell's foggy numbness had disappeared. Slept had washed away his shock, and although he was still grieving for a man he liked, he wasn't a zombie.

He did, however, wake with a newfound zeal to make sure the library was put back in order—if it could be done by the two of them —before Jackson had to worry about it.

Kyle was already worried about that phrase "if it could be done by the two of them" because what sort of mess was Wendell expecting that couldn't be taken care of by two competent men?

He'd stalled Wendell for a short while with Lisa's breakfast offerings and coffee.

But he hadn't found the fortitude to ask what Wendell had meant, and now he stood outside the library, waiting for Wendell to return with cleaning supplies, desperately trying not to imagine the worst.

How was it possible to dread an empty room this intensely?

"Ready?"

Kyle yelped and jumped a foot. "Don't sneak up on me!"

Wendell's eyebrows rose. "Sorry."

"No, I'm sorry. I didn't mean to snap. I was lost in my head a bit, and didn't hear you come back."

"It's okay." Wendell smiled at him. "Ready?" he asked again.

"As I'll ever be." Which was to say, not at all, but he wasn't about to admit that out loud.

Wendell carried a large bucket filled with soapy water in one hand and another bucket with assorted sprays and tools and gloves in another.

Kyle had not anticipated needing... well... accessories. Worry twisted his belly, but he made himself follow Wendell into the room, and rounded the bookcase.

At first glance, he didn't see anything beyond a jumbled mess of books on the floor, furniture shoved aside and a side table tipped over.

He had to admit, between Lisa putting the notion of murder in his mind, and Wendell's cryptic cleaning commentary, he'd unwillingly started to imagine a huge pool of blood on the area rug in front of the fireplace. Maybe even arterial spray.

He had to stop watching murder mysteries. Which was probably the reason he'd had that weird brain glitch the other night up in Marsh Mist.

Wendell stood over one of the wingback chairs. "I don't think this can be saved. Do you suppose it's antique?"

"The chair? I doubt it. Sandra was expecting people to use it. I know she wanted sturdy, but I doubt she'd have set out something valuable for guests to use."

Kyle stepped a little closer.

"Why? What's wrong with it?" Kyle asked. But then a second later, a distinctive and unmistakable smell hit his nose. "Oh. Never mind."

"Yeah," Wendell sighed. "Like most things in life, death is not exactly clean and tidy. However, I think we got lucky. Everything appears to be contained on the chair. But if it's not an antique, I'm going to make the call that we don't try to salvage it. Even in this town, and its appreciation of the paranormal, I doubt there's many who'd want to sit in this chair after someone died in it."

Kyle nodded emphatically. "You've got that right."

"I'll be back in a few minutes."

Kyle's stomach tightened, but he nodded. He wasn't about to let Wendell think he didn't have the guts to stay by himself in a damn library.

Wendell carefully lifted the chair and left the room. Kyle gave the chair's negative space a wide berth and gathered up an armload of books, which he started reshelving. How the hell had the EMTs managed to dislodge so many of them?

When Wendell returned, Kyle hadn't quite finished with the books. Wendell stared critically at the carpet.

"Let's move everything off the carpet. Just in case, we ought to have it cleaned professionally. We can roll it up and I'll put it in the storage shed for now."

"That's a good idea." Because the smell hadn't entirely dissipated, and Kyle had started to suspect that perhaps not all of the bodily fluids had been contained to the chair.

Being careful where he stepped, Kyle helped Wendell clear the carpet. Wendell picked up an edge and gave it a light shake, sending a few pens and a couple of coins flying. They'd been camouflaged by the ornate floral pattern.

A scant few minutes later, and Wendell had left with the rolled up carpet, and Kyle went back to organizing books.

Weirdly, the same Shakespeare book he'd found upstairs had also been one of the books in the jumble. Kyle glanced at the upper shelf where Wendell had returned it. There was a single space open, like a missing front tooth.

Had Chester taken the book upstairs? But Chester hadn't been staying in any of the guest rooms upstairs. Or was there some internet challenge going around that required people to reference Shakespeare? Regardless, it was far too high for Kyle to reach without a step-stool, so he simply placed it out of the way for Wendell to put away later.

He also set aside the e-reader and crossword puzzle book, which he presumed were Chester's. At some point, they'd probably have to pack up Chester's cottage. Once they did, they could leave it for Daisy to clean.

By the time he'd replaced all the other books, Wendell returned and started trying to arrange the furniture so it wasn't completely obvious that one of the chairs was missing. Even with all of Wendell's cleaning products, he hadn't thought to bring a broom, so he left again to find one.

Since the pens and coins from the carpet might also belong to Chester—Daisy was scrupulous with her cleaning—Kyle got down on his hands and knees to retrieve them.

One of the pens had a logo visible—Cross—which Kyle knew cost a bundle. If it wasn't Chester's, someone would be looking for it. It had rolled right to the back, in a shadowy area, tucked between the lip of a warped floorboard and the base of one of the built-in bookcases.

When he grabbed the pen, he hit the base of the bookcase and the board wiggled. *Weird*. He poked at it with the end of the pen and it moved. So, he hadn't imagined it. He pulled out his phone and turned on his flashlight app. Maybe it just needed another nail or two.

Open it.

Kyle held still for half a second before he ran his fingers over the board. It was definitely loose. He stuck the nib of the pen into one of the seams and used it to pry it open. Then he dug two fingers into the small opening.

"What are you doing?"

Kyle yelped and sprang back, landing on his ass, heart slamming against his ribs, hand clutching a piece of wood.

"Um. I don't know, exactly." Truth. A hundred percent. "This was loose."

But so what? What had possessed him to try to pry it away from the wall?

He held the pens aloft in his other hand. "I think these might have been Chester's." As if that would distract Wendell from Kyle's deliberate destruction.

Wendell blinked at him in silence for a moment before he held out a hand for the pens. Kyle gave them up, and Wendell pocketed them. Then he gingerly took the piece of wood and inspected it.

"Doesn't look like any real harm done. I'll just put it back and we'll make sure it gets nailed in before Sandra and Bill return."

Kyle nodded, cheeks heating as he considered how fucking foolish he must appear.

He scooted back a bit, still on his ass, to give Wendell room to kneel down, and let his head fall back against the bookcase behind him. This whole thing was really messed up, but at least he was no longer alone in the library, where someone had died.

"There's something in here." Wendell set the board aside and stretched his hand under the bookcase, and Kyle yanked him back.

"What?"

"Dude. You don't go sticking your hand in random dark spaces in Florida. There could be venomous spiders. Snakes. Or, or... vermin."

"I'm sure Sandra keeps up with her pest control."

Kyle shook his head. "That may be true, but seriously, you've got a broom right over there. Don't take the risk."

The last thing anyone needed right now was a trip to the hospital.

"You're right. Thanks." Wendell popped up and grabbed the broom, then used the end to coax out whatever he'd seen below the bookcase.

For a brief moment, Kyle let himself get excited by the thought of a pirate's treasure trove, but unless one of the previous occupants had found some treasure and decided to hide it under a bookcase, there wasn't much chance of finding pirate booty in the Orange Lady.

Then Wendell jerked the broom and the object skidded into view, leaving a trail of thick dust behind.

It was grimy and rectangular, and looked to be free of cobwebs. But Wendell had taken his warning to heart and grabbed a pair of work gloves from cleaning supplies he'd brought in, as well as a rag.

He swiftly wiped away the dirt, revealing an old wooden box with a tiny latch.

"Huh. A cigar box."

Oh. Kyle hadn't ever seen one before, but he liked it.

"Is there something inside?"

Wendell gave it a shake. "Seems like."

Kyle rolled his eyes. It wasn't a damned bank vault. "So open it."

Wendell sat the box carefully between them so they'd both be able to see what was inside.

Probably wouldn't be anything interesting, but old love letters could be fun.

Kyle casually pulled a book off the nearby shelf, just in case he needed to swat whatever was inside, but that didn't stop him from leaning in so his shoulder brushed Wendell's.

Like he was trying to draw out the anticipation—must be

Wendell's storyteller gene—Wendell flipped the latch and raised the lid like there was a prize for how slow he could move.

Then gravity took over and the lid fell back. The inside was amazingly free of dust.

Wendell pulled the gloves off and pulled out the documents inside.

"These are... driver's licenses?"

"Driver's licenses? Who needs that many licenses?" Kyle asked and grabbed a few out of Wendell's hands. They were old, not like today's slick almost credit-card style. Some were laminated, some weren't.

He flipped through them, and a cold, dark sensation spread through his belly.

"These are... all different people," Kyle whispered.

"I know. This is weird," Wendell replied as he flipped through his stack.

Underneath them all, was a brown envelope. Wendell hadn't noticed it yet. Or at least, he was too engrossed in the licenses to pay it any attention. Kyle reached out and snagged it, leaving his pile of licenses in the box.

Nothing was written on the outside, and what was inside had a bit of bulk to it.

Kyle opened the flap and dumped the contents of the envelope on the floor.

Polaroid pictures spilled out, slipping and sliding. Each one featured two people, close up and washed out in color, in OG selfie style. As he picked up each photo, Kyle realized one person remained the same, but the second person and background images changed, as apparently had the time period, as the one man slowly aged throughout. He had a full head of dark hair, and bright blue eyes that, despite the other fading colors, seemed clear and intent, like he was looking at Kyle and not the camera when he'd taken the photo. Presumably this was the owner of the camera.

Kyle picked up another one. It appeared to have been taken at a

Mardi Gras celebration. Likely in New Orleans, if that black smudge in the corner was one of their distinctive and intricate iron balconies.

The sweet-faced blond man with the owner of the camera smiled widely, eyes glassy with inebriation. Kyle flipped the picture over. In precise lettering with blue ink, the name Trevor H.

Kyle picked up another one. In this one, a pixie-faced young woman, dressed like a flower child, smiled drunkenly at the camera. The background appeared to be a music festival. Maybe. Or just a picnic at a park.

Given the age of the photo, it was entirely possible she was also OG. OG hippie. Her name was listed as Annemarie L.

The bad feeling he'd always associated with this room returned in a rush, and ten times as strong.

"Hey, any of those licenses belong to a Trevor or Annemarie?"

"What?" Wendell looked up from his intent perusal.

"Do any of those licenses match up with these pictures?" Kyle held the two photos aloft, and he was resolutely not thinking about the many, many other names inked on the backs of those dozens of photos.

Wendell flipped through the licenses.

"I have an Annemarie London and Trevor Henning. Why?"

Fingers trembling ever so slightly, Kyle held out the photos. Wendell held onto the two licenses he'd extracted and set the others down before taking the Polaroids.

Wendell flipped them over and scanned the names before flipping them back and peering at them next to the licenses. Then he glanced down at the two piles.

"Well. We've both seen Criminal Minds, right?"

Kyle nodded. "This isn't good, is it?"

"Nope. I don't think so."

"Uh, that's not Chester in those pictures, is it?" Bit of a coincidence, wasn't it? Chester dying right beside this box of probable horrors.

Wendell peered at the images again. "No, I don't think so. Back when these were taken, Chester might have been around the same age as this guy, but their features and builds are completely different."

Kyle didn't know why he was relieved by that, but he was.

"What do we do now?"

Wendell sighed. "As much as I hate to do it, I think this might be a police matter."

No police.

"Did you hear that?" Kyle asked. He rubbed at his ear, which had a funny cold spot.

"Hear what?"

Kyle blinked. He can't have heard anyone whisper anything. There was only him and Wendell in the room.

"It's not like, urgent, or anything is it? I mean, this box has to have been here since before we were born. Or at least, before I was born." Kyle smirked at Wendell, trying to dispel the somber mood.

Wendell snorted out a laugh like Kyle had caught him by surprise.

"I think this has been here longer than I've been alive, too." Wendell elbowed him gently. "And no, I'd guess not urgent."

"Maybe we should see if we can, I don't know, figure out if this is actually sinister. Maybe... this guy was a bartender and all these licenses got forgotten at a bar over the years?"

Wendell shrugged but didn't look at all convinced. "It's possible. Remotely." He sighed. "But if we turn this over to the police now, we're never going to see it again. This might be evidence of a real mystery, and my writer's soul can't bear to let this opportunity go."

Kyle smiled at him. "Maybe we can try and figure things out together. The internet has to be able to get us pretty far along, right?"

"Right. First things, first, though." Wendell pulled on the work gloves and gathered everything up to put it back in the box. "Let's finish tidying up in here, and then I'll pick up some latex gloves for us. Fingerprints might still be valuable, even after all this time. The police might forgive us for waiting to turn this stuff in, but I bet they'd be much less forgiving of us fucking up any evidence."

"Assuming there is any need for evidence. This still could be completely innocent."

"I hope so, but I have serious doubts."

So did Kyle, but he also loved mysteries. Just so long as they didn't have to solve this one in the fucking library.

"Maybe we take this back to your cottage. The light's better, and it's more private."

"What about Jackson?"

Kyle didn't want to involve anyone else. "I don't think we should burden him with this right now. He was pretty torn up by Chester's death." They'd all been shook up, for sure, but Jackson had taken it harder than Kyle would have expected.

"Yeah, I think you're right. We can tell him about it later, when we're ready to involve the police. He'll have to know, at that point, because it wouldn't be fair to spring them on him again, without any warning."

"Sounds like a plan."

No police.

Nope. Kyle definitely wasn't hearing anything. That was his brain misinterpreting the wheeze of the air conditioner. It was a bit elderly at this point. Sandra had been muttering about it needing a new... compressor or something... the last time he'd run into her at the market. This was how ghost stories got started. Faulty mechanics and twitchy brains making two plus two equal thirteen.

SEVENTEEN

16 Days to Haunt Fest

WENDELL HAD BARELY KEPT his curiosity in check while they'd rapidly returned the library to normal, and put away the cleaning supplies. He'd carried the cigar box back to his cottage like a newborn baby, and instead of ripping it open and satisfying the questions whirling about in his brain, he carefully placed the cigar box into the safe in his cottage and locked it up. He ignored the tiny twinge of guilt at his actions. He was ninety-nine percent sure the police would want the contents of that box, but he hadn't lied to Kyle. He'd never had an opportunity like this before, and might never again.

The story potential, and the potential for sparking his muse, were invaluable. And as Kyle said, the stuff wasn't recent. Even if the cops wanted to blame them for something, the most they'd get was a slap on the wrist. How could they get anything else? Especially since the police might never have the box if it weren't for their actions.

A short delay to try and find out more about the people in the photos wasn't too much to ask. He'd be properly respectful of the responsibility he held.

"Want to go get supplies with me?"

Kyle looked at his phone. "It's after lunch. Lisa dropped off a bunch of food for you and Jackson. Maybe we eat first, then supplies?"

He wasn't particularly hungry, which wasn't like him at all. But it made sense to continue eating like normal.

"We should check on Jackson. Get him to eat something too." Wendell had not liked Jackson's reaction yesterday.

Kyle nodded. "Yes. We work on the box this afternoon, and tomorrow, too. At least, until my ghost tour tomorrow night."

Before Chester's death, they'd made plans for a nice dinner out at Flamingos for tonight, which Wendell hadn't eaten at yet. But realistically, he didn't think he'd be in a good mood for a date night.

"Would you be okay if I cancelled our reservations for tonight?" Wendell asked.

"Of course not. I'm sure you're not up to a night out, and I'd rather we both enjoy the evening when we go."

The 'when' in Kyle's statement gave Wendell hope for the future. And Kyle's complete lack of irritation about the broken plans only confirmed that he was as wonderful as Wendell believed.

Just before they left his cottage, Wendell reached out and pulled Kyle into his arms. No kissing, no grinding, just a simple hug. Wendell pulled all the comfort out of it that he could.

"I'm really glad you're here with me."

Kyle squeezed him tight around the waist. "Me too."

This was so much more than a vacation fling. However amazing and unexpected that was.

They stepped out into the bright sunshine. In the face of the almost blinding light, and tropical heat, it was hard to believe the last twenty-four hours had happened.

Wendell was quite worried about Jackson, but he'd apparently had sleep aids and assured them he'd be okay after a good night's sleep. Wendell knew from past experience they could knock you on your ass, but it was shortly after noon. He should be conscious and moving about. Soon.

"Do you know anyone who might be interested or able to keep Jackson company? I don't want to leave him alone. I mean, we could have him hang out with us, but he might have a different opinion on bringing in the police, and quite frankly, he's in charge of the inn. If he wants to call them, we'd have to accept that."

Wendell wanted desperately to dig into that box. He'd been distracted at first by inspecting the old licenses, marveling at the differences from today. Initially, they'd been a historical oddity, nothing more. It hadn't even occurred to him to question why anyone would keep a bunch of different licenses hidden in a box. Or how or where one would obtain such a collection.

Not until Kyle had handed him the Polaroids.

Then there had been a flash of insight born of watching, reading, and writing too many horror stories. Seeing too many police dramas. An academic thrill and atavistic revulsion occupying the same space in his head.

But he wasn't going to focus on that now. There was also Chester's personal effects that would need to be gathered up and sent to his home. If Jackson wasn't up to that, Wendell would have to get that done first.

"Stay with Jackson. Keep him company." Kyle muttered quietly beside him as they walked along the beach path toward where Jackson was staying. "Maybe keep him distracted."

Okay, *distracted* hadn't exactly been Wendell's plan, but it wasn't a bad idea, all things considered.

They stood in front of the door, but Kyle put out a hand to keep him from knocking.

"What?"

"Look, I might have an idea. I just don't know if it's a good idea. Most everyone is going full tilt to prep for the tourist onslaught. So the people I might normally call on for this kind of help are going to be crazy busy. But there are a couple of people who often aren't as busy at this time of year. Thing is, they're both sort of assholes. I mean, I can probably get one of them to come over, but I can't guarantee Jackson will enjoy the experience."

Wendell mulled over that for a moment. He didn't know Jackson all that well, but it was clear he'd arrived in Florida in a rather fragile state. The only problem was, he did not enjoy drawing attention to that in any manner. Solicitude was not particularly appreciated. A bit of antagonism would be better than sympathy, and Wendell needed a distraction of his own to deal with his feelings. Commiserating with Jackson wasn't going to help either of them.

"Sounds like it might be a great idea."

Kyle's eyes widened and he stared at Wendell like he'd maybe lost a few of his marbles.

"Really?"

"Honestly, dealing with an asshole might snap Jackson out of his funk better and faster than someone walking on eggshells around him." Wendell hoped. He wasn't exactly a psychologist. But he did know he'd go nuts sitting around and thinking sad thoughts about Chester. He needed to get out and do something to take his mind off it. If it wasn't the box of photos, it would have been something else. "It would definitely be a distraction, in more ways than one. Call them."

Wendell would normally suggest texting, but someone without much to do for the tourist influx might actually be an older person who didn't deal with technology.

A weird mental bias, actually, considering his own grandmother loved gadgets.

"Uh. No." Kyle grimaced. "I'll go see them in person."

"In person?" That was even more unexpected. "Why?"

"Well, for starters, a personal appeal for a favor like this will go down easier. And secondly, one of them has absolutely no qualms about answering the phone while he's taking a shit or having sex. It's... disconcerting."

A laugh burst out of him. "Disconcerting." Wendell laughed some more, and Kyle started to chuckle as well.

"I hope you know you're going to see that in a future movie somewhere. I am one hundred percent using that."

Kyle shrugged. "You go ahead. He'll never know he was the inspiration. I'll go talk to them, see which of them I can coerce into the job, while you get whatever supplies you want."

Wendell nodded and stepped forward to knock on the door.

There was a lengthy silence before Wendell pounded his fist on the door, harder and longer this time. Because if he didn't see Jackson's face soon, he was calling the police back to do a welfare check.

After another minute of silence, they heard a sort of shuffling on the other side of the door before the handle rattled, and then it swung open with startling swiftness.

Jackson blinked sleepily at them, eyes red-rimmed, hair in complete disarray, the crease of a pillow imprinted on his cheek. Wendell bit his tongue to hold in an inappropriate laugh.

He'd expected fancy silk pajamas or a smoking jacket or something. Jackson, for all that he seemed utterly practical, had an air about him that, if he had a British accent, Wendell would have had no trouble believing he was English aristocracy.

But Jackson was wearing cotton pajama bottoms with unicorns on them, and an old Depeche Mode t-shirt.

He looked young and vulnerable like he'd walked out of a college dorm. After an all-nighter or a keg party.

"Hey, man. How are you doing?" Wendell asked.

Jackson smiled ruefully. "Better, thanks, although I did have a hard time getting to sleep."

"Lisa brought over some lunch. You should probably eat something," Kyle said.

Jackson's eyes went wide. "It's not lunch time yet, is it?"

Then his stomach let out a loud grumble, and Wendell snickered.

"It's actually past lunch. C'mon. We haven't eaten yet, either."

Jackson stared down at his pajamas and plucked at his shirt.

Wendell shook his head. "There no one here. You can get changed later."

They stood there in silence while Jackson considered things. Or maybe while he just let the mental fog disperse as he came to full wakefulness.

"I am hungry." He slipped his feet into a pair of flip-flops by the door and grabbed a key ring from a nearby table before he joined them in front of Jackson's cottage.

The sudden absence of tension made Wendell realize how worried he'd been about Jackson. He was utterly relieved to see that Jackson seemed just about back to normal.

They walked the short distance to the back of the inn, the noise of insects and frogs loud in the absence of any guests at all. Then they paused for half a beat, while Jackson fumbled with the keys to unlock the inn's back door.

Inside, there was a desolation in the atmosphere, as though the building was not ever meant to be devoid of human presence. Wendell wouldn't be surprised if this was the longest the building had been empty in years. And it felt wrong.

But it would be bustling soon enough. And the new clients would hopefully dispel the melancholy of losing this one.

In the dining room, Jackson heated water for tea and coffee. Normally at this time of day, in this heat, Wendell would be downing iced tea or diet soda, but hot drinks equated to comfort in his mind, and clearly Jackson felt the same. They all probably still needed a bit of comfort.

Kyle brought Lisa's prepared lunch out of the kitchen, along with a couple of cheery yellow-frosted cupcakes.

"What mythical monster are those named after?" Wendell asked.

Kyle let out a little sigh. "Honestly, I think Lisa was phoning it in that day. She just calls it the Yellow Dragon. It's lemon frosting, lemon cake, and lemon curd filling."

Jackson perked right up. "Lemon? I love lemon."

Kyle smiled. "I guess Lisa's also got a touch of the sight."

Also? Wendell wondered who else in Kyle's life had "the sight" but that was a topic for another time. It was good to see Jackson so engaged.

"To be fair to Lisa, though," Wendell said. "I can't think of many yellow critters off hand. Yellow Dragon isn't a bad name at all."

"Eh, maybe," Kyle replied. "But dragon is definitely her go-to if she can't come up with a better creature."

"Dragons are cool. I think she's got a good idea," Jackson murmured.

They ate mostly in silence, Kyle avoiding anything that was heavily processed, too starchy or too fattening, but he scarfed down an impressive amount of vegetables. He even swiped a fingerful of frosting from Wendell's cupcake, giving him an impish grin that made Wendell want to forget everything else and take the man back to bed.

But they were on a bit of a time crunch if they wanted to figure this all out, or at least, figure most of it out before work and tourists got in the way. Tonight, he'd make their evening special, with or without a date night. Chester's sudden demise made him all the more sensitive to the notion of living in the moment, even if part of him felt it was a bit disrespectful.

And he very much wanted to live in the moment, and as much of the future as possible, with Kyle. There was nothing about Kyle that didn't make him happy.

He reached out under the table and rested his hand on Kyle's knee. Which got him a big sappy smile, and he could do nothing but smile back.

"Okay, okay, you two. This cupcake is plenty sweet enough," Jackson said after clearing his throat.

Wendell grinned ruefully at Jackson.

They finished eating, and Jackson made a shooing motion with his hands. "Go on, get out of here and have some fun. I'll get this cleaned up."

Jackson sighed heavily, still looking tired.

Oh, he hated to bring this up, but he couldn't leave just yet.

"What about Chester's room? Please don't work on that by yourself. Let me help you."

"I can help too," Kyle said.

Jackson waved a hand. "That doesn't have to be done today. I readily admit, I am not ready to tackle that on my own, but there's plenty of time before anyone checks in. Today, I just need to figure out how to break this to Sandra, before someone else tells her. Assuming they haven't already."

Wendell didn't know if the police had an obligation to inform her of the incident, but even if they hadn't, he suspected the Sandy Bottom Bay gossips would be whispering in her ear, even from hundreds of miles away, before too long. Jackson was right to get on top of that.

"And you're sure I can't do that for you?"

Jackson sighed. "As much help has you've given me—which I truly appreciate—this falls squarely within my responsibilities. But you've correctly figured out I don't want to. So I think I'll have another cup of coffee before I tackle that."

He suited actions to words and got up to refill his mug.

Since Wendell was more eager to get back to the mysterious cigar box, and far less eager to go through Chester's effects or have an uncomfortable conversation with Sandra, he took Jackson at his word.

Kyle stood outside the battered mobile home that Drew's twin brothers, Rob and Wyatt, shared. He'd already stopped by the auto body shop, and as suspected, neither of them were there. Not many people bothered with auto repairs until after Haunt Fest was over. For emergencies, the Drummond twins had a phone number—not the cell phone that Rob answered without any regard to the caller's sensibilities—and one of them would arrive to open the shop.

Much of the town had been surprised at how reliable the twins ended up being, and presumed it was the support and financial backing of the town's matriarch, Helen Somerset, that had enabled them to get their acts together. Personally, Kyle believed they'd been scared more or less straight by the shit that had gone down two years ago when Drew almost died. When Drew's brother, Rob, almost died. When the *mayor* had murdered people to cover up his nefarious business dealings.

But the why didn't matter. What mattered was that neither twin would have anything to do between now and the end of Haunt Fest aside from some last-minute handyman jobs—which was how they rounded out their income while the auto body shop was in its infancy. Again, Kyle was skeptical that they weren't still involved in some shady business, but perhaps even they had seen the folly of engaging in illegal activities when their brother was married to a cop... who was also the son of the town matriarch.

Rob and Wyatt weren't dumb, no matter how they presented themselves to the rest of the world.

Kyle gritted his teeth. Procrastination was not an admirable quality. He marched up to the door and knocked.

This was a terrible idea. But he was committed. And frankly, a little desperate. He didn't know of anyone else he could convince to do this on short notice. He just hoped Wendell was right, and that an asshole would be exactly what the doctor ordered for Jackson.

Kyle listened. There was definitely someone moving around inside, but he didn't hear any movement coming toward the door. He knocked again, more insistently. Wendell wasn't the only one who could pound on a door.

Finally, the door was yanked open by a large, well-built blond man fresh out of the shower. Thankfully with a towel around his waist.

"Hey Wyatt. Are you here alone?"

"How'd you know it was me?" Wyatt grinned and patted his chest. "It's because I'm better-looking than Rob, right?"

Kyle rolled his eyes. He was one of the few people who could tell the twins apart, but in this case, he hadn't even needed his usual cues. Rob wouldn't have bothered slinging a towel around his waist before opening the door.

"Yeah, sure."

Wyatt shook his head like he was exasperated by Kyle's unenthusiastic response, but he backed up and let Kyle inside.

"Want a drink?" Wyatt asked. He got himself a soda out of the fridge—which in itself was progress. Kyle would have assumed he'd already started on the beer.

They sat down at the tiny kitchen table that extended from one wall of the motor home.

"Seriously, though, are you alone?" Kyle asked again.

"Why? Want to test your moves on me?" Wyatt waggled his eyebrows and smirked.

Kyle's cheeks heated just a bit. Wyatt especially had become far less of an asshole in the past year. He had really taken the danger to his brothers to heart. Before, he'd been a real dick, and while he accepted that both Kyle and Drew were gay, there had often been a sharp edge to his teasing.

But in recent months, he'd... softened? Rob had become more withdrawn, while Wyatt's interactions had been more genuine and less like he was deliberately trying to piss people off. And more and more often, he'd made jokes about men, especially Kyle, wanting him. Perhaps those were Wyatt's attempts to prove he was truly unconcerned about "the gay". For most people, that would still be dick-ish behavior, but for Wyatt, it was almost unprecedented personal growth.

"I am not interested in your bod." Objectively, it was a nice bod, but not one Kyle wanted any part of. "I wanted to know if Rob was here." He glanced at Wyatt's towel-clad hips. "Or, if you have a, uh, lady-friend here."

Wyatt burst out laughing. "A lady-friend? How old are you, a hundred?"

Kyle gritted his teeth. He should have known attempting to be polite was utterly pointless.

"As for your question. I am alone. Rob and one of his *lady-friends* took a road trip down to the Keys. Don't know when he'll be back."

Then Wyatt was his last chance. As annoying as Wyatt could be, Kyle did prefer his chances at getting Wyatt to do what he wanted, and to be properly responsible about it. More so than Rob, at any rate.

"Did you hear what happened at the Lady?"

"I heard about your *man-friend*." Wyatt winked at him. Fine, he supposed lady-friend was a stupid term. But he knew the twins well enough that girlfriend definitely wasn't the right term either.

"I'm not here to brag about my boyfriend." Although he did love saying that. However temporary it would prove to be.

"No? Are you sure?"

Kyle had no idea what Wyatt might mean by that.

"Of course, I'm sure." He waved a hand. "Stop distracting me. I mean about the death."

Wyatt sat up straight. "Who died?"

"One of the guests. Just a heart attack or something. Natural causes, I assume, based on what I heard the cops saying. But Jackson found the guy and was really upset."

"Jackson," Wyatt repeated.

"Yeah. Jackson. He's in charge while Sandra and Bill are on vacation." Vacation maybe wasn't quite the right explanation, but he didn't want to get sidetracked down another rabbit hole. The twins got their fair share of gossip, like anyone else in town, but more often than not they ignored it out of lack of interest. Wyatt might not even know Bill had had surgery, much less left the state to recuperate, and it wasn't Kyle's job to fill him in now.

"Right. I might have seen him around. So he found the body?"

Kyle nodded, knowing that this might be a little sensitive, however much Wyatt wouldn't want to admit it. It was the reason he'd rather ask Rob for this favor.

"That sucks. Is he okay?" Wyatt asked with more compassion than Kyle would have expected. Then again, it hadn't even been two years since Wyatt discovered the body of his friend, although that had turned out to be murder. Nevertheless, he should have realized Wyatt would be sympathetic to Jackson's situation.

"It hit him pretty hard, actually. Wendell and I have some things to take care of, and I was hoping you could go over there and keep Jackson company. Maybe help him get the place ready for Haunt Fest."

Wyatt curled his lip. "I hate dealing with all those guests at the inn. They're so demanding."

"When have you dealt with guests at the inn?"

"Sandra was replacing light fixtures in all the rooms and hired me to do that. Everyone was a pain in the ass. 'Where's the dining room? Where's the beach? Where's the ice machine? When are you going to be done?' Asking me about fucking ghosts every ten seconds." Wyatt took another swallow of soda.

"Well, there aren't any guests at the moment." Or ghosts. Kyle was sure of that. Definitely sure. "Jackson cancelled all bookings until tomorrow evening."

"So he's rattling around that place all by himself?"

"Well, mostly. Wendell's in one of the cottages."

"And you're there more often than not."

Kyle wanted to object on general principle, but it was the truth. He'd spent as much free time with Wendell as he'd been able to.

"How do you know that?"

Wyatt lifted a shoulder. "People tell me shit. Shit I never wanted or needed to know. But I pay attention to things about you and Drew. Because you're family."

Kyle could hardly be mad at him about that.

"And you let me know if I have to go talk to Eddie." His voice had hardened, and Kyle's sentimental warmth vanished. This was exactly why he'd hoped to dial down the antagonism with Eddie. Because if the twins got involved, things were going to get messy.

"Eddie and I are fine."

"Really? Heard he ran into you in the bakery."

"Stalking me much?"

That made Wyatt laugh again, and Kyle wanted to dump the can of soda over his freshly washed head.

"Like I said, people tell me things. Sometimes, people want to stoke the chaos."

Although he'd never heard Wyatt say anything like "stoke the chaos" in his entire life, it did indeed sound like the people who told stuff to Wyatt might be troublemakers.

"Stop. We're off track again. Can you go and look after Jackson for me?"

"What, so you're free to bang your bf without guilt? I don't think so."

Kyle bit back a scream. He definitely didn't want to tell Wyatt about the cigar box. But without doing so, he did seem a little selfish. He could still make this happen, though.

"I am looking after your brother's business, you know. I'm not entirely at loose ends. And I have plenty of ghost tours booked up. The least you could do is give me hand, here."

"What about your bf? Isn't he on *vacay*?" The wry twist to Wyatt's words was bitter, but Kyle wasn't sure if it was directed toward him or someone else. Also, vacay was a new word for Wyatt, too, as was the repeated bf. Something was going on with Wyatt. Drew might know, but it wasn't urgent enough for Kyle to bother him on his honeymoon.

"He's actually here to work as well." As soon as inspiration struck, at any rate. "Are you going to help out?"

"Dunno. What's in it for me?"

Kyle stared at him. "What's in it for you? How about, I don't text Drew on his honeymoon? Because if I do, and he has to call you from Paris, he is not going to be pleased."

Wyatt clamped his lips together and his nostrils flared with irritation. Not like Kyle would have actually bothered Drew on his honeymoon, but Wyatt still had a lot of guilt where Drew was concerned and Kyle was not above using it for his own ends.

Especially since he hadn't quite forgiven the twins for the part they'd played in almost getting his best friend killed. They'd gotten off lightly, in Kyle's opinion, and when they were done paying as per Kyle's more draconian standards, then he'd leave off the guilt trips.

"Fine. I'll go over there. You don't need to bother Drew. When did you want me to go?"

"As soon as you get dressed."

"What if I had something else planned?"

"Do you?" Kyle couldn't keep the skepticism out of his voice.

"No. But I don't know what the hell I'll do when I'm there. Small talk isn't one of my things."

"Oh, I know that. He's gay, so don't be a jerk about it. Better to try and keep your mouth shut entirely."

The tension left Wyatt's jaw and he looked like he was about to start laughing again, but didn't.

"Once upon a time, you wouldn't say shit to me if your ass was on fire. Now you're telling me to keep my mouth shut? I maybe miss those quiet days."

There was no rancor in Wyatt's tone, but that didn't stop heat from licking up Kyle's neck into his cheeks. Once upon a time he had a very intense and R-rated crush on both Wyatt and Rob. Together. Which was the reason he'd never been able to speak in their presence.

But the crush was long over. Not that he would ever admit its existence to either twin. Not even under torture.

"If you can't think of something to say, think of something to fix. There was a lightbulb in the library that blew out the other day, and I don't think it ever got replaced. That's a handyman thing, right? Find more of those to do. Have him help you. I'm sure you're smart enough to think of something."

Kyle flounced out of the mobile home, Wyatt's renewed laughter floating behind him.

Somewhere, somewhen, Wyatt had found his funny bone. Or more like, stolen it from someone else. Kyle wasn't sure he liked this Wyatt who laughed with genuine humor.

The door swung shut behind him with a bang. Kyle didn't know why, but he stopped and turned around. For a split second, all sound was deadened, like he was wearing earplugs. He blinked, and the dented, whitish siding of Wyatt's mobile home appeared to be streaked with blood. Arterial spray, if Kyle recalled his murder shows correctly. His pulse rate rocketed and a chill wrapped cold tentacles around him.

"Wyatt?" Kyle managed to croak out the one word, but too quietly for anyone to hear him. He took a step toward the door, and blinked again.

Everything was back to normal. He took another step. Other than the dents and dings he'd seen when he first arrived, there was no additional staining. Squirrels rustled in the trees, insects buzzed in the air, a warm breeze ruffled his hair.

Another blip, courtesy of his over-active imagination. Maybe he needed to rethink his position giving ghost tours.

He took a couple of deep breaths to get his heart rate down to near normal, then he headed back to the center of town.

EIGHTEEN

16 Days to Haunt Fest

WHEN KYLE HAD TEXTED WENDELL, he'd said he was already back at the cottage. Which made perfect sense, as it had taken Kyle longer than he'd expected to track down Wyatt and arrange for him to visit with Jackson. Since he was passing the bakery, he grabbed cookies for the next night's ghost tour, so hopefully they'd have some uninterrupted time to investigate the contents of the cigar box.

The longer they had it in their possession, the more trouble they'd be likely to get into once they turned it over to the police, but Kyle hadn't been able to suppress the feeling that they should avoid the police, at least right now. Wendell had agreed, which meant Kyle didn't have to explain his feelings, but Wendell's agreement could change at any point.

The bell on the door jangled as he stepped into the bakery. It did smell delicious, but without much of a sweet tooth, he didn't find it as intoxicating as Wendell did. He picked out his cookies, and grabbed an extra for Wendell.

With a smile, he paid, then turned for the door.

"Kyle." Eddie's voice was flat and disdainful.

"Eddie." Kyle attempted to match the tone.

Whatever Eddie said next was lost as Kyle's mind was filled with an image of him snatching up one of the nearby chairs and swinging it at Eddie's head. His knees wobbled, and he put out a hand to steady himself, wrapping his fingers around the cool metal of the chair beside him.

He snatched his hand back and slammed it against his chest, sucking in air, as Eddie's now-concerned expression filled the field of his vision.

"Are you okay?" Eddie asked, not a trace of contempt in his voice.

"Yes." The quaver in his voice was not particularly convincing, so he said it again. "Yes. I'm fine. Thanks. Uh, low blood sugar, I think."

He held up his bag of cookies. "I'll have one of these."

"Are you sure?"

"Yep, all good." Kyle skirted Eddie's outstretched hand and raced out the door. He didn't know what was up with his brain, but neither was he ready for a world in which Eddie Price was nice to him. That was maybe just as scary.

Outside in the sunshine, the image of him doing violence was unthinkable. He slayed with sass, killed people with awesomeness. Violence was not his go-to and he didn't understand why he was having these thoughts. Maybe Chester's death had affected him more than he realized. Or it was just the unsettled atmosphere at the inn.

That must be it. Maybe he could convince Wendell to sleep at his apartment. If not tonight, because he might not want to leave Jackson on his own, then tomorrow night after Kyle's ghost tour. It might do them good to get away for a night, especially since there might not be too many more chances until after Haunt Fest.

He sucked in another deep breath, and resolved to only think happy thoughts. After all, he hadn't quite realized it until he'd spoken to Wyatt, but despite an awkward start, he hadn't been crippled by his customary shyness with Wendell. And he cared more for Wendell than he'd ever cared for any guy he'd dated. Maybe that was a sign that Wendell was right for him.

Maybe that meant he'd have to figure out how a long distance relationship might work. Los Angeles might be fun to visit on a regular basis.

But that was definitely not something he needed to worry about now. He had not known Wendell long enough, no matter how promising the start.

Right now, he needed to focus on the mystery, prepping for Haunt Fest, and getting Wendell into bed. Simple.

In less than a week, Drew would be home. Maybe he could do a reading. Tell Kyle if he had anything to worry about.

The sunshine helped clear his mind, and he headed right back to the inn.

Instead of trying the lobby door, which would undoubtedly be locked, he slipped around the side of the building and let himself in through the gate.

He paused when he got to Jackson's cottage. Should he warn Jackson of Wyatt's impeding arrival? Because he was confident Wyatt would show up. The twins were extremely good about not risking Drew's disapproval, and Kyle knew how to put them firmly on Drew's bad side. And he fucking would if he had to.

Maybe it would be best to get Wendell to text Jackson. That might reduce any arguments. He suspected Jackson wouldn't approve of a "companion" but with a writer available, surely they could make it sound like a plausible necessity. That a handyman would be doing some work during the unexpected lull.

Kyle nodded to himself, and continued down the beach path to Wendell's cottage. He knocked on the sliding door, but couldn't see inside as Wendell had pulled the curtains closed.

Then the door whooshed open. "Come in, come in," Wendell said, and gave him a quick kiss.

The joy of that natural display of affection blinded Kyle for a moment as he entered the cottage. Then he rocked to a stop and blinked.

The living room had been transformed. Kyle had been expecting latex gloves and maybe a notebook. Wendell had bought a lot more supplies than that.

Ellie, who owned the stationary store, must be dancing a fucking jig right now.

Wendell had rearranged the furniture, and set up two easels, each of which held a giant pad of paper. Markers, pencils, rulers, push pins, sticky notes, several notebooks, and masking tape were heaped in a haphazard pile on the coffee table. A weatherproof box, presumably to store the cigar box, sat on the floor beside the table.

Wendell had gone all the way out.

Then he spied a skein of red yarn, and he plucked it out of the pile.

He turned it over in his hands. Then glanced up at Wendell.

"What is this for?"

Wendell looked slightly abashed. "In case we need to... make connections between things."

"I hate to break it to you, but I think those boards they show on TV and movies, where they string red yarn between things is probably only set dressing. I can't imagine real detectives would use such a thing."

"Yeah, I know." Wendell let out a sigh. "I haven't exactly needed to research police investigative techniques, but I got caught up in the excitement of it all. I even bought a map of the US, which is what the push pins are for."

"Okay, well, that might actually be useful, although we don't really know if where these people lived is important. We get a lot of tourists through here, and have for a long time. Where they came from might not matter."

Kyle wasn't about to mention it might not be that easy to jam a push pin into a spot on a map that had been taped to a regular wall. As Wendell's had been, right beside the door to the bedroom.

"Yeah, I realized that after I got back here. I had this idea... well, I guess it's silly."

Kyle squeezed Wendell's hand. "It's not silly. Even if it doesn't give us any additional information, it might still be interesting to see."

Wendell smiled at him, and Kyle stretched up for a kiss.

They lost a few minutes that way, but then remembered they were on a bit of a time crunch.

"Let's get started." Wendell pulled out a package of latex gloves and they both pulled on a pair.

First thing they did was catalog the documents and match up the photos with the licenses. There were forty-three individuals represented. Based on the expiry date of the licenses, none of them were over thirty when those licenses were in use.

A few photos had recognizable or suggestive images in the background, enough so that they were able to take a stab at location.

Three were most likely taken in New Orleans, one had a partial sign that may have been for Salem. Two had the old clock tower visible, and were clearly local. Another one was taken near the founder's residence and two more at the lighthouse. Two more could have been taken by the old cemetery, but cemeteries had a sameness about them, and without any legible headstone inscriptions, it wasn't a guarantee that the photos had been taken in Sandy Bottom Bay.

But the rest of them? Bonfires or beaches or wooded areas, and that was only if the background wasn't so overexposed or so blurry as to be useless, at least to their eyes.

They'd jotted down names, addresses, birthdates, possible locations, and basic descriptions. Wendell photographed everything on his phone. Kyle had a sneaking suspicion that some of the photos were going to get printed out at the nearest business center, assuming Wendell didn't ask if Drew had a printer at the store he could use. It would be the final finishing touch to making this cottage look like conspiracy theory central.

When they were done, they put the documents carefully back in the cigar box, then into the weatherproof box, then into Wendell's safe.

Just the mere ritual of preservation, which neither of them suggested might be overkill, was enough to convince Kyle that they both suspected the same thing. This was not a typical box of mementos, or a long-forgotten stash of licenses left behind by careless or drunk bar patrons.

But Kyle wasn't ready to admit what he thought aloud. And clearly, Wendell wasn't ready either.

With the cigar box safely away, they pulled off their gloves. Wendell flopped back onto the couch and stared at the notes they'd made on the easel, notebook in hand.

Kyle stretched, his back sore after so long hunched over the photos.

He walked over to the kitchen and washed his hands.

It would be so easy. Just grab one of the knives. No one would hear.

Kyle gripped the edge of the sink, knuckles whitening. He then turned around. Wendell hadn't moved, gave no indication that he'd heard what Kyle had.

Had Kyle actually heard anything?

He was not going crazy. Not now, when things were going well in his life. He didn't know where that little voice came from, but he was chalking it up to imagination. Exhaustion. Stress. He was *not* hearing voices. Not. He utterly refused.

"So, uh, what next?" By some miracle, Kyle's voice sounded rock steady. If only his emotions were the same.

"It's getting late. I'm tired, and I think we've done all we can do with this. Tomorrow we can start on the internet, see what we can find about these people. Maybe create a timeline based on license issue or expiry dates."

"Are you hungry? I know we'd planned a date night, and maybe that doesn't feel appropriate, but we still need to eat."

And Kyle needed to get away from this inn for a while. Reorient himself.

"I guess I could eat. And I can use a break, too. Angry Parakeet?" Wendell stretched and tilted his neck like he was working out a kink.

"Sounds good."

"Let's check in on Jackson before we go. Did you find someone to keep him company?"

"Shit." Kyle glanced at the time. "I completely forgot to get you to text Jackson about that."

"You wanted me to text? Why me?"

Kyle wrinkled his nose. "Well, it might not be the most ideal solution, but it is a solution. Of sorts. Anyway, I thought it might be better coming from you since you at least have semi-official status here at the inn. I'm just, well..."

"My boyfriend?" Wendell asked with a warm grin.

"Yes. Your boyfriend." Kyle took a moment to bask in the joy of that, before he sighed. "And if I told Jackson, I would be your overstepping, interfering boyfriend, wouldn't I?"

Wendell lifted a shoulder. "Yeah, maybe. Well, let's get over there now and make sure to smooth over any waves."

Kyle didn't want to mention it, but if Wyatt had showed up already, unannounced and as brash as usual, the waves might be of tsunami proportions.

They could hear the yelling the moment they opened the door to the main building.

"What the hell is going on?" Wendell asked.

"Sounds like Wyatt is here. And in the library." Because of course they were going back to the library. If exposure therapy worked for phobias, Kyle was clearly doing it wrong because his dislike of the library had only grown each and every time he'd been inside it.

With a resigned sigh, he followed Wendell into the library, where Wyatt and Jackson were yelling at each other.

Or more specifically, Jackson was yelling at Wyatt, who was oblivious to Jackson's heightened emotional state.

"I don't even know who you are! Why are you just randomly... changing lightbulbs?"

"I already told you. I was asked to come by and take care of some work around the inn. So here I am."

"By who? Sandra did not mention this to me. You can't just change lightbulbs with impunity."

Kyle smothered a laugh while Wyatt crouched in front of the electrical outlet attached to the lamp with the lightbulb that had shattered in their presence a few days ago.

"I'm not. The problem here goes deeper than a blown lightbulb. Faulty wiring in the outlet, maybe. Or an overloaded circuit. I'll need to grab some equipment and supplies to fix this right. Make sure it's not a bigger electrical issue."

"Oh for fuck's sake, Wyatt. I didn't ask you to make up problems," Kyle said.

Jackson whirled on him, hair sticking up in an aggressive bedhead, jeans and t-shirt pulled on haphazardly, like he'd still been wearing pajamas when Wyatt had shown up.

"Kyle, you're responsible for... this... this..." Jackson sputtered to a stop, face flushed.

"Um. Yes. I am." Kyle had to admit, Wendell might have been onto something. Jackson might not look anywhere near as put together as he normally did, but despite his ire, neither did he look as fragile and delicate as he'd appeared this trip. Which had gotten even more pronounced after Chester's death.

"Why would you do that?" Jackson asked plaintively. "And why him?"

Kyle's face heated. How did he explain how worried they were about Jackson without sounding like a mother hen?

He looked at Wendell, who shrugged. Wendell was at even more of a disadvantage, since he didn't know Wyatt at all.

"Oh, for fuck's sake." Wyatt stood up. "Kyle asked me to come over. I've come across a dead body before. And it sucks. He didn't want you to be alone, and I know what you're going through."

"What?" Jackson's gaze flickered between them.

"And I'm guessing that Kyle wanted alone time with this dude." Wyatt waved a hand at Wendell. "I'm Wyatt. I guess you're the guy Kyle's banging?"

The slight heat in Kyle's cheeks burst into an inferno, matching the red that slashed across Wendell's face.

"Um. Wendell. Nice to meet you?"

"Wyatt, what the fuck?" Kyle ground out. At least Jackson was still mostly speechless. Kyle could only focus on one disaster at a time.

But Wyatt was not deterred, nor was he finished speaking.

"And Kyle is basically my little brother, so if you hurt him you'll have to answer to me."

Wyatt puffed up, clearly the biggest man in the room and Wendell blinked at him, like he wasn't sure what to do with this statement. A statement that only served to humiliate Kyle.

"Wyatt, shut the fuck up!"

"So, is everything under control or do I need to make this official?" A voice boomed from the doorway, and everyone turned toward it.

"Hunter, no one called the cops," Wyatt snarled. Drew's brothers did not have the most congenial relationship with the town's police force, and Scott was clearly here in his official capacity. Or so Kyle assumed, given he was wearing his uniform.

"Actually, I did," Jackson murmured. He stared back, stone-faced, when Wyatt turned a glare on him.

"Why did you do that?" Wyatt did not sound happy, but amazingly, Jackson didn't even flinch. He might be more suited to the hospitality business than Kyle had originally believed.

"Well, I didn't know who you were or why you were here! And I didn't exactly call the cops."

"Oh really? So, Hunter just showed up because he's got psychic powers?" Sarcasm bled from Wyatt's words.

"No, I mean, I did call him. I'm friends with his older brother. I called Scott directly for help."

"And I happen to be on duty right now, so yes, the cops are here. Or at least, one cop is here," Scott said, with a little bite in his tone.

Honestly, Kyle was sort of impressed that Wyatt hadn't said anything derogatory about the cops. Drew must have impressed on him the necessity of not saying shitty things about his husband's career path.

"Jackson, is everything okay?" Scott asked in his best, most official tone.

"Yes, I'm sorry. I guess it was a misunderstanding." Jackson sent an unimpressed look Kyle's way.

Scott nodded. "Good to know. But feel free to call if you need anything else."

"Sorry to bother you," Jackson said softly.

"It's no bother, I promise." Scott's tone was no longer official, and Kyle assumed they were also friends after a fashion. As much as Kyle might call Wyatt a friend, based on his relationship with Drew.

Scott left, and in the distance, they heard the front door close. Then Jackson sighed.

"I appreciate your concern. I really do. But I don't need a babysitter, pretending to fix things."

Wyatt growled. "I am a handyman. And an auto mechanic. And I'm not making shit up." He held up the cover of the outlet, and the back was black with scorching.

Jackson gasped. "Shit. That could have lit the place on fire."

"Yes. It could have. And it needs fixing."

Jackson moved a little closer to Wyatt, the tension in his frame loosening. "Can we discuss what needs to be done to fix this?"

He glanced at the single wingback chair by the fireplace.

"Maybe in the dining room? Can I maybe make you a cup of coffee or something?"

"Sounds good."

They left the room, without another glance at Kyle and Wendell.

Suddenly Kyle got a mental image of Wyatt stabbing Jackson with the screwdriver he was holding. Or was it Kyle doing the stabbing?

His heart rate sped up, and he clenched his hands into fists. He squeezed his eyes shut, trying to erase the image. So much blood. He hadn't even watched any scary movies lately.

A loud thump behind him made him jump, and Wendell let out a surprised grunt.

Kyle sucked in a breath, somehow smelling of oranges, and turned toward the source of the sound. A book lay open on the floor.

Shakespeare.

He glanced up at the empty space on the bookshelf, like a mouth missing a tooth. How had that fallen off the shelf? It made no sense.

But he was grateful for the distraction, even if he could have been concussed if he'd been two steps closer to the bookcase, because that awful image was no longer occupying his mind. He bent over to pick up the book.

"It's open on Macbeth again. Someone must have spent a long time reading that play," Kyle murmured.

"And are you okay?" Wendell asked. "That fell awfully close to you."

"I'm fine. It didn't touch me."

Wendell ran a hand over Kyle's cheek. "I'm glad. What did you mean that it was open to Macbeth again?"

"Oh, when I found the book last time, up in the guest suite, it was also open to Macbeth. Same page as before, even."

"Weird. That's where I saw it open, too. I guess the spine must be broken there." He took the book from Kyle and put it back on the shelf, shoving it back as far as it could go. "There. That's not coming down again."

Kyle caught another whiff of oranges as he took Wendell's hand.

"Ready to get going?" Because Kyle was more than ready to get the hell out of this library.

"Yes. By the way, who is Wyatt, exactly?" Wendell asked as they left through the front door, locking it after them.

"He's one of Drew's older brothers."

"Ah. He's, um, an interesting person."

"Yes, he is. But he was the only one I could think of who'd look after Jackson, and wouldn't already be overwhelmed by Haunt Fest preparations."

"And he said he'd found a dead body before?"

The story of how Drew met Cliff, solved a murder, and almost died, along with Wendell's questions, took the rest of the evening. Kyle even managed to broach the topic of Drew's new psychic abilities. Wendell said all the right things, but Kyle suspected he didn't actually believe. Not that Kyle blamed him. Drew had had to prove himself more than once, and Wendell hadn't had any proof yet.

Everyone in Drew's circle who believed in his new talent kept quiet about it as much as they could, but it hadn't been quiet enough. Drew's readings throughout October were already booked up, and he had many more bookings that were months out, when he rarely got advance bookings before. And many more locals signed up for regular readings, although that had been the mainstay of Drew's business after he'd inherited it from his grandmother.

Kyle hadn't gone digging, mostly because Drew would prefer not to know, but he suspected there were message boards and paranormal blogs that had mentioned the psychic in Sandy Bottom Bay. And he suspected Drew's increased notoriety had partially fueled Eddie's feud.

Regardless, it had been a pleasant evening, and they stood in Wendell's bedroom, he hoped it would get even better. He did, however, firmly close the door. No way did he want to catch glimpse of those photos posted in the living room. He wanted to pretend that everything was normal. Especially while he and Wendell were going to entertain themselves in the very best way.

NINETEEN

15 Days to Haunt Fest

THE NEXT MORNING, Kyle slipped back to his apartment to grab a couple of changes of clothes and his costume for his scheduled ghost tour.

He'd slept better with Wendell than he'd slept for a long time. Sure, it might have had something to do with the orgasmic stupor, but mostly it was the sense of safety he had in Wendell's arms. It was relaxing like nothing he'd known in his life.

He wasn't sure he wanted to give up this relationship when Wendell returned to California, and he really wasn't sure what to do about that. In the meantime, he'd bury his head in the sand and pretend everything was okay. It was definitely not something to worry about right now.

They had other things to think about. Worry about. Like that box of photos. And they didn't have long to think about it, because there were guests expected to check in this evening. Daisy would be back this afternoon to give the library a once-over. Then... it would be almost non-stop work for both of them until the end of October. If they didn't find out anything today about the people in the box, they might not have time in the coming weeks to devote to it at all.

Wendell let him in through the front door of the inn and locked it behind them.

"I'm going to find Jackson, make sure everything is okay here."

Kyle thought he'd seen Wyatt's truck in the parking lot, so Jackson was probably fine. He wasn't sure if Wyatt thought he was getting paid for this gig, though. Jackson might have offered to pay him for the work. If he did, that might explain Wyatt's return for a second day. After all, if he could stretch an hour's worth of work into two days, that would be Wyatt all over.

Not that Kyle had any idea how much time it would actually take to fix whatever electrical issue Wyatt had found, but if it were truly extensive, even Wyatt was responsible enough to call in an actual electrician rather than try to mess around with it himself.

"I'll take our stuff to your cottage." Wendell had already given him the second key for the door. Sweet, but access to the same hotel room wasn't quite on the level of getting a key to a boyfriend's apartment. Or so Kyle assumed, since he'd never had that sort of relationship with anyone he was sleeping with. Drew didn't count, because they were like brothers.

Maybe one day.

They split up at the back door, Kyle heading down to the beach. He dropped his bag off at the cottage, and waited a few moments, staring at the information they'd compiled so far. But after a few minutes, he grew restless and returned to the inn.

There were sounds of activity in the library. Always the damn library. Kyle sucked in a breath and made himself go into the room. The chill in the room from the overactive air conditioner made him shiver.

"Wendell?"

But there was no one there.

"Are you going to start a fire?" Wyatt's voice behind Kyle made him jump.

"Fuck, Wyatt, don't scare me like that."

He turned around.

"Scare you? I've been talking to you since I walked in the room."

He had? Kyle tried to gesture dismissively, only to find the fire poker in his hand. He opened his fingers and it dropped to the floor with a clatter.

"What? Um... how?"

"Your bae fucked you senseless last night?" Wyatt asked.

Kyle blinked at him. He had zero recollection of picking up the poker, but Wyatt's use of the word "bae" went a long way to clearing his mind.

"Aren't you too old to use slang like that?" Because ew. Terrible slang, and he had no interest in discussing his sex life with Wyatt.

Wyatt shrugged. "Whatever."

"What are you doing in here?" Kyle asked.

The expression on Wyatt's face said he thought Kyle was asking a stupid question, but at least he didn't say so aloud. Who knew Wyatt was capable of rudimentary tact?

"I'm fixing the outlet. Remember? I needed some stuff I didn't have on hand. And I'm checking for other faults."

"Oh. Yes." Kyle stared down at the poker on the floor. He made himself squat down and pick it up.

No one would miss him.

Kyle slammed the poker back in its spot beside the hearth and darted back to the door.

Sure, there were a lot of people who thought most of the Drummonds were a waste of oxygen, but Drew would miss his brothers. And so would Kyle.

He didn't know why he was having such random, poisonous thoughts, but he was definitely going to have to find a therapist after Haunt Fest was over. Clearly the stress was getting to him.

Rubbing his chilled fingers together, Kyle stood well outside the library. Should he just head back to Wendell's cottage? Or try to find where he and Jackson had disappeared to?

He wasn't much interested in hanging out in Wendell's cottage by himself. Instead of fruitless searching, he sent Wendell a quick text.

Kyle: *Where u?*

The response came through with gratifying swiftness.

Wendell: *Jackson's*

Kyle: *B right there*

Kyle wasted no time getting over to Jackson's place. Jackson let him in, and guided him to the kitchen.

Sandra and Bill's house was tiny, but cozy. It was clearly a home, not part of the inn. But it was small. Not much bigger than Wyatt and Rob's mobile home. Then again, Drew's parents had more or less raised three boys in that mobile home, whereas this house only had to accommodate three people, Sandra, Bill, and their son, before he'd left for college out of state and stayed there.

Not that Kyle had any room to talk. His apartment now was the biggest space he'd ever lived in, after he'd left home, and it was itty bitty.

Jackson poured Kyle a cup of coffee without even asking, then plunked down in a kitchen chair. He waved a hand at Kyle to indicate he should also sit. Wendell was already seated, with a full cup of coffee. He smiled tiredly at Kyle.

"What happened? What did I miss?" Had Wendell mentioned anything about the box of photos? He'd thought they'd been in agreement about keeping Jackson in the dark, at least for now, but clearly something had altered Wendell's previously cheery mood.

Jackson ran a hand through his hair, making it stick up in all directions.

"Just been on the phone with Sandra. It was a really uncomfortable conversation, but we managed to convince her that she didn't need to come back," Jackson said with a sigh.

"Had she spoken to the police? Did they need her for some-thing?" Kyle asked.

Wendell shook his head. "The police had already told her that she didn't need to be here for any official purposes, but she was defi-nitely worried about us holding down the fort."

Jackson leaned back in his chair. "I'm worried about us holding down the fort too, but Sandra doesn't need to know that. She and Bill have enough on their plate right now."

"Is there anything I can help with?" Kyle asked.

Drew would be back in a few days, and despite the rapidly approaching Haunt Fest, Kyle would have more available time with Drew covering the store.

Jackson smiled wanly. "We've got guests checking in later today. Not to Chester's cottage thankfully. But we still have to gather up his personal effects and return them to Chester's next of kin. The police have had some difficulty locating them, unfortunately."

"Do you want us to work on that now?"

Jackson let out another sigh. "I should probably do it myself, but let's be real. I don't want to. I think that's obvious to both of you. And I really appreciate what you've done for me. I... well, I'm not in the best place right now, and frankly, I saw the situation here as a bit of an escape. I wasn't expecting this at all. But I can get a hold of myself and do it. Eventually."

Kyle flicked a glance at Wendell. He'd been blindsided by Chester's death, but not like Jackson had been. Kyle was almost a hundred percent certain Wendell would have an easier time with the job than Jackson would, especially with Kyle helping.

"Please don't force yourself to do it. I can take care of it." Wendell volunteered before Kyle could say anything.

"And I can help. It's not an issue. Does it need to be done before Haunt Fest?"

Jackson's jaw clenched and his eyes got shiny. He took a couple of deep breaths before he spoke. "Thank you both. I appreciate it. If it's done before Haunt Fest, Wendell, you won't have to move to the hotel for that one weekend. I can just assign out Chester's cottage to the guests who'd been originally slated to stay in Kelpie's Roost."

"Oh. Well." Wendell stared at Kyle. Kyle was pretty sure he was thinking about the easels and all the paper they'd posted around the cottage. Which might only get worse after today. "That would definitely be more convenient."

Kyle held back a snort of laughter. This definitely wasn't the time or place for merriment, especially since Jackson wasn't going to hear anything funny in Wendell's dry comment.

Then he got control of himself. "Then it's settled. Wendell and I will pack up Chester's belongings. Before Haunt Fest."

Kyle wasn't about to commit to an actual date before he'd had a chance to review his schedule with Wendell. But they'd shoehorn it in somewhere.

"Not today?" Jackson's good-natured smile let Kyle know they were off the hook.

"We can if you need us to."

Wendell nodded his agreement. "We are at your disposal."

Jackson shook his head. "No. It really isn't necessary. In fact, let me cover the new guests coming in. You have some fun today. Maybe go out for a nice dinner. Tomorrow will be soon enough for work. And the tourist crush will be on us before we know it. Take a break now, while you can."

"Are you sure?" Wendell asked.

Kyle didn't say a word, not about to stick his oar in now. Because this definitely wasn't his decision, even if he was already hoping for dinner at Flamingos. It was out of his price range, but Wendell had suggested it before, and Kyle shamelessly wanted to go.

"I'm sure. Wyatt said he'll be around most of the day, and if I need anything, I'll just rope him into it."

Kyle bit his lip to hide his amusement of the mental image of Wyatt in bondage at Jackson's feet. But he was really glad he'd coerced Wyatt into helping out at the inn.

"Okay then. We really appreciate it," Wendell said, and stood up.

Jackson shook his head. "Nope, you're doing me a big favor by clearing out Chester's room. This is the least I can do in return."

Kyle stood, and Jackson was right behind. After the tiny crucible of emotion they'd lived through, he felt a lot closer to Jackson than he'd ever have expected. At some point, he'd get Jackson to tell him exactly what went down with his husband. But for now, that wasn't what Jackson needed.

Instead, he threw his arms around Jackson and gave him a hug.

Jackson sputtered out a laugh, and hugged him back. "You have fun."

Kyle pulled back and winked. "Oh, we will."

Jackson rolled his eyes, but he was smiling, too. "Be good."

Kyle gasped and clutched his fists to his heart. "Never say so!"

Which got both Wendell and Jackson to laugh, which lightened the mood in the small bungalow tremendously.

"Go on. Get out of here before I get jealous. I'm going to check in with Wyatt, see if he needs any help."

Kyle and Wendell waited while Jackson locked up and walked with him along the path until it diverged, and Jackson headed to the inn while Kyle and Wendell walked hand in hand back to the cottage.

Wendell stretched, his spine cracking as he did so. He checked the time.

They'd been at this for hours, and Wendell was starving. They'd managed to work through lunch, which wasn't like him. And so far, despite his reluctance to say it aloud, there was truly only one conclusion to draw.

"Think we can get a reservation at Flamingos early enough to get you back here for your ghost tour?" Wendell should have asked earlier. This was going to be their last mostly relaxed night until, if all he'd been hearing was true, after Halloween. More than a month. It was shameful he'd let himself be distracted by photos, when Kyle was the most adorable man he'd come across in a long time. Sexy, sweet, smart, and for a change, interested in Wendell the person, not Wendell the conduit to a casting director.

"Ha. I booked it on my phone while we were still in Jackson's kitchen. We've got an hour to get ready."

"An hour? It won't take me an hour to get ready. We're not eating at Buckingham Palace."

Kyle snorted. "It might not take you an hour. But I've got some primping to do."

Wendell's heart warmed, and he tugged Kyle to him.

"You don't need to do any primping. You're perfect just like this."

Kyle's expression softened, and his cheeks pinked right up. Wendell kissed him.

"You know, an hour is definitely long enough for another activity."

Kyle's eyes narrowed. "You don't say. It takes a bit for me to primp, whether you think I need to or not."

"We could make it quick." Wendell wasn't sure if his hopeful tone would be enough to convince Kyle. Because changing his clothes and brushing his teeth wouldn't take nearly an hour.

Kyle tapped his lips thoughtfully. "Shower with me."

He'd already showered this morning at Kyle's, but that had been alone. Usually, in drought-stricken California, he'd feel too guilty to shower more than once a day, but here? With the prospect of a naked, wet, Kyle? He would shower all the damn day. There had to be a way to accomplish it without hurting themselves, right? His imagination, and other things, were up for the task.

"Sounds like a plan."

He followed Kyle into the bathroom like a compass needle aiming for magnetic north.

Wendell wandered out of the bedroom after Kyle had shooed him out, nearly thirty minutes and a cascade of water later. Sex and blowjobs weren't great in the shower, in his past experience, but hand jobs? They were mighty fine.

But it wasn't easy to focus on the pleasure while staring at the pages of information they'd compiled.

They'd spent hours combing through the internet, and found surprisingly little to add to the data they'd compiled from the photos and licenses. No social media accounts for anyone in that box, but given the age of the documents, that might not mean anything.

But they'd found very little else to go on. A few of them had been listed as missing, with family still wanting information about their loved ones' whereabouts. Last known destination? Sandy Bottom Bay for Haunt Fest.

Those were a very small percentage of the whole. The others were almost like they'd vanished without a trace. There were some paid services they could have signed up for, newspapers, databases, and the like. Wendell could have afforded the fees, no problem, but the effort to dig up information was excessive, for a random research project.

Or maybe not so random. Because there was now no doubt in his mind. Hell, there had been almost no doubt when he'd first laid eyes on those photographs. But even that tiny shred of hope that this was all perfectly innocent and normal had been eradicated by hours of chasing down a whole lot of nothing online.

Having birth dates and addresses should have made it easy, despite all of the licenses having been issued well prior to the availability of the internet. Or so he'd thought.

Now, he was having serious misgivings about having concealed this from Jackson and the police. And he had a newfound respect for detective work. It was fucking hard. Police databases might make things easier, but wow, this wasn't nearly as interesting as the research he normally did for his scripts.

Kyle came up behind him.

"They're all dead, aren't they?" he asked.

Wendell sighed. "Yes. I think so."

He didn't state the obvious, but he was going to have to call the police. Because these people weren't just dead. They'd been murdered.

And he'd have to let Jackson know about the impending shit show that would undoubtedly follow. But it didn't have to be tonight. Since he'd already waited this long, maybe it could wait until after Haunt Fest. Maybe. He'd have to think about it, but not now.

He turned around, and sucked in a breath. "You look amazing."

Kyle had made the most of his primping time. Eyeliner lined his eyes, traces of glitter highlighted his features, lips were glossy and a rosy shade deeper than Kyle's normal lip color. His clothes were tight enough Wendell wasn't sure he could breathe—Wendell certainly couldn't catch any air in his lungs.

"Thank you." Kyle's smile faded as he glanced over Wendell's shoulder. "I feel a little guilty, though, getting ready to go out and have a good time."

Wendell picked up his hand, and threaded their fingers together.

"We can't do anything for them right now. If nothing else, this tells us that life is short, and we need to live it while we can."

Kyle's attention returned to Wendell, and he met Wendell's gaze. "I guess you're right."

Wendell cupped Kyle's cheeks and planted a ghost of a kiss on those shiny lips. No sense mussing up Kyle's careful make up job until later, in bed.

"Try to put this out of your mind. We're going to eat, have a good time, then you're going to lead your ghost tour and I'm going to go along."

"You're going to come? Tonight? That's great!"

Wendell smiled. He was looking forward to it, because he was starting to suspect that his inspiration for his next script was going to come from Kyle, not Sandy Bottom Bay, or even the sad box of photos. So, he might as well be wherever Kyle was going to be. And it had nothing to do with his growing feelings for the man.

Okay, of course it did. But there was no reason he couldn't get a little inspiration from the man he was rapidly coming to care for. In fact, it made it all the better, in his opinion. And after Haunt Fest was over, he was almost certain he'd be ready to tackle a new script.

"C'mon. We don't want to miss our reservation."

It would be great to have a pleasant, low key evening.

TWENTY

15 Days to Haunt Fest

KYLE SMILED at the big group gathered on the Orange Lady's porch. He was the tiniest bit out of breath, because he and Wendell had gotten so caught up in their conversation over dinner that they ended up running late. Kyle was sure he could talk to Wendell forever.

The sex was awesome, too. Wendell was the whole package.

He'd had to dash through some overgrown palm fronds on the little-used path along the side of the building to get to Wendell's cottage, because some of his tour patrons had already begun to gather, and he didn't want them to see him out of costume. Sure, it wasn't an elaborate costume, but nevertheless, it wasn't something he cared to do.

Fortunately, his makeup only needed slight modification from what he'd worn to dinner, and then a quick change into his pirate-esque garb.

Then back through the inn, and out the front door. Which was the first time he'd actually done that for a tour. He'd only had a chance to wave at Jackson and flip the bird at Wyatt's snide remark about a butt pirate before he'd swooped outside to make his grand entrance. Much more dramatic. He was a fan.

Wendell had joined the group milling about on the porch, which had grown to a small crowd while he'd been changing. His messenger bag was positively bulging with cookies from Lisa's bakery, and he handed them out to everyone, along with his regular spiel about the Lady.

Normally he did a little more of an introduction about himself and the festival and the town, but just in case anyone had read about Chester's death, he didn't want to give any potential sensation-seekers the opportunity to ask about it.

He hustled them off the porch as quick as he could, then headed toward their first stop, the founder's residence. On the way, he gave his usual plug for Drew's shop, but it was quick, because despite Drew's extraordinary new talents as a psychic, this was a ghost tour. Last he looked, ghosts and psychics were unrelated.

"Here we are at the founder's residence. Sandy Bottom Bay was settled by a group of sailors who'd run aground on the rocky shoals just north of town. Samuel Blunt, considered to be their nominal leader, built this fine home the year after the town was established in 1836. Some say they were actual pirates on the run from justice in the Caribbean, and Samuel Blunt their pirate captain."

There weren't exactly gasps of shock in the crowd, but Kyle loved how even the mention of pirates got a pleased reaction from every tour group. He gave a jaunty little swing of his hips in what he hoped was a swashbuckling fashion. Perhaps he ought to invest in a fake sword to really sell the pirateness of it all.

"There is some circumstantial evidence to support the idea. Piracy was on the wane in the 1830s, due to vigilant naval activity. Any pirate wanting to save their skin might want to consider a new career. Additionally, there is no official record of the ship that suppos-edly crashed on the rocks. Some historians claim it was really the pirate ship Annihilation, and Samuel Blunt was really its captain, Black-hearted Barney. And of course, this group of sailors had a lot of funds to put into building their town, far more than you'd expect."

The crowd shuffled a bit, and Wendell smiled encouragingly.

"Sandy Bottom Bay Historical Society has refurbished the founder's residence as it would have appeared when it was originally built by Samuel Blunt. But he did not get to live in it for long. As you might imagine, a town founded by pirates did not have many marriage prospects. They utilized the tradition of mail order brides. One of Samuel's men was jealous of both Samuel's new bride and his status in the town, and believed if he got rid of Samuel, he could step right into both roles."

Kyle paused briefly to let the anticipation amp up.

"Late one night, the man snuck into Samuel's house. Samuel didn't go quietly, and both men died. It is said that you can sometimes see them fighting in the upstairs window."

Kyle waved a hand, with a dramatic flourish, at the window in question, in the main bedroom upstairs. If this story was true, poor Mrs. Blunt had been woken out of a sound sleep to find her husband and another man fighting to the death right beside the bed. He shuddered.

"What happened to the wife?" One of the guests asked.

"Was Samuel's pirate treasure ever found?" Another asked.

"Glad you asked. Samuel Blunt's treasure was never found. But Mrs. Blunt returned to her northern home a very wealthy widow. If her husband had kept any of the treasure in his home, she found it, and kept it as her inheritance. If there was a treasure, Blunt's share is undoubtedly gone."

There were a few more questions, and Kyle rattled off the times people could tour the founder's residence. Most of the historical venues on his route weren't open by the time his ghost walk started.

After he told the group which direction they were going next, he let them begin shuffling along. Over time he'd discovered that the leaders of the pack were eager and unlikely to stray or get lost. It was the slow pokes and stragglers he had to worry about. They were all adults, or accompanied by adults, of course, but if people got lost or left behind it had a detrimental effect on his online reviews.

A flicker of light caught his attention and he glanced up at the haunted window.

As the hairs on the back of his neck stood up, he gasped. It wasn't a light he'd seen, but the pale image of a man. Two men. Fighting.

The quartet in front of him stopped, and one of guys said, "What?"

Kyle glanced away.

"Did you see that?" Kyle asked before he could stop himself.

As one, the four tour guests twisted to look up at the window again, and one of the women tittered nervously.

"There's nothing there," the other woman said.

Kyle clenched one hand into a fist and forced himself to look back. They were right. The window was as blank and dark as it always was on his tours. He pulled in a deep breath, trying to slow his racing heart as clandestinely as possible.

"Better luck next time," he said, forcing a lightness into his tone.

"Good one, man," one of the guys said. Kyle hurried them along, more than ready to leave the founder's residence behind. He resolutely did not look back.

Alongside the old cemetery, with its moss-covered headstones, Kyle moved through the group so that he was once more at the head.

Wendell gave him a quizzical look, but Kyle shook his head, and continued with his spiel. He heard the quartet whispering quietly with some of the other guests. Hopefully not about his impending madness.

"Beyond the cemetery is the ruins of the old church, dedicated to St. Brendan, one of the patron saints of sailors. The church was commissioned by the founders in 1842, but burned to the ground in 1912. It was relocated several blocks east, but the rectory, which was unscathed by the fire, is now a local history museum."

Kyle mentioned a few notable early residents of Sandy Bottom

Bay who now resided in the old cemetery, and the hours of the museum. He resolutely did not focus on the graves, for fear of seeing another apparition. To think he'd long wanted to see a ghost. Now that he maybe was, it was awful. Because he wasn't sure if he was developing a mental illness or if he believed he was truly seeing spirits. And right now, he was still hoping it was an aberration brought on by stress.

"Further beyond, along a curve in the coastline, is the lighthouse. It was not erected by the founders, but it was built as a warning beacon for the very same shoals the founders ran aground on. It is also said to be haunted, by one of the lighthouse keepers who went mad and committed suicide."

And the least said about that the better, at the moment. Fortunately, he was well used to modifying his presentation to fit the audience. This time, however, he was modifying it to suit his own rattled imagination.

"There are also tours of the lighthouse during the day, although it was decommissioned several years ago with the ready availability of radar and sonar."

"Are we going to walk by there now?" One of the teens accompanying their family asked.

"No. I know it looks not too far away, but the appearance is deceptive. It's quite a long hike from here, and there's not much to see in the dark."

They talked a bit more about pirates, and where treasure could possibly have been hidden—a much more benign topic of conversation for his state of mind, and he was glad to play right into that. All groups were different. Some of his audiences would have pressed for more macabre details about the suicide or mysterious deaths or other hauntings that weren't on the tour, but this group was more into the pirate aspect. And he couldn't be more grateful.

An hour later, they arrived at the final stop on the tour. And the only location still open for the tour guests. Entirely intentional.

"This is the old saloon. As far as we know this is one of the oldest buildings in Sandy Bottom Bay, and likely the most popular."

As expected, that got him a few laughs.

"There are said to be a number of ghosts haunting the premises, whether it be because they died in bar fights or because they just couldn't face an afterlife without alcohol, but please feel free to go in and try some locally brewed root beer, a close cousin to the sassafras root beverage that might have been served here back in the day. They also have an alcoholic version, for those of you wanting a little more kick in your soda."

That got him more scattered laughs, and he gave his farewell speech and collected cash tips from several tour guests.

Thank all the stars in the sky that he'd done this tour hundreds of times and could recite the basics in his sleep, because he had no fucking memory of stopping at the apothecary, the clock tower or the old jail and courthouse. Based on the time, however, he must have continued on his tour as normal, because this was the usual time he offloaded the guests at the saloon.

But there was a blank in his mind during the last hour. Sure, he often did his tour by rote, but this didn't feel quite the same. Especially since there was one major difference this time—Wendell. Who was hanging back until Kyle had answered the last of the questions, and saw the final group of guests head into the saloon.

Wendell came up next to him. "That was great. I loved it. But is everything okay?"

"Um, why do you ask?"

"You just seem a little shaken? Upset? I don't think anyone else noticed. Did I throw you off by being here?"

"No. Not at all." Wendell was a safe place. He'd become one surprisingly fast, but Kyle couldn't deny the truth of that. He stepped closer and let Wendell pull him in close. He snuggled in.

"Shit, you're freezing." Wendell rubbed his hands along Kyle's back. "I can't believe you got cold on that walk. Even after dark it's still a lot warmer than I would have ever expected."

Kyle hadn't realized how chilled he was, not until Wendell wrapped him in the firebrands masquerading as strong, solid arms.

He couldn't stop the trembling, but he was sure Wendell had attributed it to temperature, not fear. Because he was starting to think something was very wrong, and he didn't know what. He couldn't think of any way to ask what had happened without exposing the giant glitch in his brain.

The worst thing? He wasn't going to have time to deal with any of this, not until after Haunt Fest. Maybe not even until after Halloween. Even then it would be tricky, but he definitely needed to make an appointment with a doctor.

He stayed in Wendell's embrace, and concentrated on his breathing, trying to get his heart rate back under control.

Between his decision to talk to a doctor and some deep, calming breaths, it didn't take too long before he was, well, less rattled. Enough so that he could take a stab at normalcy.

He hoped his brain wouldn't glitch this bad again until he could see a professional.

"Did you want to go inside, rest up, maybe get a drink?" Wendell asked.

Kyle took a deep breath, and stepped back. "No, I don't go into the saloon after. No one local drinks there. It's really aimed at tourists, and it's just a little weird to hang out there with the tour group after the tour is over. No one really knows how to interact. Do they invite me to drink with them? Do they ignore me? Do they bombard me with questions until last call? It can get awkward fast."

Wendell grinned at him. "I take it you didn't always have that rule."

Kyle let out a faint chuckle. "You are right. But I learned fast. And the saloon is very kitschy. It's too over the top." Then he laughed for real. "I find it too much competition."

Wendell smiled widely. "You're not too over the top for me."

The sincerity of those words hit him right in the gut. There had been more than one guy who'd thought Kyle was too much. Too loud, too camp, too gay, too whatever. True, he did like being the center of attention, but he was pretty sure he could lay that at his parents' door. With their chronic indifference, he'd spent a lot of his formative years waving the metaphorical flag trying to get their attention, and failing that, anyone's attention. Now, it was just a part of who he was, and the fact that Wendell might even like it? Not a bad thing.

Drew appreciated that Kyle's nature often kept him out of the limelight, and Kyle suspected Wendell might be of the same mind.

"So, what now?" Wendell asked.

"Maybe we can call it a night? I'm a little tired." Not necessarily physically tired, but it had been a difficult couple of weeks, and it was only going to ramp up. He'd be tired even if he wasn't losing his fucking mind.

"Sure thing." Wendell shuffled a bit, and wouldn't quite meet his eyes.

"What?" The question came out a little sharper than he intended. "Sorry. I..."

"It's okay, Kyle. You're tired. I just wasn't sure if you wanted go back to your apartment tonight. Like, alone."

Silly man. "I would like to sleep in my own bed tonight." The mattress wasn't better than the one in Wendell's cottage, but it was familiar and comfortable.

"Sure."

Kyle rolled his eyes. "But I don't want to sleep there alone."

"Oh. Oh!" Wendell finally met his gaze, and smiled again.

"C'mon, let's go."

SCREAMING SHATTERED Wendell's pleasant dream just after midnight and sent him bolting out of bed.

It took him a split second to realize where he was—Kyle's bedroom—and another moment to figure out who had screamed —Kyle.

The screaming stopped but Kyle started thrashing about, muttering about blood.

However awful this nightmare looked to Wendell, it had to be much worse for Kyle.

Wendell bounced back on the bed and tried to hold Kyle still. It was like cuddling a bucking bronco, but Wendell did his best.

"Kyle, wake up. It's a dream. Just a dream. Everything is okay." Wendell kept up the litany for several seconds before Kyle started to quiet. His face was slick with sweat, and he opened his eyes to look at Wendell.

"A person has a lot of blood in them," he murmured, eyes glazed and not entirely focused.

"It's okay. No one is bleeding." Wendell rubbed his arms soothingly along Kyle's back. Before long, Kyle's muscles relaxed and he fell back asleep curled against Wendell.

It took a lot longer for Wendell to find sleep again. He well knew how much blood a person had in them. It had been one of the first things he'd researched for his first script. When they'd started shooting, he'd wanted to show a victim fully exsanguinated. But the one-and-a-half-gallon pool of artificial blood had looked unbelievably massive, even to a bunch of people intending to film a horror movie, so they'd reduced the quantity.

But he'd never forgotten that wide pool. Unfortunately, he could only think of one reason why Kyle might be dreaming of blood. And it wasn't a residual from the ghost walk.

Wendell had been extremely selfish wanting to keep those photos out of the hands of law enforcement. He'd had misgivings almost immediately, but had quashed them in favor of trying to light a fire under his muse.

Kyle might live in a town dedicated to the paranormal. He might conduct ghost tours a few times a week. He might adore horror movies and watch murder mystery shows. But deep down, he was likely able to rationalize it as fiction.

The cigar box wasn't fiction. The cigar box represented real people. Real people who had probably died violently at the hands of another person. It was affecting Kyle adversely, and Wendell had been blind not to see it. When Kyle had zoned out partway through the ghost tour last night—although Wendell was probably the only one who'd noticed he'd lost some vivaciousness—that should have been a big clue as well.

Chester's death alone would have been hard enough for most people to deal with, never mind adding in the cigar box. Hell, Wendell had been burying some of his emotional responses too. And it wasn't fair to subject Kyle to something that preyed on his mind in this way.

Not if he wanted to keep seeing Kyle. Wendell wasn't going to be responsible for breaking his new boyfriend, that's for sure. He wanted to cherish Kyle for as long as he could.

Which meant he had some work to do, while Kyle was teaching his tot ballet at the community center in the morning.

With that decision made, Wendell's mind settled enough to let him slip back asleep.

TWENTY-ONE

14 Days to Haunt Fest

WHEN KYLE'S phone alarm woke them both up in the morning, Wendell grumbled a bit, but propped himself up on one elbow and gazed at Kyle.

Kyle stretched and wiggled a bit, drawing Wendell's eye down his lithe frame.

"Like what you see, big boy?" Kyle asked with a laugh.

"You know I do," Wendell replied and leaned over to give him a quick kiss.

Kyle deepened it a bit, but his secondary alarm went off and he pulled back, nose wrinkling in irritation.

"I guess we don't have time for anything fun this morning." Kyle's mouth shaped a delicate pout, something Wendell never would have imagined would fire his libido, but it might have been because Kyle was more genuine than any wannabe actor who'd ever tried the look on him.

"Sadly, no. Not if you don't want to disappoint your tots."

Kyle sat up. "No, I don't want to do that. It's their last ballet class until November, and I can't disappoint them." He smiled fondly, and then got out of bed and headed to the bathroom.

Not that he'd ever expected to think this in his life, but Wendell was glad they didn't have time to have sex. He was also glad he'd suggested just going to sleep last night. Kyle hadn't mentioned his disturbed sleep, but the shadows under his eyes told the story. Ideally, Kyle would find some time for a nap today, but if that didn't happen, they'd just have to hit the sheets earlier tonight. For sleep.

Kyle's obvious exhaustion only solidified Wendell's determination to clear out Chester's room on his own, then talk to Jackson about the cigar box. Hopefully, Wendell would also be able to get all the research he and Kyle had done packed away before Kyle finished with his tot ballet class.

Maybe he could even talk to Drew, as soon he returned, for ideas on how to lighten Kyle's workload.

For now, Wendell got dressed and made Kyle his favorite breakfast of fruit and yogurt. Wendell made himself some too, but he'd definitely be picking over the leftovers at the inn when he got there. Lisa's baked goods were too tasty to forego. Also, he didn't love yogurt, but eating it made him feel a bit healthier, and it made Kyle happier when he ate better.

The pleased expression on Kyle's face, and the adorable smile made it all worth it.

"You are just the sweetest man. You spoil me." Kyle kissed him, and Wendell basked in his approval. The fact that such a simple thing made Kyle so effusive made him angry that Kyle hadn't been pampered by anyone before.

For a long time, Wendell had assumed being single was what his future held. He hadn't known Kyle long, but he could picture eating breakfast with this man for the rest of his life. He wanted that. There was something ineffable about Kyle that just made Wendell complete.

A lot would depend on his muse and if it decided to cooperate, but so far, his time in Sandy Bottom Bay had been the best days of his life. If the coming weeks were as fulfilling, he would have to give some serious thought to sticking around.

Less than an hour later, Wendell was back at the inn, master key in hand, standing inside Chester's cottage.

Daisy had cleaned the cottage the day Chester had died, so there wasn't anything gross or stinky in the room. Just an odd air of emptiness and the normal contents of a vacation suitcase or two spread throughout the living area and the bedroom.

First thing Wendell did was sweep the curtains open to their fullest extent. The bright Florida sunshine dispelled the gloom. Since the cottage was almost identical to Wendell's, his perception of gloom was likely all in his head, but it still made him feel better.

He started with Chester's clothes, packing them carefully into the two suitcases, and separating out items that would likely require laundering. Jackson hadn't mentioned if the inn would do that before returning Chester's belongings to the next of kin. Maybe because Jackson hadn't even thought about it. Wendell certainly hadn't. Not until this very moment.

It was humbling in a way Wendell would never have imagined, the knowledge that one day, someone would have to sort through one's underwear and dirty laundry. That someone else would learn all your secrets, whether you want them to or not. And perhaps with no control over just who learned all those things.

He hoped that wherever Chester was now, he didn't mind that Wendell was the one sifting through the remnants of his life.

From clothing, he then proceeded to the toiletries and medications. There were a lot. Unsurprisingly, he supposed. His parents took a number of meds, and his grandmother even more. Part of aging.

All of it went into the bag specifically designed for such things.

Finally, the only things left were the things Chester loved. Books, puzzles, a couple of magazines. Chester's e-reader was already in Jackson's care, as it had been with Chester in the library. There was also a cell phone, which surprised Wendell as he'd never seen Chester with it. He wasn't sure he could ever be parted from his own, and he sort of envied Chester's ability to just leave his phone in his room. Unplugging in a way Wendell didn't know if he'd ever be able to accomplish.

The book that sat on the bedside table was a history of Florida. Unlike the other books he'd gathered, this one had a bookmark. A photo.

Although his personal connection to this tragedy had tempered his natural curiosity, it spiked when he saw the worn edge of the photo. Was it a picture of Chester's late husband?

Wendell couldn't resist. He pulled it out of the book, noting immediately it had probably been taken by a 35mm camera. He also noted it was old. From the seventies, based on the clothes of the two men centered in the photo. After all the internet research he and Kyle had done recently, he was starting to feel a bit like an expert on the seventies.

Chester had had dark brown eyes, and it was easy to see his attractive features on the young, dark-haired man on the left. Then Wendell turned his attention to the image of a younger blond man, and a third man, appearing just beyond the blond's shoulder.

A chill swept through Wendell, head to toe.

He'd seen both of those faces before. In the cigar box. He turned the photo over. In faded script, someone had written "me and Sam Kerwin, 1973".

Wendell could barely breathe. He knew that name, too. He just hadn't made the connection when he'd found Sam's license in the cigar box. When he and Chester had chatted about Chester's reasons for visiting Sandy Bottom Bay, he'd mentioned a man who'd changed his life. Sam Kerwin. Who he'd never seen again after that trip. Never heard from again.

Without social media, Wendell hadn't thought that all that momentous. Neither had Chester, obviously, based on the fond way he'd spoken about Sam.

But the man in the background of this photo, and all the Polaroids in Wendell's safe told a much more sinister story.

With trembling fingers, Wendell pulled up the pictures he'd taken of their "evidence" on his phone. It took a bit of scrolling before he found the one he was after. There was no doubt in his mind. Same two men.

Chester was fucking lucky he'd had the chance to make his move to San Francisco and live his truth, because Sam sure as shit hadn't had that opportunity. Poor bastard.

Wendell sat on the edge of the bed and stared at the photo for a little longer. The dark-haired man—the stranger—was more clear in this photo, despite the fact he wasn't the focal point of the picture. Chester's camera had been of a much better quality than the instant camera.

He didn't much care for the look in the stranger's eyes. If he'd come across that guy in a bar, he'd have avoided him like a horde of dermestid beetles. He shuddered. That guy was trouble, in all capital letters.

After carefully setting the photo on the dresser, Wendell snapped a quick picture of it on his phone, then quickly finished packing up the rest of Chester's gear. Fortunately, Chester hadn't used the safe, because it would have been a bitch to get that open without knowing the right code.

He slid Chester's photo into his shirt's breast pocket, moved Chester's two suitcases outside, then let the door close and lock behind him.

He stopped briefly by his own cottage to add the purloined photo to his stash in his safe. This provided another compelling reason to turn the cigar box over to the authorities. While it might not be concrete proof of misdeeds, not by a long shot, hopefully the police would see it in the same light as Wendell had. Chester's photo had erased the last of Wendell's lingering doubts.

If the cops didn't charge him with obstruction or something, it would be a miracle.

But before he did anything drastic, he needed to talk to Jackson.

Wendell found Jackson bickering with Wyatt in the dining room. Was this going to be a regular occurrence? The gist of their spat seemed to be over something besides the electrical outlet that Wyatt had been working on, but Wendell didn't have the brain space to care.

"Jackson, we have to talk."

Jackson jumped and turned. "Oh, Wendell, you scared me. What's up?" He gave Wyatt an exasperated look before he walked toward Wendell. Wyatt rolled his eyes in response, and stared avidly at the two of them, clearly not about to give them any sort of privacy.

And Wendell didn't want anyone else knowing how badly he'd fucked up.

"Can we talk? Privately?"

Jackson gave Wendell an uncertain look before he nodded. "Let's go to the office." Jackson turned back to Wyatt. "Don't do anything while I'm gone."

Wyatt rolled his eyes again, but poured himself a cup of coffee from the all-day carafe and dropped heavily into a seat.

Jackson sighed, and led the way down the hall.

In the office, they sat on the two chairs. It made the small room feel even smaller, but it wasn't meant for leisure.

"How are you doing? Getting along with Wyatt okay?" After Kyle had explained his relationship to Wyatt, Wendell had thought a little irritation might be good for Jackson. Wake him up a bit. But he could have been wrong about that. He wasn't a psychologist or anything.

Jackson huffed out a sound that might have been part laugh, part exasperated sigh.

"Wyatt's fine. Annoying at times, but he's been good company, actually. And he's fixed a number of things that Sandra had put on the back burner after Bill got sick. So that's been good, too. Although I'll have to be careful not to subject the guests to him. He's a bit... brusque."

That made Wendell laugh, in spite of the heavy weight on his shoulders. "I don't know him well, but that seems an apt description."

There were a few moments of silence as Wendell pondered the best way to broach the subject.

"What did you want to talk about?" Jackson asked, a little fearful. "You're not... leaving, are you? Because I don't know if I can make it through Haunt Fest without help. I can pay you."

Now Wendell felt like shit. He hadn't meant to scare Jackson. He grasped Jackson's hands and squeezed gently.

"Please don't worry about that. I am here to help, and I'm here through the end of November." At the very least.

Jackson's shoulders sagged. "Oh good."

Wendell let go of Jackson's hands and sat back in the seat. Time to rip off the bandage.

"It's still not good, I'm afraid." He proceeded to tell Jackson what they'd found in the library, and what they'd discovered about it since. And about the photo he'd found in Chester's room.

Jackson's eyes widened more and more as Wendell spoke.

"So, I think we need to call the police in. I mean, I always did think that, but I was hoping to delay until after Haunt Fest. But I'm starting to think it needs to be now."

The recitation of the facts didn't include Kyle's odd demeanor during last night's ghost tour, nor his nightmare. Given Jackson's serious expression, Wendell didn't think he needed to pile on the additional substantiation.

They stared at each other following the end of Wendell's story. Then Jackson sighed.

"Can I see it? I mean, I think you're probably right, but I'm assuming this will require a full-scale police investigation. I'm almost certain there isn't a statute of limitations for murder, and if I'm understanding you correctly, you think everyone who has a picture in that cigar box has been murdered. I don't... shit, I don't want to cause Sandra and Bill any more undue stress, but this is a big fucking deal."

Wendell blinked. He wasn't sure he'd heard Jackson swear like that thus far, which only emphasized how much he'd thrown Jackson for a loop.

Unless he'd picked up some bad habits from Wyatt, who was definitely no stranger to foul language.

"Let's go." Wendell wanted this done before Kyle finished up with his tots and other errands. Sooner it was out of the cottage, sooner it would stop freaking out his boyfriend.

When they stepped back out into the hallway, Jackson glanced guiltily around, like he feared someone had overheard their discussion. But without a soul was in sight, they quickly made their way to Wendell's cottage.

They stepped inside, and despite the morning sun, the cottage was shrouded in darkness. Wendell had made sure to close all the blinds and drapes before he'd left. He had not wanted any curious passerby to peek in.

As soon as Wendell flicked on the overhead lights, Jackson gasped.

"You weren't kidding about this, were you?"

Wendell had to admit it was a bit startling, even when it wasn't his first glance. Photocopies of licenses plastered all over the walls, sticky notes with scribbled text stuck around and below each one. It did look very much like a conspiracy theorist's lair, like many Wendell had seen in movies. Perhaps that had been more of an influence than he'd realized. He didn't even know if real detectives worked like this.

In his own scripts, real law enforcement either got killed off at the beginning, or didn't get involved until the final credits. He'd never had a reason to research investigative procedure.

"This is... appalling," Jackson whispered. He didn't seem to expect a reply, but Wendell agreed.

He'd just let the decades between the crimes and current events dull the horror to the point he'd indulged his curiosity. Which was stupid. The sooner this got turned over to the police, the sooner the families of these people would find out what happened to their loved ones.

Jackson peered at the various notes and bits of research while Wendell looked on.

"Can I see the photos?"

Wendell nodded. He opened his safe, then pulled on another pair of latex gloves before he pulled out the cigar box. Jackson raised his eyebrows, but he too pulled on some gloves.

"No sense destroying any more evidence than we have already, I suppose," Jackson said wryly.

Shit. He'd definitely screwed up. But at least Jackson was joining forces with them, more or less, if his use of the word "we" was any indication.

Or perhaps Jackson's curiosity was also getting the better of him. Wendell certainly couldn't blame him for that.

Jackson first looked at Chester's photo, then flipped through the rest of them. He didn't bother with the licenses at all. He paused a bit longer on the photo where the one guy looked like Kyle. It gave Wendell a queasy sensation in his gut, and he hated looking at it. But he knew the guy's name. Lars Eriksson. A name as Nordic as his looks.

At least Jackson didn't make the obvious comment, as Wendell had done. And whatever basis this guy had used to... collect photos, it hadn't been on appearance. Aside from general age, which had all been late teens and early twenties, there wasn't a specific physical type or gender represented.

Jackson looked at a few pictures, then stopped on the one with Sam Kerwin for an extra moment, before taking a look at the rest.

With reverence, he placed them back into the cigar box, then flung himself on the couch while Wendell put the whole thing back into the safe.

When he turned back, Jackson already had his phone out and was texting someone.

"The police here have a texting option?"

"No, not really. I texted Scott. Hunter."

Wendell's expression had to show every bit of his confusion.

Jackson's cheeks pinked up a bit. "He's a friend. I've known him for a while. When my husband and I used to come down here together."

Wendell spared a moment to wonder if Scott was the person Jackson had met for dinner on his first night. If so, he didn't see why Jackson hadn't mentioned it, but that wasn't any of his business.

"Is he coming?" Wendell sat down in the chair, leaving the small two-person couch to Jackson.

"He said he'd be over right away."

They sat in silence, although Jackson's gaze kept skimming the pictures around the room. Wendell didn't know how long "right away" meant, but Sandy Bottom Bay wasn't that large.

Wendell wanted to turn on the television, just to break the heavy silence, but that didn't fit in with the seriousness of what was about to happen.

Nevertheless, he hoped Scott was nearby.

TWENTY-TWO

14 Days to Haunt Fest

A BRISK KNOCK startled them out of their lethargy. Jackson leapt up and raced for the door. He opened the door for Sandy Bottom Bay officer Scott Hunter, in full regalia.

"Are you okay?" Scott scanned Jackson intently, as though searching for wounds or bruises.

"I'm fine. Fine."

"Then what was so urgent?"

Jackson frowned, then swept an arm around to indicate the room.

Scott looked up, and took in Wendell's research.

"Holy fu-, I mean what is this?" He stepped fully into the room. "This is fu- I mean, this is messed up."

Scott's attempts to clean up his language gave Wendell the urge to giggle, but it was likely only the stress of the situation that made him want to start laughing.

"Where did all this come from?"

"Me. Well, sort of," Wendell replied. Which got him the full force of Scott's intense glare. This was not the same affable man he'd met in the bakery.

"You did this, you say. And why would you do such a thing?" Scott's voice was hard, suspicious, hand lowering a trifle closer to his sidearm.

Wendell blinked, frozen by the unexpected menace.

Jackson, however, was not similarly ossified. He whacked Scott on the bicep with the back of his hand.

"Dial it down, and listen. Wendell should have called you earlier, but this is something you need to know, not something he did. Got it?"

"Jackson, what the hell?" Scott wasn't happy, but the threatening tension had evaporated. Wendell drew in a deep breath, stomach just a bit fluttery.

That could have escalated fast, and in a fucking scary way.

"You can't jump to conclusions, you should know that by now."

Scott closed his eyes in exasperation. "Fine, yes, but you brought me to what looks like serial killer central. What the hell is all this?"

Wendell cleared his throat, and started to speak, with more of a waver in his voice than he'd like.

"Kyle found a box in the library."

"In the library? Then what are we doing here? And where is Kyle right now?"

"Scott." Jackson's voice was sharp and scolding. "Sit down and be quiet."

Wendell bit the inside of his cheek to keep from grinning at the way Scott slumped down on the couch, like a teenager who'd gotten scolded by dad. And just like that, the man he'd met in the bakery banished the hardened cop.

"Please continue. I'll save my questions for the end." Scott gestured for him to go on.

"We were cleaning the library after Chester was taken away. Kyle found a loose section at the base of a bookcase, and inside was this incredibly dusty cigar box."

Scott's skepticism was palpable, although he stayed true to his word and didn't say anything.

"I mean, at first it didn't seem like anything bad. It had a bunch of old drivers licenses in it."

Scott glanced at the papers Wendell had plastered on the walls, and although he clearly had questions, he held them in.

"Forty-three. All different people, and from a variety of states. Weird, right? But we both sort of thought we might have been jumping to conclusions. I'm a writer of horror stories, and Kyle, um, seems to love murder shows." Paranormal or otherwise.

Scott snorted out a laugh. "That's the truth."

Wendell smiled. "Yeah, so we got kind of caught up in the mystery of it, aware we could be making something out of nothing. But below the licenses was an envelope with Polaroids in it. Forty-three. Each one features two people. One matching a license, the other is a man with dark hair, the same in every photo. And in case there was any doubt, a name matching the license was written on the photo."

Scott sat up straight. "Are you kidding me? This isn't some prank Kyle has cooked up, right?"

"I wish it was. Because it was kind of fun, until we concluded that those forty-three people had probably been murdered."

"Who was the man in the photo? The one who was in all the photos?"

Wendell shrugged. "No idea. I mean, he was probably in his thirties, although it's hard to tell. But those licenses are all from the seventies and early eighties. Kyle didn't recognize the guy, but that doesn't mean anything. He could be an eighty-year-old dude by now. And there's no guarantee he lives or ever lived in Sandy Bottom Bay."

Scott had apparently thought the time to be silent was over, but that was okay. He also no longer thought Wendell was a threat, and that was the most important part.

"That's something for the police to decide."

"Of course," Wendell agreed. "It's just that a number of the photos seem to have been taken in the area. Which I would think indicates residence, or at least, frequent visitation."

Scott scrubbed his hands over his face.

"Let me look at these pictures, because you're suggesting there was a serial killer operating in Sandy Bottom Bay and no one knew. Which is a pretty big fucking deal."

"Um, gloves?" Wendell offered him the box of latex gloves.

Scott glared. "Does this mean this evidence, if it is indeed evidence, is uncontaminated?" His voice had hardened again, just a bit.

"What is wrong now?" Jackson didn't bother hiding his exasperation.

"Because, Jackson, they figured whatever this was might be important enough to wear gloves, but they still mucked around with it instead of calling the authorities."

Wendell's cheeks flushed. It was a truth he couldn't deny, but he had to answer Scott's question.

"Sorry, Scott. We both suspected there might be evidence you'd need, but not before we'd both touched a bunch of things with our bare hands. But I bought the gloves to minimize any further damage."

"Uh huh. From continued touching." The censure in Scott's tone was clear.

"I'm sorry." There was nothing else to say, was there? They'd been in the wrong, and deep down, Wendell had known it. He suspected Kyle did too, which had only contributed to his odd behavior over the past couple of days.

Scott sighed and pulled on a pair of gloves. "Never mind that. Let's see what you've got."

Wendell opened the safe and handed Scott the photo he'd retrieved from Chester's and explained who Sam Kerwin was, and the significance of the photo.

"Anecdotal evidence of a disappearance. Not concrete, but it's suggestive." Scott peered at the dark-haired man in the background, who wasn't Chester. "I don't recognize this guy either, but as you say, there are reasons I might not."

He set the photo down carefully on the coffee table and made grabby hands for the box. Wendell handed it over.

Jackson paced as Scott sifted through the contents, and Wendell sat on the chair, unable to tear his gaze away.

After several moments, he dropped the photos back in the box.

"Jesus fucking Christ." Apparently guarding his tongue was no longer a priority. Scott looked up at Wendell. "I think you're right. What the fuck? You should have called this in earlier."

"Yes, I should have. And I'm sorry. But there's already been so much chaos, and it's just getting busier. Adding this into the mix is only going to making things harder for everyone."

"You've got that right." Scott stripped off his gloves with a snap and dropped them on the table. "I'm calling in backup, and we're taking all this into custody."

Wendell wanted to protest, but in reality, he'd suspected it was a possibility.

"And where is Kyle?"

"That's what I'd fucking like to know," Wyatt said angrily from the door. "What did you do to him, you bastard?"

Wendell stood up. "What are you talking about?"

Wyatt strode into the cottage and slammed his hand against one of the easels, sending it flying.

"This, you sicko freak. What the fuck is all this?" Wyatt's anger was just as scary as Scott's, but in a different way. Scott had been cold and calculated. Wyatt was angry like a bull and people could get hurt, even if that wasn't his intention.

Scott stood up, too. "Drummond, calm down and don't touch anything or I'm going to arrest you."

And that was waving a red flag in front of that raging bull.

"Don't touch anything? Because why? If this guy did anything to Kyle, I'm going to kill him."

"Wyatt, just stop." Jackson was apparently the beast whisperer today, because Wyatt obeyed, although he still vibrated with suppressed rage. "Wendell and Kyle found all this stuff. And it's evidence of a crime."

Wyatt took a minute to take in that information and process it before he calmed down enough to lose the hectic red color in his cheeks.

"This is some freaky shit, though. Gotta admit that, right? Looks like one of them serial killer things."

Scott looked heavenward, like he was asking for help from the divine, but knew there wasn't any help coming.

"You can't breathe a word of this to anyone, Wyatt," Scott ordered, then looked at him and Jackson. "That goes same for the both of you. Last thing we need is a mob of reporters in the midst of Haunt Fest."

Wendell and Jackson both nodded, but Wyatt clenched his fists.

"I'm not agreeing to nothing until I know where Kyle is. He's like family," Wyatt said stubbornly.

"Kyle's at the community center teaching ballet to small children," Wendell said.

"And you're sure of that?" Wyatt's bluster was fading, much to Wendell's relief.

"I will confirm it in just a minute, if that will make you calm the fuck down, Drummond." Scott waved his phone at Wyatt. "Now don't touch anything, and don't go anywhere until I say so. You don't want to get mixed up in another murder case, do you?"

There was no love lost between Scott and Wyatt, that was for sure.

Scott stepped into the bedroom to make his phone calls. They could hear him talking but not what exactly was said. Wyatt plopped down on the couch, while he and Jackson sat in the other two chairs.

Wyatt leaned over the coffee table and peered at the cigar box. "Who the fuck got murdered?" He reached out with a thick finger, and Wendell sucked in a breath to remind him not to touch anything, although he doubted he'd have more success than Scott had.

But at the last moment, Wyatt drew back before he'd laid a finger on anything.

"Well?" he asked.

Wendell blinked. "Well what?"

"Who got murdered? The old guy?" The tone had a strong suggestion of *are you stupid* but Wendell answered anyway.

"Not Chester." Weird that he died right by the cigar box, though. Kyle would have never found that box if it hadn't been for Chester.

"Then who?"

Wendell sighed. Scott might be pissed at him later, but he'd rather avoid Wyatt being pissed at him now. Wyatt was a large man with an unpredictable temper.

Wendell started the story from the beginning, only to be interrupted.

"Hold on, hold on. If I know the cops round here, and I do, this is gonna take a while. Got anything to eat?"

Wendell stowed the box in the safe, then ransacked his kitchenette for snacks and drinks. He didn't have much besides finger foods because he'd been grazing heavily on the leftover food at the inn, or going out places with Kyle. But he had chips, dip, baby carrots, and hummus. Along with a few sodas.

Enough to keep Wyatt from gnawing his arm off, at any rate.

Wendell continued with the story while Wyatt ate, and Jackson picked at his cuticles, shifting restlessly in his chair.

"So, this really is some serial killer bullshit," Wyatt proclaimed, although Wendell hadn't actually articulated that supposition. Not yet.

"Um. Maybe?"

Jackson cleared his throat. "Probably."

It wasn't lost on Wendell that Wyatt might actually watch a lot of the same shows Kyle did, because he came to the serial killer conclusion quite rapidly.

"Is Kyle in danger?"

Wendell shook his head. "I can't imagine so." Unless it was from stress and an overactive imagination. "There's no evidence of any victims later than the eighties."

"Ancient history. Not sure why Scott's in an uproar. Wouldn't whoever did be dead of old age?"

Jackson took over at that point, which was just as well because Wendell's throat was dry as a Brit's sense of humor after reciting the same story twice. He grabbed a can of root beer and downed half of it, although he wasn't at all hungry.

Jackson sighed. "If these people died around here, their families could still be looking for them, wondering what happened."

Somewhat chastened, Wyatt sat back and listened while Jackson finished telling the story.

Scott emerged from the bedroom, electronic tablet in hand, and pulled a chair from the kitchen table close to the rest of them.

"I have some follow-up questions, which we can take of while we wait."

Wendell didn't bother asking who they were waiting for. He assumed it was whomever would be confiscating all the research he and Kyle had done.

This was not going to be a good time.

Thirty minutes later, Wendell's cottage was overrun with cops.

It was a small space, so three extra cops seemed like an invasion.

They were taking every scrap and entering it into evidence bags. Once Scott was finished with his current interrogation—Wendell was a little surprised Wyatt and Jackson hadn't been booted from the room—they'd be going back to the library to look at the spot the cigar box was found.

Exhausting. He couldn't imagine how horrible it would be if he were an actual murder suspect.

"What the fuck happened? Is Wendell hurt?"

They all heard Kyle yelling outside. Wendell leapt up to greet Kyle as he came barreling into the cottage, pushing aside one of the officers.

"What the fuck is going on here?" His face had lost all color and the freckles that spattered his cheekbones stood out in a way Wendell had never seen before.

"Hey, it's okay. I'm here. Everything is fine."

Kyle turned his head, and his pupils wide and dark, almost like he'd been drugged.

"You're okay."

Wendell gathered him up in his arms and held him close. Kyle clutched him like a drowning man on a life raft.

"What is going on?" Kyle whispered into his chest.

"Long story short," Wendell began. He needed to make it short or his throat was never going to forgive him. He was a writer, not a talker. "I found a photo in Chester's room. One of the victims. It was a man Chester had met, who disappeared without a trace. But we have a trace now, and well, I couldn't justify keeping this from the police and Jackson any longer."

Kyle squeezed him tightly. "I just had these images of everyone dead. Blood all over the place. As soon as I saw all the police cars in the parking lot, it was all I could see."

Blood again. Wendell should have turned these photos over to the cops the second he suspected they were a serial killer's trophies.

"As you can see, we're all fine." He started rubbing Kyle's back, trying to soothe him.

"Oi, get a fucking room," Wyatt called out.

Kyle pulled away and glared. "Don't make me call Drew."

Wyatt held up his hands, pretending he was scared.

Scott coughed weirdly, more like a muffled laugh.

Then Kyle's phone buzzed. He took a couple of steps away from Wyatt and yanked his phone out of his pocket, then frowned. The angle was wrong, and Wendell couldn't see who was on the caller ID display.

"Hey. Is something wrong?" Kyle tone was confused, but he listened. Then spoke again, tone gentle. "I'm fine. You don't need to worry about me. Enjoy your last few days in Paris."

There was another pause. "Please don't come home early. There is really nothing wrong."

Kyle said a few more words, then hung up the phone.

"That was your friend, Drew?" Wendell asked, and Kyle nodded.

"Good timing," Jackson said.

"Not really," Wyatt said. "My baby bro is psychic. He probably felt a disturbance in whatever gives him his woo-woo juice."

So much to unpack. But weirdly, Scott didn't even flinch, just continued making notes.

Wendell looked at Kyle. "Really psychic? He called entirely unprompted?"

"So he said. But I wasn't kidding when I told you about him before. He does seem to have a gift. A knack."

"He's the real deal, my man," Wyatt said. "Saved our bacon because of it."

Wendell would like to believe, but he'd definitely need to see evidence with his own eyes before anyone changed his mind. Getting proof would be wildly cool, though.

"For real?" His surprise was more about Wyatt's wholehearted support of Drew's talent. Not at all what he expected from the man, but then, he still didn't know Wyatt at all.

Kyle nodded. "I'll see if I can get him to do a reading for you. It doesn't always work, which is probably a blessing for his mental state, but yeah, when it happens, he knows things he shouldn't know."

Wendell was definitely willing to be convinced.

"I need to ask you a few questions, Kyle," Scott said.

Kyle grimaced. Jackson stood up.

"Okay if I go back to the main building? I think the guests that checked in last night are out sightseeing, but just in case, I'd like to smooth any troubled waters. And close off the library so there won't be any looky-loos when you come back to check it out."

"That's fine," Scott said. "But don't go poking around in there."

Jackson nodded, but Wendell suspected he was holding back an eye roll.

Wendell ushered Kyle to the chair he'd been sitting on while getting grilled by Scott.

"Sorry for not warning you. Can I get you something to drink?"

The tender little half-smile on those kissable lips was something Wendell would love to see for the rest of his life.

"Thanks. A diet soda would be great."

Wendell grabbed a cold drink for Kyle from the fridge, then turned back.

He blinked and rubbed at his eyes. Weird. For a moment there, it looked like Kyle's hair had dark, almost black roots.

Another blink. Kyle's hair was its normal sun-kissed blond.

What a bizarre thing to imagine.

TWENTY-THREE

5 Days to Haunt Fest

MONDAY EVENING, Kyle drummed his fingers on the table and craned his neck toward the entrance of the Angry Parakeet yet again.

"I'm sure they'll be here soon." Wendell's tone was conciliatory, a tone Kyle had become increasingly familiar with as the days passed.

Mostly because Kyle had been more and more unpredictable, even to himself. He was low-grade angry, all the time. It had started the day he'd come back to Wendell's cottage to find it full of cops. Once he'd ensured no one was dead, bleeding out all over the seafoam green area rug, like the image his mind couldn't stop supplying, he'd been incandescent with rage.

But a part of him knew he had no reason to be upset. Wendell was well within his rights to inform Jackson and the police about the cigar box they'd found. And probably should have done so earlier. That logical piece of his mind managed to keep a grip on his outward behaviors. Scott and Wyatt for sure would have called him out if he'd been acting too weird.

Inside his head? That was a whole different thing. Inside he seethed and growled. And he didn't even want to see that damned cigar box anymore. It was giving him nightmares, something he'd thought he was immune to, since not one horror movie had ever disrupted his sleep.

But this near-constant emotional battle was exhausting; hiding his fears kept him perpetually short-tempered, and he was counting the days to the end of Haunt Fest. He had a doctor's appointment scheduled for the following day, and he hoped to get a referral to a psychologist. One who could see him fast.

"Did you want to order something to munch on while we wait?"

"No." Kyle grimaced. That had come out waspish and curt. "Sorry. I mean, dinner will be enough of a splurge for me, appetizers would be too much. But get something if you want it." He took a long look at his boyfriend and smiled. Wendell made things better. Mostly. Not that a boyfriend could cure whatever mental illness he was currently developing, but Wendell's presence tended to have a mitigating effect on the ping-pong of his emotional state.

Today, though, Wendell was meeting Drew, and his husband Cliff, for the first time. Drew had been home almost a week now, but things had been too hectic for the four of them to get together, and there wasn't going to be a better time between now and the end of Haunt Fest. Kyle was eager for Drew and Wendell to meet, and hadn't wanted to postpone. It was important that they like each other, and the fact that Drew was late wasn't going to make a good impression.

Not that Wendell would judge. He was far more laid back than Kyle was about things, and as long as Drew didn't stand them up entirely, Wendell wouldn't hold it against him.

Kyle's anxiety was all out of proportion, but he didn't know how to control it, aside from dropping down into a few yoga poses by the table. Even if he'd been tempted to subject his favorite pair of jeans to the Parakeet's sticky, beer-scented floors, yoga was becoming less and less effective at keeping his emotions on a slow simmer. Anything that went wrong sent everything boiling over, and he was snapping at everyone.

When Sally came by, Wendell ordered hummus, instead of his favorite potato skins. Which made Kyle smile in genuine pleasure. Either he was trying to make a good impression on Kyle's best friend —who would never judge a person's taste in food—or he was hoping to entice Kyle to nibble with something he was more likely to eat, especially since the Parakeet served their hummus appetizer with carrots and cucumbers as well as the pita bread that Kyle would never touch. Or maybe both.

Whatever the reasoning, it was done with Kyle in mind, he had no doubt of that. And it was so sweet. He'd never been involved with a guy who cared about what was best for Kyle, and he liked it a lot.

On the other hand, it was possible his current attitude was not adequately conveying how much he appreciated Wendell's company. He'd really have to explain things to Wendell and soon. The last thing he wanted to do was drive Wendell away. And he'd learned enough about Wendell by this point to feel—mostly—confident that a burgeoning mental illness wouldn't drive him away.

Kyle tried a couple of meditative breaths, because that was a concern for another time. He had plenty to worry about with just this meeting.

He opened his mouth to speculate on what was keeping Drew, but a heavy hand fell on his shoulder.

"Hey there, Kyle," Cliff said behind him. Kyle stood and gave him a quick hug.

"Good to see you!" Cliff looked super relaxed, not a look he wore all that often.

Drew followed close behind, and Kyle's eyes burned. His best friend looked so damn happy, he could barely stand it. Also, his hair was ruffled which probably explained why they were late and why Cliff was all relaxed.

"Didn't you get enough sex on your honeymoon? Had to have some afternoon delight right before leaving the house, did you?" At least his tone sounded every bit as teasing as he meant it, because these days, that wasn't always a guarantee.

Drew's face lit up as red as his hair, and he spluttered out an apology. Kyle rolled his eyes, but couldn't stop grinning. Meeting Cliff had been so good for his friend.

"Oh, shush. Like I'd begrudge someone a good orgasm."

Cliff turned a laugh into a cough, and Kyle realized Wendell might be a little alarmed at their dynamic.

He turned back to Wendell, who had also stood up, but there was a tiny smile playing about his lips.

Good. He'd never once told Kyle to dial it down, and it didn't look like he was going to start.

Kyle ran through the introductions, and they all sat down around the table. Sally returned and fresh drinks were ordered, along with meals. Cliff and Drew were familiar enough with the menu to not need any time to think about it.

They chatted a bit about Paris—Kyle was the only one at the table who'd never been, and it sucked. And not in the good way. Although London was first on his bucket list, and all those West End shows, he'd have gone to Paris in a heartbeat. As soon as he'd gotten a steady income, he'd gotten a passport. So he'd be ready, perpetually hopeful.

Then, Cliff sat back in his chair. "So I hear you two engaged in a little obstruction of justice while we were gone. That's a courting ritual I'd never have come up with."

Kyle blinked at him for a moment, but this time it was Wendell sputtering out an apology. Kyle smacked Cliff gently on the bicep.

"Be nice to him. I like him."

Cliff just laughed.

Kyle turned to Wendell and squeezed his hand. "He's teasing. I might have forgotten to mention Scott is his partner at work. Scott would have ratted us out in a hot second."

"Seriously, though, what you found was really creepy. Do they think it was from a serial killer for real?" Drew asked.

"You know we can't talk about specifics." Cliff softened his refusal with a quick kiss to Drew's temple.

Wendell looked disappointed, too. Since turning over the cigar box, they'd heard a big fat nothing about any sort of progress or information. Despite having run into Scott a couple of times over the past week.

Kyle and Wendell had been quite busy, but still managed to have the occasional lunch or dinner out, and of course, spent every night together in Wendell's bed. It had been a little easier to sleep without seeing pictures of all those dead people, but he wouldn't say he was totally rested.

Better than sleeping alone, of that he was certain.

"You know, Wendell, you look a little familiar." Cliff squinted across the table. "Sure I haven't arrested you at some point?"

Wendell laughed. "No arrests on my record, I swear."

Kyle might have scolded Cliff for that, but he had actually sounded as if he were joking. Interrogation in the form of a joke, at any rate.

"Hmm. It'll come to me eventually, I guess."

Oh. Cliff had been *serious* about Wendell looking familiar. Weird. Maybe Cliff was a deeply closeted horror movie fan.

"Both Kyle and Wyatt said you're a real psychic, Drew. Do you think I could maybe chat with you sometime about it? For research." Wendell deftly changed the subject.

Drew tilted his head slightly, appearing confused. Shit. Kyle had never actually told him what Wyatt did for a living.

"You've met Wyatt? I'm sorry," Drew said.

Wendell smiled. "He's a little rough around the edges, that's for sure. But Jackson likes having him around, and he's sort of growing on me."

In that moment, Wendell won Drew over, Kyle was certain of it. Drew's brothers could be big, insensitive goobers, but they all loved each other and looked out for each other. And they looked out for Kyle, too. More like his family than his own parents.

"Anyway, you wanted to interview me? Are you a journalist?"

Wendell darted a questioning look at Kyle. He shrugged.

"I tried to keep the text messages to a minimum while he was on his honeymoon, and this is the first time we've talked in person since he got back."

"Oh, well, I write movie scripts."

Kyle couldn't help himself. "Drew, he wrote *Dead Eye Dance*. And *The Missing Sarcophagus*. And he's working on another script right now." Those script notes had taken some serious explanation when the cops had found them, and fast talking to let Wendell keep them. Kyle didn't know why they hadn't been digital, but Wendell said sometimes writing things out by hand primed the pump. Regardless, Kyle had been excited that Wendell had made some progress overcoming his writer's block.

"For real? That's amazing! Those movies were so scary," Drew said. "Of course you can interview me."

"Thanks," Wendell replied.

But Cliff tilted his head. "You're a script writer. From Hollywood."

"I actually live in Burbank, and our studio is in Glendale." Then it was Wendell's turn to squint at Cliff. "Wait a minute. You look familiar too."

They peered at each other. Cliff snapped his fingers. "Industry parties. I've seen you at a few of those."

"I don't go to many, but I went to a few when we were trying to sign..." He glanced at Kyle. "Uh, trying to sign the dude who shall not be named."

Cliff snorted. "Yeah, that guy. Those would be the parties I was at. I was his dirty secret."

Wendell made a face. "You dated that jerk? He's such an asshole."

"Well, I figured that out quick. Maybe not quick enough, but live and learn."

"I'm glad. Wow. I always knew there were unplumbed depths to his assholery. And keeping a secret boyfriend while sexing up his costars is pretty fucking low." Wendell slapped his hand over his mouth. "Shit, I mean..."

"It's okay. I know he cheated on me. It's one of the reasons I gave him the boot and moved here."

"Have you actually *met* before?" Kyle was not at all sure how he felt about that.

Cliff shook his head. "No, we were never introduced. Uh, B, never introduced me to anyone. Anyone who asked, I told them my name, but I think most partygoers thought I was private security, not an actual guest."

That brought a grimace to Kyle's face. A little to close to what he'd experienced himself while away at college, and it sucked.

"I'm sorry you had to go through that."

Cliff smiled and ruffled his hair like Wyatt and Rob often did.

"Hey, dammit, I spent a long time on this."

Wendell patted his hand comfortingly, but he was absolutely trying to fight a grin.

"Dick," Kyle whispered, but they could all tell he was teasing. Thankfully, his brain appeared to be cooperating this evening.

"So, about that psychic thing, when would be a good time to meet up with you? Would it make sense for me to have a reading done?" Wendell asked.

"I have a lot of readings booked for the next month, but I have some time tomorrow morning. Can you make it at ten?"

Wendell blinked. "Of course, that would be amazing."

"Perfect. I'll do a quick reading, then you can ask me questions."

Kyle was pleased Drew seemed a little more comfortable with his newfound abilities, but perhaps that was because he didn't get true psychic flashes every time he did a reading. But Kyle suspected, if the online store continued on its current trajectory, Drew might be able to reduce or even eliminate his tarot readings, if he wanted to. Kyle wasn't entirely sure if he'd want to lose that connection to his gran, but fewer readings? That Drew would be able to get behind.

The rest of the evening went smoothly. Wendell fit right in. Drew and Cliff asked intelligent questions about Hollywood, and Cliff seemed to appreciate comparing notes on things they'd both liked about living on the West Coast.

Kyle was happy, and was able to enjoy it—mostly. Hearing about how cool some of the LA places were gave him a tiny splurge of jealousy. In all too short a time, Wendell would be returning to his real life in Tinseltown. Kyle wasn't sure he'd want to live there, but he wanted to see it. He didn't want Wendell to go back.

On the other hand, he utterly adored the way Wendell would occasionally grab his hand and hold it, with little regard for who might see. No, Kyle *loved* that. Wendell smiled broadly when Kyle got overexcited while telling a story, and didn't complain or scold when he splashed soda on the table while using his drink hand to emphasize a point.

Wendell might be the best thing to ever happen to him, and every day ticked down the countdown clock to Wendell leaving. But he refused to entertain any dark thoughts. He'd had far, far too many of them lately.

TWENTY-FOUR

4 Days to Haunt Fest

WENDELL TOOK a deep breath when he walked into Drew's shop the next morning. He'd been there a few times with Kyle, but it didn't feel the same. Not when he was going to have a tarot card reading.

He wasn't entirely sure why he'd never done this before but he was quite excited. The fact that Drew's brother seemed to be a hundred percent convinced his talent was real surprised Wendell. Wyatt did not seem like the sort of person who believed in much besides football and beer. But he might also be judging a book by its rednecked cover.

Kyle had told him about the events two years ago, and he also seemed convinced Drew had developed a paranormal ability. If events had truly unfolded the way Kyle had described, there were a lot of points supporting their belief. But Wendell was very much in the "if I see it, I'll believe it" category.

The goal was to keep an open mind. And enough borderline

weird stuff had already happened since his arrival in Sandy Bottom Bay that he was certain he'd be able to do just that.

The scent of incense in the air added to the mystical vibe. Sure, it had smelled the same every time he'd met Kyle here, but knowing he would soon pass through those dark velvety drapes, delicately embroidered with mystic symbols, added some extra atmosphere.

He stepped closer to the drapes and peered a little closer at the symbols. He might not have researched police procedure before, but symbology? Yeah, he'd delved pretty deep into those waters. If one squinted a bit and loosened up some of the definitions, the unifying theme seemed to be one of wisdom. Or perhaps knowledge. Both? The symbols were from a wide variety of traditions.

Regardless, whomever commissioned these drapes had done their homework. A closer inspection revealed it was unlikely to have been Drew. These curtains, while in good repair, were showing their age, which was most likely older than Drew was himself.

He glanced up and saw the tiny security camera. He had sort of wondered how Drew prevented stock from walking out the door while he was doing readings. After meeting Cliff last night, he also had the impression that Cliff—or possibly Kyle—would have been the ones to insist on security. Drew had an almost bewildering naiveté about him.

The draperies parted to his right, startling him, and revealing an unfamiliar shape outlined by the dim light.

"Please, come in." The shape stepped back, and Wendell passed through the opening.

Wendell blinked, trying to adjust to the lower light level. Candles of differing heights and thickness were arrayed along a modified sideboard and hutch, similar to the one his gran used to hold the holiday china.

The incense smell changed along with the light. It became sultrier, heavier, spicier. Not having a window visible made a big difference. It was like he'd stepped into another world or another time.

"Please, have a seat," Drew said softly behind him. It was Drew's voice, but also not the voice he'd come to know over dinner last night.

Regardless, he took a seat at the table covered in black cloth, with a stack of well-worn tarot cards in its center.

Drew sat down across from him with swish of fabric.

"Please shuffle the deck while thinking of a question you'd like guidance for or a problem you'd like to overcome. Then choose five cards without turning them over."

As Wendell reached out for the deck, he glanced up at Drew and almost gasped.

The affable, good-looking, boy-next-door red head had been utterly replaced by an ethereal mystic. A turban swathed his head, hiding any trace of his red hair, aside from faintly gingery eyebrows. Thick black eyeliner ringed his eyes, utterly changing his appearance.

He had to hand it to Drew. Or rather, Malachi. The man knew how to put on a show. The trappings of the reading were excellent. Hollywood often portrayed tarot readers as tawdry and over the top. But Drew had perfected the atmosphere and props in a way Wendell had never expected.

He held onto the cards for a moment, pondering what he wanted the cards to tell him. Until this moment, he hadn't given any credence to those who believed, but there was a tiny part of him that thought this might be for real. Or wanted it to be for real. Which was probably the true magic Drew had, tapping into that want.

Asking about his relationship with Kyle didn't seem right. Malachi/Drew was still Kyle's best friend. Especially since he wasn't sure if he'd be expected to tell Drew what his question was.

He shuffled and started thinking about the scraps of scripts he'd jotted down since arriving in Sandy Bottom Bay. The bits he was most interested in weren't a good fit for the horror enterprise he and his siblings were trying to build. The town's inspirations were many, but he still wasn't able to grasp a concept that resonated.

How was he going to overcome his writer's block? He knew damn well the answer wasn't Kyle, even though meeting Kyle had been all kinds of amazing. So yeah, that was his question. Overcoming his writer's block.

Repeating the question in his mind, he continued to shuffle the stack of oversized cards. No sense doing this half-assed.

After a few moments, he counted out five cards and separated them in a small pile beside the rest of the deck.

When asked, Wendell said he wanted guidance to overcome roadblocks with his writing.

Drew arranged the cards facedown in a simple cross pattern, presumably placing each card based on the order Wendell had selected them.

The next twenty minutes saw Drew turn over each card, and explain how it related to the question Wendell had posed, and how Wendell could perhaps overcome the roadblocks in his life.

Unexpectedly, he found himself on a much better mental footing than he'd been when he came in. Much more optimistic, and ready to dive into the script—after Haunt Fest—that was calling him, regardless of what it meant for the studio. The itch in his brain, the one that put fingers on keyboard, was back. And he could fucking kiss Drew for that. If he weren't with Kyle, and he didn't think Cliff would arrest him or something.

Wendell sat back in his chair with a smile. "That was amazing."

Drew had probably had some additional info from Kyle, so it wasn't a total cold read, but neither had Wendell seen any indication of supernatural ability. Drew had been insightful, but also skillful at guiding Wendell to draw his own conclusions. He probably did a fantastic cold read on complete strangers.

Drew smiled back. "Thank you. C'mon, let's go into the back, get something to drink, while we do the interview." His voice was no longer Malachi's. Utterly fascinating.

"Lead the way."

Wendell followed him through more drapes to a door, which opened into a tiny but homey kitchen. Kyle had already told him how Drew had inherited both house and business from his grandmother, and he saw a lot of touches in the kitchen that had to have been grandma's, along with several modernizations.

"Beer? Water? Iced tea?"

"Iced tea would be great, thanks." Bit early for beer in his opinion, even though he'd fully acclimated to this time zone.

Drew hung his silky robes on a hook by the door, revealing a black t-shirt. He took off the turban and hung it over his robes, then ran his fingers through his bright hair, then grabbed some glasses and a pitcher of tea from the fridge.

He poured them both a glass, then pushed a sugar dispenser that looked like it had been appropriated from a nearby diner, toward him.

"Unsweet is good, thanks."

"It can get fucking hot under those robes." Drew took a long swallow from his glass and immediately refilled what he'd drank.

"I bet."

"So what did you want to know?"

Wendell took a swallow of his own tea to give him time to get his thoughts in order.

"I have to admit, I would assume people wouldn't want you to know the question they asked. I mean, wouldn't they be 'you're a psychic, you should know'?"

Drew laughed. "Yes. I have a couple of standard responses to that, depending on the client's attitude. And there was a time I wouldn't have asked. But these days? I want to know, up front, if they're coming to me hoping I'll solve a serious medical, legal, or psychological problem. Because if they think they've got cancer, I've got to convince them to go see a doctor, you know?"

"Some might say believing in psychics was a serious psychological problem."

"You sound like my husband."

"Yeah, I might have only just met him, but he strikes me as a true skeptic."

"It took a bit for him to realize that most people who 'take me seriously' see me more as a confidant and sounding board than someone who is going to magically fix all their problems. I do get a few people who can't afford to see a mental health professional, and I've done my best to get them referred to local practitioners who are doing discounted and pro bono work."

Again, Wendell was impressed. He didn't know if all professed psychics were that responsible, but he suspected there were a goodly number who weren't.

"I must admit, I'm glad the Death card didn't come up, even though I know it's not a literal representation of death or dying."

"Yes, I remember your use of tarot cards in *Time of Death*." There was the tiniest hint of reproach in Drew's voice.

Wendell chuckled. "Sorry I made your job harder."

"Can you keep a secret?"

"Of course. Especially since you're Kyle's best friend."

"Two years ago, when all that stuff happened, well, that card seemed to cause more trouble than it's worth. I don't keep it in my deck anymore."

Wendell stared at him. "You, you just took it out."

Drew smirked. "Yup."

The man wasn't nearly as innocent and unworldly as Wendell had assumed.

"That is diabolical. Sneaky as shit."

"But it has made my readings a lot less stressful."

Wendell had no doubt that was the truth.

Drew glanced at the time on the stove. "Sorry, I have to get ready for my next client. But I can answer any other questions later."

"Thanks, I appreciate it." Wendell waited while Drew recreated Malachi's appearance, then Drew led him back into the reading room.

Drew headed to the sideboard, and gave Wendell a cheeky grin before he lifted a heavy metal pyramid inscribed with hieroglyphics. He picked up a card from underneath.

"Shut up." Wendell strode over and held his hand out. Drew

extended the card, and their fingers touched as Wendell took the Death card.

Wendell froze. Drew's face had gone slack, his eyes unfocused, his entire body stiff. He'd seen someone look like this once, right before they'd fallen to the floor with a seizure.

The card fluttered to the floor as he prepared to keep Drew from hitting his head when he went down.

But he never did. After several interminable moments, Drew blinked rapidly and shook himself like he'd dozed off for a few minutes.

"Dude. Are you prone to seizures? Should I call a doctor or an ambulance?"

Drew took a deep breath. "Let's sit down a minute. I... well... that never gets any easier."

Wendell hovered behind him, and they took their seats at the reading table again.

"Are you okay? Should I call Cliff?" Not that he'd know how to do that, but he had Kyle's and Scott's numbers. One of them would be able to pass on a message.

Drew patted his hand, like Wendell was the one who needed comforting.

"Look, I know you're every bit the skeptic Cliff used to be."

"Used to be?" Wendell would have bet large sums of money Cliff was the poster boy for skeptics.

"He's been... convinced that I can see things that, well, I shouldn't be able to see. I get glimpses of the past or future. Sometimes it's images, sometimes it's ideas, thoughts. I don't know what triggers it, though. Touch, yes, but I don't have to avoid touching people. It actually doesn't happen all that often."

Wendell didn't think Drew could fake the physiological responses he'd witnessed, but what if he was having mini-seizures and was somehow interpreting that as having psychic visions?

"I've had all sorts of brain tests. This all started after I got a concussion. It's not medical, I promise you."

He couldn't not ask. "What did you see?"

"Not much. And honestly, it made no sense to me at all. I just know that when you find the knife, you're going to need Eddie." Drew wrinkled his nose.

"Eddie?"

"Yeah, Eddie Price. He's—"

Wendell held up a hand. "I've met Eddie already." Was this some complicated way to bury the hatchet without anyone losing face? Because how the hell was he supposed to use this as confirmation one way or the other?

"Well, I don't know what sort of knife you're supposed to find, but I have the strong sense you'll know when you see it?" Drew sounded confused. Which made two of them. "Also, I feel like oranges are some sort of signpost. But I don't know what that means."

"Okay, I'll definitely keep that in mind. But are you sure you're alright?" Because Wendell had his doubts. Which might be more because of how unnerved the incident had made him, along with the mention of knives. Oranges were far less scary, and so was Eddie.

"Fine. I promise." Drew's voice was firm and confident, and Wendell was going to have to accept that answer. Even if there was a medical issue at the heart of this, Drew was a grown man who could take care of himself. And he already appeared as normal as he had when Wendell had arrived.

Drew grabbed Wendell by the arm. "I know you don't believe me. But I also know how much you care for Kyle. I love him. He's been like a brother to me since we were kids. If you ignore what I've said, Kyle could get hurt. And I don't mean emotionally." Drew's voice was low and urgent. Sincere.

A warning with ominous elements, and as vague as a foggy morning... no better way to get buy-in as a psychic. The next time Kyle slipped while cutting onions, Drew could point to that as "proof" of his prescience.

That didn't mean Wendell wasn't rattled. If this was Drew

bamboozling people, he was a fucking master. Or maybe he was doing his best to spark Wendell's creative juices.

But there was no chance to ask any more questions. The tinkle of the bell on the entrance rang, which was Wendell's cue to leave, if Drew's shooing motions didn't make that obvious.

"Thanks again." He'd have to work out the payment later. He wasn't about to soak up a reading for free just because he was dating the man's best friend.

He slipped out through the draperies and passed a woman in her fifties or sixties wearing a pastel pink linen suit and pearls.

He nodded at her, and she gave him a benevolent smile in return, and he was reminded he was overdue for a chat with his family. At least Lucinda had stayed true to her word and had backed off. If he'd had to deal with her badgering him about a script with everything else, he might have gone mad.

The overhead bell tinkled as he left, and he jogged back to the inn, letting the bright Florida sunshine soothe his jangled nerves.

When Wendell got back to the inn, Jackson had everything well in hand. He was really starting to thrive, and seemed to enjoy the increasing pressure that more guests brought. It might have been a way to avoid the stresses in his life that had brought him here at the drop of a hat, but for the time being, Jackson appeared to be happy and well.

Kyle had a bad headache when they woke up this morning. Not a hangover, since he'd stuck to club soda and lime at the restaurant last night. But he'd not wanted breakfast this morning and grunted miserably from the covers when Wendell spoke to him.

No one needed Wendell for anything, and he was starting to get hungry.

Right now, the inn was only half full, but that would change on Friday, three days from now. Once they were full up, he'd likely be trapped in the inn with those guests. It was what he'd signed up for, but more and more he was losing interest in the haunted hotel idea.

But he'd made a promise to Sandra and he wasn't about to let her or Jackson down. No matter how little he needed the research now.

He checked his app for the food truck status. No burritos today, but there were po' boys. Po' boys did not seem like a Kyle-friendly food anyway, which made this an ideal lunch option. Get out for a walk, get some good food, and maybe he could swing by the bakery and see what cupcakes were on offer today.

A long walk and an excellent po' boy later, Wendell stared at the vibrant frosting tops of the cupcakes in the bakery case. He wasn't sure he had room for one, but he was going to get one anyway.

"Hey, there, Wendell," Tony said. The lunch rush was over, so Tony leaned against the wall on the other side of the cupcake case.

"Hey Tony. How's it going?"

"Eh. Getting busier by the day. Worse than Christmas, around here."

Coming from a bakery, that had to be saying something.

"I'm looking forward to seeing what it's all like." And he was, even if he might spend most of Haunt Fest behind the inn's front desk.

They chatted a little longer. Wendell had started to get to know Tony when he showed up with the bakery's deliveries each morning. He wasn't sure if he'd call Tony a friend at this point, but colleague and close acquaintance would apply.

"So what's the Gryphon?" The lush purple frosting had caught his eye right off. But the name gave him no clues.

"Ube and caramel."

"Sounds delicious. I'll have that, please." There had been a diner not far from his apartment in LA that frequently had ube cookies that he loved. He was eager to try an ube cupcake.

"Tea?" Tony asked.

"Yes, thanks."

"Go have a seat. I'll have things out in a minute."

Wendell sat near the door, and smiled at the white-haired woman at the far table, the only other patron in the bakery at the moment.

She had a half-full cup of coffee that she was ignoring in favor of her knitting. Or was it crocheting? His knowledge of the textile arts was almost nil. But her needles were flying, and Wendell was mesmerized at how quickly she added stitches.

He did his best not to stare, but he couldn't help glancing over. Tony brought his tea and cupcake, and Wendell lingered over both, amazed at how many stitches had been added to the woman's item. He couldn't tell what it was supposed to be, but the colors were gorgeous.

He'd lingered a bit, half hoping he'd see Scott, but after an hour he was ready to give up. They hadn't heard one peep from the police after they'd gathered up the evidence related to the cigar box. Maybe they hadn't had any more luck than he and Kyle had had, tracking down the victims in that box. Not that they were under any obligation to keep anyone at the inn, maybe not even Sandra, informed of their progress.

But if he'd casually bumped into Scott, at say, the bakery, it would only be natural to *ask* about it. Wouldn't it? Clearly, he was doomed to disappointment in that regard. Maybe another time.

He gathered up his dishes and took them over to the counter. Tony took them with a nod, and Wendell turned to leave. Then he had an idea, and turned back to Tony.

"Hey Tony, if I was looking for someone who lived in town during the seventies, and has a good memory for faces, who would I talk to? He hoped the "still have all their faculties" was implied because he didn't want to say it and offend anyone.

"The nineteen-seventies? You're in luck." Tony jutted his chin toward the woman in the corner. "Barbara Mayhew. She and her sister have lived here their whole lives. Pretty sure she's been around long enough to suit you. More research?"

Wendell nodded. "Sort of, yes. Thank you."

This might backfire big time, or it might get him in trouble, but time had not assuaged his curiosity.

"Excuse me," he said as he approached. "I was hoping you might be able to help me."

"You're that writer fella at the inn. Stepping out with our Kyle."

"Um. Yes. That's me. Wendell." Whatever she meant by "our" Kyle.

"Sit down, Tony," she called out imperiously. "Another cup of tea for my young friend."

Tony saluted and got to work.

"That's not necessary."

She dimpled at him. "Not often I get to have tea with a strapping young man."

Wendell smiled back. "Thank you. Can I get you something to eat? A cupcake or something?"

"I could do with a little toast and cheese."

He hadn't seen that on the menu board, but he suspected Tony was happy to cater to this regular. Just as he was about to stand up and put the order in, Tony appeared table side, juggling a cup of tea, a carafe of decaf coffee, and a small plate with cheese on toast. He set everything down, refilled Barbara's cup, and left again, but not before winking broadly at Wendell.

Barbara Mayhew was definitely a regular.

"Mrs. Mayhew," he began.

"Nope. Call me Barbara."

"Oh, thanks. I'm Wendell."

She nicely refrained from saying that she already knew his name.

"Going to be good to Kyle?"

Wendell smiled again. He sort of loved how almost everyone he met seemed to care about Kyle's wellbeing. "That's my plan."

"Good, good. What did you want to know?"

Right. Small talk was over. Maybe one's patience with it diminished over time. If that was the case, Wendell would be blurting out one word answers and demands by the time he was Barbara's age.

"I'm sure you must have heard about the death at the inn, one of the guests."

"I did. Shame. But I didn't know that fella."

"No, I wouldn't have expected so. But I chatted with him a bit, and he had fond memories of a man he'd met when he was here, in the early seventies."

This was where things got a little dicey. Because if he told her the full truth, that might be considered interfering in a police investigation. So he needed to massage the truth a little.

Barbara chewed on her toast as he thought out his next words.

"Anyway, I had to gather up his belongings for his next of kin, and I found an old photo of a man. I think he was local, and I guess... I don't know. I wondered if anyone knew who he was."

Wendell pulled up the picture he'd taken of the photo from Chester's room, and expanded it so that all was visible was the dark-haired man in the background.

"Do you recognize this man?"

Barbara took the phone and tilted it, squinting. Then she pulled a pair of glasses out of her shirt pocket and put them on, then looked again.

"Huh. Looks like Matthew Trask."

Good. A name to start with. "That's great. Thank you."

She harrumphed, something that was instantly recognizable, even though Wendell had never experienced it in person before.

"Not sure who'd have fond memories of that man, though."

Wendell blinked. "There was... something wrong with him?"

"Nothing to hang your hat on, no. But he was reclusive. Didn't talk much to people. Was too slick when he did. Had some sort of job as a traveling salesman, and even I know that was a job going nowhere back then. So he wasn't always in town. His brother, Luke, owned the Lady back then. Matthew had permanent residence in one of the upstairs rooms when he was in town. But he was a free-loader. Didn't help out with the inn, as far as anyone knew. Didn't get involved, except to party with the tourists. Bit of a ne'er-do-well, my grandmother would have called him."

"Interesting. What happened to him? Does he still live in town?"

"Bit ironic, that. He died of a heart attack in the library of the inn. Just like that poor man."

"He's dead?" Despite the fact that every townsperson seemed to know the circumstances of Chester's death, no one had mentioned there had been another, similar death years ago.

"Yes. I want to say it happened around eighty-four or eighty-five. He was young, too, mid-forties, if I recall. Luke didn't want the stress of the inn to catch up with him and sold the place soon after. It languished a bit, passing through a few owners, until Sandra and Bill bought it. They moved from up north somewhere, wanted to get away from the winters."

"Does Luke Trask still live around here?"

Barbara shrugged, wiped her fingers on her napkin, then picked up her needles again. "Don't think so. I think I heard he'd died fairly young too. I don't think they had any other family."

"And it couldn't be Luke in that picture?"

Barbara laughed. "Nope. Luke was a red head. Not like young Drew, mind you. Darker. But not dark like this. Definitely Matthew."

Wendell couldn't be certain without police resources, but he was confident he'd found the identity of the killer. He could do some more digging online, see what he could find. And next time he saw Scott, he'd sound things out. He didn't want to keep information from the police, but if they'd already identified Matthew, they wouldn't be too pleased with him clumsily trying to do their job for them.

"If you're still having issues with writer's block, you should consider taking up knitting. Working with your hands can free up your mind."

Wendell blinked at her. Most of the people he'd met didn't even seem to know he wrote movie scripts, let alone mention his creative stumbles.

"How did you know?"

"Knitting is harmless. People talk about all kinds of things with and around knitters." Her smile was serene and wily at the same time.

"I don't know how to knit."

"The community center has classes all the time."

Wendell laughed. "I will keep that in mind. And thank you for the information."

He drained the last of the tea, said his farewells, and tried to pay Tony for Barbara's coffee and toast, but found it was all on the house anyway. Which didn't come as a big surprise.

Lisa and Tony were good people.

Wendell walked back outside, wondering what he should do with this information. But first thing would be to find out if Kyle was awake and if he needed anything.

Back in his cottage, Wendell found Kyle sitting up in bed reading.

"Feeling better?" He climbed on the bed with Kyle.

"Yes, thanks." Kyle put his e-reader down, and cuddled up next to him.

Wendell hadn't missed the dark shadows were still present under his eyes, and his face was still pale. He pulled Kyle close.

"Is it this bad every year? You seem so stressed." And on edge. Almost nervous, but that couldn't be right.

Kyle cleared his throat. "It's always stressful. This year does seem to be, um, quite bad, though."

"Maybe there's something we can do next year to lighten your workload. Because this can't be healthy for you."

"Next year?" Kyle's voice wavered.

Wendell shifted them so he could look deep into Kyle's eyes. "Next year. I don't know how this will all work out, and this is obviously not the time to have that discussion, but I don't want this to end. You're... what I've been looking for. I love you."

Kyle's eyes filled, but nothing spilled over. "I love you too. And I want all that. We'll figure out how it'll all work. Together."

"Together." He kissed Kyle's lips gently.

Then Kyle drew back. "Now, stop being so sweet, because if I start crying, that headache is going to come right back."

"I will try to be moderately horrible for the next hour or so."

Kyle let out a watery laugh. "I'd appreciate it."

"Did you eat? Can I get you something?"

"I've got water, but I wouldn't mind some of those crackers we bought the other day."

"Of course." Wendell hopped up and got the crackers that were so full of grains and things they were practically bird seed that barely clung together in a cracker-esque form.

Far too healthy for him, but Kyle was happy with them, so Wendell was also.

If only he could relieve Kyle's stress as easily as he brought him a box of crackers.

TWENTY-FIVE

3 Days to Haunt Fest

T MINUS 48 hours until the inn was full to capacity, and another twelve hours or so until the official start of Haunt Fest. Part-time workers had been engaged and would be trickling in to help the closer they got to liftoff. Wyatt was lurking around somewhere, supposedly helping. Whether or not he was making himself useful was questionable. But Jackson seemed to like having him around, enough to find him tasks to do, so Wendell wasn't about to complain.

Kyle was having a nap in Wendell's cottage before he had to get ready for the ghost walk tonight.

He'd claimed he wasn't tired, claimed everything was fine, but one good blow job, and he'd passed right out. Wendell was starting to get worried. A bit worried. Everyone in town seemed on edge, though. This might be normal. If Kyle didn't improve after the crucible of Haunt Fest, Wendell was going to insist on a doctor's visit. Which might be terribly high-handed, but after Chester's sudden death, he wasn't about to lose Kyle. Not when he'd just found him.

Most of the guests were out doing touristy things, which meant they had a bit of a break. Wendell wanted to find out more about Matthew Trask. He hadn't even told Kyle about his discovery, because he'd seemed so brittle in the aftermath of his migraine. And they'd both been busy today, crossing paths here and there, like Wendell had crossed Kyle's dick about thirty minutes ago.

Jackson took advantage of the temporary lull to escape to his own place. Wendell thought about sitting in the library, but he wasn't ready to spend leisure time there. Too soon.

He plunked down at a table in the sunroom and started a search for all things Matthew Trask on his phone. Much like his 'alleged' victims, very little digital information came up.

Then someone screamed, followed by a heavy thud. Bigger and louder than last time. His stomach clenched, but he bounded out of his chair.

"What happened?" He yelled as he ran, unsure exactly where the scream had originated, but something had him heading toward the library. "Is everyone okay?"

Was that a faint cry for help? He put on more speed, and skidded around the corner, and saw a person huddled on the floor at the base of the stairs that led up to the guest rooms.

He skidded to a stop by the person, and fell heavily to his knees.

"Kyle. Oh my God, Kyle." He wanted to ask if he was alright, but Kyle was out cold. His chest lifted and rose, alleviating one fear. Wendell stretched out a hand, and froze. He wasn't supposed to move him, he didn't think.

He glanced up the stairs. He couldn't be sure, but it looked like Kyle had fallen down. What if he'd broken his neck? Wendell didn't dare move him.

But there was blood on the floor and he didn't know where it was coming from.

"Help! Help!" Wendell hadn't brought his fucking phone with him, and he didn't want to leave Kyle alone, but he needed to call an ambulance.

Wyatt pounded into view. "What's wrong?"

"Wyatt! Call an ambulance. I think Kyle fell down the stairs." Wendell's voice cut out for a moment. "It's bad."

As contrary as Wyatt often was, he didn't argue for a second, just pulled out his phone and called. Wendell didn't know where was safe to touch Kyle, so he settled for stroking the fingers of his outstretched left hand and whispered encouraging words.

Wyatt paced as they waited. Which fortunately wasn't long. As soon as they heard the sirens in the distance, Wyatt raced to the front door.

The same EMTs who'd attended Chester's death trundled down the hallway, with a lot more haste than they'd done for that call.

They brusquely got Wendell out of the way, and he stared, sick to his stomach as he watched them check vitals, then secure Kyle's neck.

The blood on the floor had them worried, too, and they quickly discovered a compound fracture of Kyle's right forearm, which had been hidden from Wendell's view under Kyle's torso.

Fuck.

He started to shake as they swiftly loaded Kyle onto the stretcher, and he tried desperately not to focus on Kyle's fracture. He'd written, and seen, the film version of a compound fracture multiple times, but he couldn't bear to see that damage on the man he loved.

Large hands grasped him on the shoulder, maybe a little too tight. But then, Wyatt thought of Kyle as another brother. This had to be hard for him too.

Wendell tried to speak, but only a croak came out. He cleared his throat and tried again.

"Who is his emergency contact?"

"Don't know. Drew probably."

They followed the stretcher out to the ambulance. Wendell couldn't stop shaking.

"I'm following him to the hospital," Wendell said as the ambulance sped out of the parking lot, lights flashing.

"No, you will not." Scott Hunter stepped out of the police cruiser that had somehow arrived without Wendell noticing.

"What? Of course, I will."

"Sorry." Scott shook his head. "You've just had a shock, and I can see from here you're shaking. I need to ask you a few questions, then I'll drive you to the hospital, because I don't think either of you are in condition to be behind the wheel." There was sympathy in his voice, and concern, but steel also. They weren't getting around Scott's official edicts.

"Where's Cliff?" Wyatt looked like he needed a hug, but he also looked like he'd kill anyone who came near, and Wendell wanted to live to fight another day.

"I dropped him off across the road first. He'll let Drew know what's going on, get him to the hospital."

That was one less thing to think about.

Daisy had already left for the day, there were no guests in their rooms, as far as Wendell knew, which only left Jackson.

"What about Jackson?" Wendell asked.

"Is he inside?" Scott glanced over his shoulder at the inn's front entrance.

"He was going to take a shower while the guests were out," Wendell replied.

"We'll make sure he knows what's going on."

Another deputy pulled into the lot, and Scott directed him to find Jackson and let him know what happened.

Scott took down a few notes, and although Wendell hated the delay, trying to focus on the answers to Scott's questions sanded the edge off his adrenaline high. A slight queasiness took up residence in his stomach, which could either be from the adrenaline spike or plain old worry. Probably didn't matter much. He knew it wasn't going away until he found out if Kyle was going to be okay.

When they were done, Scott offered the passenger seat to Wendell for the trip to the hospital, and he wasn't about to object. Even though he wasn't sure if he was offended Scott considered the possibility that either he or Wyatt had tried to murder Kyle, or pleased Scott concluded it was no more than an accident.

"Wyatt, you can take the back."

"Oh, fuck no," Wyatt spat out. "Seen enough of the backseats of your damned cruisers. I'll find my own way there."

"No driving. Not for at least an hour."

Wyatt glared at him, then stamped inside the inn.

After they were on their way, Wendell looked over at Scott. "What did Wyatt mean by that?"

Any two other people, Wendell might have assumed a sexual encounter that hadn't gone well, or a past relationship situation. Not that Wendell's gaydar was impeccable, but they didn't interact with each other in the way people did who'd been intimate. In his opinion, Wyatt was almost aggressively straight, but he'd seen that as camouflage more than once, so that didn't prove a damned thing.

"Wyatt and his twin, Rob, have had a number of brushes with the law in the past. They're both working on straightening out their act, mostly because they're trying to stay on Drew's good side, but when they were younger? Saw the backseat of a cop car more than once."

That explained some of the veiled references he'd heard during his first meeting with Drew and Cliff, references that he'd meant to ask Kyle about, but had promptly forgot when they were next alone together and naked.

In a surprisingly short time, they were at the hospital. It was small, and seemed new. At least they didn't have to drive halfway to Tampa.

Scott pulled up next to the walkway near the emergency entrance and threw the car in park, but didn't cut the engine.

"Aren't you coming in?"

"Can't. I need to go back to the inn. Get everything I need for my report. But Cliff will be here with Drew."

"Oh, I guess that makes sense." Wendell opened his door, but paused. He was almost afraid to get out. What if Kyle was in a bad way? The break had been awful, and he'd been out cold. None of that was good news, but it could still be a lot worse than that.

"Give him a hug from me, okay? I'll be in to visit as soon as I get a chance."

Wendell couldn't stay in the car forever. And he wanted to see Kyle. More than anything.

Inside the hospital, after a bit of confusion, he was directed down a chilly corridor to a waiting room. Drew was wrapped in Cliff's arms as they sat together. No one else was in the room.

"How..." Wendell's voiced cracked. "How is he?"

Drew's eyes were rimmed in red and his face was blotchy. He glanced up, and Wendell's gut clenched, fearing the worst.

Drew sniffed, and Cliff gave him a squeeze.

"He regained consciousness in the ambulance, and they said his vitals were good, but they took him immediately into surgery to fix his arm."

"So he'll be okay?" Wendell held his breath as he waited for an answer.

Cliff shrugged. "No one will commit to anything, but they seemed optimistic."

Wendell dropped heavily into a chair as his legs had become rubbery.

"I was so fucking scared. He was so damned still."

Drew reached out and grabbed his hand. Drew's fingers were like ice, but Wendell's weren't much warmer. "At least you and Wyatt were there. What if he'd been alone?"

That didn't even bear thinking of.

Like he'd been summoned, Wyatt raced into the room.

"How is he?"

Cliff tensed up just a bit. There was definitely some friction between Drew's brother and his husband. Which might be nothing more than Wyatt's checkered past that Scott alluded to in the car. Nevertheless, Cliff repeated what they knew about Kyle's status.

"This is so fucked up," Wyatt said as he dropped heavily into the chair beside Wendell. It had definitely not been an hour, but Wendell wasn't going to question if Wyatt had actually driven or gotten a ride to the hospital.

Cliff might not be too keen on Wyatt, but Drew clearly was comforted by his presence. Made Wendell long for one of his own siblings to sit with him. He appreciated Wyatt's proximity, though, as he knew Wyatt better than either Cliff or Drew, and there was some slight comfort to be had by that familiarity.

He'd appreciate some handholding even more, but that would probably get him a hospital bed alongside Kyle if he even suggested such a thing.

Despite Wyatt's edges that were so rough they might well be serrated, he genuinely cared about Kyle and his wellbeing, and that alone was enough to get in Wendell's good books.

A nurse entered through a set of swinging doors and strode over to them.

Her gaze roved over them and lit on Wyatt.

"Are you Kyle Grainger's brother?"

Wyatt bounded to his feet. "I am." The conviction in his voice would have had Wendell believing him, and he started to understand why Cliff and Scott might take issue with some moral flexibility in Wyatt. Then again, Wyatt was the only blond here, and his coloring was far more similar to Kyle's than it was to Drew's.

Drew glared at him and also rose. "I'm Drew, his emergency contact."

The nurse redirected her gaze. "I just wanted to let you know you should go home, get some rest. He's still in surgery, and by the time he's out and recovered, visiting hours will be over. You won't be able to see him until tomorrow, no matter what, so you might as well try and get a good night's sleep. He's in good hands."

Drew nodded, and the nurse returned the way she'd come.

Cliff stood up and took Drew's hand. "Let's go home." He looked at Wyatt and Wendell. "Can we give you a lift?"

"Thank you." Wendell didn't know what else to do but agree. He didn't know how reliable Ubers or taxis were here, and if Cliff and Drew weren't staying, he probably shouldn't either.

He wasn't sure how much rest he was going to get, but it wouldn't hurt to try.

Back at the inn, Wyatt got out of the car with him.

"We can drive you back to your place," Cliff said.

"Nah. My truck is here."

Wyatt patted Drew awkwardly on the shoulder and closed the door.

Interesting. Wyatt had actually obeyed Scott's orders.

Drew gave them a halfhearted wave, and they drove off. Not far, obviously, since they lived across the road.

Wendell wasn't looking forward to telling Jackson everything. Because this had been a lot. He glanced over at Wyatt, who looked just a little bit lost.

Then he remembered the dribs and drabs Kyle had told him about Wyatt. Wyatt, who'd found the body of his best friend. Wyatt, whose partner in crime, aka his twin, had left town for some indeterminate time. Wyatt, whose brother just got married.

"Um, Wyatt, if you wanted to crash on my sofa tonight, that would be okay." Wendell wasn't sure he wanted to be alone with his thoughts, and maybe Wyatt didn't either.

There was a pregnant pause was Wyatt simply stared at him, like he was processing Wendell's words.

Then he smirked. "Sure, yeah. But hands off the merchandise." He gave himself a smack on the ass, then sauntered into the inn.

Wendell sighed wearily, then followed him inside.

He found Lisa, Tony, and Barbara at a table in the dining room, which was normally empty at this time of day. These three were some of the people closest to Kyle so it didn't surprise him that they were already on the scene. They all had mugs in front of them, and a couple of plates that had crumbs on them. A fourth mug on the table indicated that Jackson was close by.

He followed Wyatt to the coffee station, but chose peppermint tea instead of anything caffeinated. Sleeping would be elusive enough without any stimulants. Should also help with the queasiness that hadn't much abated. He might write about gore, but seeing all that blood in real life, from a man he loved, was disturbing in a way he'd never anticipated.

Once he'd gotten his drink, he pulled a chair up to the table and sat down. Wyatt had slipped away, but Jackson had already returned.

"Where'd Wyatt go?"

Lisa shared a look with Barbara. "It's taking some time for Sandy Bottom Bay to get used to the newly law-abiding Drummond twins, and vice versa," Lisa said. "There is some awkwardness with people they've, um, had interactions with in the past."

Both Barbara and Tony wore neutral expressions, so Wendell wasn't sure which one of, well, the three of them who'd had previous altercations with Wyatt. Maybe all of them.

Jackson opened his mouth, maybe to defend Wyatt, maybe to ask for specifics, but then he cut his gaze to Wendell.

"How are you doing?"

"Me? Don't you want to know how Kyle is doing?"

Jackson waggled his phone. "Cliff is keeping us updated, via Scott. But you've... well, this has to be hard on you." Empathy shone bright and clear in Jackson's eyes.

The other three around the table nodded in agreement, and Barbara took a break from her knitting to pat his hand.

"Oh. Uh, yeah, I think I'm still in shock. I, mean, I can't even figure out what happened."

"When Scott came back from dropping you at the hospital, he was very thorough. He scouted the stairs, and checked where the carpet is tacked down. He didn't see anything that would have caused Kyle to trip. He took a lot of photos, but I think, unless Kyle says otherwise when he's able to answer questions, he's chalking it up to a tragic accident," Jackson said.

Wendell blinked. "What else would it be?"

Jackson's cheeks reddened. "Negligence. If it was a loose floor-board or carpeting."

"Oh. I see." His mind was definitely fuzzy as he hadn't even considered the ramifications of such a serious accident on commercial property. "Maybe his knee gave out."

Lisa nodded. "I expect you're right. It never returned to a hundred percent after his accident."

She gave him a little smile. "Drew texted me while he was on his way to the hospital, and I closed down the bakery to come right over."

"That was very kind of you," Jackson said. "The past few weeks have been more difficult than I expected. And Tony cleaned up, which was a real help, since I expect to see guests returning any time now."

Something in Wendell's gut unclenched. He hadn't been actively worried about seeing Kyle's blood on the floor, but his subconscious had clearly been in a tizzy about it.

"You two are honorary Sandies now. We'd help you out even if it wasn't for Sandra and Bill." Lisa smiled gently at them.

Sandies? Somehow it didn't surprise him that the name for residents of Sandy Bottom Bay was something he hadn't expected and wouldn't have guessed. Not that he could immediately come up with better idea.

He loved the idea of being an honorary Sandy, and it made sense for Tony and Lisa to feel that way. He and Jackson had almost daily dealings with the bakery, and had gotten on quite well with them. But Barbara? He'd just met her the other day for the first time, despite clearly being a regular at the bakery.

Like she could intuit his confusion, she looked up from her knitting and gave him an impish smile.

"You're wondering why the dotty old lady tagged along?"

Wendell pressed his lips together. There was no polite way to answer that question, and from the sparkle in her eyes, Barbara knew it.

But she took mercy on him.

"I'm the one who developed the ghost walk itinerary for the chamber of commerce, and I was their first tour guide. I trained Kyle on all the knowledge he needed. But he definitely has more panache and charisma than I ever did."

If the group's goal was to get his mind off Kyle's injury, they were doing a great job.

"Why? I mean, I guess someone had to develop the tour, but..." Wendell didn't even know what he was trying to ask. It had never once occurred to him to wonder about the origins of Kyle's performance.

Barbara waved a hand in an almost dismissive gesture. "I used to be a cultural anthropology professor at one of the universities in Tampa. My focus was on oral traditions, and I developed a related interest in folklore and ghost stories. The ghost tour derived from a paper I was writing on the subject of local oral traditions, which in this town is all ghost stories."

"I'm utterly fascinated. But that still doesn't explain why you're here, aside from concern for Kyle. I don't think any of us can learn the patter quick enough to take over the tours. In fact, I should probably call someone at the chamber of commerce to let them know they'll have to find someone else to run the tours, or maybe cancel them."

Barbara rolled her eyes. "Dear boy, that's why I'm here. I'm going to do the tours while Kyle is incapacitated."

Wendell frowned. "But that's a really long walk." He'd definitely got in his steps that day.

"I'm not in my dotage, you know. I walk over five miles a day, when I'm not engaged in my ethnocultural studies of the textile arts. And I'm also on the local art council." She shook her knitting at him with a stern look. And he suddenly had no trouble imagining her as a professor. One that was a tough grader.

Wendell was amazed Sandy Bottom Bay had a local art council, but perhaps he shouldn't. If nothing else, someone had to govern the museum.

"Thank you, Barbara, for taking this on. I know Kyle will be worried about it."

"He's a good boy. As are you for taking care of him."

Wendell bit his lip. He didn't really feel like he'd taken good care of Kyle at all, between the nightmares and the broken bones. But he wanted to.

They talked a little more, Lisa telling a few stories about her and Drew and Kyle in high school, and Wendell shared a few mishaps on various sets that he'd witnessed. It was nice talking to people who were interested in what he did but weren't starry-eyed or wondering what he could do for their careers.

The guests staying at the inn were unexpectedly self-reliant, and although they heard several of them come in and go out, none of them rang the bell or texted Jackson. They ordered Chinese food and had a quiet, amiable dinner that Wyatt joined them for.

After dinner, Wyatt asked Wendell quietly if he could go crash, and Wendell gave Wyatt a key to his cottage, figuring he'd just use his master key to get in later. Wendell wanted to crash too, but he wasn't sure he'd be able to sleep yet, so he'd rather let his new friend group keep him distracted.

All too soon, though, Barbara packed up her knitting and traded out her fleece-lined Birkenstock sandals—which made Wendell sweat just looking at them—for a pair of heavy-duty running shoes and thick socks. Lisa handed her a trademark bakery bag with the cookies Kyle normally handed out for a tour.

"What are these?" Barbara pulled out an individually wrapped gingerbread mummy.

"A little bit of flair Kyle has added to the tour. He gives out cookies, and my business cards, to all the tour guests."

Barbara smiled and shook her head. "See? Panache. In spades." She took the bag, then offered the bag with her knitting and sandals to Lisa. "Can you take this into the bakery tomorrow for me? I think between my purse and the cookies, I'll have more than enough to carry."

As much as he just wanted to curl up on his bed and go to sleep, even if it wasn't quite eight o'clock, Wendell had to speak up.

"I can go along on the tour, you know. Carry your stuff for you."

"No, no, I'll be fine. Today is a bit helter-skelter, but tomorrow I'll have time to put together my regular tour kit, which involves a tote on wheels, a collapsible stool, a big umbrella and a rain poncho."

Wendell smiled. "Are you sure?"

"I am. I've already turned down Lisa and Tony's offers. I remind you, I am not infirm or in my dotage."

The thread of steel in her voice told Wendell he'd be smarter not to offer again.

"Then I think I will head to back to my cottage."

Lisa and Tony stood. "We need to get going. Mornings come very early for bakery people."

Everyone gave him a hug, and Jackson saw them out while Wendell cleaned up the remains of dinner and the dishes.

He had just finished putting the last mug in the dishwasher when something struck him. Barbara had designed the ghost tour. Designed. He ran for the front, hoping she hadn't already left the porch of the inn, because he didn't have the energy to chase her down.

He skidded to a stop by the front door. Jackson was nowhere in sight, but Barbara and the group were still on the porch. After taking a moment to catch his breath, he slipped out the door and waited until Barbara had told everyone about the history of the Orange Lady Inn and her namesake.

The story was much as Kyle had told it, but as Barbara had already admitted, without the same flair. Barbara might love to study storytelling, but Kyle was a natural at actually doing it.

He waved Barbara over once she'd finished her spiel, and he pulled her aside.

"Sorry, I just thought of a question." He'd have to be quick, before the tour group got restless. "Why doesn't the tour mention Matthew Trask's death? Shouldn't he be a ghost here as well?"

Barbara waved her hand dismissively. "No. He died of a heart attack. Death by natural causes doesn't make for a good ghost story." She straightened up, like she was about to deliver a lecture on how events got incorporated into an oral tradition, but one of her flock approached with a question, and Wendell went back inside the inn, then headed for his cottage.

That certainly explained why no one had mentioned the similarity between Chester's death and Trask's. Probably no one but Barbara and others of her age group remembered it, and likely not without someone or something triggering that memory. Like showing around a picture of the man.

Damn, the walk to his cottage seemed way longer than normal.

Each step, his limbs got heavier and heavier, like he was walking through thick, sucking mud. He wasn't sure he'd ever been this tired before.

At least his cottage was the first one. He let himself in, and got a little jolt at the sound of a buzzsaw drowning out the sound of the crashing waves on the beach.

Then he realized it was Wyatt, sacked out on his couch and snoring fit to wake the dead.

Wendell was either going to lay awake worrying about Kyle or he was going to pass the fuck out from emotional exhaustion. Either way, the snoring was going to be immaterial, especially as it was rhythmic enough to act as white noise.

He trudged into the bedroom, stripped down to his boxer briefs, turned off the light, and tumbled into bed.

And stared at the ceiling.

Kyle's bad dreams had been filled with blood, and now Wendell feared his would be as well.

He snatched up his phone and pressed a button.

"Wendell? Are you finally ready to give up on this nonsense and come home?"

"Luce," was all he got out before his voice cracked and the tears started. Lucinda might not be his most sensitive sibling, but they were definitely the closest of the four of them.

"Oh my god, Wendell. What the fuck is wrong? Who do I have to kill?"

He let out a watery laugh, although it wasn't enough to stop the waterworks entirely.

"No one. There's no one to kill." He was barely coherent, but he managed to get the words out.

"Then you tell me what is going on right now, or, or... I don't know what I'll do, but it will be dramatic."

Wendell laughed a little more. Lucinda was normally a very practical, level-headed person, but she was also hands-down the fiercest defender of their family. If Kyle had ever thought himself too over the top, he just needed to see Lucinda in defender mode to feel better. There had been that one time with a school bully. Lucinda's response had attracted the attention of the FBI. And they hadn't been pleased.

"Well, I met someone."

There was a hitch in Lucinda's breathing. And before she assumed he just got dumped, Wendell told her about Kyle. How he felt. And the accident.

There had been more tears, and although Lucinda wasn't the greatest at giving comfort, she did her best, which was all Wendell could ask for.

Eventually, his tears dried up, and they started talking about how his trip was in general. Luce considerately did not ask how his writing was going, although he was going to have to tell her sooner or later.

Tonight was not either of those times.

"Wendell? Wendell?" Luce asked.

"What?" His tongue felt thick, and his throat was scratchy. He grabbed the glass of water beside his bed and took a drink.

"You almost fell asleep on me. Time to go to bed, okay?"

"Okay." He finished off the water.

"Things will look better in the morning, I promise. And text me if you hear anything about Kyle, okay?"

"Okay," he said again.

"Night, baby bro."

"Night, Luce." His phone slipped from his fingers to land near his shoulder.

Wendell flipped onto his side and curled his arm tightly around the pillow Kyle had slept on.

Then his eyes dropped closed, and everything faded to black.

TWENTY-SIX

2 Days to Haunt Fest

WENDELL SAT up straight in bed, sunlight streaming in through the windows. His eyes were swollen and sore, but that was secondary.

"What the hell was Kyle doing upstairs?"

"What was that then?" A voice called from the kitchenette.

Wendell gasped and pulled the sheets up to his chin like a Victorian maiden while his pulse skyrocketed. Who the fuck was in his cottage?

Oh. Right. Wyatt.

"Nothing," he called out. But it wasn't nothing. Wendell checked the time. If he hurried, he could make it to the hospital for the start of visiting hours. After a quick check of his phone—no texts or phone calls telling him Kyle took a turn for the worse—he took care of the morning's biological necessities then pulled on jeans and a t-shirt.

Showering would only make him late for visiting hours.

When he left the bedroom, he was pleased to note Wyatt was at least wearing briefs. He'd have been happier if he'd been fully dressed, but at least he wasn't naked.

"Don't you have any coffee here?" Wyatt asked, voice still thick with sleep. He must have awakened not long before Wendell had.

"Nope. Only tea. I don't often drink coffee, and when I want some, I can just grab it from inn's dining room."

Wyatt grunted.

"Say, do you remember seeing Kyle come into the inn yesterday afternoon?"

Wyatt blinked at him. It was a particularly doltish expression, but something about it made Wendell suspect it was a deliberate attempt to make people think Wyatt was stupid. And despite all the bro banter and coarseness, Wendell thought Wyatt might not be at all stupid.

"No. Didn't see Kyle at all, until, well..." Wyatt swallowed heavily, and Wendell did the same.

"Is that weird? I mean I went into the sunroom, and I saw you in the kitchen when I passed by."

"Yeah, I saw you too."

The response was hardly needed, since they had nodded to each other in greeting.

"Wouldn't you have noticed Kyle coming in too?"

"No," Wyatt grunted. Then his face made a funny contortion, like he realized Wendell wasn't actually the police trying to get him to incriminate himself. He cleared his throat. "Maybe I would have noticed Kyle coming in, or maybe I wouldn't. I'd been outside just before I was in the kitchen, mucking with the generator, and that's around the corner."

Wendell pursed his lips. That would have been before Wendell had entered the inn, having just left Kyle in the cottage. Kyle would have had to come to the main building sometime after Wendell had already gotten there.

Then again, Wyatt had been working. Kyle could have slipped in without either of them knowing. Or Jackson.

Either way, that didn't explain why Kyle had gone upstairs. He'd have no reason to be in the guest areas, unless Jackson had asked him to run an errand for a guest. And based on Jackson's reaction to Chester's death, Wendell believed Jackson would have been completely wracked with guilt if Kyle had been performing a service for the inn when he'd fallen down the stairs.

Wyatt cleared his throat, and Wendell realized he'd gone silent, lost in his thoughts.

"I'm heading to the hospital now. Let me know if you want to crash here again tonight." Wendell was leaving the invitation open, because he'd definitely been more comfortable not being alone in his cottage last night, momentary scare this morning notwithstanding.

Wyatt grunted and lifted a shoulder. "Tell Kyle I'll be in to see him later."

The response was gruff, and didn't address Wendell's invitation at all, but he sensed Wyatt didn't hate the idea. Not a surprise, really. He likely wasn't used to living alone, not if he usually shared a place with his twin.

Wendell grabbed his travel mug and sped to the inn to fill his mug with coffee before he hopped in his rental and drove to the hospital as fast as the speed limit would allow.

Kyle tried to blink his eyes open, but his eyes were gritty and his lids heavy, and he gave up, leaving them closed for the time being. It was like he'd just pulled an all-nighter. But it had been a long time since he'd done that, for anything. He rarely drank to excess, not even in college. Sleep was just too important to squander on anything besides good sex. And unless he'd just boinked a cement mixer or steamroller, he had not had a good time last night.

His bed was also screamingly uncomfortable. He shifted and let out a groan.

Holy fuck, but every damned thing hurt. His arm was heavy and oddly immobile. And his mouth was so dry it was like the Sahara desert had died there.

There was no hope for it. He needed to open his damned eyes.

He squinted against the light. It was as bright as day, but didn't have the warmth of sunlight. Had he fallen asleep with the lights on?

Then his eyes focused, first on the IV bag hanging above his head, tubing snaking toward his left side. He lifted his left hand, which was the IV's destination.

Hospital. That explained some things. He turned his head gently, to see his right arm. It was immobilized in a cast, and a contraption held it slightly elevated. He suspected it would take some effort to move it, and based on the dull ache that was becoming an insistent throb, he was not in any hurry to move his arm.

Thank fuck Drew had arranged for real health insurance for the both of them last year for the business, or Kyle would have had to rip out the IV and haul ass out of there before he was bankrupted.

"Oh, you're awake." Wendell burst into his room, and Kyle tried to smile, but that hurt too, as his lips were every bit as dry as his mouth.

He tried to work his throat, but couldn't create any saliva or understandable sounds.

"The nurse said you might want some water, let me help you."

The next few moments were spent getting as pampered as he could in a hospital bed. Wendell raised the head of his bed so he was more or less sitting up, then directed a straw at his mouth. He wasn't allowed to suck it all down in one go, but it wasn't long before he felt more human. A well-battered human, but one less likely to dry up and blow away.

"How are you feeling?"

"Sore," Kyle croaked out. And it was slowly getting worse. At least there would be some drugs on offer. He hoped.

"I'm sure you are. You scared the shit out of me, you know. I came running when I heard you cry out."

Wendell sat down beside him, on his left. Instead of holding his hand, which might dislodge the IV, Wendell slid his palm under Kyle's and let it rest there.

His hand was so warm, like a heating pad. It let Kyle relax a trifle.

"Uh, what happened?" Kyle couldn't help but glance at his brand new cast, but he hadn't had much chance to inventory any other injuries.

"You fell down the stairs at the inn. Somehow, you managed to avoid getting a concussion, which is a minor miracle, but you had a compound fracture on your forearm, both radius and ulna were broken." Wendell shuddered and paled slightly. Kyle shuddered right along with him. He'd seen another dancer with a compound leg fracture and it had not been pretty.

Thankfully, he didn't remember seeing his own fracture.

"What about my knee?" Because if he'd re-injured his knee, there might not be any recovering from that.

"Drew told them about that when you were brought in, but my understanding is that you mostly have contusions. A couple of bruised ribs as well, but no serious leg injuries."

Okay. Bruised ribs and a broken arm he could deal with. It wasn't like he had to lift other dancers anymore.

"And Barbara is taking over the ghost tours until you're ready to go back."

"Good." He hadn't even remembered about the tour, but he definitely would have fretted about it as soon as it crossed his mind.

"How, uh, long?" Kyle waved a finger around in the hopes that would get his point across about how much time he was missing.

"You fell yesterday afternoon, had surgery that same night, and now it's just after ten in the morning."

That wasn't so bad. And he was so thankful he didn't have a concussion. Barfing his guts out like Drew had with his would have been agony with his broken arm. But like Drew, he also had a very handsome companion to care for him.

Wendell stroked his arm lightly with his other hand.

"What happened, do you remember? Why were you upstairs?"

Kyle blinked at him. Wendell offered more water, which Kyle took while he tried to piece together the previous day. His heart started beating faster, and he gripped Wendell's hand tightly with his own, now clammy hand.

Unlike Drew, this hospital visit was going to cost him the man he loved. Because... because... he mostly knew what happened before he fell. But he needed Wendell's help.

"You have to help me."

"Of course. What do you need?"

"And you can't tell Drew." Because he'd tell Cliff. And he didn't know what Cliff would do.

"Anything. What is it?"

It was starting to get hard to breathe, but he needed to get this out.

"I... I don't remember why I went upstairs. I don't remember leaving the cottage, I don't remember going upstairs." He tried to talk quietly, and quickly. He had to get this out while there were still alone.

"You have to tell the doctors. They must have missed a brain injury if you're having memory loss."

"No!" The vehemence of the word tore at his throat, but Wendell anticipated him and had the straw at the ready. Kyle sipped gratefully but every second not talking was wasting time.

"Why don't you want to tell the doctors?"

"Because I didn't lose time after the accident, I lost it before. I... think I might be losing my mind." He hiccupped, and his eyes burned but he was able to keep the tears at bay.

"What are you talking about?"

"One minute I was in your cottage. The next thing I knew I was standing on the inn's upstairs landing. I don't know how I got there, or why I was there, but I had a knife in my hand."

"A knife?" There was a weird note in Wendell's voice, but Kyle had too many problems to try and ferret out why. Hell, it might just be because he agreed with Kyle's assessment of his mental state.

This time, he couldn't stop it, and a tear rolled down his cheek.

His right cheek, so he couldn't do anything but let it drip down his face, roll down his neck, and soak into his hospital gown.

"Yes," Kyle whispered. "I don't know where it came from. And I heard a voice." This was the worst part. "It wanted me to hurt people."

Wendell sucked in a breath. Too bad that wasn't the end of it.

"I didn't know if I could stop it. Block out the voice. I dropped the knife. But part of me wanted to pick it up again. I... I... did it myself. I figured if I hurt myself bad enough, I couldn't hurt anyone else."

Wendell's face was as pale as the sterile wall behind him.

"Are you saying you fell down the stairs on purpose?" Wendell's voice was as hushed as Kyle's now.

"Yes. I didn't know what else to do. But I'm afraid. I need help. Please, find someone, a psychiatrist, who can help me."

"I will get you whatever help you need. But why can't I tell Drew?"

"Because he'll tell Cliff. And I don't want to get arrested. Promise me!"

"Oh honey. It'll be okay, but I promise not to tell Drew."

It wasn't going to be okay. How could it be okay?

"Kyle, have you considered that this might be the morphine talking?"

Being with Wendell had always been comfortable. Safe. But safety was an illusion. If his mind was truly playing tricks on him, nowhere was safe. There was no escape. He started to tremble.

"It's not. This happened. I'm... I'm losing my shit. This wasn't the first time I heard that voice. I see blood all the time. I can't take it."

This time the tears started and he couldn't stop them. They shook his body, ratcheting up the pain, which made the tears worse, and then he started gasping. There wasn't any air in his lungs.

"Kyle, oh my God, Kyle. Breathe." Wendell's words barely registered over the cacophony of beeping, then a nurse thundered into the room.

More shouting, words he couldn't understand, but he kept his gaze on Wendell's frightened face, even as his vision grayed at the edges.

Then everything in him relaxed and he slipped into blissful sleep.

Wendell stumbled out of Kyle's hospital room, stunned. He leaned against the wall, then slid to the floor, his legs too wobbly to keep him upright.

What the ever-loving fuck was going on right now?

The pair of nurses who'd responded to Kyle's heart monitor finally emerged, and saw him on the floor.

"Are you okay? Did you fall?"

"Um. No, just... is he okay? What happened?"

Wendell clenched his trembling fingers in a fist.

"C'mon. We'll get you into a chair."

They helped him up, then one of them guided him to an empty room while the other disappeared. When she reappeared, she had a small, institutional cup of apple juice in her hand.

"Drink this. You'll feel better."

Wendell obeyed, and she left again, leaving him in the company of the male nurse.

A few moments later he'd regained his composure, and he asked his question again.

"What happened?"

"Not supposed to tell you unless you have his permission." The nurse glanced furtively around. "But that had to have been scary. It was just a panic attack. He's fine. Trauma, even accidental trauma, can sometimes have unexpected consequences."

A panic attack.

"He was talking about some weird stuff."

"It could be a side effect of the pain killers he's on. We'll keep an eye on him, but Sarah is going to keep him from having visitors until this afternoon. So if you're feeling better, you should go home. Take a break. Come back later today if you want."

Wendell nodded. "Thank you."

"You sit here until you're back on an even keel."

Wendell nodded again, and then he was alone.

Was it coincidence Kyle's drug-induced hallucination had included a knife? Drew must have mentioned something about Wendell's tarot reading, and it stuck in Kyle's subconscious. Wendell hadn't actually mentioned any details to Kyle. He hadn't had a chance, and honestly, it had all seemed like a bit of a lark.

But he couldn't stay here all day. Going back to the inn and helping out Jackson would keep his mind off Kyle's obvious terror. He hoped.

At the end of the hall, coming toward him, were Drew and Wyatt. He rushed up to them.

"They've said no more visitors until this afternoon."

"What? Why?" Drew asked.

"He had a panic attack after he woke up." More or less the truth.

"A panic attack. That doesn't seem like Kyle."

Wendell shrugged. "I agree, but it could be a reaction to the meds. Or maybe something like PTSD?" Or simply fear that his mental health was in severe jeopardy. But he'd promised not to tell Drew about that. And Wendell still thought it might be a hallucination that could be blamed on the painkillers.

"But he's okay, aside from that?"

Wendell nodded. What else could he do?

"Okay. We'll come back later."

As he walked out with them, he put an arm on Drew's to slow him down a bit.

"Did you tell Kyle about my tarot reading?"

"No, of course not."

"Of course not?"

Drew huffed. "I get a lot of people telling me very personal things. I would never get any repeat business if I told everyone else those same personal things. It drives Kyle crazy, mind you. He soaks up gossip like a sponge."

Interesting. Drew had already proved to Kyle, on an ongoing basis, that he could be tight-lipped.

"And you don't tell Cliff anything either?"

"Generally, no. He's not much interested in the woo-woo part of my business. But I have told him some readings, when there's been danger involved."

Ah. There it was. The reason Kyle didn't want Drew to know.

"Okay, thanks. I appreciate that."

"Maybe we can come back over together this afternoon?"

"Sounds good. Text me."

At least Wyatt had driven Drew over. Otherwise there would have been a parade of three cars heading back to the same block on Main Street. Not particularly good for the environment, even if Wendell's car was a small hybrid.

Wyatt was close on his heels when he headed slowly into the inn. He almost snapped out a snarky question about Wyatt not having another job to go to, but that wasn't fair. Kyle had asked him to do some work around the inn, and Jackson clearly liked having him around, even when the two of them squabbled.

Wendell was about to find Jackson, ask if there was anything he could do. Instead, he walked to the infamous staircase. The blood on the floor was gone. There was no trace of the incident.

But something was wrong.

Then he noticed Wyatt was standing next to him.

"What?" He was careful not to snap, because Wyatt did *not* deserve that.

"That's what I was going to ask you."

Wendell sighed. He definitely needed some perspective.

"Can you keep a secret?"

Wyatt huffed. "If I couldn't, I would be in jail right now."

"What about from your brother? Drew, I mean."

That made Wyatt even more somber. "Drew is a good person. Rob and I, we did our best to protect him, keep him shiny and happy. Our parents weren't good people. Most of our family is in jail or dead. But Drew somehow ended up untarnished by the Drummond legacy."

There was a Drummond legacy? Something to follow up at a later time. His gossip hound boyfriend could fill him in when he was feeling better.

"Okay?"

Wyatt huffed in exasperation. "Neither of us could ever tell Drew everything, because if he knew everything Rob and I got up to, he'd be very unhappy. So yes, if needed, I can keep a secret from Drew."

"First of all, let me tell you about the tarot reading I had."

That took all of two minutes. Wyatt's expression mostly remained placid, except for a brief moment after Wendell mentioned potentially needing Eddie Price's help. But the complicated expression was gone too quickly for Wendell to decipher it. Nor could he tell if Wyatt found anything of import in the reading, regardless of his previous verbal support of Drew's gift.

"Anyway, this morning, Kyle told me he, um." This was hard to say aloud. "He said he did it on purpose. Fell, I mean."

That got him a reaction from Wyatt. Anger. "What the fuck are you saying?"

"He said he fell, to stop the voice that was telling him to hurt someone. He said he didn't remember how he got upstairs, but he had a knife in his hand."

"There was no knife when he fell."

"I know. And most of me thinks it was the drugs talking."

"Except for my brother's tarot reading."

"Except for your brother's tarot reading." Even though he still wasn't convinced Drew had any sort of gift, except for an exceptional ability to cold read people.

"Then I guess we need to look for a knife."

There was a giddy relief in knowing he wasn't alone, that someone else thought it might be worthwhile looking for a knife.

The stairway was wide enough for both of them to walk up side by side.

At a glance, nothing appeared out of place.

"Scott searched up here already."

"Yeah, but he would have been looking for things that made Kyle fall. Not a knife."

"True. But he's a cop. Surely he would have said something if there was a knife just lying on the floor, wouldn't he?" Wendell asked.

"Yeah he would. He's not nearly as dumb as he seems."

Wendell thought there might be an epidemic of that going around, because Wyatt followed that back-handed compliment up with a logical conclusion.

"Which means if Kyle had a knife up here, he hid it somewhere before he fell. Did Kyle have a master key for the guest rooms?" Wyatt asked.

"No. I had mine in my pocket, and Jackson keeps his on his person, too."

"And are there any guests here at the moment?"

"Let me text Jackson and ask." Fortunately Jackson responded promptly. "He thinks everyone's gone out."

"Then we don't have to be quiet, but we'd better be quick."

It was immediately obvious that Wyatt had hidden things a time or three in his life, because his search was far more thorough than Wendell expected. Cushions flew off the chairs, and the chairs were upended. Carpet was lifted.

Wendell had opened drawers on the credenza but Wyatt pulled them right out, and upended the credenza as well.

So far, nothing. At least Wyatt was as capable of returning order to the madness as he was at creating it.

Then Wendell went over to a large waist high vase with huge sprigs of eucalyptus in it. He'd only intended to move it away from the corner so he could better see into the shadows behind it, but something clunked inside as he shifted it.

"Wyatt, help me with this."

"Yeah, that would be a good place." Wendell lifted out the eucalyptus and Wyatt tilted the vase over.

An old hunting knife slid to the floor. Its blade was about four inches long, darkened and pitted with age. The edge had seen many, many sharpenings over its lifetime. The hilt appeared to be made of bone or antler.

The only saving grace was there were no obvious bloodstains on the blade.

Wyatt set the vase down and bent over to grab the knife.

"Don't touch that!" Wendell's voice was sharp.

Wyatt paused for a moment, hand outstretched, then he stood. "Good idea."

Wendell did not want to think Kyle had actually hurt anyone with that wicked-looking knife. But if he had, the last thing anyone needed was his or Wyatt's fingerprints in the mix.

He grabbed the pad of paper from the credenza with the inn's letterhead. He tore off a sheet and used that to pick up the knife. But what to do with it now?

"Let me grab a paper bag from the kitchen."

Wendell waited, and prayed no one would encounter him because even if Miss Piggy was holding this knife, it would be terrifying.

Wyatt returned in extremely short order—he was also faster on his feet than Wendell realized.

Once the knife safely was in the bag, Wendell wondered where he should put it. And what exactly this meant for his newly shifting worldview.

"Guess you're off to see Eddie Price?"

Wendell blinked. "Yeah, I guess I am."

TWENTY-SEVEN

2 Days to Haunt Fest

UNDER NORMAL CIRCUMSTANCES, he'd never wander into a store with a knife. This one was at least in a paper bag nestled carefully inside Kyle's messenger bag that he'd left in Wendell's bedroom.

But under normal circumstances, he'd have laughed off Drew's ill-omened fortune.

Yet here he was, standing outside a medium's door, knife in his bag, wondering if he should have made an appointment, and wishing Kyle had already managed to find the time to clear the air with Eddie.

Maybe he should have ignored it all and started looking for a mental health professional, like Kyle had asked him to.

But there had been too many oddities in the recent days, and now he was determined to contribute to the pool of oddities.

With a firm hand, he pulled open the door and stepped inside. It was cool and dark inside, and he was the only one there.

Eddie also had a few items for sale, but they were more in the jewelry and books line than the stuff in Drew's store. He wasn't sure how their feud began, especially since he could easily see them combining forces, from an efficiency and economic perspective.

But what did he know about the vagaries of running a paranormal business?

He didn't feel quite as benevolent about Eddie's chosen profession as he did about Drew's. Mainly because it seemed a bit predatory to profit from grieving people.

Then again, funeral homes also profited from grieving people and maybe didn't give as much comfort as Eddie could, charlatan or not.

Just as he was wondering how long he could wait before he started calling out, Eddie emerged, silent and startling, from a well concealed doorway. Both he and Drew had that shit down pat.

"Oh, hello," Eddie purred as he approached. Then he blinked, and recognition dawned. The flirtatious air disappeared like it had never been there, replaced with concern.

"I heard about Kyle. How is he doing?"

"Um. That's sort of what I came to see you about."

Eddie paled and stumbled, reaching out a hand to the counter to steady himself. "He... he... *died?*"

Wendell gasped, and hurried to reassure Eddie. "No, no, I don't need your professional services."

Then he frowned. Why had Drew sent him here? "At least not for Kyle."

Eddie wiped a hand across his face, still looking none too steady. Wendell should have realized the implications of coming to a medium and talking about Kyle.

Considering how still and broken Kyle had looked after his fall, it wasn't something he even wanted to think about.

"Can we talk?"

Eddie pulled a sign out from under the counter and propped it in the window before locking the door.

"Come on back."

He led Wendell to a little room that had been decorated like a Victorian parlor, probably because that was what everyone imagined when they thought of attending a seance. Or at least, that's what Wendell did. But Drew's space has been modified from a home, and Eddie's had been modified from blocky office space. He'd done a good job of hiding the corporate vibes, but it was still a bit more clinical.

Eddie did have a giant crystal ball in the middle of his table, which managed to not look completely hokey. There were more chairs in this room than Drew had, and the table was round and much larger.

Drew likely didn't do readings for large groups, where Eddie might well perform seances or whatever for several people at the same time. Oddly enough, Wendell had never included a medium in any of his films, and therefore had only the most basic idea of what one might do to earn a living.

Wendell sat, not sure where to begin, and what might be relevant, with respect to Drew's command to come and see Eddie.

Eddie sat in a chair next to him, instead of on the other side of the table. The man was handsome, if a bit older. Closer to Jackson's age than Kyle's, if he had to guess. Maybe around his own age.

"Look, I don't know why you don't like Kyle—"

"Please, let me stop you there." Eddie shook his head ruefully. "I don't dislike Kyle, I like both him and Drew."

Truth rang in his words.

"But what about the rivalry? Competition for business?"

"There isn't really much overlap in what we do. Never has been. I started this business when Drew's grandmother was doing tarot readings. She helped me quite a bit in the beginning, when I was starting out. The rivalry is... well... mostly a misunderstanding. One that I should have corrected before now."

Wendell did not get the impression Eddie was going to elaborate on the specifics, but he definitely got the sense of loneliness. Could Eddie have been playing into the rivalry as a means of social interaction? Even in a place as quirky as Sandy Bottom Bay, someone who claimed to talk to the dead might not be a social butterfly.

"Tell me, what can I help you with?"

If Wendell wanted to test Eddie's veracity, he would have held information back. The more info Eddie had, the more likely he'd be able to con Wendell. But he wasn't here to test Eddie's alleged gift. He was here to help Kyle any way he could. And Drew, who cared for Kyle like a brother, thought Eddie might be the answer.

Wendell told Eddie everything, including Chester's death and finding the stash of photos.

When he finally completed his story, his throat was a bit raw from speaking. He was accustomed to storytelling on paper, not vocally.

Eddie didn't offer, just grabbed a bottle of water from a bar fridge disguised as an antique Victrola and handed it to him. Wendell drank gratefully, then stared at Eddie, waiting.

"I can tell you're a skeptic, so I don't want to tell you what I suspect. But I'll need to see the knife, and also visit Kyle."

"I brought the knife with me." Wendell used a rag he'd swiped from Daisy's cleaning cart to extract the knife from the brown paper bag. He set it down on the table, and Eddie recoiled.

"That is... whoa. Not to be too dramatic, but there is some evil associated with that knife."

If it made Kyle fling himself down the stairs, Wendell was in complete agreement.

"Please, put it away for now." Eddie shuddered. If he was acting, he was one of the best Wendell had ever met.

Wendell did as asked. "Do you think we should wait until Kyle is out of the hospital before you go see him? He's really quite fragile." Although Wendell had sworn Eddie to secrecy, he was not sure he'd done the right thing by telling Eddie everything Kyle had said in the hospital.

"I think that it would be better for Kyle's wellbeing to get him the help he needs as soon as possible. If that's not me, then you're free to contact whatever medical professional you want."

"Then let's go. Visiting hours will be starting soon." Wendell hoped this visit wasn't going to trigger another panic attack.

"Is there anything else personal in that bag?" Eddie asked.

"No." He'd emptied everything else out in his bedroom before he'd placed the knife inside.

"Good."

Eddie closed up shop, and they walked out to where Wendell had parked his car. He dropped the messenger bag in the back seat, and then drove them to the hospital.

All the way there, he did his best not to think about why Eddie might be able to help Kyle. If he did, he'd have to question his own sanity.

When they arrived at the hospital, Eddie waited outside in the hall with the messenger bag while Wendell slipped inside. Several flower arrangements and stuffed animals had been delivered, making the barren room appear fractionally more inviting.

At Kyle's bedside, Wyatt sat alone, the silence between them awkward and strained.

Which might be because Wyatt was unaccustomed to giving comfort, or he'd just said something uncouth. Odds were fifty-fifty between the two options.

"How are you feeling?" He came right over and kissed Kyle gently on the lips, garnering a strangled groan from Wyatt.

But at least he didn't swear.

"Shut it, Wyatt," Kyle said. He was clearly feeling more like himself, although when he looked at Wendell the strain he was under was still obvious.

And now that Kyle's fears were out in the open, more or less, Wendell realized he'd been seeing evidence of that strain for days, not simply the result of the upcoming festival.

He also looked a lot more banged up as the bruising had started to darken.

"I'm doing better. They changed my pain meds, and I'm not so woozy now."

"Where's Drew?"

Wyatt rolled his eyes. "Said he'd be here soon, but he made me come in right when visiting hours started."

Made him. He had a strong suspicion that Drew had nothing to do with Wyatt's presence. More like he'd been worried about what Wendell had told him, about Kyle hurting himself on purpose. For all that he tried to appear gruff and insensitive, the man wasn't heartless. One just had to dig deep to find evidence of it.

The silence between the three of them became awkward because Wendell had no idea what to say next. He also wasn't sure if he should try to get Wyatt to leave them alone for a bit. But he already knew almost everything. Kyle had asked him to keep Drew out of it, not other people.

Likely that request had been implied, but Wendell couldn't have done this on his own. He just didn't want Kyle to get too upset because he'd followed the letter, not the spirit, of the request.

Best get on it before Drew showed up.

Wendell stuck his head outside and beckoned for Eddie.

Eddie walked in tentatively. Wyatt's nostrils flared and he didn't greet Eddie or even look at him. Whatever bridges needed to built to end the feud needed to include Wyatt too. But Wendell was thankful for Wyatt's restraint. He had a feeling that restraint wasn't Wyatt's strong suit.

"Eddie?" Kyle's confusion was obvious.

"Hey. You look, um..."

Great. Eddie's bedside manner wasn't any better than Wyatt's.

"Yeah, I know." Kyle sounded exhausted. As expected. Healing took a lot of energy, and pain sapped it.

Eddie looked pained then pulled his shoulders back like he was preparing for battle. "We'll have to talk, later, when you're better, but I am really glad you weren't hurt any worse."

Kyle's lips quirked upward, a visible indication that he also heard the sincerity in Eddie's words.

"Thanks for coming to visit me."

Eddie cleared his throat. "Uh, well, as to that..." He glanced at

Wendell briefly before he reached into the messenger bag and pulled out the knife.

Wyatt swore and Kyle sat up straight. His sunny blond hair again looked like he was auditioning for a nineties boy band, complete with frosted blond tips and dark roots, same as it had when the cops had taken possession of the cigar box. At the time, Wendell assumed it had been a trick of the light. He was no longer under that misapprehension. Then Wendell's gaze dropped to Kyle's face, which looked odd—longer and thinner. But it was hard to tell because his mouth was contorted in a snarl of rage.

"Give that to me!" Kyle's voice didn't sound right, either. Then he reached out as best he could with both arms, his blood pressure soaring and the monitors beeping frantically.

"What the fuck?" Wyatt said what they were all thinking.

"Get that out of here," Wendell said. He didn't know what Eddie had been hoping to accomplish.

Kyle tugged at the sling holding his arm immobile, and Wendell was seriously afraid he was going to fuck up the good work the surgeons had done.

Eddie evidently felt the same, as he stuffed the knife back in the bag and ran out of the room.

Wendell exchanged a look with Wyatt, and they both glanced at Kyle.

His appearance had returned to normal, but he was pale and sweaty. Then his eyes rolled back and he fell back against the bed, out cold.

Not dead, according to the beeping on the monitors, which had returned to normal, or so it appeared to Wendell's uneducated eye.

A nurse rushed in, the same guy from... shit, was it just that morning? Mere hours ago?

He gave Wendell a narrow-eyed look. "What happened?"

Wyatt cleared his throat. "Kyle tried to move his arm. Like he forgot about all that." Wyatt pointed at the cast in the sling.

The nurse winced. "That'll do it."

He checked Kyle out and while he did so, Wendell slipped out of the room, Wyatt following him. Wendell definitely didn't need the nurse asking any more questions, but Wyatt definitely proved he could think on his feet.

Out in the hall, Eddie was nowhere in sight.

"Just what the fuck was that in there?" Wyatt whispered.

"No idea. Let's find Eddie. He has to know something."

Wendell and Wyatt had finally caught up with Eddie outside the hospital. By mutual agreement, they decided the best place to talk without risk of being overheard was the food truck park.

With his stomach still in knots, and very much not hungry, Wendell chose a simple order of French fries. Hungry or not, fries were one of his comfort foods. And he suspected comfort would be required while they talked.

Wyatt decided on two giant hotdogs and some tater tots. And a beer. Eddie just got a bottle of diet soda.

They sat on the picnic bench farthest from anyone else. It also helped that it was almost two, so the lunch rush was well over.

"I'm gonna say it again, what the fuck was that?" Wyatt's words were a bit garbled around a giant bite of hotdog, but the sentiment was spot on.

Wendell looked at Eddie. "We all saw that, right? Like with his hair?"

"And his face," Wyatt chimed in.

"And his voice." Eddie completed the trifecta of fucked-the-hell-up.

"So, what is going on? Because I'm going to take a wild stab and say Kyle's problem isn't his mental health." Wendell was about ready to turn in his skeptic's badge. He'd been teetering on the edge since they'd found the knife, but this was outside of enough. "And I'm sure I saw his hair do that same thing the day we turned the cigar box over to the police."

Wendell thought back on that day for a moment.

"He was angry when that happened. I thought it was just

because I'd called the police without discussing it with him. But what if it was something else?" Something else that Wendell did not want to put a name to, like verbalizing it would call down the bad karma on them.

He wrote horror films for a living. He'd seen and written this plot twist a million times. It never ended well.

Eddie held up his hands in a placating manner.

"I have some good news, some bad news, and some worse news."

Wendell thought for a moment. "Good news?"

"I don't think Kyle's having a mental breakdown."

"Duh." Wyatt filled a wealth of scorn in that one word.

But Eddie called it. It *was* good news. Wendell had a bad feeling the bad and worse news were going to far outweigh the good.

"Bad news?" Wendell asked.

"I'm certain Kyle is being haunted by the man you believe was a serial killer. The one that lived in the inn. I've never felt a presence that horrifically evil. Matthew."

Wendell squinted. "I don't think I told you his name, did I?"

Eddie rolled his eyes. "I'm not a fraud, any more than Drew is. I heard his name with my... talent. You did say you had a picture of him, correct?"

Giving up his assumption that all paranormal claims were giant shitburgers was not going to be a simple matter. He was still hard-wired for skepticism.

Wendell pulled out his phone and showed it to Eddie, which he'd failed to do earlier when he'd first enlisted Eddie's help.

"See? This man's hair is almost black. And his face is long and narrow. The fact that we could see that overlay is, well, bad news."

"Right. Okay, then. If he lived around here, died around here, he must be buried around here. We just, what, need to find out where, dig him up and like, salt his bones or something?"

Wyatt stared at him open-mouthed, and Eddie squinted at him.

Wendell's cheeks heated up a bit.

"You've watched too much *Supernatural*," Eddie said.

Guilty. But it wasn't like there was a manual for possession, was there? Besides some arcane Roman Catholic text, which probably wouldn't do much good for a couple of non-believers like him and Kyle.

"As a rule, spirits don't cling to their mortal remains. They're attached to places or things. Which is why I did not want to have this discussion at the inn." Eddie had been quite vehement about it when Wendell had suggested it.

Wyatt smiled. "The knife. What do we do, break it?"

"Well, that brings me to my worse news."

Shit.

"I was able to sense that there's something else holding his spirit to this plane. The camera."

Wendell had never quite understood the expression 'his heart sank' until this very moment.

"The camera he took the victims' pictures with."

"That would be my assumption, yes. I, um, don't suppose you know where that is?"

"Fuck, no." Wendell thought about it for a minute. "What do we do when we find it? Burn it?"

"You're a savage, you realize that, right?" Eddie's tone held a hint of humor in it, despite the fact that nothing was funny right now.

"Sorry." Peril of the day job, but he didn't want to get into that now. "What do we do, then?"

"We need to bring Kyle, the knife, and the camera together, and do a banishing ritual. Depending on how strong the spirit is, banishing may end up destroying the items, but destroying the items is not a reliable way to banish a spirit."

"That sounds dangerous. For Kyle, I mean." Kyle's reaction to the knife had been disturbing. "Won't he react worse with both items?"

Eddie shrugged. "Probably. But the ritual doesn't take long. And we have to try. I mean, as soon as we have the camera."

"We might not have the camera, but we'll find it." They had to. There was no other choice. "On the good news front, I'm glad it's the camera and not the pictures ol' Matt's spirit is tied to." And Wendell could barely believe he'd uttered that sentence in all seriousness.

"How so?" Eddie asked.

"Because no one wants to break into the police station and steal them back," Wyatt replied.

"Exactly," Wendell confirmed.

"So, where's the camera? What if it's in a landfill somewhere?" Wyatt asked.

Eddie shook his head. "Nope. It's close. But I don't know where."

"Can't you just wander around and find it?" Wyatt asked.

"I'm not a damned bloodhound. I can't just find things like I've got a GPS in my brain. I know it's close because *Matthew* knows it's close."

They glared at each other, and when Wyatt picked up his last tater tot, Wendell thought for a second he was going to throw it at Eddie.

He didn't. Another win for restraint.

"Guys. Calm down. This might not be so bad." He hoped he was right. "Kyle found the knife, I mean, obviously with Matthew's help. But he found it at the inn. Odds are, the knife was hidden with the camera."

"What about where you found the cigar box?"

Wendell shook his head. "No, I checked that spot thoroughly. There was nothing else there."

"Then it must have been upstairs at the inn somewhere," Wyatt said.

"That's what I think, too," Wendell replied. "That would explain why Kyle was up there and where the knife came from. Maybe there's a hiding spot on the upper landing. Or more likely, one of those rooms must have been Matthew's room when he was alive. Or perhaps there's some other hiding spot on the upper landing."

Not that he had any idea how to figure out which one was Matthew's room.

"Are you going to help us search?" Wyatt asked Eddie.

The question made Wendell's eyes tear up and he turned away so no one would see. He wasn't going to have to do this alone. If nothing else, Wyatt was going to stick it out with him, and that meant a lot. He didn't care if Wyatt was doing it to help him, or because he cared about Kyle; he wasn't going to let people give Wyatt shit after this.

"I want to get the knife into a protective container to try to mitigate Matthew's influence. Then I need to review my banishment ritual and make sure I've got all the necessary supplies on hand. I haven't had to banish anyone in a long time."

"Whatever," Wyatt mumbled under his breath.

Eddie glared at him, because the response had not been at all subtle. "If you haven't found the camera by the time I'm done with that, I will of course help you search."

"Let's get going. The sooner we find that camera, the better." Wendell stood and the others followed his lead. "Wyatt, I'll meet you back at the inn?"

They split off, Eddie walking back to his office space.

TWENTY-EIGHT

2 Days to Haunt Fest

BACK AT THE inn on the second floor landing with Wyatt, déjà vu hit Wendell like a punch.

This was so fucked up.

"Where did you find the cigar box again?" Wyatt asked.

"In a gap underneath a bookcase. I guess we could start tapping for hollow spaces?" To be honest, he was a bit overwhelmed. There was no way someone had missed an old camera anywhere obvious for the past forty or so years. It wasn't going to be stuck in a drawer or on top of a cabinet.

"And how big is this camera?"

Wendell pulled up a picture of the style of camera that most likely had taken the photos, based on the dates they'd deduced from the film codes on the backs of the Polaroids.

"Huh. Bigger than I'd thought. Definitely not going in a base-board gap."

"If I only knew which of these rooms would have been Matthew's."

He whirled around, staring at the doors. Two of the rooms were currently unoccupied. With any luck, they'd find what they needed in one of them. He stood at the mid point between the two doors, hoping Jackson wasn't going to come looking for them. Jackson was a great guy, and becoming a good friend, but there was no way Wendell could explain this paranormal stuff to him and expect him to believe it all.

Wendell could hardly believe it and he'd seen Kyle's partial transformation with his own damned eyes.

He shifted his gaze between the two doors. Marsh Mist or Pixie Light.

The scent of oranges tickled his nose.

"Can you smell oranges?"

Wyatt frowned and stepped closer. "Yes." He shifted to the right. Then to the left. "Here."

Wendell also moved to the left. The orange scent got stronger.

"This is it."

"Are you sure?"

"Drew said oranges would be the sign." He'd been expecting a carving or a sticker or something, but the scent was too distinctive to ignore.

With his master key, he let them inside. Wyatt had very cleverly brought his toolbox with him—they had a ready-made excuse if anyone asked what they were doing. Admitting they were looking for a haunted camera was either going to get them locked up, or, in this town, get them an over-eager audience.

Inside, there was a lot of heavy furniture, but he didn't suppose any of it had been around since the seventies. Anything wooden had been painted white, and any spare wall space had been covered in wallpaper, white with tiny blue flowers.

"Look for something that is more permanent than furniture. Loose floorboards. Bathroom cabinets. Divots in the wallpaper."

Although if they had to rip up wallpaper, Jackson was going to have some words for them. Probably all four letter ones.

These guest rooms didn't have any closets, just wardrobes, so that ruled out the false-backed closet idea he'd used in *Dead Eye Dance*.

Wyatt started in the bathroom, and just in case, Wendell tapped the back of both wardrobes, but they were solid wood. He pulled back the area rug and explored for loose floorboards.

After an hour or so, he was starting to get discouraged. This was a lot harder in real life.

But he couldn't give up. Kyle depended on him.

In desperation, he slowly turned a full circle, looking for anything. Maybe he was wrong. Maybe one of the other rooms was the right one.

Then he noticed a book laying open atop the heavy antique desk. He'd given the desk a cursory glance, but none of the drawers were large enough to hold a big camera, even if it had somehow lain undiscovered all these years.

But that book hadn't been there before, had it?

When he got closer, he realized it was that Shakespeare book, open again to Macbeth. Open to that exact same page. In a book with over a thousand pages.

This could no longer be attributed to coincidence. Not now that he truly believed in ghosts. This had to be the Orange Lady, Katherine Mercer, who helped lovers in need. He and Kyle were definitely in need.

So what was it about this desk?

"Wyatt, help me move this."

They lifted the desk to the middle of the floor. He still couldn't see anything significant about it. Then he glanced at the wall it had covered.

"Wait, are those gaps?" The bottom half of the room was covered in narrow slats of wood. Bead-board or wainscoting, he thought it was called.

The important thing about it, though, was it had been painted white, to better go with the cheery nautical theme in the room. But a section about two feet wide had what looked like deeper grooves on either side. The paint had been applied so thickly, it was hard to tell for sure, and if it weren't for the darker contrast between white and shadow, he might never have noticed it.

He pointed them out to Wyatt.

"Look like gaps to me." He scrutinized the baseboard and the wall, and the strip of wood that marked the top of the wainscoting. "Hang on."

Wyatt grabbed a couple of screwdrivers and a hammer from his toolbox.

He inserted the edge of a screwdriver into one of the deeper grooves and tapped gently with the hammer. He repeated the process all along both vertical sides, and then inexplicably right above the baseboard and below the wainscoting trim.

Then he set the hammer down and picked up the second screwdriver.

Wendell waited, almost breathless, but this had already taken longer than he wanted. Any minute now, Jackson would be up here wondering what all the noise was about.

Wyatt jammed one screwdriver into each vertical groove then applied pressure and pulled.

With a creaking sound, the entire panel pulled free, leaving a dark, gaping wound in the wall.

"What the hell?" Wendell edged closer.

"Probably a forgotten secondary access to the attic," Wyatt replied. He flipped the panel over. "This doesn't look like something your guy would have cut out himself, unless he was a skilled tradesman."

"Actually, I don't know what skills he had. Barbara thought he'd been a traveling salesman, but that means next to nothing about any carpentry experience he might have had."

"Guess so."

"Regardless, I bet no one in recent memory was aware of this access panel. If it wasn't something the killer cut out himself. I guess this is where Kyle found the knife."

Wyatt shook his head. "No way has this been opened since it was painted over. It would have been even harder to see the seams with dark wood, but before it was painted, it would have slipped out a lot easier."

"He must have had another hidey-hole up here somewhere."

If it weren't for the dangerous, diabolical nature of the items hidden, Wendell would have been utterly thrilled by this scavenger hunt.

Wendell pulled out his phone and flicked on the flashlight app before sticking his head inside the hole.

"It's very dusty. I think you're right. No one has been in here in years. Decades. But I don't see a camera."

"Maybe you need to do more than stick your head in." Wyatt's tone was just a tiny bit scathing.

"Is it safe?" He'd seen memes of people falling right through their ceilings.

"Just step on the wooden beams. Should be fine."

Should be. Comforting. But he didn't have time to get a building inspector up here.

He crouched and crab-walked over the baseboard lip, ducking his head to squeeze inside. He was able to stand up in this part of the attic, but it sloped down to almost nothing just a few feet away. It wasn't a proper attic, just some empty space under the sharply sloped roof on the side of the house.

"I wonder if Matthew had a way to get in and out of this house through here."

"If it were me, I would. But stop wasting time and find that camera."

Wendell did his best not to think about whatever Floridian critters that might have taken up residence in the rafters as he shone his light around.

"I don't see anything." But following Wyatt's lead, he tried to put himself in Matthew's place. Sure, he'd want a good hiding place. But it still needed to be accessible. He wouldn't want to alert the whole building.

Then he turned around, and aimed his light at the wall right above the opening he'd stepped through.

Fucking hell. There it was. Dust-covered. It was blocky and old-fashioned, but recognizable as an instant camera. On a ledge right above the opening. With practice, a person might only have to stretch a hand in to access the camera.

"I found it." Wendell stretched out his hand, then paused. This was yet another item he probably shouldn't touch with his bare hands.

He stuck his head back out through the opening. "I need something to grab it with. I don't think I should touch it."

Wyatt cast his gaze about, then grabbed the hem of his shirt and hauled it over his head.

"What are you doing?"

"You can wrap it in my shirt."

Unexpected. Wendell would not have expected Wyatt to bare any excess skin in the presence of a gay man.

And also, there were better ideas than Wyatt stripping. Because *that* wouldn't get noticed when they went back downstairs.

"Why don't you just get me a towel from the bathroom?"

"Oh. Yeah. That works." Wyatt put his shirt back on, and dashed to the bathroom, returning with a towel.

Wendell used it to wrap the camera, careful not to brush any bare skin against it. He sent up a silent apology to Sandra, Bill, and Jackson because it was likely no bleach in the world was going to get the dirt and bad vibes out of this towel.

Burning was the only thing that would get the evil out of the fabric, of that he had no doubt.

He exited the attic and put the bundle on a dresser, texted Eddie the good news, then helped Wyatt return the room to normal.

By the time they were done, Eddie had texted back.

Wendell met up with Eddie in the hospital's parking lot.

"Where's Wyatt?" Eddie's tone was odd, and Wendell couldn't tell if it was because Eddie was surprised Wyatt wasn't around, or that he was glad Wyatt had stayed away.

"Jackson needed some help, so Wyatt stuck around to take care of that."

Eddie nodded. "I have a box for the camera. It will be safer."

He opened his trunk, revealing two innocuous-looking black boxes.

"Where's the knife?"

Eddie tapped one of the boxes. "In here." He opened the other box.

"Are those, like, Faraday cages?" He'd researched them briefly when writing *The Third Eye*, but ultimate chose a more dramatic way to trap the demon.

"Faraday boxes, yes. Not just for blocking normal electromagnetic fields anymore," Eddie chirped with a sarcastic lilt.

But it made sense. If ghosts were comprised of energy, a Faraday cage could well interfere or contain it.

"Put the camera in this one."

Wendell used the towel to maneuver the camera into the box, which Eddie promptly snapped shut.

"What now?"

Eddie slung a backpack over his shoulder, then handed one of the boxes to Wendell before picking up the second box.

"Now, we go visit Kyle, and hope we can get this done before someone notices what we're doing and kicks us out."

That didn't sound promising. "Why can't we just wait until he'd released?"

Eddie faced him, a solemn expression on his face. "Because I'm afraid this particular spirit can gain strength from causing death. I think he might have been the true cause of Chester's death, and that gave him the ability to latch on to Kyle. Who probably has some undiscovered sensitivity to the paranormal, which has allowed Matthew to speak to him."

Chills ran down Wendell's back. "You mean, you think Matthew is going to kill him."

"I think if he's immobilized in the hospital, Matthew might see if he can find a better prospect. Hospitals are full of people, one of whom might be easier to influence. And if he needs a boost of energy, he might take it from Kyle. Didn't you say Drew had texted that the doctors didn't want to release Kyle yet? Thought he wasn't bouncing back as well as expected?"

Wendell nodded. That had been an unexpected blow when he'd checked his messages after he'd arranged the meeting with Eddie. Kyle had developed an infection that had to be treated with intravenous antibiotics.

"I think if we can banish Matthew, Kyle will have a dramatic turnaround. Spirits can be very draining."

Wendell didn't want to take a chance on Kyle's life. And Eddie was the expert here. So far, Eddie hadn't steered him wrong, and Wendell was starting to believe in something he'd never believed in before.

The afterlife.

"I'm going to prepare everything for the banishment ritual. When I say so, you open the boxes, but don't touch the camera or the knife. Got it?"

"Got it. Let's go."

When they arrived that evening, no one else was in Kyle's room. The barely touched remains of his dinner sat on the table. More flower arrangements had arrived, overdone enough that it almost looked like a movie set.

Kyle was asleep. On one hand, a bit of a relief so they could get to work without explaining things to anyone. On the other hand, he wasn't sure he wanted to do this without Kyle being aware of it happening.

Wendell grimaced. He needed another hand. Because thirdly,

what if Kyle was awake but Matthew tried to take over like he'd done in the morning? There was no other explanation he'd been able to come up with, aside from that one.

The choice was taken out of his hands, however, since one of the myriad things that Eddie took out of his messenger bag clanked when he put it on the floor.

Kyle stirred to wakefulness, eyes bleary, probably from a combination of exhaustion and pain killers. The shadows he'd started seeing under Kyle's eyes hadn't eased any. In fact, they looked darker and deeper. Under normal circumstances, he might attribute that to the stark, unforgiving hospital lighting.

But these weren't normal circumstances. And he feared Eddie had the right idea of things. Kyle wasn't going to get better with a phantasmal parasite hanging around.

"Hey there." Wendell crowded in close to Kyle's left side, hoping to keep him distracted, at least until Eddie was ready.

"Wendell? I'm glad to see you." Kyle's voice was scratchy and the words were mumbled, but his eyes started to clear a bit as he shook off the grogginess.

"I'm glad to see you, too." He gave Kyle a quick kiss, earning him a sweet smile.

"Wendell, I'm ready," Eddie said. Which Kyle didn't miss.

"Eddie? What are you doing here?"

Wendell suspected after this was over, he'd have some explaining to do, because there was no love lost between Eddie and Kyle.

Definitely a problem for later.

"We're going to fix things. I hope," Wendell whispered.

Kyle frowned.

"Now, now." Eddie's voice had an impatient edge.

And immediately, Kyle's roots started to darken.

Shit.

He sped over to where Eddie knelt on the floor. In front of him, a thin piece of rock, probably slate. Strewn across it were bundles of dried herbs and grasses. The two Faraday boxes flanked the stone.

Wendell couldn't spend any longer analyzing the products Eddie had prepared. A low growl emanated from Kyle, which raised the hairs on the back of his neck.

Matthew wasn't happy, and was getting unhappier by the second.

Wendell flipped the lids on the boxes. Eddie started murmuring under his breath, then grabbed both knife and camera simultaneously, pulled them out and placed them side by side on the slate.

He grabbed a lighter, and set fire to a small pyre of dried plants. Flames didn't flare up, but the herbs started to burn and smoke—they couldn't have been quite as dry as they appeared. Eddie threw salt over everything, then something that sparked and flared when it hit the tiny flames. He grabbed another bundle of herbs, lit them enough to create smoke, and wafted it over Matthew's two items.

The growl from the bed became a howl, the machines began beeping more aggressively, and Eddie sprinkled the slate with something else. His mumbling got louder and more commanding, although Wendell couldn't understand any of the words.

Then the room shook, and something popped, like when Wendell flew and the pressure in his ears was suddenly relieved, but this was outside his body.

Water and flowers shot up out of their vases and cascaded all over the floor. Eddie gave a final shout, Kyle screamed, and they both slumped down.

"Kyle? Are you okay? Eddie?" None of Kyle's machines had flatlined, which was Wendell's main concern.

Eddie roused himself first.

"Did it work?" Wendell couldn't stop himself from asking, even though he knew their time alone could be counted in mere seconds.

"I think so."

That wasn't emphatic enough to satisfy Wendell, but he was relieved to note Kyle's monitors were returning to normal and his hair no longer had dark roots.

"Help me with this. I hear someone coming," Eddie hissed.

The camera was a mangled mess, and the knife was broken in

three pieces. Wendell hoped that meant they were safe to touch, but there wasn't time to ask. He grabbed the remains of the camera and knife, threw them in their respective boxes, then kicked the two boxes under Kyle's bed, while Eddie shoved his accoutrements into the bag. They were just in time, because a nurse came pounding into the room.

She looked familiar, but Wendell hadn't encountered her before.

"What is going on in here? Kyle needs his rest." She quickly assessed the patient. "I don't know how he slept through that, but you are damned lucky he did."

Wendell's knees almost gave out, hearing that Kyle was merely asleep, and not anything more serious.

"I think you need to leave."

Then she focused on the flowers and water on the floor, and all over their heads.

"No, really, what is going on in here? Did you have a fight or something?"

"Um." Wendell didn't know what to say.

"It's okay, Sarah," Kyle mumbled from the bed. "It's all good now."

"It sure isn't. Eddie, you need to accept that Kyle's moved on. Wendell, you need to not be so jealous. And this is a small town, so you're both going to need to learn how to get along. You can start by cleaning this mess up, together. I'll send someone in with cleaning products. And after that, I better not see you in here until tomorrow."

Sarah stomped out of the room. Wendell glanced at Eddie. Then Sarah stomped back in. "And no smudging sticks in the hospital. Ever."

Then she whirled away and was gone.

Wendell caught Eddie's gaze, then started to laugh. Eddie laughed with him, and they clutched at each other, trying to hold themselves upright as they recovered from the extremely specific chastising.

"Hey, don't want to break up the party, but when did you two get so chummy?"

At least Kyle just sounded tired, not upset.

They both approached his bedside, and started to explain. They'd only gotten started when a maintenance worker showed up with a cleaning cart, and it took pretty much the entirety of cleaning to finish their explanation.

Kyle fell back asleep almost immediately when they were done, a peaceful smile on his face.

Wendell smiled at him, then turned back to Eddie. "So for real, is Matthew gone?"

"He is. I can't sense him in Kyle any longer. We'll have to make sure Kyle feels the same, but I'm confident this worked. If he goes back to the inn and doesn't sense anything, then we're all good."

"I can't thank you enough." Wendell hesitated for a moment then grabbed Eddie in a hug. The man held himself stiff for a second before he hugged Wendell back.

"No thanks needed. I would never leave anyone under an influence that malign. Especially not Kyle," Eddie said as he pulled out of Wendell's arms.

"Oh? Especially Kyle? Do I *need* to be jealous?" Wendell was teasing. Mostly.

Eddie laughed ruefully. "It's really not like that. I like Kyle, I do. And I'm grateful, because I think this incident can put us on a new path. One that isn't adversarial. But I'm not interested in him."

"Well, don't tell Sarah, or we might need to come up with a believable explanation."

Eddie laughed again. "I think we can go this with for now. Half of town thinks I've been carrying a torch for Kyle for months. It won't be anything new for them."

"Hey, who is Sarah? She looked really familiar."

"Sarah is Scott's sister."

"Oh shit."

"Yeah, she'll definitely tell him about this. He will tease the shit out of you forever."

From what Wendell had learned about Scott, that checked out.

"Let's go. He really does need his rest. And we both need a shower."

Eddie grinned. "Too true. Let me know when Kyle is going back to the inn. I'd like to be there, just to make sure nothing unexpected happens."

Wendell clapped him on the shoulder. "I will. Thanks again."

T minus 24 hours before the inn was full up, which also gave him a short while to decompress before getting bombarded by tourists.

His stomach growled, reminding him he hadn't eaten since... he didn't recall when.

TWENTY-NINE

1 Day to Haunt Fest

KYLE CAREFULLY GOT out of the Uber in the Orange Lady's parking lot. He thanked the driver, who'd resolutely ignored the blood spattered jeans Kyle had been wearing. His shirt had been disposed of, presumably having been in worse condition than his jeans. After hitting up the hospital gift shop, he'd bought an oversized hoodie and asked the cashier to cut off the right arm. Even then, she'd had to help him into the hoodie, and had to zip it up for him like he was an inept toddler. But it was a relief to be out of the hospital.

Kyle watched the Uber drive away, hoping he wasn't going to have to call him back immediately, then turned to stare at the building.

His doctors had been surprised, and very pleased, with his progress overnight and had discharged him this morning. He could have called Drew or Wendell or any number of people to come get him. Even Eddie, if he hadn't been hallucinating that bizarre little scene by his bedside yesterday.

But he hadn't wanted to. Mostly, because he'd already burdened so many people who were already at maximum capacity for the upcoming Haunt Fest.

Aside from that, he also didn't want anyone to know if he was too chicken to set foot back in the Orange Lady. Had he dreamed Wendell saying things were going to be better? Or did he need to run right back to hospital, check himself into the psychiatric ward?

His mind had been invaded by such poison, he wasn't sure he trusted himself. But when he woke up this morning, he'd been as surprised and pleased as his doctors. That heaviness in his mind, the darkness, the innate viciousness, had disappeared.

The question was, could he distance himself from it all enough to go back into the inn? Could he enjoy himself with Wendell, sleep with Wendell, and not worry? Could he *trust* the apparent return of his normal mindset?

There was only one way to answer all his questions. He sucked in a deep breath and walked steadily to the door, one foot in front of the other.

Ignoring the flutter in his belly, he pulled open the door. Breakfast was just about over, so he hoped the guests had mostly dispersed. He expected Wendell and Jackson would be in the vicinity of the dining room, overseeing things. It gave him a few minutes extra to figure out how he felt.

He took a shaky breath. Turns out, he felt weak as shit. He fumbled his way to the first chair in the sunroom, and let his light-headedness ease. Fortunately, the room was empty. The guests must have decided to go out and experience sunlight outdoors, rather than in here.

The sunroom wasn't scary and didn't trigger any negative emotions or thoughts. Then again, it never had, but Kyle had feared the worst. And the worst was not coming to pass, so he let himself carve out a sliver of hope.

But he wasn't ready to walk down that long fucking hallway to find Wendell. He pulled out his phone and texted him.

The pounding of feet heading his way warmed him inside. Wendell's excited expression when he ran into view made Kyle smile. He might never stop smiling.

"Kyle. Oh, I am so glad to see you." Wendell approached him carefully, hugging him gently from the left side then kissing him.

Forget smiling forever, Kyle wanted to kiss Wendell forever.

Wendell pulled up a chair close to him. "Did you break out of the hospital?"

Kyle let out an amused snort, which only cause a small twinge in his arm. "No. They released me."

"Why didn't you call me? I would have come to pick you up."

Wendell looked hurt, and Kyle couldn't have that. He grabbed Wendell's hand with his only functioning one.

"I was afraid. I was afraid I wasn't going to be able to face coming inside here, and I didn't want you to see yet another breakdown."

Wendell squeezed his hand back. "I want to be there for you. Good and bad. That's how this is supposed to work. Support and caring. I love you."

Eyes burning, he sniffled. "I love you, too. I just had to prove it to myself. And I still haven't tried the library yet. Or upstairs."

Wendell's eyes narrowed. "No going upstairs. Not for a while."

"Yes, sir!" Kyle liked how that made Wendell smile.

"Did you want some tea or coffee? Something to eat?"

"Yes. Tea please. And something light to eat."

"You wait here, I'll be right back."

When Wendell returned with a plate of fruit, oatmeal, and a cup of chamomile tea, Kyle fell in love all over again.

He also came bearing a Jackson, who attempted an awkward hug and effusive apologies.

"Jackson, please. It was an accident." More or less. But if he'd been influenced by a spirit, which would explain Eddie's presence along with burning sage in his hospital room, then accident was going to be the easiest explanation.

If it hadn't been a spirit, people would know the truth soon enough.

The two of them fussed over him for a few minutes, then Jackson slipped away to give them some alone time. Too bad alone time wasn't going to mean sexy times anytime soon.

But he was happy just to bask in the sunroom holding Wendell's hand.

Until his stomach insisted he ingest some of the food Wendell had provided for him. He had to unlace their fingers so he could eat.

"I think you said Barbara was taking over my ghost tours, right?"

"Yup. She said she'd do them until you recover."

He sighed. "I wonder how she'd feel about training someone new."

Wendell stared at him thoughtfully. "To reduce your workload?"

Kyle discovered shrugging was not something he should do for the next little while. "Not exactly. I just don't think I can face spending, well, any time at all talking about ghosts. Not now. Maybe never again. Is that... that's okay, right?"

"I want you to be happy and healthy. I don't want you doing ghost tours if it's not going to make you happy."

After shoving a fat strawberry in his mouth, Kyle noticed Wendell had a funny expression. He chewed madly, anxious to hear Wendell's thoughts.

"What's wrong?"

Wendell's rueful half-smile did not make him feel better.

"I've been considering a change in career, too." He huffed out a breath. "I don't think I can write horror movies anymore. Not after everything that's happened."

Kyle blinked. "What do you want to do instead?"

"I'm making notes for an action adventure script. And I'm really excited about it."

Unable to restrain himself, he laughed. "Is it really that different?"

Wendell rolled his eyes. "I know, I know. It's still scriptwriting. The problem is how I'm going to break it to my family. Lucinda and Byron and me... our studio was built on horror. If I write something else, I might have to shop it elsewhere. I don't mind that for myself, but I would hate to feel like I wasn't pulling my weight for the company."

"Oh, I see. Well, if your family cares about you, they'll understand, I'm sure." Kyle bit his lip. "Do you think, um..."

"I can't wait for you to meet them." Wendell stared into Kyle's eyes. "Which brings me to my next... dilemma."

"Oh?"

Wyatt popped into the room. "Hey man, you're out of shower gel." Then he did such a classic double take, it completely derailed Kyle's shock at the statement. "Good to see you, Kyle. Feeling better?"

"Yeah. Thanks, Wyatt."

"Um, talk later." Wyatt disappeared in a waft of scent Kyle associated with Wendell.

"Is your next dilemma how to tell me that Wyatt is for some reason using your shower? And your shower gel?"

Wendell's cheeks went flaming red. "It's not what you think."

Kyle laughed. "With Wyatt? Yes, I know you weren't sleeping with him."

The red started to fade from Wendell's face.

"Wyatt crashed on the couch for the past couple of nights. I think he's missing his brother, and I was missing you."

"That was really nice of you to let him stay." Especially since Wyatt had a habit of rubbing people the wrong way.

"Anyway, my next dilemma is wondering how to ask my boyfriend how he'd feel if I moved to Sandy Bottom Bay. Permanently."

"Permanently?" Was this for real? Kyle could barely breathe. He hadn't allowed himself to hope for this, and it was like getting swept out to sea. "What about your family? Your career?"

"I can write from anywhere. And I can visit. Or video chat. I don't actually have to be in Los Angeles to function."

Funny how he thought, with respect to his career, it would be harder to change genres than move across the country, but Kyle didn't have any idea how the film industry worked.

"I would be fucking thrilled if you lived here full time."

Wendell smiled and leaned in to kiss him, but Kyle held up a hand to stop him.

"Wait a minute."

"What?"

"First, let me go into the library. I want to know... I want to know that, what was his name? Matthew. I want to be sure Matthew is gone before we start making long-term plans. Please?"

"Of course." Wendell stood up.

"Um, I'm still a little shaky," Kyle said as he rose.

"I am here for you." Wendell wrapped an arm around his waist and let Kyle set the pace. Which was fucking slow, but so what? He'd only left the hospital an hour ago.

"And what if... my problems weren't caused by Matthew?" Kyle's voice shook. Despite how good he felt, mentally, he was still so fucking scared that his own mind could betray him.

"If that's the case, we'll make sure you get the help you need. I promise."

Wendell's use of the word "we" made Kyle's eyes burn with unshed tears. This man was everything he'd ever wanted.

At the door to the library, he paused.

"Let's do this." Kyle stepped across the threshold. He shook off Wendell's arm. He needed to do this on his own.

He walked all the way to the fireplace and sat down in the wing-back chair, propping his cast gently on the armrest.

The room was just a library. The heaviness and oppressive air he'd always sensed were gone. He would have no qualms about sitting in here reading.

When he looked up, Wendell was staring at him expectantly.

"It's gone. I don't hate this room anymore."

Wendell nodded. "Eddie thought you might have had a latent sensitivity to the ghosts. If he was right, and Matthew had enough strength to kill Chester, you might have been sensing him all along."

"Yeah, that could be." A thought hit him. "Shit. Does that mean I'm a medium, too?"

"I don't know. You'd have to ask Eddie, but it never sounded to me like he was suggesting that."

Kyle hoped not. "I have to admit, the weirdest thing about all this was realizing that Eddie wasn't a charlatan. All those times I called him that. I have some apologies to make."

"Plenty of time for that. But that reminds me, I totally forgot to message him."

Kyle lifted an eyebrow. "You need to message Eddie?"

"Yeah, he wanted to supervise your return here, just to make sure Matthew was truly gone."

"You'd better get on that. I'd like to know."

Wendell glanced up at the shelf that had an empty space where the Shakespeare book was supposed to be.

"Shit. I meant to bring that back down and put it away. Will you be okay here for a few minutes?"

"I'll be fine."

Wendell sped out of the room, head bent over his phone as he typed furiously.

He dozed, finding the room cozy and comfortable in a way he never had before.

All too soon, Wendell returned, book in hand.

"You know, I never believed in ghosts before. Or psychics, or mediums. But after a month in Sandy Bottom Bay, I think I'm a believer."

Kyle nodded. "Yeah, I don't think we have a choice, do we?"

Wendell swiped a hand across the aged blue cover. "We kept finding this places. Open to the same page in Macbeth. I tried to explain it away, but this last time? If it weren't for the book and the scent of oranges, I don't know if I'd have ever found Matthew's camera. And I hate to think what would have happened to you if I hadn't."

Wendell set the book aside and dropped down on the floor beside Kyle's chair.

"The scent of oranges?"

"Yeah, I thought about this all night last night. I think the Orange Lady helped me. Helped us. Haven't been lovers in much more trouble than us, have there?"

"That's the truth. And you think it was the Lady? But why Macbeth?"

"I think she was trying to warn us. Or communicate. As an educated woman, she likely would have been familiar with Shakespeare's works. Macbeth isn't the bloodiest of Shakespeare's plays, but it does have more than its fair share of murder. And it's not like she'd know the contents of a biography about Dahmer, or something."

"I guess that makes sense."

"I owe her a debt of gratitude." Wendell stared up at the ceiling. "Thank you, Katherine."

Kyle couldn't argue with that logic. "You also have my thanks, Lady."

The scent of oranges filled the room, stronger than ever, before it faded. They smiled at each other, then Wendell levered himself up and returned the book to its rightful place on the shelf.

Jackson appeared in the door. "I like that citrus smell. Where is it coming from?"

Kyle exchanged a grin with Wendell. "Don't know. Maybe someone's perfume?"

"Maybe. Wendell, there are some people here to see you."

"To see me? Not Kyle?"

Kyle was okay with that. As much as he liked being the center of attention, he'd prefer it not happen while he was feeling fragile and definitely not at his best.

"No, they were pretty clear it was you they wanted to see.

They're in the sunroom. Mostly because I told them there weren't any chairs in here, but one of them was definitely impatient."

Wendell tilted his head thoughtfully, like he might have an idea who wanted to see him.

"Did you want to stay here or come with me?"

Kyle thought about it for a second, but the truth was, now that Wendell was going to move to Sandy Bottom Bay, he didn't want to be parted from him.

"I'll come with, as long as you don't mind my slow pace."

Jackson waved a hand in a dismissive gesture. "I'll go ahead and offer them coffee. You take your time."

Jackson grinned at him, then jogged to the chair to give him a little hug, then jogged back out.

"He's in a good mood," Kyle said as Wendell helped him to his feet.

"Yeah, I think he's enjoying being busy, especially now that you're on the mend."

"Then he's going to have a fucking great Haunt Fest."

Wendell laughed. "I hope you're right."

Partway down the hallway, Kyle glanced up to find Eddie striding toward them.

He was smiling, something Kyle hadn't seen all that often since that ill-fated week they'd spent in bed together.

"Why don't you go on into the sunroom? Eddie can escort me in there after he checks me out."

"Are you sure?" Wendell asked.

"Yeah." Kyle had a few things to say to Eddie, that he didn't necessarily need an audience for, but he did want to get it out of the way.

Wendell handed him off to Eddie, then strode at a much faster pace toward the sunroom.

"He's a good man, isn't he?" Eddie's tone was almost wistful, but Kyle hadn't seen anything like lust when Eddie looked at Wendell, so he didn't have to defend his position as Wendell's boyfriend.

"He is. Look, Eddie, I need to thank you for helping me out. And apologize for... well, for all the shit I've done and said. That wasn't fair."

"I'm sorry too. I had some other stuff going on, and I took out my irritation on Drew and you. Truce?"

Kyle laughed. "Truce? I'd shake your hand but my shaking hand is wrapped up in this." He lifted his cast to emphasize his words.

Which brought him to his next issue—a lot scarier than mending a long-standing feud.

"Is Matthew gone?"

"Gone. It's amazing how different this place feels. You're going to be just fine. Honestly, just the fact that you were released from the hospital so fast should be all the proof you need."

Kyle wiped away the faint sheen of sweat that had popped upon his forehead.

"But I've got a long recovery ahead of me. And I really need to sit down again."

"Oh, of course. Sunroom?"

"Please."

They shuffled slowly down the hall, Eddie's arm every bit as supportive as Wendell's but not nearly as comforting.

In the sunroom, a positive gaggle of people sat with Wendell, drinking coffee.

Gaggle might be exaggerating. There were three, and they looked enough like Wendell for Kyle to guess who they were. He was torn between just introducing himself or scuttling away to hide in Wendell's cottage.

He certainly wasn't fit to make an entrance like he normally would. And he was still wearing his oversized hospital hoodie with nothing underneath and blood spattered jeans. Hopefully they were dark enough blue to hide the worst of it.

One of the women looked up. "Oh, you must be Kyle. Come sit down. You look like a ghost."

A giggle slipped out. "Not quite yet."

Wendell shook his head, but leaped up to help Kyle to a seat. Kyle craned his head around but Eddie had already gone. Kyle would follow up with him later. Because they'd called a truce. Maybe that meant they were even friends now. He'd have to think on that when he didn't have three of Wendell's family members staring at him.

"Um. Hi. Yes, I'm Kyle."

Jackson appeared and handed him an insulated mug with a lid on it. "Peppermint tea."

"Thank you." Kyle took a sip to cover his trepidation. He appreciated that Jackson brought him something easy to maneuver in his weaker hand, which was made all the weaker by exhaustion.

"We are so pleased to meet you," the other woman said. The man nodded.

Kyle flicked a pointed glance at a grinning Wendell. He shook himself.

"Oh, sorry. This is Felicity, Byron, and Lucinda. My siblings."

As Kyle expected. He'd even figured out which one was Lucinda and which one was Felicity, based on Wendell's brief descriptions.

Lucinda looked svelte and as polished as a movie star. Byron looked a lot like Wendell, except for a big bushy beard. Felicity looked like a cross between Wendell and Lucinda, and she had a definite "mom" vibe. But Lucinda was clearly the spokesperson.

"Kyle, I can't tell you how glad we are to meet you. I'm, I mean, we're so sorry it had to be because you got injured." Beautiful and sincere. A killer combination, even for a guy who was all the way into other men.

"Thank you. It's nice to meet you all, too. But what are you doing here?" Stupid question, because he was deathly afraid of the answer.

It was a different sort of fear than when he was being haunted. Partially possessed? Whatever. This time he was afraid Wendell's siblings were here to take him home. Or talk him out of having a relationship with a guy who had no prospects, a bum knee, and a temporarily non-functional right arm.

Giving up Wendell wasn't an option—he hoped—but he dreaded that Wendell might have friction with his family over him.

Lucinda smiled gently. "Wendell called me the night of your accident. I rallied the troops, and here we are. I'm only sorry it took us so long to get here."

"You... all flew out here because I got hurt?" She was speaking words he understood, but strung together the way they were didn't make any sense.

"Of course. Wendell made it very clear how he felt about you, and we deduced you both might need some support," Lucinda continued.

"Exactly. Had one of our actors break an arm on set, not as bad as yours, but he had a hard time functioning the first while," Byron added in.

"And it helps to have family around at difficult times," Felicity finished.

Apparently healing made his feelings rush to the surface, and his eyes welled up. His own parents had only sent an arrangement of lilies, like he'd died. And that was honestly even more than he'd expected.

Having Wendell's family come together for a crisis, especially when they hadn't even met him, was amazing.

"Thank you. That's amazing. I'm sure Wendell appreciates it, and I'm looking forward to getting to know you."

Wendell was so happy right now, he was practically glowing.

"It's too bad you won't meet my parents this time. They're in the middle of a cruise in South Asia and it would have taken them more than a week to get here," Wendell said.

Kyle appreciated the foregone conclusion that he would be meeting them eventually. It smoothed his fears down to nothing.

"That's right. We told them we had everything under control," Lucinda said.

Kyle narrowed his eyes, then looked at Wendell. Who was still grinning.

"Under control?" Kyle repeated. "Where are you staying?" Because Wendell had already canceled the hotel suite for the weekend.

"This is a bed and breakfast, isn't it?" Lucinda shrugged. "We can just get a room here, right?"

Wendell's mouth dropped open as comprehension struck.

"Luce, the inn's full up. The hotel is full up. The festival starts tomorrow."

Lucinda stared at him like she couldn't comprehend such a thing. Normally, Kyle would suggest the motel out by the highway, but given the festival's increased popularity, they might have to drive almost back to Tampa to get a hotel room or two.

"It'll be a tight squeeze, but you could stay at my apartment," Kyle offered. He wasn't lying. His place was tiny.

"Oh, that's so sweet. But," Felicity frowned. "Do you have that many guest rooms?"

Wendell rolled his eyes. "Kyle will stay with me. You and Luce will have to share Kyle's bed, and Byron... you can take Kyle's couch, or you can take the couch in the cottage with us. Up to you."

A hint of a blush colored Felicity's cheeks, and she pursed her lips. Byron's expression didn't change, like he wasn't fazed a bit by flying across the country just to bunk down on someone's couch.

"Thank you, Kyle. We appreciate it." Lucinda narrowed her eyes at him. "You really are just adorable."

Now it was Kyle's cheeks heating up. Lucinda's words didn't seem like just a compliment. Not while she was scrutinizing him like a bug under a microscope. At least he didn't get the sense she was attracted to him. Because that would be awkward and uncomfortable.

"Have you ever thought about becoming an actor?" she asked.

"Not really. I went to school for musical theater, but I injured my knee and had to change careers." Somehow, after all he'd been through, with a fresh cast on his arm, college seemed like a long, long time ago.

"No, Lucinda," Wendell said emphatically. "Let him recover before you harass him to audition."

Kyle blinked. Is that what she'd been doing? He'd actually done a bit of acting for another student's movie for film studies. He definitely didn't like it as much as theater, that was for sure. He thrived on attention in the moment. Watching himself on the big screen in the dark with a bunch of film studies majors hadn't been nearly as emotionally satisfying. But maybe a bit part would be fun. And it would let Wendell visit his family and friends on the West Coast.

He'd definitely keep the possibility in mind. For later. At least eight weeks later, depending entirely on how long his damn arm took to heal.

Kyle's energy was waning, so he continued to sip his tea while the siblings chatted about LA things that Kyle had no knowledge of. He was on the edge of dozing when Lucinda let out a rather unexpected and undignified squeal. He blinked his eyes open to see her gleefully scrolling through her phone.

She glanced up. "Oh, this is the best news."

"What?" Wendell asked.

"Remember that entitled shit stain that we had hoped would play the lead in Shadow Stalker? Bre—"

Wendell held up a hand to stop her. "I remember. But around here, we don't use his name, for fear of summoning him, like a demon."

Kyle snickered at how serious Wendell sounded. But also, the topic of discussion sent a jolt of renewed energy through him. Because it was obvious Lucinda didn't like Cliff's ex-boyfriend anymore than anyone else Kyle knew.

"Oh, that's a good rule of thumb." Byron was clearly no more of a fan than Lucinda. "Wait, why would anyone around here care?"

"Funny story, in two parts," Wendell said with a grin. "First off, remember that security dude that hung around his industry parties for a few months, making us all wonder why he thought he needed private security?"

Lucinda and Byron both nodded.

"He wasn't security, he was the secret boyfriend. Who got fed up with Br-, I mean, the nameless one's bullshit and moved out here. Found Kyle's best friend and got married."

"Are you shitting us?" Lucinda was positively crowing. "I remember asking once what happened to his security guard and he started cursing so much I thought the guy had stolen from him or something. No better revenge than living well, or so I've heard."

"And Cliff is definitely living well. He's very happy." Wendell smiled, warming Kyle's heart. He was sincerely pleased that Kyle's friends were happy.

"Okay, but you said two parts. What's the second part?"

"His last episode of *Phantoms* was filmed right here. And he alienated everyone in town."

Kyle lifted his lip in a snarl. "He was a total creep."

Lucinda and Byron stared at him and started laughing. Felicity smiled, but it was clear she'd never met the shitstain in question. Which wasn't a surprise. Wendell had told him that although she was a silent partner in the studio, she wasn't actively involved in Hollywood or the movie business.

"So, what brought *that man* to mind?" Kyle asked.

Lucinda dabbed at her eyes before she continued. "I'd started hearing rumors of issues on the set of his new film a couple of weeks ago. You know, the sequel to that action movie that he did after *Phantoms*?"

"What did he do?" Wendell asked.

Kyle had a good idea. "Probably tried to put his dick where it didn't belong."

"That's what I'd expect, too," Byron agreed.

The only sad thing about that was how limited people's memories were. Rich and famous people rarely saw significant repercussions to their actions. Kyle was pretty sure he deserved repercussions, not adulation and money from his movie roles.

"Ha. You'd be wrong. At least in this case. My friend, Steph, works on set, and gave me the heads up, although it's probably going to be all over social media soon. He was just arrested for embezzling funds from the production."

Kyle blinked. "For real? Arrested?" He couldn't have asked for better repercussions. "Can I text Cliff and Drew about it?"

Lucinda shrugged. "I don't see why not. Steph's word is gold."

Kyle shifted, then grimaced. Normally he'd use his right hand to pull out his phone. And he'd already discovered trying to use his phone with his left hand did not go swimmingly. But he fumbled it out of his pocket and grappled with it like he was trying to catch a goldfish.

"Maybe I'll text them later." Kyle slid his phone onto the table, and picked up his mug again.

"Hey, I'm glad you're all here, though. I have something to tell you." Wendell's words made Kyle tense up. Was he going to tell his family now about his future plans? Would they change his mind? Or would they hate Kyle because of it?

He wanted to suggest waiting, but maybe it was better to rip the bandage off and find out what mess lay below.

"What is it?" Lucinda's tone was suspicious, and she flicked her gaze between the two of them.

Wendell cleared his throat, suddenly appearing hesitant.

"You obviously know how much I care about Kyle." He sent a sweet smile Kyle's way, then turned back to his siblings, who were nodding but looking like they were waiting for a bomb.

"I know it's fast, but I'm going to move here, to be with Kyle."

Felicity smiled. "That's so sweet." Lucinda and Byron nodded.

"You can write from anywhere," Lucinda added. "And you hate all the schmoozing, so you'd only have to come back for important events, and family stuff."

Kyle blinked. He knew his own parents wouldn't care if he took a long walk off a short pier, but this support was completely unexpected. He'd half-expected anger or maybe pleading not to do it, or even for him to be accused of being a gold digger. Then again, he had maybe been reading too many romance novels lately.

"It's fast, but I love your brother." Kyle didn't know if that would help, but he needed to contribute something to this discussion.

Byron laughed. "He didn't tell you about our parents, did he?"

"Uh, no. What about them?" Maybe that was where all the objections would come from? It was obvious that Wendell lived in a much different tax bracket than Kyle. Did rich people sue over love affairs? Did they try to buy off unsuitable suitors with big fat checks? Not that money would convince Kyle to break up with Wendell. He had everything he needed right now.

"They met in Europe when they were both on vacation with friends. Instead of coming home on their expected return date, they eloped to Denmark to get married."

"They what?" Kyle fell in love with Wendell at breakneck speed but apparently they wouldn't beat any records in this family. "How long did they know each other?"

"A week," Felicity said, with the same motherly smile. "As they've always said, when you know, you know."

Kyle assumed she was speaking from experience, since she was the only one of the siblings who'd gotten married.

"Wow. Uh, that's amazing. So they won't mind?"

Lucinda reached over and patted his cheek. "You are so damned cute. No, they won't mind. In fact, they'll be thrilled Wendell has finally found his someone. I mean, they might be upset he's moving away, but most of us travel quite a bit anyway, and they're both still working. We don't have regular Sunday dinners together or anything."

Kyle squeezed Wendell's hand. This was a bit like a dream.

"Um, that's not all I wanted to talk about." There was more trepidation in Wendell's voice, which didn't surprise Kyle. He'd been more worried about telling Wendell's family about their relationship, but Wendell had been more worried about this.

"I don't want to write any more horror scripts. Or at least, not for a long time. I'm burnt out. I need to try something else."

To Kyle's surprise, this didn't appear to shock them.

Byron tilted his head. "Then what are you planning to do?" His words were careful, precise, and without inflection, like he trying really hard to keep emotion out of them.

"Look, I'm sorry. I know we've been working on building this horror empire, but I can't. I've got notes for an action adventure script that I'm ready to start writing as soon as the festival is over. I'm really sorry, but I think we're going to have to bring in other scriptwriters for the studio."

"Oh thank fuck." Lucinda flopped back against the chair, and Byron's shoulders relaxed, visibly dropping. Felicity's smile just got bigger.

"Wait, what?" Wendell appeared every bit as confused as Kyle was. "I thought you'd be more upset."

Lucinda gathered herself and leaned forward, a serious expression on her face.

"Baby bro, we could see the burn out coming a mile away. There's no way a single scriptwriter could produce all the stories for the size of studio we're projecting to become. But you've been so determined. And we were worried. You were avoiding social functions—more so than normal—and working such long hours, with less result."

Wendell sputtered. "So, when you kept bugging me about when I'd have a new script ready?"

Lucinda glanced at Byron. "Well, we both agreed you needed to come to this realization by yourself. He didn't agree with my methods, though. I thought if I applied extra pressure, you'd figure it out sooner rather than later."

"Uh, yeah, not sure I was a fan."

Lucinda did look abashed. "Sorry about that."

"I'm just glad you're not disappointed in me."

Kyle squeezed Wendell's hand again, hopefully conveying that if nothing else, Kyle wasn't disappointed. But it was clear to Kyle that no one in this room felt that way.

"Of course not." Byron's voice was firm. "And there's no reason why our studio has to restrict itself to horror."

"Uh, yes. I absolutely want first dibs on whatever you come up with next," Lucinda said just as firmly.

"Oh Wendell. You've always been such a worrier. I know I don't weigh in on the business all that often, but I agree. Write what you want. We're established enough that we can attract other writers for the mainstay of the studio offerings." Felicity could be as firm as her siblings.

"And if for some reason we can't produce your non-horror scripts, we will definitely help you shop them elsewhere. We're family before business." Lucinda clearly didn't want any argument on that point. She turned her sharp gaze on Kyle.

"Welcome to the family, Kyle."

The others added their welcome, and Kyle basked in their approval. One thing he'd become very sensitive to over the years, probably primed in his cradle by indifferent parents, was insincerity. And this family, including Wendell, didn't have a whiff of it.

He sagged in his seat as a wave exhaustion swept over him along with intense relief, his brief spurt of energy depleted.

"Maybe it's time to go back to the cottage?" Wendell's words were gentle, caring.

"Yes, please. I need a nap." Kyle suspected naps would be a regular part of his life over the next several weeks.

"Hey, Wendell, I think maybe I'll bunk down on your couch, if you don't mind." Byron gave him a worried look. Kyle suspected Bryon's choice stemmed entirely from the possibility Kyle might need more help than Wendell could give, and he appreciated Bryon's restraint in not saying that aloud.

And unnecessary, too. Drew had already texted him to tell him he'd commanded Wyatt to be available for whatever Kyle needed. Considering how much he'd helped Wendell, Kyle might have to let go of his irritation with Wyatt. Rob, on the other hand, was still AWOL and on his shit list.

"Of course," Wendell said. He texted Kyle's address to his sisters, and handed Kyle's keys over to Felicity before helping Kyle to stand up.

He did feel very safe being escorted by both brothers to the cottage.

Apparently projecting safety was a Weston family trait.

THIRTY

290 Days to Haunt Fest, aka December 15

WENDELL GRABBED Kyle around the waist from behind and
squeezed him. Kyle smiled and leaned back into the warm man who'd
been sheltering and loving him for over three months now. They
were closer than ever.

"Almost done," Wendell said as they both looked at the stack of
boxes.

"Good thing I don't have a lot of stuff."

Kyle was so excited it was like his blood was carbonated and he
was about to fizz over.

After Haunt Fest, which had been another overwhelming success
—and which Kyle had mostly slept through, healing his broken arm—
Wendell had started writing seriously again.

Now, at his scheduled departure back to Los Angeles, he had a
completed script to offer his siblings for possible production. Kyle
was going with him to celebrate the holidays with the Weston family,
and to help Wendell pack up his LA apartment.

Then they'd be coming back to Sandy Bottom Bay. Where Wendell had bought a little house on the edge of town. With both their names on the deed.

Kyle's apartment was all packed up. His suitcase—newly purchased—was ready for his trip to California. Their flight left tomorrow morning from Tampa.

He finally had everything he wanted.

Then his phone rang. He wrinkled his nose. "Who's calling me?"

Just about everyone he knew didn't bother calling, they just texted.

He slid out of Wendell's embrace and strode over to the dresser where he'd left his phone and picked it up.

Sandy Bottom Bay Police Department?

With a quick tilt so that Wendell could see the caller ID, he clicked the green icon and selected speaker. Whatever the police had to say, he wanted Wendell to hear it as well.

"Hello?"

"Hey Kyle."

"Oh, Scott. You scared me. Why aren't you calling from your mobile?"

"Because this is an official call. I'd like both you and Wendell to stop by the station sometime today. Maybe in the next hour."

Technically it was a question, but Kyle didn't think Scott would be impressed if they chose not to appear.

"Is there something wrong?"

"We'll tell you all about it when you arrive."

Kyle glanced at Wendell, who shrugged and nodded.

"Uh, okay. See you in about an hour."

He hung up and stared at Wendell. "What do you suppose that is about? I mean, neither of us has done anything illegal, right?"

Wendell grimaced. "Not that I know of. I mean, when we were trying to exorcise Matthew's ghost, there were some potentially questionable acts, but surely they would have followed up on them before now. Even so, I don't think anything was more than a misdemeanor, if that."

Kyle's stomach roiled. "It's weird, though, right?"

"Don't worry. If necessary, Luce can get us a good lawyer."

That eased his mind somewhat, but he was hoping they wouldn't have any reason to call a lawyer.

"C'mon. We'll do a final walk through to make sure we got everything, then we can head over to the police station and get this over with."

If this little "interview" interfered with their flight, Kyle was going to have very sharp words for Scott.

An hour later, they were sitting in a sparse conference room. It didn't look like the interrogation rooms he'd seen on his murder shows, but neither was it designed to give one the warm and fuzzies.

Jackson was also there, unexpectedly.

"Hey. Who's minding the inn?" Wendell asked.

"Janine. She's a great help." Janine had been a seasonal worker for a few years, but her kids were older now, and she wanted something more to fill her time. With Sandra's permission, Jackson had hired her on for more regular hours.

"What is this all about?" Jackson asked.

"I don't know." But seeing Jackson relieved some of Kyle's anxiety. The more of them there were, the less likely they'd need a lawyer for anything.

Scott entered the room holding a file folder thick with documents and a serious expression on his face. He closed the door behind him and sat down across from Kyle and Wendell.

"So, Chief Walker wanted to do this himself, but he got called away."

Kyle narrowed his eyes. "Why are we here?"

Scott sighed. "We're following up on that box of photos you found." Scott stared at Kyle, but now he had a glimmer of understanding about why the three of them were here in this room.

The funny thing was, he and Wendell had mostly put it out of their minds. They both sort of knew what had happened, so as soon as Matthew's ghost had been banished, it was no longer top of mind. Especially since Kyle had completely resigned from leading ghost tours and Wendell had stopped writing horror.

But the police didn't know about Matthew's ghost, mostly because police didn't believe in that sort of thing, so they must have continued investigating. And they'd never shared their conclusions with Jackson, mostly because they wouldn't have been able to prove anything.

"Oh?" Wendell asked. "I figured it was something that would take a long time to make any progress on."

"Before Chief Walker was hired? We probably wouldn't have investigated it at all. It would have been tucked away in a drawer somewhere. But the chief was so pissed off when he saw that box. Because, as we all suspected, it was as near to proof as we could get that a serial killer had been operating in Sandy Bottom Bay."

"But the chief wasn't even living in Florida when those photos were taken, was he? I don't even know how old he is, but I don't even know if he'd have been a cop then." Kyle didn't know the chief at all, but he did know he was a fairly recent hire.

"No, he's from Pittsburgh, only moved here six years ago when the chief position opened up. But after combing through the old files, it was clear that the police force back then took the easy way out. A number of fatal stabbings over the years had been classed as death by misadventure, and the book closed on them without resolution."

"And they were all people pictured in the cigar box?" Kyle was a bit amazed. "No one wanted to find their killer?"

"Well, that's partly why the chief was so angry. We only have local records for twenty-six of the people in the photos. Unsolved murders that were never investigated. And when we went digging, we found out why. Everyone in that box, and I'm including the ones that we don't have local files on, were... abandoned in some way by their families. They were drug addicts, or runaways, or some, like Sam Kerwin, were gay and had been disowned."

Kyle's heart could barely take it. Matthew had taken advantage of people who were lost and alone in this world, and had killed them.

"Sam Kerwin was in your files? He was murdered?" Wendell's voice was quiet. For a number of reasons, but mostly his connection to Chester, Sam was the one that had gotten under Wendell's skin. Not that Kyle blamed him a bit.

"Yes, he was one of the twenty-six murder victims here in Sandy Bottom Bay."

Wendell sniffed and scrubbed at his eyes. Jackson looked equally distraught.

The victims were all well beyond help, but they'd all been so young and happy in the photos. It was horrific, no matter how long ago it had happened.

"What about the rest of them?"

"Another eight we've identified via the chief's contacts with other departments across the country. Killed in the same manner in Salem, New Orleans, and Savannah. We have no more John or Jane Doe files that match the photos in the box, although there are some older unsolved murders that could well be early victims of our serial killer."

"By my count, that's nine still unaccounted for." Wendell ran a hand through his hair in agitation.

"Yes. We've sent out feelers to other departments, but it could be awhile before we hear back. Decades-old cases are not going to be a priority, especially if the department doesn't have any dedicated cold case officers. And there's a possibility that those people's bodies were just never found, whether they were killed here or elsewhere."

"That's terrible." Kyle wondered if Eddie might be able to help with that. Assuming their ghosts were still around. And assuming his ability worked that way. Although they'd called a truce, he'd been too busy to sit down with Eddie and have an honest discussion about what it meant to be a medium.

Maybe there'd been some deliberate avoidance as well. Kyle's experience with ghosts thus far had more downsides than benefits.

"The other reason that the deaths weren't investigated with any sort of vigor was that, according to the medical examiner's report, all victims had been under the influence of cocaine at the time of their deaths. They were all assumed to be victims of the drug trade. Once we had their names in hand, yeah, some of them were addicts. Chief thinks it more likely that the killer lured them into a false sense of security with the drugs."

Kyle squirmed as he recalled the couple of times he'd done E at a club. He had not known the person who'd given him the tabs, and he'd definitely been pre-disposed to be friendly. That could easily have been him, once upon a time.

Wendell laid a hand on his knee, settling him.

"What about the killer?" Wendell asked.

Scott leaned in, his expression softening a bit. "Well, that's why we called you in. The chief is sending out a press release later today, including the identity of the killer."

"You know who killed them?" Jackson asked.

"We were also able to confirm the killer had been all relevant cities at the time of those murders, and let me tell you, that was not easy to determine. Based on fingerprints and some other evidence, we are certain that the brother of a former owner of the inn killed all those people. A man by the name of Matthew Trask."

Scott narrowed his eyes at them. Well, not Jackson, because he was completely taken aback. He pointed at Kyle and Wendell. "You two knew that already, didn't you? How did you know?"

Wendell looked a bit sheepish. "Um. I took pictures of the photos with my phone and I showed Barbara Mayhew his picture. The guy that was in all the photos. She recognized him, so we just assumed he was the killer."

Which was the truth, but glossed over the fact that the town's medium had confirmed it because Matthew's ghost had tried to possess Kyle. But if Scott didn't ask the right questions, there was no reason to volunteer that information.

"Oh for fuck's sake."

Kyle opened his mouth with a snarky comment about how long it had taken them to make the identification, but Wendell poked him in the side and gave a slight shake of his head.

"Well, I didn't know that." Jackson was not happy.

"Sorry about that." Wendell's apology was sincere. "It seemed wiser to keep it quiet, considering it could have a negative impact on the inn's reputation."

"Anyway, yes, there could be some negative blowback. There could be a significant press presence in the next few days. We've already contacted Sandra about this."

"Oh, shit. Jackson. We can't leave you on your own with this." Wendell was just the sweetest man.

"No," Jackson replied. "You need to go on your trip. You do not need to stay here with me. I can always get Wyatt to help out."

Scott snorted scornfully at the mention of Wyatt. Unlike Kyle, Scott had definitely not softened on Wyatt.

"That won't be necessary," Scott said. "We've assigned deputies to assist Jackson. I promise, he won't have to deal with this on his own."

"Thanks, Scott." Jackson sighed. "Is there anything else?"

"Not really. Once the furor dies down, the chief wants to get a drug sniffing dog out there, just to make sure there isn't an old stash of cocaine on the premises. We wouldn't want anyone to find that accidentally. Sandra has already granted permission."

Wendell made a funny face, but didn't say anything. Kyle was going to have to follow up on that later.

"Can we go?" Kyle asked.

Before Scott could respond, the chief burst into the room

"Oh good, you're still here." His deep voice was a bit overwhelming in the small room. He'd probably make a great actor.

The three of them just nodded and waited.

"I wanted to thank you all. Without you, these cases might never have been solved. I just wish someone had realized back then that there was a problem. If Matthew Trask hadn't died of natural causes, who knows how many people he would have killed?" The chief shook his head, as though he hadn't meant to say all of that. "Truly, though. You have my gratitude."

His cell phone buzzed and he glanced at it before rushing out of the room again.

Scott picked up the file folder that he hadn't opened once during their meeting.

"You're free to go, and Jackson, let me know if you start getting a lot of calls or trespassers."

"I will, thanks."

The three of them walked outside together and stood in the sunshine. December was still rather warm, but Wendell was more comfortable in the cooler temperatures.

Jackson whirled on them. "You know something. Something Scott doesn't know. You are going to tell me everything."

Kyle shrugged and glanced at Wendell. "You probably won't believe it."

"I don't care. I want to know what you know."

"Can it wait until we get back from LA?" Not many people were aware, but despite everything, Jackson was negotiating the purchase of the inn from Sandra. He would soon no longer be a temporary resident of Sandy Bottom Bay, just like Wendell.

"Yes, but promise me. The truth!"

Wendell nodded. "We can do that, but like Kyle said, you might not believe us."

"Don't care. If nothing else, we might be able to add another legend to the Orange Lady's reputation." Jackson winked and headed for his car.

Kyle and Wendell had walked from Kyle's apartment, but instead of walking back, they headed to the bakery for a treat before they drove out to Tampa.

When they settled in, Kyle turned a stern look on Wendell.

"And you know something you haven't told me." Which was weird, because he had been certain Wendell had told him everything that had happened while Kyle had been in the hospital. Another reason he loved Wendell so much. The man had no poker face. He would never be able to cheat on Kyle and keep it a secret. Although Scott hadn't noticed. Maybe it had to do with how attuned the two of them were to each other.

"I didn't actually realize I knew it until Scott mentioned drugs. When we were searching for the camera, we found a small hiding place behind the bathroom mirror. There were some small bundles wrapped in black plastic. But they were obviously not a camera, and I assumed they were there to protect, I don't know, a pipe or something from moisture. I sort of forgot about them."

Protect a pipe from moisture? Kyle made a mental note to keep Wyatt on speed dial for any handyman needs in their new home.

"So you didn't look at them?"

Wendell shook his head. "No. I was focused on finding the camera."

"Well, if it was Matthew's drug stash, we'll find out about it soon enough."

Wendell drained the last of his tea, and scooped up the last smear of frosting, licking it off his finger.

Kyle couldn't help but suck in a breath. Would that ever cease to be sexy as hell?

"C'mon. Let's get out of here. We have a plane to catch."

"We do." And a family to see. One that had opened their arms to Kyle with no hesitation. He couldn't wait.

Wendell stood up and held out his hand. Kyle grasped it. This was forever.

EPILOGUE

On stage, Kyle sang with all the flourishes one would expect of a Pirate King. Wendell just about burst with pride. Kyle was meant to be on stage, and Wendell had never been more aware of that than this second. This might not be Broadway, which was where he'd last seen *The Pirates of Penzance*, but the Sandy Players were already amazing, and they were only a couple of minutes into the performance.

The past seven months had been wild. After their trip back to LA to celebrate the holidays and to pack up Wendell's apartment, he and Kyle had returned to LA twice while Wendell and his siblings prepped for the production of his new action adventure movie. It still had a hint of the paranormal, because despite his encounter with Matthew Trask's malevolent ghost, he wasn't able to completely change course.

While in LA, Luce had gotten Kyle a couple of short contracts for bit parts on two different crime dramas, as well as a commercial for mobile phones. The camera loved Kyle, but it was as obvious as neon that Kyle didn't love the camera as much as he loved the stage.

And his return to it had been more dramatic than his exit.

Three months ago, after the investigation into Matthew Trask had been closed, Wendell had sponsored a memorial service for his victims. He'd arranged for a photo wall, with accompanying mini-bios of each person. The townspeople come out in droves. Some for ghoulish curiosity, but most of them had been truly respectful.

Debra Pearson, the local theater director, had attended with her sister, Barbara Mayhew. Afterward, she approached Kyle in tears, apologizing her behavior. No one, not even her sister, had known Debra had had a romantic liaison with one of the victims, Lars Eriksson, the one who'd looked like Kyle. She thought he'd run out on her, and because of it, had treated Kyle with disdain.

It hadn't taken any time at all for Kyle to become as fast friends with Debra as he was with her sister. Within a month, they were busily planning a musical production, with Kyle in a starring role.

They'd modified the choreography to go easy on his knee, but until they started rehearsals, Wendell had never heard Kyle sing. He was amazing, and Wendell could hardly believe he'd been prepared to go without performing for the rest of his life.

All too soon, act one was completed, and Wendell clapped harder than anyone. He, Drew, and Cliff had scored seats right up front, and so they were the last to file out for intermission. It didn't take long to find the throng of people near the bar who were all there for Kyle's opening night performance—and there were a lot.

But the ones that had nearly made Kyle cry when he found out they'd be there were Wendell's family. They'd all bought plane tickets as soon as the dates had been confirmed, including his parents. When Wendell realized his whole family were going to be at the performance, he started putting another plan in motion. Because Kyle thrived on being the center of attention, and Wendell loved it when Kyle thrived.

"Oh, Wendell, baby, he was just glorious," his mom said as she hugged him.

"I know," Luce agreed. "This is why I keep trying to get him to accept a movie role."

Byron laughed. "I'm not sure you'll convince him. Not after what I saw in there. He was having the fucking time of his life."

Luce pouted. "I know."

His family merged with Drew and Cliff and the rest of Kyle's friends. Everyone except for Drew was surprised at how good Kyle had been, and Wendell was so pleased for his boyfriend.

Scott ribbed him a bit for wearing a tux, because Wendell was definitely the most overdressed person in the playhouse, although his father and brother were both wearing suits.

"Well, you know. This is my boyfriend's first opening night. I had to do it up special."

He hoped Kyle would appreciate the effort—he'd had to leave for the theater long before Wendell had gotten dressed, and it would be a bit of a surprise. Thankfully, the playhouse had a fully functional air conditioner, because July in Florida was too hot, even at eight in the evening, for formalwear.

They barely had time to finish their drinks before the lights flashed, telling them it was time to return to their seats for act two.

Act two was every bit as good as act one. Wendell had leapt to his feet with the rest of audience to deliver a resounding standing ovation. Kyle's wide smile had been a beautiful sight to behold, face flushed with exertion under the thick stage makeup.

The curtain dropped, which was Wendell's cue. He slipped out to the aisle and made his way to the stairs on the right of the apron. He stood in shadows, but he was able to see Kyle return for his triumphant curtain call. His boyfriend was fucking glorious.

In a somewhat unusual turn of events, Debra strode out to the front of the stage. Most of the cast wasn't confused by her appearance, and all of them melted backstage, except for his two costars, who each wrapped an arm around Kyle's shoulders to keep him on stage.

"Good evening," Debra called out. "Thank you all for coming, and I'm thrilled you enjoyed our debut performance of *The Pirates of*

Penzance. Special for opening night only, our Pirate King has one more scene to play."

With that introduction, Debra stepped back, while Kyle's costars pushed him forward. Kyle had no idea what was going on, but he flourished his sword and posed jauntily.

Wendell grabbed the large bouquet of red roses from the stage-hand, as he'd pre-arranged, and swallowed down his nerves. For this, he could do big, visible, and sweeping.

One deep breath, and he bounded up the stairs. He offered the roses to Kyle.

"You were amazing," Wendell said. Kyle took the bouquet, eyes shining, as he took in Wendell's tux.

"You *look* amazing," Kyle said back. He had definitely projected more than Wendell had, but Wendell was suddenly aware of a hush in the audience.

A quick glance to his side left his eyes a bit dazzled. No wonder the cast didn't get distracted by the audience. They were no more than dark amorphous shapes. Which quieted the butterflies in his stomach. Somewhat. There were a *lot* of butterflies

He dropped to one knee while he retrieved a small box from his pocket, almost dropping it with fingers numb from nervousness. He wasn't worried about Kyle saying no—not too much—but more about screwing up such a big moment in front of so many people. He wanted this to be perfect for Kyle. He flipped open the box and held it up. Inside was a brushed platinum band with an inlaid square-cut diamond. Not flashy, but excellent quality and would provide plenty of eye-catching sparkle for man who loved to shine.

Kyle's cheeks pinked up and his eyes widened. He lifted a trembling hand to his lips.

"Kyle, you've been a bright light in my life from the very second I met you. I love you more every day and I want to spend the rest of my life with you. Will you marry me?"

Tears fell from Kyle's eyes as he sniffed. Then he smiled, wide and happy. "Of course, I will. I love you so much. I've never been as happy as I've been with you."

His *fiancé's* obvious pleasure made Wendell warm inside. It amazed him that he'd managed to find such bliss and contentment.

Wendell stood and slid the ring on Kyle's finger. Kyle wrapped his arms around him, bouquet still in one hand and crinkling against his tux, then kissed him so soundly his ears rang.

Then they pulled apart, and Wendell realized that sound was applause. Along with a couple of wolf-whistles that sounded suspiciously like Wyatt. He turned and smiled ruefully at the audience, the one he could barely see.

"C'mon fiancé," Kyle said. "A bow is customary after a stunning performance."

He let Kyle lead him in a pirate-worthy bow.

ABOUT THE AUTHOR

KC Burn is a Canadian transplanted to Florida who writes happy-ever-afters about men loving men, whether they're psychics, space travelers, aliens, professors, construction workers, cops, amateur sleuths... you name it, she'll probably write it. She's got a pair of black cats, aka muses/nuisances, and a supportive, understanding hubby.

ALSO BY KC BURN

Contemporary

Cop Out (Toronto Tales #1)

Cover Up (Toronto Tales #2)

Cast Off (Toronto Tales #3)

Tartan Candy (Fabric Hearts #1)

Plaid versus Paisley (Fabric Hearts #2)

Just Add Argyle (Fabric Hearts #3)

Banded Together

Tea or Consequences

Rainbow Blues

Pen Name - Doctor Chicken

First Time, Forever

Set Ablaze

Sci-Fi

Spice 'n' Solace (Galactic Alliance #1)

Alien 'n' Outlaw (Galactic Alliance #2)

Voodoo 'n' Vice (Galactic Alliance #3)

Union of the Snake

The Tithe

Paranormal

Wolfsbane (MIA Case Files #1)

Blood Relations (MIA Case Files #2)

Craving (MIA Case Files #3)